ALSO BY JAMES BRUNO

TRIBE
PERMANENT INTERESTS
CHASM

HAVANA QUEEN

A NOVEL BY

JAMES BRUNO

HAVANA QUEEN, a novel by James Bruno

First Edition, April 2013

This work has been reviewed and cleared by the U.S. Department of State. The opinions and characterizations in this book are those of the author and do not necessarily reflect official positions of the United States Government

This is a work of fiction. Names, places, characters and incidents are either the product of the author's imagination or are used fictitiously, and any resemblance to actual persons, living or dead, business establishments, events, or locales is entirely coincidental.

Produced by Pedernales Publishing, LLC.
www.pedernalespublishing.com

For information email angkor456000@yahoo.com or contact:

Bittersweet House Press
P.O. Box 306
Canastota, NY 13035

ISBN: 978-0-9837642-6-7

Printed in the United States of America

To Lou & Mil, Dom & Elia, and Ramón & Mercedes
For forging an enduring Cuban-American friendship
at Lafayette Restaurant

ACKNOWLEDGMENTS

I thank Maria Elena de la Noval for her support, feedback and continuation of a friendship of families that pre-dates the Cuban revolution. To the great literary satirist, Gloria Nagy, I owe special thanks for her mentoring, encouragement and infectious sense of humor. José Ramirez and Barbara Rainess worked wonders to create a winning book cover and formatting. I am indebted to Eileen DuJardin for educating me on the fine points of cow magnets. The security review process was made less onerous by the courteous and professional staff at the State Department's Office of Program Information and Services. My apologies go out to the hotels Meliá Cohiba, Riviera and Santiago for my staging a variety of nefarious activities in my story at their splendid establishments. I thank my anonymous U.S. Marine contacts for their insights into the finer points of various weaponry. Finally, I extend heartfelt thanks to my friends and colleagues in the intelligence community, who also choose to remain anonymous, for their insights into espionage tradecraft, thus, lending added authenticity to my story.

FOREWORD

I had the good fortune of being assigned to work on Cuba during a stateside tour of duty in the mid-'90s. My job had three geographic legs: the U.S. Naval Base at Guantanamo, the Republic of Cuba and Washington, DC. Each month, I flew to GTMO to join the Base Commander for meetings with Cuban military officers on "The Line," i.e., the boundary between the Naval base and Castro's Cuba. These meetings are the only direct substantive contacts the U.S. government has with the Cuban military. Think *A Few Good Men* minus the melodrama, though once the small charter craft in which I flew to GTMO was forced into a corkscrew landing due to billows of black smoke surging skyward from brush fires set off by exploding land mines on the Cuban side. At other times, I flew to Havana where I had the unusual job of traveling the length and breadth of the island with another U.S. diplomat to monitor the human rights of Cubans returned to their homes after failing to make the dangerous journey to reach U.S. soil. We were surveilled constantly by Cuban government agents, whose harassment included slashing our tires, stealing items of clothing and smearing feces on our room doorknobs. In Washington, I attended regular meetings at the White House, sometimes in the Situation Room, of the Cuba Policy Working Group. Overall, it was one of my most challenging and fascinating Foreign Service assignments.

The Cuba itch, however, came to me much earlier in life. In the 1950s, my parents befriended the de la Noval family while on vacation in Havana. After Fidel Castro's takeover, the de la Novals joined the exodus of citizens fleeing their country. My family sponsored them as refugees, helping them to gain a new foothold in the United States and reinforcing a close friendship which continues to this day.

As a former official of the federal government with top secret clearances, I am required to submit for security review to the U.S. Department of State all of my writings prior to publication. This review process has resulted in redactions and text modifications in order to protect what government reviewers deemed sensitive information. These modifications do not, however, impact the integrity and authenticity of my works. It is my aim to present readers with as authentic insights as I can into the workings of our national security apparatus without violating mandated safeguards on classified information. I do not, however, submit to gratuitous censorship. The clearance process is one of negotiation between author and official reviewers in which I have the readers' interests and enjoyment at heart. Given my training and experiences, my novels possess a sense of realism rarely matched in the political thriller genre.

Si yo me pierdo, que me busquen en...Cuba

Federico García Lorca

HAVANA QUEEN

PROLOGUE

"Rudolph Valentino stayed here. Also Charlie Chaplin. And there was Clark Gable and *el gran maestro* Caruso. Rico Caruso? What was his full name? When he sang at the Campoamor. And they say Greta Garbo—"

"Who gives a shit?" Jorge shot back. "Why do you keep saying all these famous people stayed here? That was a long time ago. And all those people are dead anyway."

"And Winston Churchill! Him too!" Yesdasi continued.

"Wrong, *chica*. He stayed at the Nacional. But I said, stop this!"

Yesdasi snapped out of her reverie and blinked. "Why should I stop? We live in a place where many famous people stayed. Just think—"

Before she could slip back into her reverie, Jorge grabbed her chin with his rough worker's hand. "Yesdasi! Look at me! Look into my eyes!"

Yesdasi frowned. Her dark eyes were those of a little girl who had been told she may not have another cookie.

"Listen to me. We live in a shithole. Correction. We *exist* in a shithole. Look!" He made a sweep with his free hand. "One hundred fifty families are crammed into this dump. It hasn't seen a lick of fresh paint in fifty years. The plumbing is shot. Shit and piss pool on the ground floor. No electricity half of the time."

"La Reina is still majestic, Jorge. This place has soul. One day…"

"The queen is dead! Long live the queen!" Jorge backed

away, wagging a finger at his wife. "One day we'll be in Miami! Away from all this."

"The hell we will. Dream on, Jorge. You're forty-two years old. Make the best with the cards we're dealt."

Jorge slumped onto a hard wooden chair beside the ancient crooked dining table. He leaned forward and covered his face with his palms.

The door opened, and an old woman ushered in two boys in red-scarfed *pionero* uniforms. She pulled fruit out of a rattan shopping bag.

The kids ran to the Chinese-made television and tuned to *SpongeBob SquarePants*, via a pirated signal from an illegal rooftop dish.

"Bananas again?" they moaned.

"Hush!" their grandmother responded. "You're lucky I could find those. That *Yuma* TV is spoiling you kids. You think this is America? See how *fat* those American kids are."

Jorge kissed his mother on the cheek.

An astute woman, she instantly read the faces of her son and daughter-in-law. "You two been arguing again?"

"Ah, it's nothing, Mama," he said.

"Same old stuff," Yesdasi added.

He nodded. "We're packed like sardines in this old hotel. Plants are growing out of its fissures. We're like rats in some old Roman ruins. Five hundred worthless pesos a month gets us next to nothing. I don't think about me and Yesdasi so much as the boys. I want them to have a future."

"Watch your mouth, *hijo*," Mother said. "That CDR bitch down the hall has ears like a bat."

"'*Siempre contigo, Fidel!*' Right down to the bottom of the Caribbean on this sinking ship with *El Jefe*." Jorge snapped a mock military salute.

Yesdasi grabbed her husband by the sleeve and pulled him onto the small balcony. "Listen to your mother, Jorge. The last thing I need is a husband in jail. Just watch it."

Jorge's grimace melted into a smile. "God, I still love the fire in those beautiful eyes." He pulled her close. "Remember how we danced? We loved *salsa* even more than sex." He kissed her, and they lingered in an embrace. A tile from the balcony above fell on Jorge's head.

"Shit!" he yelled and looked up.

"Hey, Ortega! Keep it down, will ya? I'm trying to get some rest," a man admonished from the neighboring unit.

"Rest from what?" Jorge retorted. "A job at a Ministry of Construction that carries out no construction?"

"Ah. Go screw yourself!" the other man shouted back.

"Never mind him." Yesdasi placed a finger over his lips.

They looked out over central Havana, a vista of drab decaying buildings, broken streets and a scattering of vintage vehicles. Jorge shook his head.

Carlos turned a corner. Out of breath, the pudgy fellow labored under a fully packed army duffel bag. His short legs and fat ass lent a duck-like waddle to his gait. As he approached the minivan, his younger cohort quickly got out and opened the rear door.

He was about to heave in the duffel, then stopped in mid-motion. "What in God's name is this crap?" A tall pile of tangled cables and plastic parts lay in the van's rear compartment.

"I don't know," Oscar said. "Got it from an Army guy in return for some *Playboys* my girlfriend picked up cleaning rooms at the Cohiba. I think it's bulldozer parts. I'll figure it out later. Somebody'll buy them. Come on. Let's get a move-on!"

Carlos threw in the duffel and got behind the wheel. The side of the van read, "Hospital Comandante Manuel Fajardo." They screeched off.

Once on Avenida Salvador Allende heading toward central Havana, they relaxed.

"So what's in the duffel?" Oscar, slumped in the passenger's seat, feet propped on the dashboard, fingers rapidly tapping out some infernal *reggaeton* tune on the dash.

Carlos lit a cigarette and inhaled deeply. "Nipple shields, wound cleanser, hooks and retractors, drip collectors, diabetic lancets, some diagnostic shit… shipment donated from Sweden. Just came in."

Oscar squinted. "Wha'?"

Carlos exhaled smoke. "Hey, trust me. This stuff'll move. I'm trying to get my hands on some lorazepam. It's all the rage among kids with fat remittances from Miami. Can't sell it fast enough. They say the high is short, but intense. Sort of like an orgasm."

Traffic, as always, was light. A hodge podge of '50s Chevies, DeSotos, and Studebakers huff-puffed along the route with Russian Ladas, military vehicles, Soviet-era trucks, hotel taxis, and an occasional sleek diplomatic limo.

"So, Carlos, if you don't get caught, what's your plan? With the money, I mean?" Oscar asked.

Carlos glanced at his partner and took another drag on his cigarette. "You know, I hate stealing. From the state, from anybody. I was raised right. I'm a *guajiro*. Cut sugar cane as a kid out in Camaguey. We had nothing, but we never stole. Lived off of the sweat of our brow. I do this…" He jerked his thumb back toward the loot. "… because I have to. We all do. But my goal is to open up a *paladar* in five years. It'll be the best private dining in Havana." He took his hands off the wheel and bracketed an imaginary placard. "Siboney is gonna be the name. I already got a chef lined up. Suppliers. The whole shooting match. How about you?"

Grim determination formed across Oscar's face. "Me. I'm getting out. Got an uncle in Fort Lauderdale. He owns a bedding store. Says a job is waiting for me if I can get there okay. Who knows? Maybe he'll make me his partner one day."

"You'll get yourself killed, kid. Fish bait in the Florida Strait. Not worth the risk. Apply for a visa. I hear the wait is under ten years now."

"No. Can't wait that long. I'd rather be fish food than waste my life here. But I got a plan. Uncle Frank is gonna buy me a plane ticket to Quito. No visa needed for Cubans there. Then I head north. Simple as that."

The hospital van pulled in at the apartment building. LA REINA stood in bold stone relief over the outside columned entrance. Carved almost a century ago by Italian or Catalan stoneworkers, the letters were caked in black soot. Seraphim and angels graced the sides, their wings long since broken. Little paint remained on the cracking walls of the former lobby. The tops of the sweeping interior archways were hidden as the result of the installation of a makeshift extra floor to accommodate more residents. Such additions, inserted wherever the original ceilings were high, were called *barbacoas*, or barbecues, because they resembled the middle-level grills of those devices.

Carlos and Oscar climbed out of the van and hauled their booty up the curved entrance stairway.

A young black woman with screaming twin babies asked in a hushed voice, "Carlos, you got the nipple shields? I'm sore."

"Sure do. Right after the CDR block meeting tonight, when I usually make sales."

The men dragged their contraband over to the birdcage lift in the center of the dark foyer.

An eighty-something man leaning on a cane shook his head. "Lift is out. Gotta climb. Not me, though. I can't do no ten floors with this heart." He patted his chest.

"Fucking thing's out again?" Carlos kicked the elevator shaft folding door with all his might. Jugulars bulging, face beet-red, he lifted his head and bellowed, *"Me cago en tu madre!"*

A creaking sound echoed off the walls, followed by a deep groan that sounded as though it came from the belly of a monster. Silence followed. Residents stopped what they were doing. Flakes of plaster and dust floated down like snow and settled on their heads and clothing.

Carlos and Oscar looked at each other, frozen in place.

On the eleventh floor, the Ortega boys averted their eyes from *SpongeBob* at the first tremor and looked at their mother and father. Wide-eyed, the parents rushed to scoop their children in their arms.

The mother of twins did the same ten floors below in the stairwell.

Carlos shouted to Oscar, "Let's get the hell out of—"

La Reina's implosion was all encompassing, merciless, and swift.

CHAPTER ONE

U.S. Naval Station, Guantánamo Bay, Cuba

The day was beautiful, cloudless, and serenely quiet at The Line, the northeast perimeter gate of the U.S. Naval Station at GTMO. Base Commander Captain Wally T. Andrus fidgeted as he waited for his counterpart to appear from the Cuban side. His watch read 0958. His team—USMC detachment commander Colonel John Compoli, aide Lieutenant Commander Steve O'Malley, and Spanish interpreter Marine Corporal Lance Rueda—peered silently through the chain link fence. The American side featured a guard shack flanked by concrete-filled cinder blocks and oil drum berms garishly painted in red and yellow. Atop the guard shack was a sign: "North East Gate–Marine Barracks–Ground Defense Security Force." Old Glory fluttered atop the flagpole as if indifferent to the host country on whose territory it was planted. Opposite, some thirty yards away, was a high archway topped by a sign boldly proclaiming, "Republica de Cuba – Territorio Libre de America." The Cuban flag and pole were inexplicably smaller than their U.S. counterparts.

The monthly meetings on The Line were actually convivial. So much so, in fact, one would not discern that the venue was one of only two points held over from the Cold War where enemies met. The other point was Panmunjom in the Korean DMZ. Berlin's Glienicke "Bridge of Spies" belonged to the history books. And while the Allenby Bridge, the India-Pakistan

Wagah Border crossing ,and the Cypriot Green Line could offer moments of tense drama, they lacked the gravity of junctures where empires, or their surrogates, met and sometimes clashed.

In the movie *A Few Good Men*, the fictional Colonel Jessep famously said, "I eat breakfast three hundred yards from four thousand Cubans who are trained to kill me." Andrus loved throwing out that line when hosting visiting VIPs at the base commander's residence or at the Windjammer Club.

Three Cubans in olive drab marched out of one of the single-story buildings flanking the archway. Their leader, a gray-haired, dark-complexioned man with a paunch, nodded, signaling they were ready to meet. The two delegations, lined up in rank order, strode toward a white line in the asphalt exactly in the middle of the boundary. Falling into place on either side, they halted, stood at attention, and saluted. They then shook hands all around.

Brigadier General Marcos López y López gestured for the Americans to join them at a long, narrow table with folding chairs on the Cuban side, under the archway. The *comandante* of Cuba's Eastern Military Region was accompanied by Frontier Brigade Commander Col. Henrique Marcial Arribe, Intelligence Officer Carlos Amenares Sánchez, and a young female interpreter wearing out-of-place pink lipstick, private's insignia, and a name patch that read, "Navarro." All were with the *Fuerzas Armadas Revolucionarias*, or FAR, except for Amenares, a member of the Ministry of Interior's feared secret police. An orderly stood ready to serve refreshments.

As the delegates took their seats, the orderly served strong *cafecitos* and simple biscuits. The meeting venues alternated between the two sides. When the U.S. Navy hosted, in true blue USN tradition, a fairly lavish meal was served inside an air-conditioned tent. The FAR delegates relished those affairs, as evidenced by their repeated helpings of the heavy American fare. The FAR, like the rest of Cuba, lacked the resources to put on a small banquet for their Yankee counterparts.

As the proceedings began, flies buzzed around increasingly sweaty brows. The overhead sun was relentless, and the archway's shade provided little relief. The agenda was typically mundane: fence repair notification, new construction around Camp Delta, scheduling the orderly repatriation of Cuban escapees, weed eradication, and coordination of measures to put out brush fires, which were usually started by an animal blundering into a Cuban minefield—the U.S. had removed its minefields. The purpose of the monthly get-togethers was to prevent potential flare-ups from erupting between the two adversaries.

Capt. Andrus took stock of the Cubans as his interpreter translated his opening remarks. López y López, a battle-hardened veteran of Angola, was around sixty, and clearly on his pre-retirement final tour of duty. Despite his jovial demeanor, his eyes were steely. The squinty-eyed, slouch-shouldered, humorless Amenares had the air of a man who spent his time preying on people on behalf of himself as well as the state. Col. Marcial, quiet and observant, stood in stark contrast to his cohorts. A six-foot-two, muscled Afro-Cuban, he was lantern-jawed and handsome. His handshake was viselike, the grip of a powerful man. He had the right qualities for a soldier whose job was to be the first to confront the American superpower should the balloon go up. Andrus figured Marcial would probably be the guy first in line to run three hundred yards to kill him while he ate breakfast.

Seventy-five minutes later, the two delegations rose, gathered their papers, and proceeded back to the white strip separating the Republic of Cuba from America's oldest overseas naval base.

The earlier ritual was repeated with smart salutes, followed by handshakes. The last to shake Andrus's hand was Marcial. Again, the tight grip was held a few seconds longer than customary. Marcial fixed Andrus with a firm, direct gaze, but there was something more in those midnight eyes and that demi-grin. Searching? Assurance? Something.

When Marcial released his hand, Andrus felt something in his palm. Paper. Marcial held his gaze a second longer. Warning. Caution. In any case, a visual man-to-man message. Andrus pulled out his handkerchief to wipe his brow, a ploy to deposit the slip of paper in his pocket.

Andrus waited until his chauffeured sedan was a full mile on the road back to headquarters before retrieving the paper and opening it.

I want to defect.

"It's a dangle. No doubt about it. We play along. Feed him crap. Mess with their minds. Teach the bastards a lesson. They won't know which way's up when we're through with them." Bart Morgenstern pulled his squat, overweight body out of his chair and leaned forward, knuckles pressed on the conference table. "I don't buy it for a minute."

Nick Castillo liked the brilliant, slovenly Brooklyn native. Morgenstern's body might be slow, but his mind was not, and he deviated one hundred eighty degrees from the usual buttoned-down, colorless FBI headquarters types. He was arguably the best counterintel analyst the agency had. He had been on Hanssen's trail before anyone else, and he was feared and loathed in Beijing for all the PRC moles he'd exposed in Silicon Valley. A French *Sûreté* official once likened him to a truffle hog, saying he could sniff around and root out enemy spies without missing a beat.

"Maybe he's a double agent. But maybe he's not," said Lena Moreno, one of Castillo's young agents in the Field Intelligence Group—FIG—in the bureau's Miami Field Office. "We've at least got to test him."

"But we can't box him like other assets under assessment," Morgenstern retorted. "Box" was shorthand for giving a polygraph. "And the Cubes know this. He's under their control.

Totally. Believe me. We can't afford to be taken in again. I say we just ignore it. Otherwise, we feed him shit."

Morgenstern referred to a constant stream of phony Cuban defectors and turncoats who'd been showing up at U.S. embassies, military bases, and in the United States for decades. Havana's spymasters sent in those ringers for several reasons: first, to flush out and identify American intelligence officers; second, to gain insight into how the CIA manages defectors and those it recruits to spy for them; third, to feed disinformation in order to get Washington to make bad policy decisions; and last, to screw with the heads of American intel officers, leading them into a wilderness of mirrors, building paranoia to the point that even true-blue Cuban turncoats would not be trusted. Once it had achieved its goals, Havana would sometimes feed stories to the world media on how it had tricked its North American nemesis once again. Many a career had wound up in the political graveyard as a result.

"Here's the thing," Castillo said. "Our CI Division and the CIA's CI Center are taking this guy seriously. They assigned the case to this office because he passed the note to the GTMO base commander who was standing on our side of The Line. Whatever. This is a joint op. We validate him. Or not. If so, we run him. If not, we drop him."

"And the Castro boys whip up the eggs we'll have on our collective faces," Morgenstern interjected.

Castillo picked up a bound stack of FBI Intelligence Information Reports and CIA raw intel. The cover sheet showed "TOP SECRET" in bold orange-red letters. Flipping through them, he summarized, "On Sunday, another building collapsed in central Havana, killing a record eighty-six people; thirty-five were children. Riots broke out on the Malecón. Demonstrators taunted Havana's party boss, who went to try to calm tempers. A building collapses in Havana every three days, on average. The economy is going down the tubes fast. Food is short. Crime is way up. People there are talking about mass migration to Florida. The Cuban people want change."

"Yeah, but—" Morgenstern started.

Castillo raised his voice, cutting off Morgenstern. "And here's why it may be different now. Fidel Castro is eighty-eight. Raúl Castro is eighty-three. The Cuban revolution is fifty-five. The actuarial tables meet the revolution."

As the new Assistant Special Agent in Charge–ASAC–Castillo knew that the country of his forebears would be pulling him into a maelstrom. And he dreaded the prospect.

CHAPTER TWO

Havana

The GAZ jeep coughed and choked along broad Paseo Avenue, black fumes billowing from its exhaust. The patched-up Soviet-era military vehicle struggled to maintain forty miles an hour. The young Army private chauffeuring it shrugged apologetically at his passenger. Col. Marcial smiled back and took in the sights. Having been stationed in eastern Cuba for the past seven years, he seldom visited Havana.

Looming ahead was the José Martí Memorial, a towering phallus of a monument visible from most parts of the city. The great poet and patriot brooded in carved stone at the bottom of the memorial. Next to the memorial sprawled the trapezoidal Palace of the Revolution and Communist Party headquarters. The Castro boys ruled Cuba from there. Built in the 1950s under the Batista regime, the stark office labyrinth had been inspired by European Fascist architecture.

A vast vacant asphalt parade ground, devoid of any organic thing, lay across the avenue from the Palace. Marcial recalled many an hour of standing at attention and marching on the grounds in the unrelenting southern sun. If anyone actually could spare an egg, it would fry quickly on the stove-hot surface.

The GAZ chugged left onto Salvador Allende Avenue, past the glass and concrete National Theater, then right on Calle 19 de Mayo and took another sharp right into a parking lot. The private quickly got out and stood at attention as Col. Marcial stepped out on the doorless side. Two eight-story rectangular office buildings towered above, even more devoid of character than the Mussolini-inspired Palace. More East German-imbued, the Ministry of Interior headquarters was a place almost every Cuban steered clear of by choice. As he approached the main building, the visage of Che Guevara in bronze piping mounted on a concrete façade covering the entire height of the building gazed valiantly at the horizon. *Hasta la Victoria Siempre*—"Ever Onward to Victory"—declared a large scrawl under Guevara's chin.

A young MININT lieutenant met Marcial at the entrance, saluted, and ushered him to the elevator. The elevator doors opened on the eighth floor to a reception area connected to a large office suite. A plaque on the wall read, "Vice Minister – Directorate of Intelligence – Brig. Gen. Alfredo García Menéndez."

García greeted Marcial with a firm handshake and a hearty pat on the back. "My God, Marcial. Don't you ever age? You look younger. How long has it been?" The balding Vice Minister clenched a *lancero* cigar between his teeth.

"El Salvador," Marcial said.

"Ah. That long? Those were the days, eh? Jungle battles fulfilling our internationalist duty. Now… now we manage tourist hotels and taxi fleets. And how is… María?"

"Marisol," Marcial corrected.

"Right. Marisol. How is she? Beautiful girl."

"We're divorced. But Yuri is well. He will graduate from José Maceo this year."

"Another *camilito* in the family. Wonderful," García said.

Camilitos were graduates of any of the eight military academies, the so-called Camilo Cienfuegos schools. García and Marcial had been classmates at the prestigious General Máximo Gómez Academy in the capital.

García ushered Marcial into his office suite. "You know

Amenares," García said, signaling to the mirthless MININT major.

Amenares offered a limp hand. Marcial shook it.

García gestured at a hazel-eyed woman dressed in civilian clothes. "And here we have *compañera* Larisa Montilla from the U.S.A. Department." He did not elaborate further.

The forty-something woman shook Marcial's hand, but said nothing. She had light brown hair tied back and an erect bearing.

Marcial took in the office, which was sparsely furnished with the only decorations being a photo of *El Jefe* pinning a medal on a younger García, the obligatory official photo of President Raúl Castro, and two African masks on the far wall.

Angola. The Lomba River. Under attack. Marcial's mind raced back over two decades. South African long-range artillery had rained down, chewing up their encampment. Lt. Alfredo García Menéndez shouted orders to fleeing Angolan MPLA guerrillas to return to their positions. Explosions. Lt. Marcial pinned down, trying to call in MiGs to strike at the enemy positions. Limbs, blood, brains flying through the air. Total chaos.

"Henrique," García said. "I said, would you like coffee?"

Marcial broke out of his daydream. "No, thank you, General." *Moros y cristianos,* the national Cuban dish of black beans and rice, Marcial thought. He was the black bean in an office of otherwise all-white attendees. It always seemed to be that way at the senior levels. Yes, Fidel opened up opportunities to Afro-Cubans. But when it came to truly running things, the sons, and some daughters, of Europe retained the levers of power, as things had always been.

"So the transfer went okay? The American captain took it? No hitches?" García asked.

"Yes," Marcial replied. "It went easily. He took it and slipped it into his right pants pocket."

Garcia said, "Now we want you to stay in Havana until the next scheduled meeting on The Line.

"But my command—"

"Not to worry. It's in the hands of your capable subordinate, Lt. Col. Blanco. You will be put up in bachelor's quarters."

"I thought I was to just pass the note. That's it."

"There may be more asked of you."

"I'm a simple soldier. Not a spy."

"You are a patriot, Colonel."

"Why me?"

García looked at Montilla. Her eyes revealed nothing that Marcial could detect.

"You have a sterling record," García said. "And you satisfy a certain profile. They will find you more credible."

"Profile. You mean because I'm black? That's it?"

"It's more complex than that, Marcial," García said.

Marcial stared at the floor, elbows on his knees, hands clasped, and slowly shook his head.

García stood up. "We will be in touch," he said as he shook Marcial's hand.

Marcial took the jeep to his temporary quarters near Ciudad Libertad in the western outskirts of the city. He changed into civilian clothes and headed with his driver to the Malecón, the broad esplanade bordering the sea. He loved the Malecón. The sea breeze invigorated him; the expansive aquamarine sea liberated him. He closed his eyes and breathed deeply. Marisol. Hand-in-hand, they had walked for hours. Up and down. Sometimes talking, but often silent, yet close, as lovers were. He had been a cadet. She was a student nurse. Their needs were simple then. Long talks over ice cream at Coppelia. Swims at Bacuranao Beach. Salsa dancing. Los Van Van concerts. Lovemaking on the rocks below the Malecón. Things had been so uncomplicated then.

Marcial directed the driver to pull over near the old mob-owned Riviera Hotel. Straight out of the 1950s, just like so many of the cars. A city frozen in time. He hopped out onto the sidewalk next to a skateboard park. A dozen boys zoomed around, pushing the envelope of their skills, shouting both encouragement and ridicule. A bunch of girls watched, cheered, and flirted. When his big olive-green military vehicle pulled up with the MININT-uniformed driver and ministry plates, the skateboarders cruised to a stop, and the girls looked away. Smiles turned to scowls, sullen faces, and defiant eyes. The driver got out to open the door for Marcial.

"Comemierda!" someone spat. "Shitcater" was an epithet often reserved for communist officials, but always behind closed doors.

"Hey! Who said that?" the driver shouted.

"Jaime, you can go back. I'd like to walk now. Thanks," Marcial told the young driver.

The GAZ roared off, belching black diesel exhaust in its wake. Since the 1994 social unrest known as the *Maleconazo* when Havanans had taken to the streets to protest fast-declining economic conditions following the abrupt end of Soviet and East Bloc subsidies, the regime had been able to keep a lid on things. Every hundred meters, an officer of the *Policía Nacional Revolucionaria* kept watch; patrol cars crept along the road. Encased surveillance cameras mounted on lampposts and buildings were pervasive. Marcial could see that the authorities were on heightened alert.

Marcial continued down the Malecón. Like all country boys, he found Havana grand and majestic. A dowager, once stunning, now faded, falling apart. The city possessed a majesty and proportion outsized to the confines of a small island nation as if, like Rome or Vienna, it were once the capital of a great empire. The Cuban character was similar, too big, too ambitious for an island people. A sense of grandeur reflected in the imaginations of those who built Havana. And in the leadership.

His leisure stroll took Marcial past the José Martí stadium. The sea was rough with big waves crashing against the rocks. The few cars and rickety trucks that passed along the esplanade did little to interfere with the gorgeous view of the sea against a cloud-strewn sky. There were also few people. The Malecón was a place for nocturnal activity. At night, it bustled with strollers, kids, lovers, foreign tourists, hustlers, and whores.

Ahead lay a place reviled by a few, but fascinating to many. An off-limits magnet. A foothold in Cuban soil of a land of contradictions, hope, and danger. The United States Interests Section building was seven stories of concrete and glass, vintage 1953, but unlike most of Havana, upgraded and functional. Concrete berms, a black iron fence, a few forlorn palm trees, and bored Cuban guards encircled the complex. A barren concrete plaza lay before the structure. *Socialismo o Muerte!* proclaimed a billboard.

Opposite the building's front was a small forest of twenty-meter-high flagpoles topped by black flags, each with a single white star, fluttering defiantly before the U.S. mission. The José Martí Anti-Imperialist Plaza had been erected to counter propaganda emitted from a scrolling electronic sign on the American building during the Bush II era.

The U.S. Interests Section of the Embassy of Switzerland wasn't an American embassy, nor was it truly a part of the Swiss diplomatic representation. But it operated more or less like an embassy. A place that was, yet wasn't.

Marcial had never fought Americans. He'd battled counterrevolutionaries and their South African allies in Angola. He'd assisted freedom fighters in Central America. But he'd never even met an American before his assignment as Frontier Brigade Commander at Guantánamo. Though he would never utter a word about it, he found the American naval captain and his cohorts friendly and hospitable. They seemed open, constructive, and jovial. But that didn't mean anything. His job was to protect the Republic of Cuba from the Americans' nefarious schemes. He dreamt he would one day be saluting the Cuban flag on the naval base that the Americans occupied illegally.

The note-passing episode had left him uneasy. That was work best left to professional spies. Dirty work. Not soldier's work. He could accept it, assuming it had been a one-time deal. But it wasn't. Gen. García made that clear. Marcial looked up at the U.S. Interests Section again. *If only you knew...*

He took a right off the Malecón. When he stopped to buy a cold soft drink, he noticed a figure some twenty meters to his rear. A man in a blue shirt was leaning against the wall of the Riviera. Nothing out of the ordinary. Just another un- or under-employed male watching the world pass by. A common sight.

But Marcial was trained to spot anomalies, to track details. He finished his drink and headed into central Havana. He found it refreshing to be in a big city again. Havana dwarfed Guantánamo City and was relatively more prosperous. Though the unpainted, decaying apartment complexes, rutted streets, and torpor among the inhabitants signaled anything but dynamism. Yet wherever one went, the syncopations of salsa, rhumba, son, reggaeton beat from windows, door stoops, and sidewalks. Couples threw themselves into extemporaneous dance.

Every other block or so was a vacant lot, standing walls devoid of internal structure as if bombed out, or a small mountain of rubble where buildings once stood. They'd been picked clean of anything salvageable. Stick-thin mangy dogs roamed in search of anything edible.

When he had been a captain, Marcial had a buddy, also a captain, whose family had been wealthy white landowners in the old days. Some of them had stayed on to serve the revolution. On Friday nights, when they'd had one too many glasses of rum, his buddy would rail about "The Lost City of Havana, a shining gem, now a pile of ruins." Marcial himself had no reference point to pass such judgment. He was a simple *guajiro*, a son of semi-literate farmers from Oriente, three generations from slavery.

Marcial stopped and pretended to tie his shoe, while surreptitiously checking behind him. The man in the blue shirt hovered nearby, looking away as if pondering the universe. Marcial stood and gravitated in the direction of the clamor of voices. Another mound of rubble lay before him, a small mountain of bricks, spidery rebars, and plaster dust with water pipes jutting out like fractured bones of a felled beast. Two concrete angels lay shattered on the curb like celestial corpses.

"Housing now! Housing now! Housing now!" a group chanted where the front entrance of the *Reina* used to be.

Across the street, a phalanx of middle-aged women, all dressed in white, made a circular march in silence. They carried photos of loved ones.

A crowd was gathering. A young woman with a tape recorder was making the rounds. She wore a T-shirt which proclaimed, "DON'T HIT ME. I'M JUST A BLOGGER." She shoved the mic in front of Marcial's face. "What about you, friend? How do you feel about this? Over a hundred buildings collapse in Havana every year. Eighty-six innocents lost their lives in this one. What do you have to say?"

Marcial waved her off and backed away. He turned to another rubbernecker, an old man with no teeth. "What's this all about?"

"These people are survivors," the man said.

"Of what?"

"Heh, heh. Where you been, *compañero*? Under a rock? This is the Reina. Collapsed last week. Record number killed. People had enough. They're pissed. Everybody's afraid of being crushed to death in their own homes. The whole goddamn city's falling apart."

"Who's that young woman? She with *Granma* or something?"

The old man scoffed. "Shit no, *compañero*. That's Yamilé. Some say she's a hero; others that she's a *gusana*. Troublemaker she is. She puts out all kinds of criticism against the government over the computer."

"You mean the internet?"

The old man shrugged. "Whatever."

"And those women over there?"

"The Ladies in White. You really been under a rock, huh?"

"Why are they walking in a circle like that?" Marcial asked, ignoring the old man's digs.

"More *gusanas*. At least that's what those clowns in the CDR over there say." He nodded in the direction of a group of counter-protesters shouting angrily at the demonstrators. "The Ladies in White, they want their loved ones released from jail. They come to show support for the Reina victims. Yamilé comes to spread the news, and the CDR types launch another repudiation rally against the whole lot. What's this country coming to? *El Jefe* needs to crack down."

The thirty counter-protesters of the local Committee for the Defense of the Revolution waved placards reading, "Fatherland or Death!" "Down with Counterrevolutionaries!" "*El Jefe* Leads – We Follow." They shook their fists and shrieked at the demonstrators.

The CDR activists marched closer to the homeless protesters. A pushing match ensued. One of the pro-government agitators broke from formation and shoved Yamilé, who went careening out of control against Marcial, knocking him down onto the sidewalk.

Marcial shot back up, grabbed the shoving man, and threw him down onto the street with all his might. The man landed face first, and a couple of teeth flew from his mouth, followed by a stream of blood.

Several of the man's comrades rushed into the fray. "*Gusano* traitor!" they yelled and proceeded to pummel Marcial. The homeless Reina demonstrators joined in, attacking Marcial's assaulters.

Regaining her balance, Yamilé recorded the melée with her cell phone. Within half a day, it would shoot around the world via cyberspace.

A distant klaxon came nearer. Police cars and two paddy wagons screeched to a halt. Cops rushed out to separate the brawlers.

"Leave me alone! I'm not fighting! You have no right!"

Yamilé screamed as two policewomen grabbed her arms and dragged her off to a paddy wagon.

Police pulled the pro-government ruffians off of Marcial, and he got to his feet. Just as he got up, one of the cops yanked him toward the other paddy wagon.

Marcial swung a powerful fist into the cop's solar plexus. The lawman went down, clutching his abdomen and gasping for air. Fireworks flashed inside Marcial's head, followed quickly by a stream of blood from where a billy club met his skull.

CHAPTER THREE

Union City, New Jersey
Wednesday

La Paloma Restaurant on Bergerline Avenue was only two blocks to Weehawken Cemetery, three minutes on foot. But that afternoon, it would take an hour and a half. María Mirabel de la Cruz told her son, Paco, to hold the fort while she ran some errands.

"When will you be back, Mom?" the lanky teenager asked as he practiced invisible hoop shots in front of an overhead TV broadcasting ESPN coverage of Boston battling Orlando.

"I gotta go to ShopRite to get some things for the house. Then to the shoe repair. And I need to pick up our wholesale order at Palisades Supplies."

"Yeah, sure. Okay," Paco murmured, half-tuned out.

"I need you to watch the *lechón asado*. We got the Cuban-American Freedom Association banquet tonight. That *lechón* has to be succulent. They love it."

Silence.

"Paco! Did you hear me?"

"Uh. Yeah. Sure. The *lechón*. Succulent."

María wagged a finger at her son. "I'm gonna call you to make sure. If you let that pork turn to leather, I'm gonna cuff you so hard! And get off your lazy ass and do something, *ocioso*. Learn how to run a business, like your father and I did.

Came here with nothing, and now we can afford to send you to Rutgers."

Paco broke from his trance long enough to give his mother a peck on the cheek. "Don't worry. Everything'll be fine. Those old dinosaurs will get to feast on their *succulent* dead pig flesh."

María laughed. Before exiting, she placed two large posters in the front window. One was of the Pope with the caption: "God Bless America." The other read, "FREEDOM – DEMOCRACY FOR CUBA. Annual CAFA Banquet – La Paloma Restaurant." She straightened the Cuban and American flags on either side of the outside entrance before taking off in her Chevy van.

She turned right onto Bergerline Avenue, drove seven minutes in congested traffic, hung a right onto 39th Street, then a left on JFK Boulevard until she arrived at ShopRite. She took her time picking up some groceries and household items. María next entered the ramp for 495 West to end up twenty minutes later in Lyndhurst at a Dominican-owned shoe repair at a low-end strip mall. After dropping off her shoes, she strolled up and down the row of shops – Carnicería de las Americas, Ortiz Gold & Jewelry, Café Caribe, Marco's Pizza. She looked into each shop window, focusing on the images mirrored from behind her. She walked through a five-foot-wide space separating two of the buildings. The path, marked by drainage pipes and litter, ended in the grubby rear delivery area of the shops. She walked in a circle, then passed back through the narrow space.

Back in her van, María drove to East Rutherford, where she picked up some pastries from Santiago Bakery. More window-shopping was followed by a pitstop deep inside the mall. Then, she headed back across the river, over to North Bergen, onto 4th Avenue, then made a sharp U-turn to double back along the same route, all the while scrutinizing every vehicle around her, noting makes, years, colors, conditions, and license plate numbers.

After a stop at Palisades Supplies for some restaurant items, María parked the van on a dead end street a few blocks from La Paloma and carefully eyeballed the length and breadth of the trash-strewn short strip bordered by a near-vacant parking lot and a small deteriorating warehouse.

Yakov Peters, deputy head of the Soviet Cheka, once said, "The best quality of a spy is patience." And the one thing constantly drummed into the heads of new recruits of the General Directorate of Intelligence in Havana was, "There is no such thing as too much security."

María had been number one in her class when running a surveillance detection route, or SDR. In her final exam, the DGI assigned twenty experienced officers to cover her. She lost all of them within ten minutes. María attributed her talent in part to her plain face and square body. She was a person no one looked twice at, except Ramón, who was equally nondescript. He made a good husband.

Conducting a good SDR entailed constant tracing and re-tracing of routes to identify that recurrent face, car, clothing, motorcycle, or physique that would give away a tail and going through choke points in order to winnow out surveillance operatives. María never took shortcuts. Life in solitary at a federal penitentiary was something she had no intention of risking.

When they had been slipped into the Mariel exodus by the DGI in 1980, María and Ramón dreaded leaving their native land for the Main Adversary—Moscow's and Havana's ideological nemesis, the United States. But they made their way into American society and the virulently anti-Castro Cuban exile community. Eventually, they would be allowed to return to retire and to collect the medals awarded to them by *El Comandante*. As Principal Resident Agent in New Jersey, María had developed over the years a wide-ranging network of deeply embedded moles and subagents who provided a wealth of intelligence and carried out active measures in the service of their Cuban masters. The steady damage done to the reactionary exile leaders was immeasurable.

María crossed Hillside Avenue on foot, skirted a row of houses, and proceeded along a path through a wooded area into Weehawken Cemetery. Again, she was hyper-alert of her surroundings. She crossed the cemetery's circular drive and walked slowly to the designated rendezvous point. She spotted the small white cross painted on a maple tree, indicating the dead drop was ready for pick-up.

Almost hidden in bushes was the grave of Albert Vadas, Medal of Honor winner for heroism in fighting the Spanish at the Battle of Cienfuegos, 1898. Kneeling in feigned prayer, she carefully surveyed her surroundings. María then made the sign of the cross, stood, and circled behind the headstone to retrieve the package left by her case officer, a DI agent working under cover as a diplomat in the Cuban mission to the U.N.

The feel of cold steel behind her left ear and a metallic click were not part of the game.

Herndon, Virginia
Thursday

Luís Gabaldón popped another dexlansoprazole. Acid reflux wasn't something he'd wish on anyone. His diet, he could deal with. Nerves, however, were another matter. And whenever his debt level got out of control or he was out on a mission, Gabaldón's stomach rebelled.

He wondered if his new case officer from the Cuban Interests Section was too green. For the third time in the last ten months, he had been instructed to meet at Ralph Fendrick's Used Auto Parts Lot in Spotsylvania, Virginia. The lot was over seventy miles from Herndon through northern Virginia's can of worms road system, which meant an hour and a half if the perennial traffic congestion was merely insane rather than homicidal. And the fact that it was already ninety degrees and near a hundred percent humidity at ten a.m. added to the aggravation.

"And don't forget to stop at Macy's after the bank to pick up my new dress. You got the ticket?" Mercedes asked.

"Yeah. And don't ask me again. You think I'm stupid?" Luís put his Dodge pickup in gear and proceeded to back out of the driveway of his ranch house, which was nearly identical to the scores of others in the cul-de-sac-pocked tract-housing neighborhood.

"Wait up!" she yelled, scampering from the front door in pink fluffy slippers, a too-long moo-moo, and curlers in her hair. "You're not stupid, Luís, just slow on the uptake sometimes. I need money for groceries. And Little Louie needs to pay for his football equipment this week. Those cleats alone are two hundred dollars. Matilda's behind on her prom preparations. She needs to order a gown and make an appointment at the hair salon."

Luís shut his eyes and massaged his forehead. He then grabbed for the bottle of Extra-Strength Tylenol he kept in the glove compartment. He prayed the fifty-megaton headache that was coming on wouldn't work with the stomach acid to cause him to vomit.

"And for a car repair shop owner, you're not too swift about keeping up on car payments. Little Louie's Grand Am is behind by two—"

Luís screeched out of the driveway, smoke shooting out as the rubber met the road in his escape from Robin Hood Drive. He pulled onto Fairfax County Parkway behind a behemoth bus filled with camera-crazy Asian tourists. Black diesel fumes filled the Dodge's cabin. Luís honked futilely.

Groceries. Hah! If you regard the rarefied, galactically-priced fare at Whole Foods as "groceries," or daily doses of designer coffee at Starbucks at four bucks a pop as "groceries," then, sure, we're the all-American family. With four cars, genuine NFL equipment for a highschooler, prom preparations that rivaled those for Oscar night, annual pilgrimages back to Santo Domingo to see family and shell out subsidies to them, two mortgages, taxes that only went up, and business and health insurance that bordered on the extortionate, they had traded steady but uncomplicated poverty back in the old country for the so-called American Dream of boundless materialism and its huge costs.

He tossed seventy-five cents into the collection basket giving access to the Dulles Toll Road. Traffic moved smoothly.

Luís had been proud of his achievements. He started his own business repairing cars. Then the contracts came—first, the Herndon police, followed by the county government car fleet. He bought two more garages. Finally, the biggest kahuna of them all: the USG. Specifically, the Pentagon. His reputation firmly established as a reliable and fair auto-repair businessman, Luís had landed a sizeable contract with the Defense Department to maintain and repair several fleets of official cars.

The money was good, but the more he made, the more they spent. Vacations, a boat, cars, and a revolving credit line that took in Macy's, Neiman-Marcus, Gucci, Redskins tickets. It was amazing, he thought. America the Beautiful, to be sure. But also America the Spendthrift. Everyone fell for it. And everyone was paying the price.

He'd be a bankrupt grease monkey had he not met Corrales. He had taken a loan from a guy he thought was a loan shark, though a nice fellow, well groomed with that smooth self-confidence exhibited by successful attorneys and CEOs. The man's Cuban accent was so close to Luis's own Dominican one. They hit it off. Corrales gave him five grand at the outset with easy terms. When that was gone, Luís went back to Corrales with head bowed, to ask for an extension of payment.

"No problem," the handsome Cuban said. "Here's ten more." And then, "Do you think you could give me copies of the Pentagon's motor pool?"

A funny request, but what the hell? After the next ten grand, Corrales asked for more detail—which cars were assigned to what officials, their daily routes, the drivers' full names and home addresses. The payments rose when Luís let a "friend" of Corrales work on some of the cars on weekends. The money was good and getting better, but again, there was a price to pay in meeting Corrales's demands while still running the business and attending to the voracious needs of his family. He slept fitfully, his back ached constantly, and his stomach churned.

On I-95 south, Luís put some soothing Latin string music into the CD player. He thought through more clearly all the demands being made upon him. Too many to have to answer to. Thank God he was a teetotaler, didn't use drugs, and had no interest in other women. He and Mercedes attended church every Sunday. All he really needed was *money*.

Luís had decided to up his demand to fifty grand. And that was only the beginning. He had other Latino friends who did business with the government. He could tap them for all kinds of info to sell. But he had no loyalty to the stinking Castro regime or to Cuba. This was strictly business. He forked over useless information about government cars in return for payment. An American business transaction. Nothing more.

Ralph Fendrick's Used Auto Parts Lot was little more than a car dump, one of many eyesore auto boneyards scattered around rural white trash Virginia, a place where one could put hands on a door for a '78 Impala or a fuel injector for an '89 Lincoln Continental. After paying his respects to Redneck Fendrick, Sr., Luís went poking around the corpses and detritus of autos past. He made his way to the back piled high with wrecks. He found the 1991 red Toyota Corolla and waited, as instructed. He heard the crush of straw under a foot and turned.

"You're not Corrales," were his last words.

Key West, Florida
Friday

After being waved through the main gate at Saratoga Avenue, Ulices Peña drove his van displaying "Peña Painting – Have Brush, Will Travel - Key West" under the U.S. Naval Air Station Key West sign. Passing the F-5 squadron belonging to Fighter

Composite Squadron One-Eleven, he proceeded to the family housing complex at Sigsbee Park. He returned a mock salute to Chief Warrant Officer Bud O'Reilly, one of his supervisors and a man never without a joke.

He assigned tasks to his five-man crew waiting at the house to be painted that day. Once the men began, Peña returned to his vehicle to complete some paperwork: paint orders, invoices, payroll tax computations, work mileage, number of fighters on the runways that morning, and observable activity at the 749th Military Intelligence Company HQ. The last two entries were made in code in tiny script on page fifty-three of a paint catalog.

His cell phone chirped. O'Reilly wanted to meet him at the administration building to go over some contract details. Ulices told his crew, started the engine, and took off. He was met in front of the small conference room by O'Reilly, who opened the door for him before leaving the building. Lt. Commander Don Watson of the Office of Naval Intelligence and FBI agent Nick Castillo were already seated at the table.

"How's Uncle Horacio?" Watson asked. "Any news?"

"No. Nothing," Ulices replied.

"No contact from the courier?" Watson asked.

"Nope. None," Ulices said.

"Coffee?" Nick asked, offering a Styrofoam cup of steaming office swill.

Ulices took the cup. "Thanks."

Nick removed documents from a yellow manila folder and laid them in front of Ulices. They were stamped SECRET – NOFORN – ORCON. No Foreign – Or Contractor dissemination.

"We'd like you to hand these over to the courier next time you rendezvous," Nick said. "I think *tío Horacio* will find them interesting."

At five-foot-four, Ulices had never pictured himself as a Latin James Bond. He was a house painter. Oil versus latex. Natural bristles versus synthetic. Brick red versus terra cotta.

Those were his areas of expertise, not passing secrets from one government to another or playing games of international deceit. But he had fallen into it.

On his last trip to Santa Clara to see family three years ago, Uncle Horacio had appeared on his doorstep. Ulices had barely ever seen Uncle Horacio. He was off in Africa, the family said, serving the revolution, or in Moscow at the Cuban embassy, or in Havana. Always anywhere but in Santa Clara.

Horacio had been completely off the radar after Ulices's parents left Cuba with their three kids in the eighties. Miami High School, vocational training, his own small business, a modest house in the 'burbs, fine Cuban-American wife, two boys, Dolphins games. Security. Ulices felt America was the greatest country on earth, and he would do anything to repay what the nation had done for him.

"So," Uncle Horacio had said, "that girl you knocked up while at high school in Santa Clara? That daughter, she had your eyes, your smile. Beautiful girl." He showed Ulices a photo.

A betting man would wager that a DNA test would confirm the connection. The child was indeed beautiful. He had loved her mother as much as a sixteen-year-old could love. But his parents' move out of the country ended the relationship, much to their relief. Ulices had never heard from the girl again.

"Idania is her name," Horacio said. "Graduated with honors in microbiology. Now she is applying for a job with the Pedro Kourí Institute in Havana. Very prestigious. World travel. Access to the special hard currency stores." Horacio shook his head.

"Yes?" Ulices prompted.

"Ah. A complication. No party ties. No connections. Priority is given for the children of deserving party members for these jobs. To reward those who have served the revolution. As for those who fled *la Patria*..." He shook his head again.

"I can arrange a meeting. I am sure she would love to see her father," Horacio said.

And he did. The meeting had been emotional for both.

Father and daughter hugged as if they'd reunited after a long spell rather than not having ever met. His heart was hers.

Dear Uncle – *Colonel* – Horacio had hooked his nephew. In return for some hazily defined favors from Ulices, the uncle would grease the skids for Idania to pursue her dreams.

It was a pact with the devil, Ulices knew. Spy for Castro in return for assuaging the guilt he'd felt for having abandoned his baby.

"You absolutely did the right thing coming to us, Ulices," Nick said.

Ulices snapped out of his reverie. "Yeah. Sure. I love this country. I owe it so much. That's why I reported my uncle's approach to the FBI as soon as I got back. But I'm a simple painter. This stuff makes my head spin. And I don't like doing secret things. Pretending to spy for them when I'm really spying for you. How long do I have to do it?"

Nick leaned forward. "Listen to me, Ulices. What you're doing is a great service to your country. The information you feed to the Cubans helps keep them off guard. And their dealings with you help us to get insight on how they operate in this country. I can't give you an end date. Maybe when Fidel is dead."

Ulices shook his head. "That one will never die." He departed with the documents, which he would lock up in a safe deposit box until he got the signal.

The signal came in the form of a phone call a week later. A male voice gave him the address of a pay phone on Roosevelt Boulevard and a time to be there. He was told to be at the Winn-Dixie supermarket on the same boulevard at nine o'clock that evening.

Ulices called his wife to say he'd be working late and asked for a grocery list. He walked up and down the supermarket aisles. Nothing out of the ordinary. He stuck his head into the ice cream freezer. Rocky Road. *Ah! Found one, the last!* As he placed the carton in his cart, he discovered a standard mail envelope had mysteriously appeared where the large envelope Nick had given him had been. A brush pass executed by a magician. He quickly stuffed the new envelope into his paint-splattered coveralls, paid for his groceries, and left the store.

As he settled into the driver's seat of his van, Ulices looked left and right. Then he pulled out the envelope and carefully opened it. In the dim illumination of the parking lot lights, he brought the single sheet of paper to his face. It was blank.

Tap, tap.

He rolled down his window.

CHAPTER FOUR

SECRET

1613Z 17 JUNE

FROM: DIRECTOR FBI
TO: MIAMI IMMEDIATE
NEWARK IMMEDIATE
NEW YORK IMMEDIATE
WASHINGTON FIELD IMMEDIATE

SECTION 1 OF 2

NO FOREIGN DISSEMINATION

UNSUBS: MURDER OF TWO SUSPECTED
CUBAN AGENTS, ONE DOUBLE AGENT
MIAMI FILE 185-11

MARIA MIRABEL DE LA CRUZ – UNION CITY, NJ
LUIS ALONSO GABALDON – HERNDON, VA
ULICES PENA – KEY WEST, FL

1. MARIA MIRABEL DE LA CRUZ'S
BODY WAS FOUND 0910, 16 JUNE, BY
GROUNDSKEEPER AT WEEHAWKEN

CEMETERY, IN UNION CITY, NJ. SUBJECT WAS SHOT TWICE IN THE HEAD. NO OTHER EVIDENCE OF TRAUMA. NO VALUABLES TAKEN. FAMILY REPORTS SUBJECT WAS RUNNING ERRANDS AFTERNOON OF 16 JUNE.

2. LUIS ALONSO GABALDON'S BODY WAS FOUND 0940, 17 JUNE, BY OWNER OF USED AUTO PARTS LOT IN SPOTSYLVANIA, VA. SUBJECT WAS SHOT TWICE IN THE HEAD. NO OTHER EVIDENCE OF TRAUMA. NO VALUABLES TAKEN. FAMILY REPORTS SUBJECT WAS RUNNING ERRANDS MORNING OF 16 JUNE.

3. ULICES PENA'S BODY WAS FOUND 2120, 18 JUNE, BY LOCAL POLICE AT SUPERMARKET PARKING LOT AT KEY WEST, FL. SUBJECT WAS SHOT TWICE IN THE HEAD. NO OTHER EVIDENCE OF TRAUMA. NO VALUABLES TAKEN. FAMILY REPORTS SUBJECT WAS WORKING LATE AT U.S. NAVAL STATION KEY WEST EVENING OF 18 JUNE.

4. BALLISTICS AND AUTOPSY REPORTS PENDING.

5. ACTION FIELD OFFICES REQUESTED TO BEGIN INVESTIGATIONS IMMEDIATELY SURROUNDING CIRCUMSTANCES OF HOMICIDES AND REPORT DEVELOPMENTS.

"Three double-tap jobs within seventy-two hours, eleven hundred miles apart. Amazing," Bart Morgenstern said. "Autopsy reports. Are they kiddin' or what? Whadda they gonna find? Lead poisoning of the brain? And ballistics is irrelevant, and I'll tell you why." Morgernstern grabbed for another jelly donut from the box on the conference table.

Nick Castillo, unshaven and baggy-eyed, reached out and held his arm. "You're bucking for a heart attack, Bart."

"Yeah. You're right. No self-control." Morgenstern shook off Nick's hand and picked up his third donut of the morning.

"I can't figure it out," Nick said. "I meet with Peña a week ago, give him his marching orders. Guy said he wasn't cut out for espionage, just wanted to be left alone. But patriotism for the United States drove him on. And he gets whacked in a parking lot. Three carefully synchronized hits, in an identical fashion. Very professional. But it can't be Havana. When have they ever carried out wet affairs inside the United States?"

"They tried to whack DGI defector Florentino Aspillaga inside the United States in the '90s, but failed. Before that, there were at least eight attacks inside the mainland United States between 1969 and 1982, by Puerto Rican terrorists. Seven were bombing incidents. Five killed, fifty-nine maimed. Funded and trained by Cuban State Security. We know that. And there's the Black Panthers…"

"Okay. But how many cases do we know of confirmed assassinations by actual agents of Cuba inside this country?"

Bart pondered. "JFK?"

"This isn't funny, Bart." Nick got up.

"DRIVETRAIN."

"Excuse me?"

"DRIVETRAIN could be behind it," Morgenstern said. "MININT operative. Very nebulous. We don't even know if it's a he or a she. All we got is some tidbits from defectors over the years. CIA gave him or her the code name DRIVETRAIN. We know, for example, that Carlos the Jackal's case officer for Latin

America was this DRIVETRAIN. He or she coordinated money, travel, weapons, and logistics for the Jackal. The Jackal's in a French prison now and won't divulge the identity at any cost. My guess is he doesn't even know. DRIVETRAIN uses buffers, cutouts, and couriers. A Green Beret was ambushed and killed in El Salvador in 1987. A MININT colonel who defected in 1991 told us it was carefully plotted by a deep-cover officer in a super-secret office of MININT called the Special Activities Unit, located in a building separate from Directorate of Intelligence headquarters on Linea Street.

"How is it you know all this stuff?" Nick asked.

"When you eat, breathe, and dream this shit year in and year out, it becomes second nature. There are guys who can tell you who batted a thousand in the 1947 World Series, or who can recite the price of General Electric stock for twenty years straight. I can tell you who's been in charge of the MININT motorpool since its inception or Raúl Castro's favorite drink—vodka, by the way. I couldn't get a real job in the private sector. I'm a geek with a very particular specialization."

"I'll say."

The door opened, and Special Agent in Charge Clement Rourke entered. With him was a woman in her late twenties, tow-headed, pale complexion, and a serious expression.

Rourke retained the military bearing he acquired as a young Marine. He was a straight shooter and highly respected among the Bureau's rank and file. "On this Triple Hit case, we need results ASAP. And since this may involve foreign state actors, we need close interagency coordination. This comes from the top. Headquarters has sent us"—he gestured at the young woman—"Ms. Kate Kovalchuk. Ms. Kovalchuk is an analyst at CIA, currently assigned as Special Assistant to the Director of National Intelligence, Admiral Forster." Rourke introduced Nick and Morgenstern to her. "She is to be given the fullest cooperation. Consider her a full FIG team member. The DNI places highest priority to this case, and Kate is his personal representative." Rourke excused himself.

"What have you turned up thus far?" Kovalchuk asked.

"Coffee?" Morgenstern offered.

"No." She looked expectantly at Nick. "So?"

"Well, first we need to divide labors, assign responsibilities."

"In other words, you've got squat. Just as I thought. Admiral Forster sent me here to kick-start a multifaceted, multisourced, robust investigation. Now."

Nick exchanged glances with Morgenstern. "This Triple Hit just happened. I'm the ASAC for this Field Intelligence Group—"

"And I'm the DNI's personal representative. This investigation has to happen, and I mean, like, yesterday. We have no time to waste on bureaucratic cake baking, people. Now, if you'll excuse me, I need to get settled in." She rose and left the room.

"Personal representative for ball busting," Morgenstern spat as soon as the door closed.

CHAPTER FIVE

Havana

Larisa Montilla was ushered into the moderately sized, simply decorated office of the First Secretary of the Communist Party of Cuba, on the fourth floor of the Palace of the Revolution. Her MININT uniform freshly pressed and her colonel's lapel pins polished, she stood at attention and saluted smartly. "*Comandante.*"

In a sitting area away from the Scandinavian-design desk, a shrunken old man slumped in a state-of-the-art wheelchair, the clinical elements of which were suppressed with black paint and tasteful cushions. "Please, *compañera* Montilla. Please sit down." He gestured at a stuffed chair to his right.

She'd been there before during the Special Period when the *liderazgo*—the leadership— had feared the worst after the fall of communism in Eastern Europe and the Soviet Union, when the pipeline of subsidies to the regime had abruptly ended and the economy had gone into a tailspin. Enemies, internal and external, became emboldened. The highly honed skills of loyal apparatchiks like her were needed to counter their schemes. Montilla had delivered by neutralizing the Miami gangster exiles bent on subverting the revolution. Shooting down the tiny Skymaster aircraft of the so-called Brothers to the Rescue in 1996 to foil their efforts to drop propaganda leaflets over the Malecón and thereby instigate another mass migration had been her idea. For that and other feats, *El Jefe* had awarded her the Order of Máximo Gómez.

His beard had thinned considerably. Age spots had sprouted across his face. His eyes were sunken. He raised his right index finger in his trademark gesture that said he was about to make a point. "José Martí said, 'Men fall into two camps, those who hate and destroy, and those who love and build.'" His voice cracked, and a wheezing spasm seized him.

A medical orderly from the fourth-floor clinic rushed over with an inhaler at the ready.

El Comandante quickly recovered and shooed away the orderly. "I have spent a lifetime *building* this country because of my *love* for the Cuban people. I will never abandon them."

"Yes, *Comandante*," she said.

"But I am mortal. And so is my brother. The reins of the revolution will soon be passed on to a younger generation of patriots. Like yourself."

"Not for many more years, *Comandante*."

He dismissed her comment with a wave. "We must plan. Lenin didn't plan enough before he died. I intend not to make the same mistake. I now hold no official positions. I am a Soldier of Ideas only. In the meantime, our enemies salivate like wolves about to pounce on their prey. They think we are weak. They think they will be able to take over. But yet again, they underestimate the iron will of the Cuban people to remain free and the steadfastness of their leaders. And... and..." There was a long silence. The old man had again raised his index finger, about to drive home another point. But like a soaring bird suddenly trapped in a net, his thought was caught in suspension. His eyes searched for his next words, but they didn't come.

Montilla shifted uneasily in her seat. The orderly fidgeted in a corner of the office. The seconds piled into a minute. Finally, the bird came free.

"And we therefore need to keep the enemies of our revolution off balance." He punched his left palm with his right fist to drive home the point. "You know, Che used to read a lot about strategy. He especially liked that Chinese strategist... uh... Santa... somebody." He rubbed his forehead, as if hoping to massage a failing memory out of it.

"Sun Tzu," Larisa offered.

"Ah, yes! That's the one. Che quoted him a lot. He used to say, 'by inflicting damage, we can make it impossible for the enemy to draw near.'" He fixed his eyes on Montilla's. "So, I want you to do more of that. Understand?"

"Yes, *Comandante*."

"The other thing he said, quoting that Chinese, was 'It is only the enlightened ruler who will achieve great results through the best use of his intelligence apparatus.' You have achieved great results for *la Patria*, Colonel. I expect you to achieve even more during this period of transition."

"Yes, *Comandante*."

"And I am promoting you to the rank of brigadier general. The first woman to achieve that rank."

"*Comandante*, I—"

"Never mind. You earned it." He held her gaze, then nodded ever so slightly, deep in memories. He leaned over, and in a soft voice, said, "You are a true child of the revolution. And I trust you more than anyone."

Three official sedans screeched to a halt in front of Combinado Del Este prison. Brig. Gen. Alfredo García Menéndez stepped out a half-second before his car fully stopped and stood before the four-story block-like main building. His adjutant produced papers for the dumbfounded gate guards and demanded to see the warden immediately. The small party of MININT officials was escorted in by a flustered prison hack. The man's tunic was unbuttoned and his shoe laces untied—clear signs he used his desk as an ottoman. The french doors of the warden's office swung open.

The warden leapt to his feet and saluted. Shock combined with obsequiousness on his sixty-year-old face.

Garcia returned the salute. "Bring out prisoner Henrique Marcial Arribe. I am taking him into my custody."

The warden picked up a phone and ordered the prisoner be delivered pronto. An uneasy silence ensued.

"What's he charged with?" García asked.

Papers shuffled. Flunkies scattered. A minute later, the warden put on his reading glasses and read the rap sheet. "Disorderly conduct, assaulting an officer of the People's Revolutionary Police, potential dangerousness through conduct in manifest contradiction of socialist norms."

"Marcial is an Army colonel," García said.

"He had no papers. We can't simply take somebody at his word," the warden replied.

García raised his eyes to the ceiling in exasperation. "No papers. Yes, you're right, Warden. What do I sign to take him out of your custody?" He was given a form, which he signed.

Marcial appeared in the company of two prison guards. His simple cotton shirt was torn and bloodied, and his shoes were missing. His face was bruised. The top of his head was bandaged, and an eye was swollen.

García looked him up and down and slowly shook his head. "Come," he said and gestured toward the door.

In the car, García exploded. "What in the world were you doing showing up at a counterrevolutionary political demonstration? Are you out of your mind?"

"I just happened to walk by it."

"And did you just 'happen' to break the jaw of a CDR activist? And punch a policeman in the stomach? And take down several more before you could be subdued?"

"They attacked first—"

"Oh. Did they now? Why would they do that? Because they didn't like your face? And why aren't you wearing your uniform? This wouldn't have happened had you been wearing the uniform. And why didn't you have identification?"

"I'm stuck in Havana with nothing to do. So I thought I'd take a tour of the city. I left my ID in my uniform back at the BOQ."

"OK, Colonel *Turista*." He pulled out a packet of photos. "How do you explain this?"

Marcial took the photos. They showed Yamilé with a microphone "interviewing" him. Others displayed him in the melee with the CDR guy and the police. "I thought she was a *Granma* reporter."

"Well, she's not! She's an enemy of the state, you fool! What's happened to you, Marcial? You were a soldier's soldier. Now you are a… a hooligan?"

"I can explain it all."

"Never mind, Colonel. You're a disgrace. I'm taking you back to your quarters. I want you to stay put. When I do give you permission to leave, you will wear your uniform at all times. Understand?"

"Yes, General." Marcial observed city life through the window. What had happened to him? He had just fallen into a mess not of his own doing. Wrong place, wrong time. Fatigue overtook him, and he closed his eyes.

Angola. Marcial was wounded in both legs. The MiGs came roaring down to attack the South African artillery positions. The MPLA troops ignored the commands of Lieutenant García and kept fleeing the battlefield. García was abandoned as the enemy troops advanced. Marcial was placed on a stretcher and evacuated. No. No. Go help García! Help García!

"Henrique. Henrique! Wake up," García said, nudging Marcial's shoulder.

Startled from his dream, Marcial fought the fatigue that weighed on him.

"Listen, Henrique. I'll confide something," García said in a low voice. "The revolution is now at a crossroads. We are going to see changes. What will they be? I don't know. But you see those police there along the Malecón and around government offices? They weren't there a month ago. There's restiveness. The rice ration has been cut again. People can't find what they need to get through the day. Foreign investors are pulling out. More open challenges against the authorities. The internet breaks down the walls that were in place for decades, bringing the world to the people. With all of our old friends either now capitalist, or like China and Vietnam, capitalist in all but name, *socialismo o muerte* just doesn't cut it anymore. People want more. They want to be able to travel outside Cuba too. And I don't need to comment on the leadership. They can't last that much longer."

"Why are you telling me this?" Marcial asked.

"One, because we are old fighters. We fought and survived together in Angola. You shed blood. I was captured. Two, you are being tasked with a delicate mission, the wisdom of which I question."

Marcial looked at his old friend with surprise.

"Yes. Those who refuse to adjust to change and are stuck in the old ways will do anything to keep a lid on things. The Cold War lives on with them. They see nothing but enemies. Foreign as well as domestic."

"You're telling me I'm on a fool's mission?"

García stared out the window at a city crumbling by the day. "Go along with it. Build trust with the people putting you up to this. The day may come when that will be needed. We are soldiers, you and me. The Army may one day be called upon to take sides. And the Army must never fight against the people."

CHAPTER SIX

Just as Morgenstern had predicted, the autopsies confirmed the obvious: two bullets in the brain of all three victims. The shots were all behind an ear. Ballistics revealed the bullets were all nine millimeter, but from a different gun in each case.

Nick's sources in the Cuban-American community and in Miami criminal gangs yielded no leads. The murderer in each case had been careful to leave behind no material evidence. FBI field offices turned up no witnesses. The family members of the victims could think of no suspects, no enemies out for revenge. None of the victims had ever been involved in criminal activity.

"So what's this 'other information' about these three being Cuban agents?" Nick asked.

Kate's neck-length blond hair, blue pantsuit, and simple white blouse broadcast sobriety and purpose. It seemed she did all she could to suppress the presence her five-foot-nine-inch athletic frame naturally projected. "Special Compartmented Intelligence indicates Mirabel and Gabaldón were sleeper agents who were activated years ago by the Cuban DGI. Peña, of course, was your asset, another in a long line of FBI double agents burned by Cuban intelligence."

Morgenstern sat brooding in a corner. "Oh yeah? How about the crowded ranks of dead CIA recruits? Not to mention the Bay of Pigs?"

"Point made," she said. "Shall we move on?"

"And so the sleepers…" Nick said.

"What about them?" Kate asked.

"Special Compartmented Intelligence reveals they're Cuban agents, you said. So who offed them, and why?"

"Don't know," she answered curtly.

"Then let me ask you this. How is it that CIA knows of two enemy spies on U.S. soil, but the FBI doesn't? CIA's turf ends where U.S. territory begins. In case you weren't aware, the Federal Bureau of Investigation is in charge of counterespionage within the United States."

"Need to know."

"I beg your pardon?" Nick shot back.

"Need to know. National security information is shared on a need to know basis. All Special Access Programs are handled in this manner, *as you know*. Someone in your agency may have known it, but it just hasn't trickled down to you. I suggest you go up your chain of command to find out. Otherwise, it's not my business."

"Okay. Then let's see the files on them."

"Can't."

"Let me guess. 'Need to know.'" Nick shook his head. "So much for breaking down the stove pipes on information post-9/11," Nick said.

Kate shrugged. "I don't make the rules."

Morgernstern, who'd been glowering in silence, snorted and shifted his large behind in his chair. "I'll tell you why they were whacked. A, they changed their minds about America and wanted to quit spying for the Castros; b, they got sloppy and proved to be too risky to run anymore; or c, they were turned. In the case of Peña, they found out he was a double and took revenge."

Kate furrowed her brow and focused her gray eyes on Morgenstern. "Cuba is a creaky ship. The leaks are spreading. The stops are coming out. Five decades of communism have taken their toll. Cuba stands shoulder-to-shoulder with North Korea as the two remaining states in the world still clinging to orthodox communist ideology. Food is in shorter supply. So are daily necessities. The Castros have one foot in the grave. People have had enough. We have reports of citizens forming ad hoc committees throughout the island to challenge the government. The security apparatus has ramped up surveillance and suppressive measures. There are mass arrests."

"So where's this leading?" Nick asked.

"Hardliners, mainly in the Party and MININT, want to crack down," Kate answered. "Moderates in the civilian bureaucracy and the armed forces are opposing severe measures. As the Castros' grip on power fades, factions are appearing and vying to take the initiative to fill the emerging leadership vacuum. The struggle would extend abroad. Hardliners and progressives are liquidating each other's agents, either to scotch their opponents' operations or just to drive home a point. We've been anticipating this for years."

"Here's another thought," Nick said. "Even with his reduced brain cells, Fidel's still conniving. He fears Washington will interfere. Part of his black genius has been an uncanny ability to keep his adversaries off guard. We've only seen the beginning."

"Could be," Kate said.

Nick stood up. "Look. Speaking of hardasses, you've been less than cooperative since arriving here. A successful investigation rides on all agencies getting along."

"Sorry if I came on a little too strong," Kate replied. "Yeah, sure."

The low-slung pueblo-style bungalows surrounded by neat postage-stamp-sized lawns bespoke suburban contentment. As Nick Castillo turned right onto LaBaron Drive, memories flooded his mind. The good and strict nuns at Blessed Trinity, when there were still nuns to teach. Miami Springs Senior High as he and other Latinos filled the changing student body. A comfortable and secure existence. Teen pushback against the "Cuban thing" and Spanish language. His first love.

He pulled into the driveway almost by instinct. Nick increasingly contemplated life's inevitable changes. The dreaded passing of generations. Loss of the nest. He relished the time he had available with his folks and was grateful the FBI had given him the posting close to home, for a few years anyway.

His aproned mother, Serafina, stood in the doorway with a smile on her ruddy face, the icon of countless childhood memories. *"Ah, guapo mío! Qué bueno a verte!"* She planted a juicy kiss on both his cheeks.

"Mom, it's only been a week."

"Solamente una semana, eh? Tengo solo un hijo. Tú tienes que hacer respecto a tus padres." She shook an admonishing finger at him.

The two-way linguistic traffic had been a feature since he was a boy. Parents addressed son in Spanish. Son replied in English. All three family members were completely bilingual, but that didn't change tradition.

The rich aroma of his favorite dish, *ropa vieja*, slow-cooked pulled beef in spiced tomato sauce, filled the air. Fried plantains and black beans and rice completed a picture of culinary heaven for Nick.

His father's handshake was the remaining physically firm feature in the man. Rolando leaned on his cane and quipped that he had "nothing to hide from the FBI." Spending ten years in Castro's prisons, starting from scratch in the U.S. as a penniless, middle-aged immigrant, and gaining hard-earned success as owner of a small construction company had all taken their toll.

They sat down to eat. Little had changed in the small dining room, from the porcelain statue of the Virgin Mary on the credenza, the cheesy tapestry of the American eagle on the far wall, to countless tchotchkes meticulously arranged inside a glass-door cabinet and, of course, the official swearing-in FBI portrait of Nick.

"I read in today's *El Herald* that the lid's finally about to blow in Cuba," Rolando said. "What can you tell us, FBI man?"

"You know better than to believe everything you read, Pop. The Herald's been reporting stuff like that for years. Who knows?"

"But this time, it's for real!" Rolando picked up the Spanish-language edition of the Miami Herald and hit the front page with his hand. "'Sources throughout the island report heightened security in the major cities. Dissidents are blogging that people are talking about taking to the streets to protest food shortages. Moreover, neither President Raúl Castro, 82, nor his ailing brother, Fidel Castro, 87, have appeared in public in weeks, sparking speculation of an oncoming leadership crisis.'"

"I've heard the same reports, Pop. Whether now is different, only time will tell."

"Your father has been asked by the Cuban-American Freedom Association to head a committee on transition for Cuba," Serafina said. "It is a great honor."

"I want to dance on the coffins of the Castros," Rolando said. "I refuse to die until those devils are out once and for all!"

Nick lifted his glass. "Let's hope so, Pop. Here's to Fidel's and Raúl's early demise and freedom for the Cuban people."

They clinked glasses.

"It would make me even more proud of my son if he joined CAFA."

"Pop, we've been over this before."

"You see us as anti-communist-crusading dinosaurs. I know! You young people are losing your ties to your mother soil. You haven't suffered like we have. We know the tyranny…"

"Pop! Please let's not discuss this again…"

Serafina interjected, "How do you like the food?"

"As always, Ma, it's terrific."

"So, Nicky, seeing any girls?" Serafina asked.

Nick shrugged. "Not a lot of time for a social life."

"You mentioned a new lady joined your team. What's she like?"

Nick furrowed his brow. "A man-hater, Ma. Worse than Vilma Espín."

"What's her name?"

"Kate, uh, Kovalchuk."

"Kovalchuk." His father snorted. "Russian name. We know about Russians. Don't bring her home."

"Ukrainian. Sounds like a Ukrainian name, Pop. Anyway, don't worry. She's an ice princess, about as warm as a snowstorm at the South Pole."

"Ukrainian. Russian. Same thing. Find a nice Cuban girl," Rolando said in between bites.

"A girl joins my office, and you two are talking like emcees on the Dating Game."

"It's just that you're thirty-five, and time is running out, darling. Before you know it, you'll be gray, fat, and bald," Serafina said. "And well, it would be so nice to have grandchildren."

"What's for dessert?" Nick asked.

CHAPTER SEVEN

Dear Papa,

Everything is fine with me. I hope all is well with you. Wow! You're in Havana! How is it? I hope you are having a good time. How long will you be there? Is this a promotion?

Things here at José Maceo are fine. My grades continue to be high. I was presented the Senior Cadet Achievement Award. I feel so proud. I wish you could be here to witness it. I look forward to graduating and beginning my career in the FAR. But I am a bit worried. Some of the guys in my class are saying they'll be ordered to fire on citizens who are unhappy with our present situation. Other guys argue that they must live up to their oath to follow the leaders' orders and to protect the revolution. They keep telling us the Yankees are preparing to invade, but as far as we can see, there are no such preparations by the Americans to do so. There's nothing about it on the internet.

I've met a very nice girl. Her name is Carmelita, and she's from Santiago. Enclosed is her photo. Isn't she a knock-out?! I plan to introduce her to you. I haven't heard from Mama in quite a while. Maybe next week. The mail moves slowly here.

Papa, please burn this letter after you read it. The stuff I wrote about my pals is just for you only. The Party probably wouldn't like it.

Affectionately yours,

Yuri

GRANMA - *Official Organ of the Central Committee of the Communist Party of Cuba*

ELECTIONS A GREAT SUCCESS

(HAVANA) The results in the recent elections of delegates to the Municipal Assemblies of People's Power were formally ratified by the Council of State. The success of the elections was greeted enthusiastically throughout the nation.

José Ramón Machado Ventura, first vice president of the Councils of State and Ministers, and Ricardo Alarcón de Quesada, president of the National Assembly of People's Power, presided over the official event in the Vitrales Salon of the Cuban Parliament, attended by members and presidents of the commissions representing Cuba's 14 provinces and the special municipality of the Isle of Youth.

WE SHALL NEVER SETTLE FOR A HALFWAY REVOLUTION

The commission presidents unanimously called on all citizens to work doubly hard to advance the revolution to new heights. First Vice President Machado declared, "If tired, go for retirement, but do not become a hindrance. Do not become an obstacle. Do not stand in the way. There is much to do, and this is a task for revolutionaries. It is not enough to have been a revolutionary yesterday; one needs to be a revolutionary today and a revolutionary tomorrow. And not being a hindrance is also a way of being a revolutionary. Those who feel emboldened in the face of difficulties to criticize Cuba and socialism will be dealt with harshly."

Marcial put down his morning reading and downed his *cafecito*. He looked at his son's letter and smiled. He felt so proud. The boy was everything a father could ask for—smart, loyal, self-directed.

Before long, with luck, Yuri would marry and make Marcial a grandfather. He shook his head. Unbelievable. How time flew.

Shifting his gaze from Yuri's letter, he frowned. Change was in the air all right. And García was right. There were those who would resist change at all costs and those who would embrace it. And there was the crux. Choices would have to be made. Two generations had been born and raised without being confronted with the need to make major choices. The prospect left him with a chill. How would he choose?

The Café 20 de Mayo was a peso-only, state-owned hole-in-the-wall that rarely, if ever, saw a foreigner. So the tipsy Italian with the young *jinetera* on his arm barged in like an Armani in a guayabera world.

"*Ola, qué tal? Ola a tutti!*" The Italian cackeled drunkenly. "*Me gusta Cuba! Me gusta moltissimo!*" He leaned heavily on the girl to keep from tripping.

The handful of patrons, all men in work clothing, looked up with a mix of curiosity and amusement. The top of the middle-aged Italian's shirt was open, revealing a bushy chest and a flabby mid-section. His was a face in the crowd: balding, nondescript, pasty. He was one of perhaps a thousand European males who alit on the island monthly in search of action with bronze- or ebony-skinned, cash-starved beauties.

The man plunked a handful of euros on the plastic table. "I want a cappuccino, *por favor!* And one for my *carita* too. And biscotti!" He proceeded to smooch with the girl.

The manager tried to explain politely that the Café 20 de Mayo accepted only *pesos nacionales* and served only Cuban coffee and sweet rolls when they were lucky to get them.

"Okay. Give us *caffè cubano*. And *ecco pezzi nazionali*. Cuban pesos. Okay?" He threw a bunch of ordinary pesos on the table and emitted a loud belch.

The manager shrugged and went to fetch the order.

The man rubbed his face with both palms. "Ahh. *Madonna!* My head hurts." He shut his eyes.

Half amused and half repelled by the episode, Marcial studiously minded his own business. He flipped through the newspaper, but kept one eye on the odd couple.

The girl, a mulatto no older than twenty, deftly slipped her hand into the Italian's pocket and relieved him of his wallet. When she rose to leave, Marcial got up and deftly stepped between her and the door, causing her to run into him. She attempted to sidestep him to make a quick escape.

But Marcial again blocked her. He held out his hand. "Turn it over."

The girl made a run for it.

Marcial's thick right forearm caught her neck, and he corralled her to him. "Give it up, I said!"

She handed over the wallet.

"Now get out of here before I call the police," Marcial said.

The girl hightailed it out of there.

The Italian still held his face in his open hands. He appeared to have fallen asleep.

Marcial stood soldierly erect in front of the slumped man. "*Señor. Señor?*" He bent slightly and gently shook him.

The man's face slipped from his hands. He focused on Marcial.

Marcial held out the wallet. "*Señor*, that girl, she tried to rob you."

It took a few seconds, but the man began putting it all together. "Oh, my God. Oh, my God." He took his wallet, stood up, and shook Marcial's hand. "Thank you very, very much. How can I repay you?" He reached into his wallet for some bills.

Marcial made a gesture indicating he wanted nothing in return.

"Oh, but please. You deserve a reward." The man spoke in a mélange of Italian, Spanish, and English.

"No, *señor*. It's all right. But please do be more careful. Unfortunately, there are a lot of bad people who make it their business to prey on foreigners." He bowed slightly and turned to leave.

"Wait!" the Italian said. "At least allow me to buy you a *cafecito*. Please."

Marcial hesitated. "Okay." Marcial took a seat at the man's table.

The Italian ordered another coffee and sweet rolls. "I'm afraid I've made such an ass out of myself. I'm normally not like this."

"What do you do?" Marcial asked.

The manager delivered the coffee and rolls.

"I travel. And I meet people," he answered enigmatically.

Marcial nodded and decided not to press further.

The Italian's demeanor changed from addled to sober. He sat erect. His hazel eyes reflected alertness. "May I ask your name?"

"Marcial. Henrique Marcial Arribe."

"Nice to meet you, *coronel*." The man broke into flawless Spanish. "You can call me Fabrizio."

Marcial was caught off guard.

"I am going to make this quick and to the point," the Italian said in a low voice. "If you truly wish to work for the other side, I can help you. I believe the future of your country depends on good men like yourself. The way things are going, you will be called upon to take action one way or the other, probably sooner rather than later. Cuba faces two futures: that of a modern democracy or that of a Latin American North Korea. Which will it be, *coronel*?"

The puzzle pieces were falling into place. The man had come in direct response to the *I want to defect* note MININT had him hand over to the American GTMO base commander.

"If it's money you require," the man continued, "this is no problem. No problem at all. We can have it deposited in an offshore account of your choosing. We can also resettle loved ones, your wife, and children, if you have any. But not immediately. We ask that you stay in place and work for us. When the time comes, we'll arrange for you to leave Cuba. You can settle in America, Europe, South America. The options are wide open. But I need a commitment from you now. As you can appreciate, I place myself in the greatest danger doing this. I'll need to depart Cuba immediately."

Marcial sat back and tried to process what the man was saying. His instructions from García had been to report immediately any approaches in response to the bogus defection note. But then, García had later confided his reservations about the whole ploy. Could Marcial trust his old friend? In Cuba, everyone learned early on that trust was a luxury best reserved for fools. And that Montilla woman… something about her discomforted him. A very clever and dangerous person, he suspected. What to do?

The Italian jotted down a phone number. "Take this and memorize it. Then destroy it. Call this number when you're ready to talk further. Or if you're in danger." He looked around, then slipped the paper under the plastic plate holding the sweet rolls. The man got up and departed.

CHAPTER EIGHT

Bangkok, Thailand

The Ecuadorian passport listed his name as Juan Antonio Rodríguez Betancourt. He sported the trim beard, horn-rimmed glasses, attaché case, and tropical suit of a global businessman. His name cards identified him as "Executive Vice President, Santander Pumps, S.A., Av. Amazonas, Quito." He told the immigration officer at Suvarnaphumi International Airport that he was doing business with assorted Thai agribusiness companies in Khon Kaen, Ubon Ratchathani and other cities. His taxi ride on the new highway into the city was smooth. So was his rendezvous with the Cuban embassy first secretary in the lobby men's room of his mid-grade hotel, the Savaly, off Sukhumvit.

He freshened up in preparation for his three p.m. appointment with his Japanese contact, an import facilitator. He ordered coffee for two from room service. Yoshio Hayakawa arrived punctually, sporting the dark blue suit, white shirt, leather-bound brief case, and mildly pleasant face of the classic Japanese company man. They sat at the small suite table near the window. Rodríguez opened the large office envelope passed to him by the Cuban intelligence officer and presented it to the other man.

NATIONAL SECURITY COUNCIL
The White House

TOP SECRET

NATIONAL SECURITY DECISION
MEMORANDUM 16

TO: The Secretary of State
        The Secretary of Defense
        The Director of National Intelligence

SUBJECT:Countering North Korean Aggressive Policies

As a result of the May 30, 2013 National Security Council meeting, the President has made the following decision...

TOP SECRET

THE JOINT CHIEFS OF STAFF
Washington, DC 20301

MEMORANDUM FOR THE SECRETARY OF DEFENSE

SUBJECT:Contingency Plan for North Korea

1. In response to your request dated 8 May 2013, the Joint Chiefs of Staff have evaluated a smaller (two-three aircraft) B-1B strike as a possible contingency option. An outline plan for a "quick strike" capability against a North Korean airfield using a limited number of B-1B aircraft is forwarded herewith...

SECRET

CENTRAL INTELLIGENCE AGENCY

Intelligence Report
Directorate of Intelligence - Asian Pacific, Latin
American, and African Analysis

SUBJECT: Exploring the Implications of Alternative North Korea Endgames: Collapse of the Pyongyang Regime

The Korea Working Group recently completed its
analysis of potential scenarios that would follow in the
wake of the collapse of the DPRK...

R 180752Z JUN 13
FM COMNAVFORJAPAN
INFO O RUAMWC/COMUSKOREA
RUAMWC/COMNAVFORKOREA
RUABP O/N SAPACOFF JAPAN
RUAUAZ/FIFTH AF FUCHUV USFJ
P R 161006Z JUL13
TO CINCPACFLT
INFO COMSEVENTHFLT
COMSERVPAC
DIRNAVSECGRUPAC
NAVSECGRUACT KAMISEYA
OCEANAV
USS GEORGE WASHINGTON
SECRET NOFORN
BEETROOT OPERATION ONE (C)
SUBJ: OPORD OPERATION EAGLE ONE
A. CINCPACFLTINST 003120.24A
B. CINCPACFLTINST 03100.3D

I. SITUATION: KOREAN PEOPLE'S ARMY (KPA) AND DPRK NAVAL AND AIR FORCES HAVE STEPPED UP AG-GRESSIVE ACTIONS AGAINST THE REPUBLIC OF KOREA (ROK). U.S. FORCE STRUCTURE AND DEPLOYMENTS TO COUNTER DPRK THREAT ARE HEREBY ORDERED…

Hayakawa, otherwise known at Lt. Col. Cha Jong Hyok, of the Research Department for External Intelligence of North Korea, was clearly pleased. "Again, we are indebted to our Cuban comrades. Your penetration of our mutual enemy weakens them and makes us stronger. With this continuing flow of inside information, the imperialists' schemes to destroy our revolutions will meet only with failure."

Col. Cha placed his briefcase on the table, dialed the rotary lock, and opened it. The case was packed with stacks of one hundred dollar bills. "One hundred thousand dollars down payment, as usual. One million will be transferred from our bank in Macao to your account at the Banco Tamanaco in Caracas." He took out one stack and fanned it with his thumb. "And I assure you that these are the genuine article. Made by Uncle Sam, not by our Great Comrade." He chuckled.

There was a knock on the door. "Room service."

"Ah. Yes," Rodríguez said. He gathered the documents and returned them to the envelope.

Cha closed the briefcase before Rodríguez opened the door. A smiling bellhop carried a tray with a pot of coffee and two cups.

"Yes. Over there." Rodríguez gestured at the desk and held out a fifty-baht note.

The bellhop put down the tray and accepted the tip. He then reached behind his back, pulled out a SIG Sauer P226, and plugged each man in the face with two rapid-fire 9mm bullets.

The bellhop calmly reholstered his weapon, collected the envelope and briefcase, and exited.

Culebra, Colombia

If they were captured, their cover story would be that they were medical workers who accidentally crossed the border while searching for an U'wa village in which to set up a clinic. The three Cuban intelligence officers had actually received basic medic training to back up their cover story. Their Venezuelan intel counterpart had a similar "legend." The five armed FARC rebels accompanying them were to be described as locally hired guns for protection against bandits.

Their actual mission was quite different. They were to link up with FARC rebel leaders inside Colombia and work with them to rebuild a guerrilla movement decimated by the Colombian government's effective counterinsurgency "Patriotic Plan," a policy that combined aggressive military tactics with sustainable rural development. The operation was meticulously designed to conceal any links with its sponsors and organizers: Havana and Caracas.

They crossed the flush Meta River in canoes before dawn to rendezvous with their FARC contacts before sundown. There were no border points or other man-made indicators of an international boundary in the heavily forested region, but units of the Colombian Army regularly patrolled the largely lawless area.

Upon reaching the Colombian side, the infiltrators concealed their canoes in the brush and proceeded inland. They followed a path through a small gorge. The shade cooled them from the Amazonian sun. The weather was calm. No signs of people. Smooth operation. After twenty minutes, they stopped to get their bearings, consulting their laminated Joint Operations Graphic maps, a product of the U.S. military.

The Venezuelan captain was the first to catch a glimmer from above, the sun reflecting off metal. His cohorts followed his gaze.

As he looked down, the Colombian *Lancero* Special Forces captain at the top of the gorge smiled. The intel the Americans had provided was spot-on. He shouted the order to his squad: *"Fuego!"*

The wrathful rain of bullets and grenades gave the intruders no chance to take cover or return fire.

CHAPTER NINE

Miami

The CAFA banquet at a suburban Marriott was attended mostly by white males in their sixties and older. They sported the tailored suits, fine grooming, and self-satisfied expressions of men who'd arrived by their own bootstraps and were proud of it. But the ranks were becoming diversified with some black and Asian faces, females, and even younger members.

Nick Castillo had agreed to attend the affair to please his father. The one condition he set was that his father make no mention of his son's employment. Blending into the wallpaper was Nick's sole ambition while there.

Several hundred people filled the banquet room. The front featured a podium, some banners calling for democracy and human rights in Cuba, and mounted high, a five-by-six-foot photograph of the murdered Cuban sleeper agent, María Mirabel de la Cruz. Beneath the picture was a banner with bold blue letters: "MARTYR OF FREEDOM – CASTRO ASSASSINS MUST GO!"

Nick nudged his father and pointed at the picture. "Pop, what's this about?"

"María Mirabel de la Cruz. One of our senior officers. Very active in the movement. She was killed in New Jersey. C'mon. You know this already. Professional hit. Had to be Castro's assassins. We want our government to take this to the United

Nations. We're doing a big publicity campaign to draw the world's attention to this heinous crime."

"Oh my God," Nick murmured.

"What?"

"Uh. Nothing."

It was a Mount Rushmore-size irony. The leading anti-Castro exile organization was honoring a Cuban spy, a deep-cover one at that. Nick's head spun. His knowledge of the case was classified. He was therefore prohibited from breathing a word about it. The dead woman's infiltration of CAFA was so complete and so credible that she was being sanctified by the very people she had set out to destroy in her service to Cuban communism. Nick felt helpless, but also profoundly embarrassed for his father and friends who would be made terminal fools once the truth came out.

Vice president GloriaYnez Ocampo went to the podium. She launched into a moving eulogy of the spy. "Mirabel fled Cuba in 1980, one step ahead of the secret police. She risked her life to seek freedom in this great country and served tirelessly for our cause. The cause of liberty. The cause of national salvation…"

María Mirabel was being beatified for anti-Castro sainthood. As Ms. Ynez went on, several of Nick's father's friends kept looking in his direction. A couple caught his eye and nodded. They knew he was with the Bureau, and they wanted to talk with him afterward, Nick assumed. What would he say? What *could* he say?

"Pop, I gotta go. Work calls," he whispered.

"But—"

"Sorry, Pop. It's important." Nick slipped away.

Nick drove directly to his office. He greeted the guards manning the front desk, swiped his ID card through the reader, and entered the dark, empty suite of offices. He sat at his desk in a corner cubicle and fired up the secure computer. After he entered a series of passwords and user IDs, the world of official secrets opened to him.

He skimmed the *SIOC Morning Report,* a daily summary of intelligence articles from FBI headquarters, then the *CIA World Intelligence Review, WIRe-CIA, Spot Intelligence Report, Daily Intelligence Summary, Weekly Intelligence Forecast, Weekly Warning Forecast, IC Terrorist Threat Assessments, NCTC Terrorism Dispatch,* and *NCTC Spotlight.*

Most of the reporting was redundant, various takes on the same events with a heavy emphasis on Islamist terrorism. Nick shook his head and harrumphed. Over 850,000 bureaucrats in some thirteen hundred government organizations produce 50,000 intelligence reports a year, and most of the time the government didn't know their asses from their elbows.

Then, a short piece from the best intelligence collector in the world, CNN, caught his eye.

"South American and Japanese Businessmen Murdered in Bangkok Hotel."

He clicked on the video stream and viewed how the incongruous pair had been killed—two 9mm bullets expertly lodged in each face. That sounded familiar. The victims' passport photos were displayed. An Ecuadorian. Name: Juan Antonio Rodríguez Betancourt. *Hmm.*

Nick ran the name through a classified database search. DEA turned up a Mexican narcotrafficker named Juan Alonso Rodríguez Betancourt. The photos didn't match. No other matches from other federal agencies, nor from Interpol. Nick switched to CI Watch, an interagency watch list of agents of hostile intelligence services and their movements, classified SECRET. *Bingo!* The LEGATT—FBI's Legal Attaché—at the U.S. Embassy in Lima had reported that a known Cuban DI officer by the name of Luís Andrés Guarín rendezvoused with a Peruvian government official presumed to be a paid asset of the DI in January in a Lima park. A "friendly service"—Nick assumed the Peruvian National Intelligence Service—with the interesting Spanish acronym of SIN had reported Andrés was a colonel in the Cuban intel service and was active as an "intel broker." He sold secrets for hard cash to other governments, notably Iran, Russia, and North Korea.

North Korea. Hmm. He ran the name Yushio Hayakawa through the same database. It was like running John Brown through the system—too many hits to make any sense. Nick clicked on Hayakawa's photo and did an image search for a face match.

After a minute, the computer spat out a fuzzy surveillance photo provided by a liaison officer of the South Korean National Intelligence Service. Place: Macao. Date: July 2006. Pyongyang operative Lt. Col. Cha Jong Hyok was reported to specialize in hard currency transactions ranging from counterfeiting to money laundering to cigarette smuggling in order to raise desperately needed funds for the bankrupt North Korean regime.

Everything became as clear as the moon over Miami in January. The Cuban agent, Andrés, was selling secret intelligence to the North Korean agent, Cha. Bangkok was the Vienna of Southeast Asia, a large bustling city with convenient travel links to the world, a perfect place for spies to do their business anonymously and get on their way.

Next, Nick scanned the Spanish-language press: *El Herald, El País, Telemundo, Diario las Americas.* The lead story in all was Venezuela's rift with neighboring Colombia over the latter's charges that Caracas was aiding and providing refuge to FARC guerrillas.

But a short piece buried inside Diario caught his eye. El Tiempo, citing government sources in Bogotá, reported that Colombian Special Forces had ambushed and wiped out a band of FARC guerrillas who had infiltrated from Venezuela in a remote jungle area. An unnamed Army source cited technical intelligence provided by the U.S. as key to the success of the operation.

Nick sat back with his hands behind his neck and feet propped on his desk and shut his eyes. Two Cuban agents in New Jersey and Virginia had been professionally dispatched. One double agent in Florida was likewise assassinated. A Cuban intelligence officer and his North Korean counterpart had been killed in the same fashion in Thailand. And a band of Cuban-supported FARC guerrillas were wiped out just after infiltrating Colombia, thanks to "technical intelligence provided by the U.S."

Who was wiping out Cuban agents? And why? Was it indeed an outward manifestation of internal Cuban political strife? Or was it an external enemy? His own government? It didn't add up.

The arrests were arbitrary. They were going after anybody remotely suspected of harboring anti-regime sentiments.

"Unfair. *Unfair, goddammit!*" Marcial pounded the table. He was back in his barracks in Caimanera, cheek-by-jowl with the boundary of the U.S. Naval base at GTMO.

News had just arrived that Yuri had been taken into custody for undefined "crimes against the state." According to the son of a fellow senior officer, Yuri had been rounded up along with a dozen other cadets. They had all been caught expressing criticism of the government. Yuri's intercepted letters and his new girlfriend had given him away. Carmelita was a *chivata*, a snitch, one of countless who occupied all levels of Cuban society.

Marcial looked out his office window at the vacant dusty street, the deteriorating buildings, and the near absence of human activity. Caimanera, a bustling bar-and-brothel playground for American GIs before the revolution, lacked a pulse. Unlike in any other Cuban town, one rarely heard music in Caimanera. It was a police state within a police state by virtue of its proximity to the enemy base occupying Cuban soil. Cuban citizens required a special pass to visit Caimanera. The token population remaining in the town was watched closely lest any try to make a mad dash to the American side.

Marcial's first reaction upon hearing of his son's arrest was to contact his old comrade-in-arms, García. But he was summoned that morning to report to Santiago immediately. The order came from his superior officer, Brigadier General López y López.

The journey by military vehicle through rain on bone-jarring roads took two and a half hours, made longer than usual by new checkpoints as part of a growing security crackdown. Marcial used the time to think about the turns his life had taken in the last weeks:

"I want to defect."

"You are a patriot, Colonel."

"Where you been, *compañero*? Under a rock?"

"The revolution is now at a crossroads."

"I believe the future of your country depends on good men like yourself."

He was angry, angrier than he'd ever been in his life. His brief imprisonment for having been in the wrong place at the wrong time. Yuri's arrest. And a creeping sense that he was being used.

It was late afternoon when he arrived at the outskirts of Santiago along lightly trafficked Avenida Raúl Pujol. A weathered billboard proclaimed, "Santiago de Cuba – Ciudad Heróica." Hero City. The Castro brothers had launched the revolution there in their 1953 ill-fated attack on the Moncada barracks. Marcial liked Cuba's second city. It was livelier, the music faster, the accent melodic, and the faces largely African.

The driver took a turn into central Santiago.

"Hey," Marcial said, "you're going the wrong way. The FAR base is in the other direction."

"That's not where we're supposed to report, *Coronel*," the young driver replied.

"Where then?"

"MININT headquarters, *Coronel.*"

Marcial's heart sank.

They approached the deluxe Hotel Santiago, its three trapezoidal pools glimmering bright blue in the sun. Behind the hotel lay the drab MININT office building. To its rear was the MININT jail in a simple shoebox structure enshrouded in trees. After being cleared into the area and parking the vehicle, they were met by a flunky who led them not to the office building, but to the jailhouse.

Waiting for him was a familiar face. Larisa Montilla was wearing the uniform of a MININT general. She greeted him with a stiff handshake, her patrician face stony. Diana, virgin goddess of the hunt.

Accompanied by two aides, she led Marcial down a corridor of cells. They stopped at an end cell, and Montilla ordered a guard to open the door.

"I believe you know this man, Colonel?" she asked.

Marcial entered the cell. In the dim light, he saw a body leaning against the wall, shackled in chains. The man's head slumped down.

Montilla signaled the guard with her chin. The guard lifted the prisoner's head with his billy club.

Marcial saw a white male with swollen eyes and flesh torn from repeated beatings. But the man was recognizable. Marcial nodded.

"His name is Salvatore Badoglio. *Maggiore.* Major, isn't it?" Montilla said.

The guard prodded the man's head with the tip of his billy club.

The man gasped. "Yes."

"Major Salvatore Badoglio of the proud Carabinieri. Retired."

Montilla's impassive face now reflected the smug grin of the victor. "Formerly an Italian national police officer. Now a CIA cut-out agent. Is this true, *Maggiore?*"

The guard prodded again.

"Yes," the Italian whispered.

Montilla turned to Marcial, her green eyes boring into him. "You met this man. Did you not?"

"Yes. At a café. He was drunk with a—"

Montilla cut him off. "We know." She signaled to the guard to lock the cell door, then led Marcial back down the hall. "We know it all, Colonel."

Once outside the jail, Montilla halted and looked again at Marcial with those haughty eyes. "Of course, you should have reported the contact immediately."

"Well—"

"But you did not."

"I—"

"He is a CIA asset directed to recruit you, Colonel."

Marcial's words froze in his throat. He had faced enemy bullets, artillery barrages, risk of capture, and poisonous jungle snakes in service to the revolution. But he had never become paralyzed in the face of fear. Until that moment.

Montilla smiled icily. "Let us call it… an oversight."

Marcial shook his head with incomprehension.

"You played your part in our operation with perfection, Colonel. The note you passed to the Americans on our behalf at Guantánamo, your meandering around Havana."

It hit Marcial like a bolt of lightning. The man in the blue shirt, shadowing him. And Marcial used as fish bait.

"We can forgive your oversight and your blundering into a protest demonstration by anti-state reactionaries resulting in your own, albeit brief, incarceration. We can chalk it up to the naïve mistakes of a non-professional operative. You are, after all, what did you say? Ah, yes. 'A *simple* soldier.'"

"What will happen to the Italian?" Marcial asked.

"I'm sure he will be useful to us at some point. A bargaining chip when we need something from the West."

"And my son?"

Montilla's face reverted to poker mode. "Ah, yes. I heard about his trouble. Foolish boy."

"I wish to appeal for his release. He is young—"

"And foolish like his father?"

Marcial's jaw muscles tensed, not the body language to telegraph at a moment like this.

"I will look into it," General Montilla said enigmatically. "In the meantime, we may have further need of your patriotic services, Colonel."

"I understand."

CHAPTER TEN

For the first time in his life, FBI agent Nick Castillo was breaking the law. He could have flown to Havana legally via one of the sanctioned daily charter flights from Miami. As a Cuban-American, he had that right. But as a U.S. government employee with a top secret security clearance working in counterintelligence, it was verboten.

If the Cubans became aware of his occupation, he would risk arrest and a kangaroo court conviction as a spy for the United States, to be kept on ice as a bargaining chip for the release of jailed Cuban agents. The Castro brothers had been frantic to obtain the release of their spies, "The Cuban Five," since the group had been imprisoned in 1998. A live FBI agent apprehended skulking inside Cuba would be like winning the lottery for them.

But Nick had to go. So he chose to slip into the steady stream of Americans who defy the law by traveling to Cuba via third countries. His flight from Cancún was to arrive at José Martí International Airport in fifteen minutes. As with the handful of other Americans aboard the Mexicana Airbus 320, Nick would politely ask that the Cuban immigration officer not stamp a visa into his passport, which was a request the Cubans routinely granted. They issued the visas on a separate sheet of paper that the illicit tourists would discard before returning to their homeland, giving no open evidence to U.S. authorities of their unlawful travel.

Nick had already lost one asset, the double agent Peña. He was damned if he was going to lose another to assassination. He had to at least warn Marcial of such a threat. Beyond that, there was little he could do for the man while inside Cuba. Not knowing who the perpetrators were behind the killings made his mission that much harder. He was convinced the CIA knew but wasn't saying. The Ice Princess Kate Kovalchuk's cagey demeanor when he questioned her served to deepen his conviction. And Special Agent in Charge Rourke, his boss, was too trusting or too busy building his public image at conferences to care.

Nick pondered the prospect of spending years, perhaps decades, in a Cuban prison with no one to yearn for him but his aging parents. No wife. No children. "It would be so nice to have grandchildren," his mother had said. His gift to her instead would be a broken heart. As for his own heart, he contemplated in his most private of moments, in bed alone, walking in a beautiful park alone, eating in a restaurant alone, whether he had a heart. Why was it that he couldn't commit? Women liked him. He liked them. But what was it in him? His work? His cherished personal freedom? No relationship lasted long. He'd break it off. What was it Alexis, the smashing Boston Irish girl, had called him when he'd dumped her after a year of living together? "A closed book." Unreadable.

A flight attendant announced seat belts must be fastened and seats brought upright in preparation for landing.

"What is the purpose of your visit to Cuba?" the bald immigration officer asked.

"Pleasure," Nick replied.

"What is your occupation?"

"Accountant."

"You are Cuban-American?"

"No. Puerto Rican."

"Welcome to Cuba, señor Castillo." The officer stamped a visa on a sheet of paper and handed it to Nick.

Fidel always harbored a special place in his heart for Puerto

Rico, Nick knew. He called the two islands "Two wings of the same bird."

Born and raised in Miami, it was Nick's first visit to the land of his forebears. His family members had all left Cuba by the '70s. A few distant cousins remained scattered around the island, but his folks had lost touch with them. His folks didn't know of his plan. Nobody did. Just a week in Cancún to unwind, he'd told co-workers and family. He had no time, however, for mental meanderings. He needed to get into town. Unable to use credit cards or travelers checks because of the U.S. embargo, Nick would have to pay for everything in cash. He carried a wad of greenbacks on him that could choke a horse.

He took a Gaviota agency microbus to downtown Havana, again blending into the tourist milieu as much as he could. He checked into a small boutique hotel near Old Havana. All the while, careful not to be obvious, Nick was hyper alert for a possible tail—a car, a motorbike, a pedestrian that crossed his path more than once.

From Bart Morgenstern, Nick had learned the name, phone number, and code phrase of their contact agent, a quiet, but disgruntled archivist in the Ministry of Justice who offered his services for free after his eighteen-year-old brother had died in prison shortly after being arrested for selling beef on the black market during the Special Period of near economic collapse. The prison authorities claimed the boy had died of an aneurysm. A close family friend who was a medical doctor examined the body and reported that death had occurred after a severe blow to the cervical vertebrae.

"CALLICO," the archivist, had passed a note clandestinely to the FBI rep at an Interpol conference in Geneva a dozen years ago. Since then, he had provided a wealth of mid-grade intel on the goings-on of the Cuban government. When CALLICO alerted his American handlers of the sudden disappearance of Salvatore Badoglio, Nick knew he had to act. Waiting for the usual Washington decision-making-by-committee was not in the cards. And the usual outcome was to shrug and write off a lost agent, like a tax deduction.

He'd heard so many stories from his family about a gay and vibrant pre-Castro Havana, of a good life for those fortunate to be middle class or higher. The rose-colored rear-view perspectives of exiles were always to be taken with a grain of salt, of course. But the tug of the home country was like a tidal pull on the soul of every generation of expatriated Cubans. As they forged their way ahead through North American society, young Cuban-Americans nonetheless felt shadowed by *la patria*, stalked by tradition, history, and family lore.

A large bronze lion greeted Nick on the Prado, the beautiful tree-lined boulevard that ran from the harbor mouth to the Parque Central. From his right, a bride in white, clutching flowers, posed for pictures at the steps of the Palacio de Matrimonio, an ornate, baroque building. Women in garish dresses and men in ill-fitting suits swirled around the beaming young woman. Nick snapped his own photo of the happy scene.

A block further, a dozen young girls in tutus practiced their pirouettes and pas de chats outside the National Ballet School. The serious focus on their cherubic faces combined resolve with innocence.

Buildings in that part of Old Havana were in bright pastels and good repair. Foreign tourists thronged favorite haunts like El Floridita, a Hemingway hangout and home of the daiquiri, and La Corona cigar factory, where busloads of visitors shelled out convertible pesos for overpriced cigars. *Jineteros* ranging from hookers to hawkers plied their trade, directing a mish mash of English, Italian, and German toward their would-be prey.

Nick doubled back nonchalantly as he pretended to consult his guidebook. In reality, he was applying some tradecraft countersurveillance to see if he was being followed. So far, there were no signs. He would make no attempt to communicate with the contact agent for several days, not until he could be certain the authorities were not onto him.

Before him loomed a monumental structure with Doric columns and a huge cupola. The impressive building, El Capitolio, was home to the Cuban parliament until Fidel installed a new tenant, the Academy of Sciences. Dominating the Havana skyline, it resembled the U.S. Capitol Building. Just as well that it wasn't the host of a dictator's rubber stamp legislature, Nick thought.

Nick went off the beaten path to find the Havana that most tourists didn't frequent. He ventured into south Old Havana. Crumbling apartment houses packed to the rafters with occupants sat forlornly amid tangles of ad hoc electrical wiring. The exteriors were stained and patched; many balconies had collapsed, leaving unhealed scars on the faces of once classic architectural beauties. Laundry fluttered from between buildings and outside windows, like white flags seeking surrender from the elements. Every time Havana got slammed by increasingly frequent mega-hurricanes, these structures and their inhabitants suffered more irreversible damage.

But music carried through the air—the bom-bom-bom of *timba*, the molasses flow of *son*, or the nerve-jangling onslaught of *reggaetón*. Wherever X and Y chromosomes were in proximity, instantaneous dancing broke out—a basic *salsa* set danced by a thirtyish couple here, a sensuous, female-centric *despelote* performed there. One was tempted to drop everything and join in, which some did. Nick warmed instantly to the joie de vivre of Habaneros. Cubans back home enjoyed music as well, but for them, it was not an escape from the deprivations of daily life, and they were too busy pursuing paychecks or business success to take time out and just break out in dance.

From the open windows of the dwellings wafted the aroma of *congrí*, the staple black beans and rice of the Cuban diet. The accent smell of meat was notably missing. Many people, young and old alike, hung out on corners or sat at impromptu tables and stools playing dominoes, the jobless and underemployed whiling away time.

But the knots of young people were what especially caught his eye. Most weren't smiling. They seemed to be speaking in hushed undertones and often looking over their shoulders. They lent an undefinable tension to the air.

He came upon a mostly vacant city block. It was apparent that the space had been recently occupied by a large building. Only the foundation remained. The debris of the building had been hauled away. Yet two PNR cops patrolled the block, which was cordoned off with sawhorses and signs warning, "Keep Out."

Curious, Nick moved to peruse the site from outside the barriers.

One of the cops trotted over to intercept him. "Off limits!"

"Just looking," Nick said.

The cop shook his head and signaled for Nick to return to the other side of the street. Nick did so. He bumped into an elderly woman with a ration book in her hand. He asked her about the guarded vacant lot.

"La Reina," she answered.

"Oh," Nick said, suddenly realizing he'd stumbled onto the building that had collapsed, killing eighty-six people and sparking protests.

"They cleared it lickety-split after the demonstrations," the old woman added. "Amazing how fast they can work when there's trouble." She held up her ration book. "And there's going to be more trouble if they don't get us food!"

"But why are they still guarding it?" he asked.

"They still come. The trouble-making *gusanos*, those *Damas de Blanco* bitches. La Reina has become a symbol, a rallying cause for those who oppose socialism."

Nick thanked her and continued on his way.

It was high noon, a hundred degrees, and Nick's stomach was growling. He wanted to avoid the overpriced state-run tourist eateries with their iffy food and indifferent staff. He searched for a good *paladar*, a private home-restaurant that served good food but which labored under severe anti-entrepreneurial restrictions ranging from high taxes to limited seating and proscribed advertising.

"Hey, pal. Need help?" came a male voice from Nick's rear.

He turned to see a wiry, middle-aged man with graying hair and half his teeth.

"You American? Right?

"Yeah, right. How'd you know?"

"Your shoes, man. They're big. Europeans wear skinny shoes. Latin Americans wear shoes with fancy designs. Americans wear big, plain shoes to get them from here to there with no fanfare."

Nick laughed.

"You lookin' for a good place to eat?"

"Yes."

"You want steak? Seafood? French? Spanish?"

"Cuban."

The man guffawed. "Cuban? You want good Cuban food? Go to Miami."

"I'm from Miami."

"No kidding? Lots of Cubans returning to visit these days. You got family here?"

"I'm Puerto Rican."

"Hmm. I could've sworn you were Cuban. You sound like a Cuban, not Puerto Rican."

"What do you expect when you live in Miami?"

"Yeah, sure. You wanna a girl? Black, brown, white? Got 'em all here. Like 'em young, or experienced?"

Nick waved him off. "Not interested."

"You gotta be married, right? The horniest tourists are the married ones."

Nick shook his head.

"You single, then?" The man looked Nick up and down. "You're handsome, tall. You even look smart. What're you? Mid-thirties?"

"Something like that."

"Divorced?"

"Nope."

"You gay? I can get you some boys…"

Nick was having enough of this hustler. "Have a good day, *amigo*." He started to walk away.

The man pursued him. "Hey! Sorry. I didn't mean to offend or anything. Look. I know a good family who has the best non-fancy *paladar* around here. Nice people. Good local food. No hassles. Come. I'll show you."

Nick's stomach growled again, and he needed rehydration badly. "Okay. But I don't want any *jinterismo*, no hustle. Got it?"

"Sure! It's called Camagüey Lindo. Five-minute walk from here." As they made their way along cratered sidewalks and klatsches of idle adults and playing children, the man asked, "You a cop?"

"No. I'm an accountant."

"Funny. I pegged you for a cop. Or maybe a soldier."

"An accountant," Nick repeated.

They passed a freestanding wall. *Socialsimo No! Libertad Sí!* was crudely painted on it. Socialism No! Freedom Yes!

A klaxon of official vehicles approached. Two PNR cars screeched to a halt. Police leapt out and chased after several young men who scattered like mice. But a teenager atop the wall brazenly hurled rocks at the cops with a homemade slingshot. Two of the officers unholstered their pistols and aimed at the youth.

"Get down here now!" the commander shouted.

The boy dropped his crude weapon and raised his hands.

"Let's get the hell out of here!" Nick's new acquaintance grabbed Nick's arm and led him down a tight alley.

"What was that all about?" Nick asked.

"Trouble. People are pissed. But it's none of our business. Follow me."

They arrived at Camagüey Lindo sweaty and out of breath. The *paladar* was inside another drab apartment house. No building sign indicated its existence, just a small plaque on a door inside a dark, dank corridor.

"Oh, by the way" the man said between breaths, "my name is Enrique." He offered his hand.

Nick shook it. "I'm Nick."

Enrique knocked on the door. A plump, fifty-something woman with dyed hair opened it. A smile crossed her face like a sunburst. *"Bienvenido, señor."*

The maximum-allowed twelve chairs at four tables occupied the neat living room. A flowered bed sheet concealed the family TV, and delicate white Mariposa blossoms graced the white-linened tables. Out of a side door, a teenaged girl brought the one-page menu. The woman's husband also entered to take the drink order.

Enrique fidgeted. "Well, my friend. Here it is." He made no move to depart.

"Yeah. Uh... thanks," Nick said.

They stood smiling at each other.

"Um... join me for lunch?" Nick asked.

Enrique broke into a big grin. "Why, with pleasure! So nice of you to invite me. Ha, ha."

The two sat opposite one another. They were the only guests.

"Two daiquiris," Enrique told the husband.

"Wait. No daiquiri for me. I don't drink during the day," Nick interjected.

Enrique would have none of it. "This man, Fausto, used to work as barman at El Floridita. He knows the secret formula. You cannot leave Cuba without a genuine Floridita daiquiri!" He raised two fingers to Fausto.

Nick shrugged in resignation. They placed their meal orders, Enrique choosing lobster, an illegal, for-export-only delicacy, nonetheless available at many *paladares*. Nick followed suit.

Minutes later, the daiquiris arrived, ice cold and garnished with wedges of lime.

The rum-based drink went down Nick's parched throat easily. Enrique ordered two more.

"I really can't," Nick protested.

"Of course you can!" Enrique insisted. He got up and raised his glass. "To Cuban-American friendship!"

Nick reciprocated with a silent raise of his glass. The third round of drinks arrived before the food did. Enrique ordered a bottle of red wine with the food.

Nick's head spun. He knew he'd imbibed more than he should. But he enjoyed the place, the food, the hosts, and even Enrique, a bit. His newfound Cuban friend told him he had worked as a foreman at a sugar mill for years, then illegally set up residency in the capital to work "in the tourist trade." He had a wife and two grown children in some hardscrabble village in Las Tunas.

The wine, on top of the daiquiris, made Nick loosen up. Everything was just swell. The food. The drinks. The...

An arm moving on his bare chest pulled Nick out of deep slumber. He cracked open bleary eyes. His head throbbed. He tried to raise a hand to his forehead, but the woman's limp arm weighed down his own arm. "Huh?" was all he could manage as he took in the figure of the woman who partially covered his naked body with hers. "What the...?"

The curtains snapped open, letting in a blast of brilliant Cuban sunshine. The shock blinded Nick. He wanted to leap up, but his body felt paralyzed, and the pain in his head was seismic. As his eyes adjusted to the bright light, he saw a man with a camera taking photos. He summoned strength to lunge forward, but was restrained by a pair of large hands.

"Señor Castillo, you are under arrest for the crime of espionage," said a clean cut, olive-skinned man with short hair and a military bearing. He tossed Nick's trousers on the bed. "Get dressed."

The woman got up, moved to the side, and lit a cigarette. She wore only a blouse and a pair of panties. Her face reflected a businesslike expression.

The man who had restrained Nick yanked him up roughly by the shoulder. He was barrel-chested and muscular.

It was all coming at Nick too fast. He could barely stand, his head ached, and his senses were dimmed. As he came slowly back to life, he strained to recall his last conscious moments. He put on his trousers and shoes. When he grabbed his shirt, the big man shoved him out the door. He fell to the pavement. When he stood, he spotted a faded *Motel Paradiso* sign.

He had no time to think as he was handcuffed and frogmarched toward a large sedan with open doors. The enforcer pushed Nick's head down, shoved him into the back seat, and joined him on the right. To his left was a man with a black moustache. The man who had told him he was under arrest got into the front seat and nodded to the driver. The car screeched off.

"What the hell is this all about?" Nick demanded.

The enforcer rammed his left elbow sharply into Nick's ribs, knocking the breath out of him. He bent over and struggled to recover his breathing.

No one said anything as the car sped away from the city. Nick's mouth felt like sandpaper, but he dared not request water. He shut his eyes to concentrate. Camagüey Lindo. Daiquiris. Wine. Enrique. *Godammit. Enrique. I've been set up.*

The cityscape became more industrial with warehouses and idle factories, then gave way to more open land, gardens and farms. A lumbering humpbacked *camello* flatbed truck with passenger seating jury-rigged on the back was taking on more riders than it could reasonably accommodate. A queue of people waited patiently hoping they'd hit the lottery and be let on. Cuba was like that. One spent a good part of one's life waiting. For bread. For coffee. For a hospital bed. For remittances from abroad. Everything but the air they breathed. And the ultra-cynics among them were certain their leaders were conspiring to socialize that sector as well.

The only other traffic was military. Convoys of Army trucks whooshed in the opposite direction, toward Havana. Open APCs carried hundreds of armed troops.

Something is happening. Something big, Nick thought. *And for better or worse, I'm in the middle of it.*

CHAPTER ELEVEN

DIRECTIVE

Council of Ministers
Havana

After months of study, the Council of Ministers, with the partici-pation of vice-presidents of the Council of State, other members of the Politburo and Central Committee Secretariat, the first secretaries of provincial Party committees, and the chairmen of the provincial government councils, as well as other mass organi-zations and senior agency officials, agreed to a set of actions to reduce considerably excessive employment in the state sector.

Reductions in force will be implemented in stages. Those workers who are relieved of their duties will receive counseling from the Cuban Workers Central. There is no doubt that the realization of these measures will have the decisive support of the workers, the peasants, and other sectors of society. These measures will be carried out in accordance with the mandate of the people of Cuba, enshrined in the Constitution of the Republic, that the socialist nature and the political and social system contained in it are irrevocable.

CUBASIEMPRE.COM

BLOG BY YAMILÉ ACOSTA

Cubans have a saying: "A lie runs until it is overtaken by the truth." In the last few weeks, the half-century-old lie that the Revolution has the full support of the Cuban people was exposed by the truth of dozens of military cadets expressing opposition to the regime. It was exposed as well by the protests sparked by the avoidable loss of life in the collapse of La Reina building in Havana. A lie lives only for so long. The truth is forever.

Our octogenarian fraternal leaders remain oblivious to the people's needs. There is no milk to be found anywhere now, yet what is Fidel talking about? Nuclear war that won't happen. The rice ration has been cut again. Where is Raúl? In Carácas trying to wheedle more cut-rate crude out of another morally bankrupt leader. Their answer: fire tens of thousands from their state jobs.

If history has taught us one thing, it is that all dictatorships run their course and they never end well. It is now Cuba's time…

Yoandi Álvarez walked back to her dorm after dark along a narrow path a short distance from Patricie Lumumba Avenue. The pre-med student pondered how she had done on the difficult chemistry exam she had just taken.

A power brownout dimmed the few streetlamps that still functioned. The air hung like a damp curtain. The day's heat surrendered no quarter to the night. Yoandi fanned herself futilely with a notebook. The city of Santiago de Cuba burned in the summer.

Yoandi stopped to fish a small flashlight from her purse. She flicked the switch. No light. Like the streetlamps, it too was a victim of the country's dysfunction. Bad batteries. Cheap manufacture. Rust.

"Mierda!" she uttered. *"Solamente basura! Toda basura!"* She would feel her way along the darkened path.

A large figure loomed before her. He lunged. His hand covered her mouth before she could scream.

Yoandi sobbed uncontrollably before two male policemen at the main PNR station in downtown Santiago.

"Go home and take a shower," the older officer said. He looked up at the clock. Ten minutes to quitting time.

His younger partner placed a hand awkwardly on her shoulder. She backed away.

"I am the fourth woman to be raped on this campus in three years!" she shrieked.

"But this is what happens to girls who run with a rough pack," the senior cop told her.

"What do you mean, a 'rough pack'?" she asked.

"You know. Those hooligans who attack the revolution. Be a good girl and stick to your studies."

Yoandi rose. "You'll do nothing! You'll let this pass. Just like with the other women! Demand bribes and sit on your asses! You don't serve the people! You serve only yourselves!" She stormed out.

"Our records show no one in this building has gone to vote yet. You still have two hours before the polls close." The CDR factotum scanned his clipboard. "Yes. Seventeen adults live in this building," he said crisply, clicking his pen.

The residents hanging around on the porch snickered while passing around a jug of rum.

The CDR man looked up. "Did I say something funny?"

"Yeah. You did," said an unshaven man with unruly hair.

He leaned back in his chair with his bare feet planted squarely on the balustrade, soles facing the CDR man.

CDR Man was getting impatient. "Your duty to vote is not a laughing matter."

"Oh yeah? So tell me this, *com-pa-ñe-ro*. Who's running?" He took a gulp of rum.

"The list is posted. You can't miss it."

"You're right, *compa-perro*. But there's a mistake." The unshaven man looked around conspiratorially at his neighbors, all five sheets to the wind. Muffled laughter erupted.

"Your disrespect will be noted," CDR Man said.

"Oh! Good. Yes! Note me down! Note all of us!" He made an exaggerated salute. "Now here's the mistake. There's only one party on the ballot."

"The Communist Party of Cuba is the only legal party," CDR Man retorted.

The unshaven one raised his index finger. "Exactly! And *that's* the mistake!"

CDR Man started to back off as the inebriated group began to edge forward. He glanced at a billboard he had helped erect some months ago beside the crumbling, subdivided villa on the outskirts of Santa Clara.

VIVA LA REVOLUCIÓN SOCIALISTA! had been defaced to read, *VIVA LA ROBOLUCIÓN SOCIOLISTA!* – with *robo* signifying robbery and *socio* being a play on the word for buddy, hence cronyism, a form of corruption rampant throughout Cuban society. The defacings therefore rendered, "Long Live Cronyistic Robbery!"

Another sign across the street had also been altered. *SOCIALISMO O MUERTE,* a Fidel-favored slogan, was changed to read, *SOCIALISMO = MUERTE. SOCIALISM = DEATH.*

Some of the porch people brought out clubs and steel pipes, tapping them menacingly in their hands. CDR Man backed further away.

Another porch denizen tossed a red scarf. "Hey, *coño!* Take this. It's my son's *pionero* scarf. Take it and tie it around your balls. Then go hang yourself!" Guffaws all around.

The unshaven one shouted, "You can't eat revolution, *compaperro!* We've all been laid off. How are we supposed to survive? Take your sham election and shove it up your red *cederista* ass!"

The agitprop from the Committee for the Defense of the Revolution scampered away.

They all had one thing in common. On their right wrists, they wore bracelets that read, *Cambio*. Change. Hundreds of students wended their way down Avenida de los Libertadores. Destination: the Museum of the 26th of July, dedicated to the Fidel-led 1953 attack on the Moncada Barracks.

Many carried signs reading AVENGE YOANDI! and PROTECT CUBAN WOMEN! and FIGHT CRIME: FIRE THE POLICE!

Some addressed university issues: OUR DORMS ARE KENNELS – CLEAN UP THE SQUALOR. POWER TO THE STUDENTS! REAL ELECTIONS NOW!

Others waved placards with political messages: *LIBERTAD!* DEMOCRACY NOW! DOWN WITH DICTATORSHIP!

Workers spontaneously joined the procession, shouting, "JOBS! JOBS! WE DEMAND JOBS!" They rallied around a woman holding up a large poster bearing José Martí's image and a quotation of the great freedom fighter: "One just principle is more powerful than an army."

Uneasy PNR cops strode on the margins of the demonstration, unsure what to do. The Santiago protest erupted in outrage at the rape of yet another female student, Yoandi Álvarez. But that tragic attack merely opened a floodgate of accumulated grievances ranging from the regime's hammerlock on academia to squalid dorms to the expulsion of students from other universities for protesting related issues. A petition demanding freedoms, circulating at all institutions of higher learning, already had forty thousand signatures, many of which had come from professors.

The clincher came when, on the other end of the island, Havana University students heckled and jeered the president of the National Assembly during what was to have been a pro-forma set piece for televised propaganda. Flustered, the old man left in a huff. Within hours, the entire scene was circulating in cyberspace, having been recorded on the cell phones of students.

"*Libertad!*" "*Libertad!*" "*Libertad!*" "*Libertad!*" The volume grew as more people joined the procession through downtown Santiago. As they approached the Moncada barracks, rocks were hurled at the building, smashing windows.

At that point, scores of Association of Combatants of the Cuban Revolution – military veterans and communist party cadre – launched a counter-protest, or "act of repudiation," a favored regime tactic to break up anti-government protests. Only it didn't work. Outnumbered and outshouted, those minions were split up and chased away by the passion-filled crowd.

As the marchers turned a corner, they confronted a wall of police in riot gear. A loud whistle gave the signal to attack. Canisters of tear gas flew toward the protesters. People scattered in all directions. The police lunged forward with shields and clubs raised. Firefighting rigs turned on their high-pressure hoses, further breaking up the crowd. They ran in all directions away from the police, down streets and alleys. Many held handkerchiefs to their faces, nearly blind from the tear gas.

A group of twenty students found refuge in Santa Teresita church, several blocks east of Moncada. A mass was in progress.

Minutes later, a booted foot kicked open the door. PNR plainclothes personnel rushed in, swinging billy clubs and shooting pepper spray indiscriminately into the faces of protesters and worshipers alike. They arrested everyone under age forty.

"Recuerde La Reina! Viva La Reina!" the ladies chanted as they walked in circular motion. "Remember The Queen! Long Live the Queen!" Rather than a monarch, however, they were extolling the fallen building that had become a symbol of a collapsing state and the mortal risks of living in it.

La Reina tied together two protest themes at the nationwide demonstration: humanitarian and economic. The white-clad ladies held blown-up photos of loved ones imprisoned for political offenses. The other set of women decried the dual currency economy that divided society into the sliver of haves and the masses of have-nots. Dollars versus pesos. Real moolah versus funny money.

State Security agents took the women's pictures, but the protesters remained undeterred. World attention provided a restraint on the regime. Arresting and beating middle-aged women on the streets was bad for business, and Cuba had become dependent on foreign investment and tourism.

Another subversive group also appeared on streets in cities and towns across the country: librarians. Unofficial, grassroots book-lovers in every province had opened home-libraries in defiance of the law over the past several years. Such was the pent-up demand for uncensored literature that the authorities wisely chose not to pick a fight with the brave librarians. They and their supporters demonstrated for freedom to operate legally. Freedom of information.

The spiritual and intellectual epicenter for the myriad budding movements was the Martí Forum. Formerly marginalized writers and philosophers, they took to heart the advice of East European dissidents-turned-leaders to act as if power would be handed to them tomorrow, because it just might. So they banded together to create a loose body to fashion a democratic constitution, policy papers, and plans for a new Cuba. The internet was their enabler. The regime's efforts to stem the flow of information was as futile as the boy who stuck his thumb in a dyke to stop the tide of onrushing water.

And there were the punks.

Julio Guerra Pérez believed in nothing and worshiped chaos. And youth loved him for it.

Orgasmos para Julio concerts drew big crowds of disaffected, jobless, pissed-off youth. Julio's gigs lacked the needed official license. He had been previously arrested for "social dangerousness" and "comportment in manifest contradiction with the norms of socialist morality." Again, only the European Union and other democracies' close attention got Julio off with a small fine rather than the customary one-to-four years of "reeducation" behind razor wire.

Since *Orgasmos para Julio* was denied the means of advertising, word passed via the punk underground whenever the band was to perform. The evening's unannounced concert on Havana's Malecón attracted not only spike-haired *punqueros* and scruffy *friques*, but swarms of average teens and gen-Yers, and of course, plainclothes policemen who arrived hours in advance. They came together like the cyclonic forces that give creation to a tropical storm.

In a strategic move, *Orgasmos* chose to stage their performance right next to two major tourist hotels, the four-hundred-room Meliá Cohiba and the twenty-one-story Riviera. They could expect hundreds of foreign tourists to be in that spot of the Malecón. A heavy-handed crackdown by the authorities risked killing the goose that laid the golden eggs.

PNR officers' attempts to keep the storm from forming by shoving the growing numbers of young Cubans to keep going were met by obscene gestures. European vacationers were also out in force, busily snapping photos with their digital cameras. As dusk approached, police wagons and sedans appeared.

At seven o'clock, the performers arrived in a two-tone '57 DeSoto. First out was bandleader Julio, twenty-one, black curly hair, fluorescent turquoise jacket, and checkered pants. From the rear, out hopped Johnny Basura and Louie Chíngame Fuerte, the former with blue spiked hair and Ubangi earrings, the latter tattooed like a road map. As they unloaded guitars, drums and speakers, five PNR plainclothesmen surrounded them.

"Identification," demanded an officer.

"Fuck. Why?" Julio demanded.

"Just hand it over," the officer repeated.

Reluctantly, the musicians fished out their ID cards.

"What is your intention being here?" the PNR man asked.

"Look for babes and get high," Julio shot back.

A crowd formed around the cops and punk rockers. It grew and grew, soon vastly outnumbering the police. The head cop returned the IDs and, with his cohorts, made a strategic withdrawal.

The crowd applauded the three young performers, who wasted no time setting up their equipment along the promenade wall. As the sun set on Havana Bay, the three adjusted their guitars. An ear-splitting sound pierced the air when they modulated the sound system. The audience grew to several hundred people.

"*Viva Cuba!*" Julio cried over the speakers.

"*Viva!*" the crowd shouted back.

With that, an avalanche of strident guitar notes and drumbeats crashed down, and the show was on.

They opened with *Comandante Comemierda*.

> *Comandante Comemierda,*
> *Comandante Comemierda,*
> *Pincho tan grande,*
> *Pinga tan pequeña.*
> *Comemos tu revolución y vomitamos tus mentiras!*
> *Siempre contigo*
> *Siempre contigo*
> *Comandante Comemierda!*

> Comandante Shiteater,
> Comandante Shiteater,
> Such a big shot,
> Such a small prick.

We eat your revolution and vomit your lies!
Always with you
Always with you
Comandante Shiteater!

Through the amped-up blast of punk music, the *eeh-aah, eeh-aah* wail of police sirens became louder.

A swelling phalanx of Combatants of the Cuban Revolution and CDR members pushed their way to the impromptu stage. "*Viva Cuba! Abajo gusanos! Revolución Sí! Reaccionismo No!*" They stormed the punk rockers in an "act of repudiation."

Fans quickly formed themselves into an assault force and shoved the pro-government group away, barely saving Julio, Louie, and Johnny from injury. A melee ensued. Fists, clubs, bricks, and knives were brandished. Blood spilled.

The police vehicles screeched onto the scene. Cops in riot gear stormed the brawl. But ill-trained in riot control, they broke formation and became dispersed among the crowd. Punk toughs managed to wrest riot clubs and pepper spray from some of the policemen and turn them onto the lawmen.

Outnumbered and overwhelmed, the cops ran for their lives. The pro-regime thugs ran too.

Foreigners recorded the happenings as well as those Cubans with cellphones or cameras.

The concert was over.

People locked arm-in-arm and formed up parade-style. They marched down four-lane Paseo Avenue, chanting, "*Libertad! Libertad! Cuba Sí! Castro No!*"

A festive air took hold as residents poured into the streets on foot and on bikes. A spirit of rambunctiousness took over and the capital was fast descending into chaos. More cops were beaten back with rocks, bricks, and slingshots.

The usual stops that kept people in their place came loose. Rumors spread that Fidel was dead and that the American government would welcome any Cuban who reached the Florida coast. As the free-for-all grew, many headed for the inner harbor, Vedado and Mariel, where there were boats. *Head for Yuma, the USA.* A rare opportunity to flee unrestrained by sea.

The more politically minded began to set up a hasty tent city in a park at 5th and 6th streets. They circulated manifestos calling for free elections.

Orgasmos para Julio were singing again. "Razor Blades for Socialism," "Marxist Menstruation," and "Pornstars for Jesus" were big hits among young Cubans.

Three hours later, a convoy of olive-drab military trucks moved in. Hundreds of troops jumped out and made formation, Kalashnikovs at the ready. As regular FAR troops deployed to the Malecón and other areas where demonstrators congregated, other vehicles unloaded blue-uniformed MININT *Tropas Especiales* decked out in riot gear. The elite *Tropas*, also known as the Black Wasps, formed into rows and stayed well to the rear. With Darth Vader helmets, truncheons, riot shields, they radiated power and menace.

A FAR commander stepped onto the Malecón. Through a truck-mounted loudspeaker, he said, "Go home! You have five minutes to vacate this area. If you don't, we will disperse you by force and arrest you. Go home now!"

The commander barked an order to his men. The double-row contingent of FAR troops snapped to assault-ready mode, shields up, truncheons raised.

The crowd of thousands went still.

The commander looked intently at his stopwatch.

No decisions emanated from leaderless groups. At that moment, each civilian weighed his or her options. Some sensed it was time to go home, as the commander ordered. Others weren't so ready to give up. Many felt the spirit of Cuban patriots of long ago, those who had fought and shed their lives for freedom. All felt fear.

In other neighborhoods, PNR cops dispersed or arrested individuals, restoring order block by block. But the Malecón was a bigger nut to crack. Government troops and protesters alike recalled the 1994 Maleconazo uprising. The disorganized protest had been ended by law enforcement within a few hours, but nonetheless had shaken the regime to its core.

Many people broke away and headed home. The large majority, however, stood their ground, uncertain what to do, yet defiant.

"*Viva el Maleconazo!*" someone shouted.

Others picked up the call. "*Viva el Maleconazo! Viva el Maleconazo! Viva el Maleconazo!*"

"*Libertad!*" still more yelled. "*Libertad!*"

The commander put away his stopwatch and gave a signal. The riot troops began to move forward in formation.

As they came within inches of defiant demonstrators, an elongated strained note from an electric guitar pierced the air. Julio stepped forward and, microphone in hand, began to sing:

> *Comandante Comemierda,*
> *Comandante Comemierda,*
> *Pincho tan…*

A shot rang out. A rubber bullet slammed into Julio's head, and he went down.

Like a herd of beasts of the veld, the crowd bolted. The riot troops lunged forward, shoving demonstrators with shields and beating indiscriminately with truncheons. Other shots rang out. Polish-made riot guns cast crowd-control nets over groups and individuals alike, as if capturing wild animals. Other shots launched tear gas deeper into the crowd. The sea breezes quickly blew the gas far into the atmosphere.

A number of the anti-government activists managed to overwhelm some of the troops and seize weapons, which they promptly used against the troops. A tidal push-and-pull gripped the mass of humanity. Neither side gained the advantage. The troops had the weapons and tactics, but the crowd had the needed numbers and fearless outrage to stand up to their opponents.

Then a flame shot through the air like a meteorite and landed in the midst of the troops. The Molotov cocktail spread burning fuel over soldiers, who fell to the ground, screaming and writhing in agony.

Distracted by their comrades' suffering, Tropas Especiales lost ground. Many lunged individually into the protesters, bashing as many as they could, but in doing so, losing discipline and making themselves more exposed.

A whistle blew, whereupon the FAR regulars marched forward, took aim and, upon receiving an order, fired at the crowd. Protesters went down. Blood flowed onto the street. Panic set in. The civilians ran for their lives. More shots rang out. More activists fell. The FAR troops enveloped the whole mass in a vise grip. Reconstituted special troops arrested protesters en masse and loaded them into waiting trucks.

Maleconazo II came to an end.

To the rear, a general in MININT-uniform surveyed the scene. She smiled.

The military tribunal sentenced Yuri to thirty years. Marcial wept.

"It could have been worse, Henrique," his FAR officer friend told him. "Two of the cadets—those who actively plotted to revolt—will be shot on Friday morning. The country's leaders feel they need to make examples."

Marcial called García. "Alfredo. I need your help. My son—"

"I know. I know," García interjected

"My kid was careless with his words, but he committed no treason."

Silence.

"Alfredo?"

"Your next visit to Havana, see me," García responded tersely.

Marcial understood. It was common knowledge that MININT bugged the phones and houses of senior officials. Arnaldo Ochoa, a legendary and popular general, had been caught via eavesdropping making critical remarks about Fidel. He was found guilty of trumped charges of narcotrafficking in 1989 and subsequently shot. Two Foreign Ministers had been fired in recent years for loose talk picked up by MININT listeners. Any officer with a brain had learned to exercise caution since those incidents.

"Sure," Marcial said.

"And, Henrique, remember our last conversation when you were here?"

Marcial recalled his friend's warning. "The revolution is now at a crossroads. Those who refuse to adjust to change, stuck in the old ways. They will do anything to keep a lid on things. The Army one day may be called upon to take sides. And the Army must never fight against the people."

"Watch yourself, my friend," García said and hung up.

Marcial had no time to dwell on the fate of his son. Santiago, "Hero City," was in turmoil. He received orders to report there immediately with a company of soldiers.

Marcial arrived at Eastern Military Region headquarters, where he was escorted to the office of Brigadier General Marcos López y López.

A burly sixty-year-old, the Army commander of eastern Cuba paced the floor with his hands behind his back and gaze fixed downward. "You're aware of what happened in Havana, eh, Marcial?"

"Yes, General."

"Well, the students here in Santiago are at it again. Daily marches in the streets. Counter-revolutionary rhetoric that gets more traitorous by the day." He turned to Marcial. "Do you know what they're saying? They're calling for an end to the socialist system we have worked so hard to build over five decades. And the end of the Communist Party of Cuba. They call Party leaders 'criminals.' Criminals! Why, I was leading their fathers to death and victory before those brats were even born! What is it with this generation, Marcial? You have a son, don't you?"

Marcial's jaw clenched as he stood frozen.

"Well, you do, don't you?"

"Yes, sir."

"Can you explain their behavior?"

"No, sir."

López waved a hand as if swatting at a fly. "Bah. Anyway, Havana has sent orders to quell the demonstrations as soon as possible by whatever means possible."

"Twelve young people were killed in Havana, sir," Marcial stated.

"Yes. Unfortunate. But necessary."

"But, sir—"

"It's one big *negrada!*" He slammed his right fist into his left palm. He then reddened and looked sheepishly at Marcial. In an unguarded moment, the older man had used a racial epithet roughly translated as a "negro mess."

"Yes, well, anyway," López continued, "I want you to take your men to Paseo de Martí just in front of the Moncada and keep the protesters from marching on it or damaging it further. Rules of engagement: whatever it takes. The counter-revolutionary genie must be kept in its bottle. If it gets outs, God help us."

Marcial saluted, about-faced, and departed.

The Black Wasps were lined up on the street curbs, like knights ready for battle in full riot gear. After Havana, they were in no mood to hold back. FAR units, comprising several hundred men, were deployed behind the PNR cops and Tropas Especiales. Marcial's troops were the cream of the crop, carefully selected for duty facing the Americans along the GTMO Base boundary. They stood alert and carefully watched the reactions of their commander as the protesters turned the corner onto Paseo de Martí.

A colonel with the 38th Infantry Division commanded two companies of troops deployed on both flanks of Marcial's men. They also manned a full commo station in a Soviet-era BTR-152 truck. The colonel walked over to Marcial. The two exchanged quick salutes.

"I'm Saustre," the colonel said. "We'll hold the flanks east and west of Martí. You can protect the center."

"Yes," Marcial replied.

"And we have an open line with MININT headquarters." He pointed at the truck. "Any orders will come directly from them."

Marcial nodded. Saustre returned to his men.

Very conscious that his men's eyes were on him, Marcial stood erect and barked, "Attention!" Instantly, they lined up in precise formation along the street edge, weapons at the ready, helmets secure.

Within minutes, the parade of protesters was upon them.

The demonstration reflected the earlier one, only with more people. Students constituted the radioactive core, but there were also faces of middle-aged workers, housewives, of pensioners. The slogans and epithets indeed were more belligerently political.

"OUT WITH THE CASTROS!" "DEMOCRACY YES! COMMUNISM NO!" "FREE ELECTIONS NOW!" "FREE ALL POLITICAL PRISONERS!" "WE DEMAND THE RIGHT OF FREE TRAVEL!" "END PESO APARTHEID!"

Marcial saw some familiar faces—FAR veterans, many jobless after the recent government layoffs. What struck him immediately was the anger. Like a fallen electrical power cable, it sizzled and crackled among the marchers snaking their way to the Moncada Barracks.

The marchers chanted, waved their placards, and raised their fists. Some called for the troops to join them. Others hurled epithets. The PNR men appeared intimidated and unsure. The Black Wasps, however, strained at the bit, hunched forward in attack mode, ready for anything. The FAR troops, to the rear of the police forces, maintained a state of readiness with calm discipline.

The spearpoint of the marchers directed itself flush at the center, held by Marcial's Frontier Brigade. Some carried placards with Julio the punk rocker's photo and the caption: "Bring His Killers to Justice." They stopped inches from the police and taunted them.

Black Wasps charged. With shields raised, they moved steadily forward, pushing back the demonstrators. Slowly they advanced. The protesters retreated steadily. Soon, the police troops had the protesters almost against the opposite side of the street. As PNR police moved in on the flanks to begin making arrests, the crowd struck back, hurling rocks and bricks. The PNR and Black Wasps attacked, bringing their truncheons down on the demonstrators.

An explosion broke their ranks. Then another. Black Wasps and PNR cops fell to the street, bleeding. Others went flying, limbs separated from their bodies. The grenade attacks unleashed mayhem. Chaos ensued.

Saustre ordered his men to aim high.

The crowd appeared not to be intimidated. "Out with the Castros!" They advanced toward the Moncada.

Saustre gave the order, "Fire!"

The demonstrators recoiled as the bullets went over their heads.

Marcial had not yet ordered his men to fire. They looked at him nervously. They were trained to shoot at Americans, not at their own people.

Marcial, ramrod straight, gazed intensely at the marchers. They became a blur. He saw his life pass before him.

Hardscrabble childhood. The FAR as his savior. More love directed at his country than at the opposite sex. Pride as a father. Sacrifices. Questions. More questions. Doubt. Proxy spy. His mistaken arrest. Yuri's arrest. Shattered expectations. Shattered assumptions. Service to a false prophet. What for? He seemed to be falling into a maelstrom. Confusion. Colonel Henrique Marcial Arribe. Butcher of Santiago. Black killer.

A volley of gunfire came from Saustre's troops. Marchers fell.

"Fire!" Saustre yelled at Marcial. "Our orders are to fire, dammit!"

Marcial broke from his trance. Saustre forced a radio transceiver on him. Marcial took it to his ear.

"Your orders are to fire, Colonel!" Montilla screamed. "Do you hear me?"

"Yes," he answered.

"They must be crushed, Marcial! Crushed!" she yelled.

Marcial shook his head and dropped the transceiver. He signaled his men to stand down. The marchers were in full retreat, running for their lives in all directions. Relieved, the Frontier Brigade dropped their arms to their sides and assumed parade rest position.

Saustre aimed his Makarov 9mm into Marcial's face. "You're under arrest, Colonel." A pair of military policemen seized him by each arm and handcuffed him.

CHAPTER TWELVE

Palace of the Revolution, Havana

The only thing on which the Russians didn't betray Cuba was their vodka. Always the world's best and, unlike oil, supplies never stopped. As the president of the republic read the dispatches coming in from Santiago, he needed to steady his nerves. Medicine of choice: Stolichnaya Gold.

His worst fears were coming true—violent uprisings in the capital and in the second largest city. The economic reforms he'd rammed through the hardliners were simply too little too late. An ossified Politburo of ailing gerontocrats incapable of change. Meanwhile, hundreds of thousands were unemployed and angry. People defied their leaders as never before. Fissures were growing in the Party, the government, and the military. The revolution was coming unhinged.

And then there was his brother. He poured himself a double and ambled down the private corridor linking their two offices. The Stoli eased the arthritis in his knees if not the migraine growing inside his octogenarian head.

His brother, clad in a red and white running outfit and a pair of Nikes, was poring intently over the daily press at his desk—the vision of a retiree plucked straight out of a gated community. He slammed a fist down. "It's going to happen! The Iranians are *this* close to having a nuclear bomb. War! The Israelis will strike, then the *yanquis*! Nuclear war! I must continue to warn the world about this!"

The president plopped himself down in one of the modern office chairs in front of his brother's desk. José Martí stared down from a large painting behind the desk. "We're in trouble."

The brother reluctantly shifted his attention away from the newspapers to his sibling.

"Blood in the streets. Riots. Food shortages. Tourists aren't coming. The sugar market's collapsed. Bickering inside the Party and the Army."

His brother scratched his scraggly beard. "Didn't you hear me? The world is on the brink of nuclear war. Cuba must prevent it. We are in a unique position. The whole world respects us. They listen to what we say. We must act now!"

"Yes. We must. But here. At home. The revolution is at risk of coming undone."

"Bah! Nonsense! We've been through worse. The end of the Soviet Union. Counter-revolution in Eastern Europe. Our own Special Period. Not to mention the Missile Crisis. Playa Girón. Blood? We've been knee-deep in blood. Our revolution will survive!" His ancient voice cracked.

The president shifted uneasily in his chair. "The world has changed. And it's changing at an accelerating rate. We risk being left out. If we don't change…" He circled the air with an extended hand, searching for words.

"We already made changes. *Your* changes. Those so-called reforms. I warned you that they would only entice counter-revolutionary and reactionary behavior. And letting those *gusano* 'dissidents' out of the country. Seventy-three more traitors to agitate against us from abroad. They spread lies. Then the tourists stop coming. I warned you. I warned you. What happened to *socialismo o muerte*? We must return to our roots. Remain true to our cause!"

The president lowered his head and twiddled his thumbs. "We've been through all this before."

"Yes, we have. You were always the weak one, despite your moniker of 'The Terrible.'"

"That's not true. Father pored attention on you. You were his favorite. Without me, this revolution would have ended up in the ditch long ago. Without me, this revolution would've sunk with the *Granma* in the Gulf of Mexico." The president wished he had another double of Stoli Gold.

"Remember Roque falling overboard? Fool. And when we landed? A fucking swamp! And you throwing up, even long after we'd landed. And Che getting himself 'wounded.' Bastard shot himself by accident. Ah. Those were the days, huh?"

"Yes. All *successful* revolutions share two fundamental characteristics: a, they begin with youthful passion, and b, they adapt. The Soviets tried to adapt too late in the game. The Chinese and Vietnamese, however, timed it just right."

His brother leapt from his chair, wincing as he did so with some deteriorating vertebra or joint protesting the fast movement. He pointed his right index finger skyward in his trademark fashion. "Change? Yes. Betrayal? No!"

The migraine was reaching seven on the Richter scale. He rubbed his temples and waited for his brother to lower himself back into the chair. "We have another problem, brother."

The bearded one raised an eyebrow.

"I am president now for over six years, yet decisions are being made independently of me."

His brother made no comment.

"The decision to fire on the demonstrators. The liquidation of agents in the United States."

The brother cocked his head and grimaced. "The state apparatus acts to defend *la Patria* both domestically and externally."

"The tracks all lead back to one person: General Larisa Montilla."

"A capable officer."

"A reckless officer."

The elder one wagged a finger. "Larisa Montilla has more balls than the entire senior officer corps. And she's a true patriot. A true revolutionary."

"Her ordering the shooting of civilians has opened a Pandora's box. All hell is going to break loose. And her stepping up intelligence operations inside the United States will needlessly provoke Washington. They've already retaliated. Just as we've been planning a new policy direction with the Americans. Her actions lay waste to any credibility we might have."

"You of all people should know better. You've always detested them. We let our guard down, and they will devour our little country alive. The clock will turn back fifty years.

"And she understands that which you fail to. The best defense is an offense. Killing a few demonstrators keeps the rest in line. Damaging or destroying the intelligence networks of our nemesis keeps them at bay. Especially at times when we are vulnerable."

"You told her to do these things, didn't you?"

"I am no longer president."

"Since when are you formalistic?"

"I am father of the revolution. I provide inspiration. Others act accordingly."

"You had Ochoa killed for less."

"General Ochoa was getting too powerful. And he talked treason behind our backs."

"You're grooming her to take over, aren't you?" the president asked.

"That is up to the Cuban people."

"And are you fulfilling a promise you made to her father?"

"God, I miss my Cohibas," the bearded one said wistfully.

CHAPTER THIRTEEN

"Nicholas Castillo, an American citizen, is missing. We have traced his travel from Cancun, Mexico, to Havana. Here is his flight itinerary, a photo, and other details. We ask the Ministry to contact relevant government authorities to ascertain his whereabouts." Richard Kerrick had been to the Foreign Ministry, housed in a genteel colonial-era building only six blocks from the U.S. Interests Section, a mere handful of times during his two years as Washington's top envoy in Cuba. Since diplomatic ties had been cut in 1961, regular political dialogue between the two governments was lacking. They dealt with each other primarily on special topics requiring urgent attention, largely issues involving immigration matters. Such was the anomaly of a technical non-relationship.

"Normally, your office sends a junior consular officer on such matters. This Castillo. He is important somehow? Is he Cuban-American?" Consular Department Chief Caridad Martínez asked.

"We are trying to gather further information. Right now, this is all we have," Kerrick replied.

Though Kerrick had heard the old saying, "A diplomat is a person who is paid to lie for his country," he preferred to *deflect* for his country. His instructions from the State Department were simply to present the name and photo and not mention Castillo's employer. The logic was that perhaps the Cuban government didn't know that key fact. The FBI had thus far managed to keep a lid on its missing man. Once the AWOL special agent returned to D.C., there would be hell to pay. That was, if he wasn't a turncoat who'd defected. Headquarters was scrambling, looking for any evidence Castillo had been a Cuban intelligence asset all along.

"We will check into it and let you know if we turn up anything," Martínez said with a smile.

Two men slammed Nick down on a wooden plank and secured his hands and feet with rope. They then tipped the lower end up so that his feet were higher than his head. A bearded torturer smiled evilly as he held up a simple white towel before tightly covering Nick's face with it.

Then, the deluge began. A steady stream of ice-cold water poured on the towel. Within seconds, Nick was suffocating. A cavalcade of mental fireworks went off inside his head. Every muscle contracted. Panic. He started to black out.

The towel was removed.

Nick opened his eyes. Water blurred his vision as he gasped desperately for air. Then the towel went back on his face. More cold water. His lungs burned, straining for life-giving air. His heart raced as his body struggled to stay alive.

The lethal towel came off.

Again, Nick struggled to breathe. "No! Enough!"

The towel went on again. Nick was certain he would die of asphyxiation in a Cuban torture chamber. He tried to summon any remaining shards of clear thought to recall the words to the Lord's Prayer.

The towel came off. Nick seized the moment to steal a few luxurious breaths. The towel stayed off. His desperate fight for air eased. He drew deep breaths. He blinked the water from his eyes to clear his vision.

A man with thinning red hair glowered down at him, then nodded to someone in the corner of the dank room.

Nick couldn't see who it was. His head was held in some sort of brace attached to the plank to keep it from moving as they waterboarded him.

"Señor Castillo, why were you sent here?" a woman's voice asked in Spanish.

Nick strained to look in her direction, but he said nothing.

Upon being signaled, the redheaded man threw the towel back on Nick's face, and the waterboarding resumed.

Nick screamed as he'd never had in his life. The cold water saturated his face, hair, neck, chest. *God, take me.*

Two men grabbed Marcial by the arms and shoved him onto the concrete floor. One of the men then stepped on the small of Marcial's back while he hog-tied the prisoner's hands. He threaded the end of the rope through a pulley hanging from the ceiling. Both men then pulled the rope with all their might.

A shock wave shot through Marcial as his arms dislocated from his shoulders. He screamed, hanging above the floor like a broken marionette. They left him there for what seemed like an eternity. Then, they dropped him. With his feet bound tightly and bent behind him, he came crashing onto his knees and forward onto his abdomen and face.

As he struggled to regain his senses, a pair of women's feet appeared in front of him.

"Tell us, Colonel. How long have you been spying for the Americans?"

Marcial shook his head, as much to try to clear his brain as to deny the accusation.

Two blows tore the flesh on his back and sent new shockwaves through him. Each torturer brandished a strip of tire rubber, ready for the signal to strike again.

"I will ask again. How long have you been spying for the Americans?"

Marcial forced himself to think. "Since you sent me to hand that note over to the American Naval Base commander."

More blows with the tire strips.

"How much are they paying you to betray the revolution, Marcial? Who did you conspire with to foment the uprising in Santiago? What operations have you carried out on behalf of Major Badoglio? We have known about your treason all along, Marcial, ever since you joined with the counter-revolutionaries in Havana. Confess everything, or you will know agony you could never have imagined.

Anger replaced fear and pain. He breathed some words through his hoarse voice. She bent down to better listen and ordered him to repeat it.

"You. I conspired with you."

A world of hurt rained down upon him.

"Nick Castillo. Born in Miami in 1978 to Cuban parents who left the island in '74. Rolando and Serafina. They are a handsome couple." Montilla handed over a couple of photos of Nick's parents in their front yard taken from the street. "So you're Havana people by origin, but now you make your home in Miami Springs. Nice neighborhood. Too bad they left. The revolution needs talented people. Tsk, tsk."

Nick looked around from where he sat on a hard wooden chair. He knew an interrogation room when he saw one. Bare walls. Single table. Two chairs. Bright fluorescent light. A mirror, no doubt two-way, with observers on the other side taking in the proceedings. They had put him in gray prison garb. He assessed his interrogator: forties, white, professional, attractive.

She paced around the small table with deliberate steps, hands behind her back. Her light brown hair was tied neatly behind her head. Her uniform fit too well and lacked the assembly-line cut of military apparel, obviously tailored.

She kept up her slow march around the table. "Yale. A stint in the U.S. Marines. Fordham Law. FBI. Since graduation. Now assigned to the Miami Field Office. Target: Cuba."

Nick kept his eyes fixed on a spider crawling on the opposite wall. The waterboarding had left him traumatized, but he was determined to remain impassive and say nothing. Yet he was impressed with their dossier on him.

"Oh. I must apologize for our initial harsh welcome. But I'm afraid we are virtually at war at the present time against enemies external as well as internal. Thus, we had no choice but to spare the niceties of formal protocol. Less cultured individuals in our service insisted on it." She shrugged.

Great. A Torquemada with a sense of humor. The worst kind of torturer was one who injected humor into his or her dark art. It showed she enjoyed her work.

"Your own CIA officers who volunteered as guinea pigs for waterboarding lasted only fourteen *seconds* before breaking. You lasted two *minutes* before passing out. Impressive. But you had us worried, Señor Castillo." She stopped in front of him and bent down, hazel irises just inches away. Whether intentional or not, her bosom was amply displayed. She wore no make-up, yet Nick caught a waft of fragrance, ever so light, hint of jasmine. "Now tell me, *Nick*. What can I do to get you to say something?"

The smile that blossomed across her smooth face sprouted dimples. Pearly whites flashed between her thin lips.

Nick remained stolid, emotionless. The spider on the wall was spinning a web. Soon it would lay eggs. The young would then devour their mother.

She held her face close enough for him to feel her breath. She pursed her lips in a pout. Her eyes sparkled. Nick wanted to either kill her or kiss her. Then it struck him.

"Drivetrain," he let out, letting his guard down.

"What?"

Nick resumed his rock-like stance.

"Hmm." Montilla straightened and resumed the circular

march. "It would be unfortunate for your reputation to be destroyed and the FBI to be forced to terminate you." She tossed several more photos on the table.

Nick looked down. The pictures were of him and the woman at the Motel Paradiso, naked in bed. The woman sat atop his groin, arched in the act of fornication. Nick's eyes were half closed, giving the impression of sexual ecstasy. Another displayed Nick atop the woman, her legs wrapped tightly around his buttocks.

"What would your folks think, Nick? Tsk, tsk."

"Fuck you!" Nick threw the photos at the wall. The spider was oblivious.

Montilla halted and smiled. "Ah! He talks. Progress!"

"Nobody'll buy this garbage. You drugged me. It's a clear set-up. You'll fool no one."

"Won't we? We'll see about that. I have another photo I want you to see, Nick." She placed a single portrait photo on the table. It was of Marcial, an official FAR photo taken in better times. "You came to rendezvous with this man."

Nick resumed his imitation of a clam.

Montilla placed herself squarely in front of him again. "You came to Cuba on a secret mission to meet with this man, an asset of your CIA. Funny your coming here happens to coincide with social unrest. Coincidence? Or consequence of your government's incessant efforts to undermine the Cuban revolution?"

Nick bolted up. "You twisted paranoid cunt!"

"Sit down!" Montilla ordered. "Or in one second, some terribly uncultured men in our service will come through that door and resume the water carnival!"

Nick slowly lowered himself back onto the chair.

"Their intention is not to leave a mark on you, Nick. After all, you're quite the catch for us. The last thing we want is to offer damaged goods in return for our people. When you do leave this country—and it may be decades—you will not have so much as a scratch. Unlike poor Marcial."

She tossed another photo on the table. It was of a beaten and brutalized Marcial. His eyes were swollen shut, lower lip swelled. "This man is a traitor. A spy for the United States. Fortunately, I intervened before the uncultured among us did any more damage. And I have the power to protect him from them. But not for long. And not without your cooperation. You can save him. You have an obligation to protect your asset, Nick. It's your duty. You owe him that. If you cooperate, I can make sure he is treated humanely in a normal prison. Otherwise, I'm afraid… he will face a firing squad. Soon."

Nick rubbed his forehead, then covered his eyes and tried to concentrate. *Holy shit. What have I gotten myself into? Stupid! And Marcial. I hold his life in my hands. If this bitch is to be believed, that is.* "What makes me such a big catch?"

"You are the key we've needed to liberate the Five Heroes."

"You're so dumb," he shot back, shaking his head. "A court sent your spies, whom you call the Cuban Five, behind bars in '98. It's called *justice* in a democracy, something you people couldn't even begin to fathom. You might as well put *me* in front of a firing squad. You're wasting your time."

"Leave that to us, Nick. Now tell me about your mission here. Who else were you to make contact with? I guess you know we also arrested the Italian, Badoglio. He's told us everything, Nick. Everything. So your keeping mum is without purpose. Save Marcial's life."

He shifted uneasily in his chair and rubbed his hands. "I have no mission. I came here on my own."

"On your own? Why?"

"For the hell of it. Spur of the moment decision while on the beach at Cancun."

"I'm afraid it's back to the water park, Nick." She opened the door and signaled to someone he couldn't see.

The two tormenters who'd worked on him earlier barreled in.

"Wait!" Nick said.

Montilla gestured for the men to remain in place. "Yes?"

"I came on my own accord, against policy, to save Marcial. Not to rendezvous, but to warn him he was in danger."

Montilla whispered for the two thugs to leave, and she quietly closed the door. For the first time, she took a seat. She placed her elbows on the table and leaned forward. "Why should I believe this?"

He hunched forward, meeting her at mid-table, their faces again within centimeters of each other. "Think about it. Would they send an FBI flatfoot to Cuba to do espionage? How dumb is that? Not our job. We're domestic. It makes no sense. Even shit-for-brains Cuban intel operatives can figure that one out."

Montilla held his gaze, a Mona Lisa smile on her face, her lovely green eyes searching his. She inched closer. He caught a hint of jasmine. Was it a gravitational force or a challenge that kept them nose-to-nose?

"You are a dangerous man," she breathed.

He held his ground. His mind raced. The casing of his parents' house. The detailed bio on him. The assassinations of agents inside the U.S. His arrest. They'd had him pegged from the moment he arrived. The arrests of Marcial and Badoglio. The USG hadn't even scratched the surface of Cuban intelligence penetration of the United States.

"Who's the dangerous one?" he countered.

CHAPTER FOURTEEN

Washington, D.C.

Philip Rensselaer Livingston was proud to be a direct descendent and namesake of one of the signers of the Declaration of Independence. He always made sure he let anyone who entered his personal gravitational field know that fact. Also, the Philip Livingston of yore had been descended from British Lords. He helped found Columbia University and served as a delegate to the Continental Congress. The Livingstons were true-blue loyal Americans. Not a turncoat among them. Until now.

The twenty-first-century Philip sat in his cubicle on the fifth floor of the State Department, shuffling through the day's take of intelligence traffic. He had one eye on the clock, waiting for the remaining ten minutes of the workday to tick down. His mind was on his sailing yacht, Elba, and a long weekend of skirting around Chesapeake Bay with Deirdre. But he needed to memorize the contents of a few more Top Secret cables. They could search his briefcase on the way out of the building, but they couldn't search his brain.

From the Continental Congress to this, he thought as he took in the cramped windowless space in which he worked. *A Livingston deserves better. But the nitwits in charge of our affirmative-actioned, politically correct, eviscerated foreign policy establishment have turned things upside down. Those destined to govern are shunted aside to make room for the rabble, mediocrities recruited based on factors other than merit.*

As senior Latin America analyst in the Bureau of Intelligence and Research, Livingston had established a reputation as a competent professional, albeit one who'd hit the glass ceiling of promotions and, henceforth, could only age in place.

The CIA's Special Report, "Leadership Transition Scenarios in Cuba: An Assessment," posed a particular challenge to memorize. The thirty-five pages were a comprehensive analysis of what the agency thought it knew about the inner workings of the Cuban government, densely printed and loaded with appendices and graphs. It drew from everything from open sources like the *New York Times*, to spy satellite photographs and electronic intercepts. It was classified SECRET. Next month, the intelligence community's National Intelligence Estimate on Cuba would come out. NIE's were the most important integrated intel product. They helped the White House formulate policy. While it would be tempting to try to smuggle an NIE out of the State Department, an even tiny risk that he would be randomly selected for a bag search was simply too great. Livingston hadn't been betraying his country for the past twenty-three years by being careless and wasn't about to start cutting corners. No. The successful spies were always careful spies.

At quarter past five, he collected his classified papers, locked them away in his office safe, and logged off his secure PC. He donned his Savile Row tweed jacket, grabbed his Ferragamo briefcase, strode out the door, and caught a cab on 23rd Street to Dupont Circle. Grimacing griffins and gargoyles leered down on him from the cornices of The Cairo building, home to the Livingstons for the past fifteen years. Deirdre pecked him on the lips as he entered their twelfth-floor condo, then served him his after-work single malt on the rocks.

Sitting in his Norwegian-made recliner, Livingston perused the headlines of that day's Washington Post. He shook his head and slapped the newspaper with his fingertips. "I can't believe it! I simply can't believe it!"

"What's that, dear?"

"Americans have got to be the stupidest people in creation. A big right-wing rally on the Mall, and what's their beef? Gay marriage! The wealth gap is the greatest it's ever been. Unemployment is through the roof. Banks are foreclosing on working people's homes. And what are the unwashed masses preoccupied with? Homos wanting to marry each other! And guns! They can't make their house payments. But by God, let them have their guns in case they encounter gays at the altar they'd have to take out. Jesus!"

Deirdre shook her head. "It is terrible. Just awful."

"Meanwhile, they're taxed nine ways to Sunday to pay for endless wars. Wars their sons are dying in!"

"Only a year 'til retirement, Phil. Then we'll sail home." She stroked his thinning hair soothingly.

Livingston stared off in the distance. "God. Won't it be great? To live in a sane country with moral leaders. A country where everybody's treated equally. A country at peace."

"But one that is under constant threat," she added.

He looked at her. "I like to think we've played some small part in lessening that threat."

"He told us we've done much more than that. Remember? In Havana? He came to see us and told us that we were 'Cuban heroes' before presenting us with the medal. I still get goose bumps thinking about it." Deirdre hugged herself as if shivering.

He started to pour himself another scotch, but she stopped him. "We've got another communication link-up, remember? Tonight at eight sharp. You've got to keep your head clear."

"Yeah. You're right." Livingston set the glass aside.

After dinner, the pair retired to the study. Over coffee, he caught up with *The Economist*. She read Jane Austen. They kept one eye on the clock. At 7:55, he took the small Sony shortwave out of his desk and tuned to 7995 megahertz. Static. He sat back and waited. She fidgeted with a pad and pencil.

At eight sharp, a woman's voice announced, *"Atención! Atención!"* She then proceeded to read off a series of numbers grouped in blocks of five.

Deirdre carefully took down the numbers, then moved to sit in front of the PC. She took out a CD case from the music collection carefully arranged on a bookshelf—*Bruckner Symphony No. 4*. She removed the silvery disk and placed it in the computer's disk drive. A decryption program uploaded automatically. Deirdre then entered the numbers.

When she was finished, she pressed Enter. The screen lit up with a message.

"They want another meeting here," she said.

Livingston poured himself another scotch.

"It says we are to meet Oscar at the Westin on M Street, Room 405, tomorrow at seven p.m. They want us to confirm by calling a phone number here that links to a pager."

"Hmm. They must be strapped for hard currency. Used to be the Hilton, Mayflower, or Four Seasons." He downed the scotch in one gulp. "I don't like it."

"But, dear, it's our duty, the moral obligation we took when you began working at State."

"I don't mean that. I mean it's dangerous meeting with Cuban spy handlers here in Washington. I told them years ago, it's better to meet twice a year whenever we make a foreign trip like last time in Quito. The FBI's been rolling up one espionage network after another over the past several years. Besides, I told them we want to retire and act as a reserve force in the future in case of urgent need. But our luck could run out. Federal employees to Federal inmates. Sexagenarian penitentiary convicts. No. Give me Varadero Beach or Cayo Coco. That's where we're headed. Exactly a year from now. Sailing home."

They hugged.

The Westin was five blocks north of the White House and the same distance from The Cairo. A fifteen-minute walk, but it took the Livingstons an hour and forty-five minutes. Applying the operations security they had been taught during their sole visit to Havana in the late nineties, when *el Líder Máximo* spent an evening with them, they meandered up and down Connecticut Avenue, checking out the chi-chi boutiques and enjoyed a coffee at Luna Books & Coffee, a funky, cramped joint off Dupont Circle, ideally suited to spot a tail.

They breezed through the chocolate-on-beige lobby of the Westin and took the elevator to Room 405. When Philip tapped on the door, it was opened immediately. Philip and Deirdre were ushered in by a thin, medium-build man on the cusp of forty, who had a full head of black hair and a warm face.

The room, decorated in the same color motif as the lobby, was crisply neat, except for a small suitcase on one of the beds and a pot of steaming coffee and some cakes on the small table in the corner.

"Oscar" asked them to take a seat and offered refreshments.

Livingston shifted nervously and kept looking around.

"I am sorry. Is something wrong?" Oscar asked.

Livingston leaned forward, elbows on the chair arm. "Yes. I don't like meeting like this. We're in Washington, D.C., the lion's den."

"I can assure you that we exercise the greatest caution and take your security very seriously," Oscar said in slightly accented English.

"Those Russian sleepers the FBI rolled up not long ago thought they were exercising 'the greatest caution' too. For over a decade, some of them. Turns out the Feds were onto them from day one. And there've been others, including yours."

Oscar stiffened. "There is always risk in this business. We wouldn't have called you if it weren't important. Believe me."

"All right. Keep it brief. And in the future, let's keep it to emails, short wave, and the occasional face-to-face meetings abroad."

"And brush passes, if necessary," Deirdre interjected.

Livingston nodded. "As necessary."

Deirdre added, "Don't get us wrong, Oscar. This is important to us. That's why we've done it so long and why we don't accept money. It's the cause. A moral cause. And the hostile, unjust policies of our own government. Isn't it, dear?" She took her husband's hand.

"Yes," Philip said gruffly.

"Okay, so let's get down to business, shall we?" Oscar said. "First, do you have something for me?"

Deirdre opened her purse and pulled out a compact disk.

Philip took it from her. "Deirdre spent several hours typing up my mental notes on a lot of stuff Havana will find useful. The White House's new strategy for Latin America. CIA's take on your country's leadership. Upcoming war games the Pentagon is hatching involving Iran and North Korea. Some covert ops chopped off on by the relevant agencies. Also, some insider dirt and state of play on personalities in the White House and the State Department. I've also identified some intelligence case officers heading for posts in Central America and the Caribbean."

"Wonderful," Oscar declared. "This indeed will be highly valued in Havana. I want to ask you a specific question."

"Sure. Go ahead," Livingston said.

"We would be most interested in your government's active measures to subvert our revolution."

Livingston furrowed his brow. "What?"

"For example," Oscar replied, "how did the CIA provoke the demonstrations recently in Havana and Santiago? How did they suborn the military cadets? How do they get funds to the illegal independent libraries? How do they communicate with Yamilé Acosta and the other bloggers?"

Livingston looked at his wife, then back at Oscar. "Uh, Oscar, first, I'm not privy to the covert action stuff. Second, what makes you think the United States government is behind the unrest in your country?"

"Why, because Washington has been bent on destroying us for five decades. And this new president of yours needs to show the media and the reactionary elements in Congress that he is tough on communists. Doing so will strengthen his hand in getting more money and resources for your military and intelligence apparatus. This will be good for military-industrial complex profits. Those corporations, in turn, will give money to his re-election campaign. We don't rule out an invasion of our island, a bigger effort than the Bay of Pigs in '61."

The Livingstons looked at each other again, then back at Oscar.

"How long have you been posted here, Oscar?" Philip asked.

"In Washington?"

"Yes."

"Four months."

"And before that?"

"Pyongyang, Beijing, Tehran, Minsk, and, of course, Havana."

"Uh, has it perhaps occurred to you that the riots and agitation inside Cuba might possibly be entirely indigenous? Like maybe some people are dissatisfied with things? Poor housing, reduced rations. That sort of thing?"

Oscar appeared puzzled. "No."

Philip was at a loss for words. "Well, anyway, I have no information implicating my government in those activities."

Clearly disappointed, Oscar went to the bed and opened the small suitcase. He took out a hardcover book titled, *Greek Tragedies: An Anthology*. He opened it. In the middle was a carved-out space from which he retrieved a thumb drive. "This is your private key. With it, you can send and receive encrypted messages." He then provided details on its use. "When not using it, always keep it hidden. I cannot overemphasize the importance of this. Also, erase the contents of your hard drive after communicating with us or preparing documents for us, as you did today. Understood?"

The Livingstons nodded.

CHAPTER FIFTEEN

Friendship Heights, Washington, D.C.

Amelia Hernández entered Bloomingdale's on Western Avenue at one thiry, spent twenty minutes browsing in the women's fashion department, then exited by the rear entrance. She sat on a bench near the rear entrance and looked left, right, and behind as Saturday shoppers hurried by. She looked at her watch and again scanned her surroundings without calling attention to herself. After two minutes, she got up, walked twenty feet to a pay phone, punched in a number, waited, then punched in another number. She hung up.

She walked back through the department store without stopping to browse, exited the front entrance, made her way through the pedestrian arcade of the shopping complex, and entered Whole Foods. She took a shopping cart and lingered over the asiagos, chevres, manchegos, and stiltons, then moved on to inspect the sea bass, calamari, and tilapia, onward to the granolas and mueslis, and finally to the fresh produce department, where she picked up some arugula and edamame beans. She paid for her few purchases, then exited and ambled north on Wisconsin Avenue, where she paused before the show windows of Bulgari and Saks Fifth Avenue and spent a minute or two gazing at the reflections on the glass.

She proceeded with deliberation to another pay phone. She again punched in a number, waited, and punched in another. She hung up. She retraced her route southward, descended into the Friendship Heights Metro station, and took the red line home to her apartment in Woodley Park, near the National Cathedral. Once behind closed doors, she pawed through her groceries. Next to the bag of granola was a handsoap box. She opened it and found two thumb drives, one marked "R1" and the other, "S2." The brush pass with the Cuban courier had been successful, and once again, the numerical codes to the pager of her Cuban handler to notify him of her exact whereabouts worked like clockwork. A one-way pager's advantage over a cell phone was that it was a passive receiver only and sent no signal, making it unable to be tracked.

When she had offered herself up as a loyal servant of the Republic of Cuba fifteen years previously while studying for her master's at George Washington University, Amelia Hernández had been full of idealism and outrage at U.S. policy toward Central America. The bloody Reagan wars had cost the lives of countless innocent peasants so the rich and powerful ruling classes could get richer and more powerful. The suppression had been carried out in the name of countering communist subversion. But as her sister and cousins in El Salvador were murdered, Chiquita Banana and Dole benefited in the form of expanded profits wrested out of underpaid and exploited country folk.

At an academic conference in Mexico City before graduation, she had discreetly approached a representative from the Cuban Academy of Sciences and expressed her interest in assisting the revolution. One thing led to another, and Amelia was assigned a handler who had urged her to apply for jobs at foreign affairs agencies. Since then, she had provided Havana with a steady stream of classified intelligence, policy papers, and inside dope on the personalities of each succeeding presidential administration from her perch inside the Defense Intelligence Agency.

Amelia sat at the metal desk in a corner of her bedroom and powered up her laptop. She plugged in a thumb drive and uploaded a decryption program. She then inserted the R1 thumb.

The R stood for Receive. After following a series of prompts, a Spanish text message flickered onto the screen.

Continue sending information as you have been doing, but always be sure to encrypt it. It is of utmost importance that you not leave any unencrypted sensitive information inside your home. Also, give to "C" encrypted thumb drives only. Until we advise otherwise, do not convey printed or photographed material. Hold on to such materials in a secure place until we give you the green light to deliver them. But on the whole, it is preferable that you type up information that you have memorized onto an encrypted drive and deliver it as you have been. As always, you can contact us immediately via the pager numbers.

Amelia deleted the message, removed the R1 thumb drive, and inserted S1. She leaned back a moment to collect her thoughts, then began to type.

The CIA has just put out a report classified SECRET covering the recent unrest inside Cuba and the likely impact on the leadership. Specifically, the report attributes the riots in Havana and Santiago to popular disaffection toward the regime as government layoffs continue, rations are further cut and freedoms are curtailed. There is no mention of outside interference.

CIA views the Cuban leadership as incapable of meeting the people's needs. What adjustments have been made are seen as too little and too late. They cite the advanced age of the leaders as a harbinger of future change. But the key question is whether the Cuban people might force changes well before a leadership transition.

CINCPAC is planning war games in tandem with the South Korean armed forces. The games are to send a clear message of strength to Pyongyang, to put the DPRK leaders on notice that

Washington and Seoul will brook no acts of aggression from the North. These games will take place next July.

The Pentagon has reached agreement with Israel to bolster joint efforts for cyber warfare against Iran, and specifically its nuclear program. A U.S.-Israeli covert ops unit will be formed to carry this out and will be situated in Tel Aviv. This program, OPERATION KLINGON, is classified TOP SECRET – SPECIAL COMPARTMENTED INFORMATION. It is manned jointly by Israel's cyber warfare body, Unit 8200, and the Pentagon's new Cyber Command.

The following are CIA case officers who will arrive to work in Havana in August:

Paul Delgado
Linda McCarthy

Delgado's cover will be Consular Officer.
McCarthy's will be Administrative Officer.

I will forward further details on these items as I acquire the information.

Finally, I have been doing this work for you for the past fifteen years now. Even though I am careful, I have fears that the FBI will eventually catch up with me. I have migraines and sleep badly. I may request an absence from this work for a while.

After encrypting it, she saved the message onto S1. She deleted what was in her laptop and powered off the machine. Amelia closed her eyes, leaned forward, and rubbed the temples of her throbbing head.

CHAPTER SIXTEEN

Sierra Maestra, Cuba

Yuri surveyed the rugged green landscape below with his binoculars, disregarding the lush natural beauty, drawing on his military skills instead to detect any unusual formation or movement, such as government troops.

He lowered the glasses, peered skyward, and listened—birds, jungle fauna chirping, pecking, or chattering away. No low hum of man-made aviation. He looked at his watch—two more hours until sundown. His *escopeteros* were due back any time. The scouts were reconnoitering miles away, on the lookout for any signs of increased government security presence or activity. They were also tasked with making contact with sympathizers who would man anti-regime cells, recruit supporters, and find sources of provisions and materièl.

Now going by the *nom de guerre* Capitán Zero, Yuri smirked. The irony was not lost on him. Proud graduate of José Maceo Military Academy, top in his class and, at twenty-two, he was the most wanted man in Cuba. He instinctively touched his right cheek. The scar was still healing. It would leave a permanent gash on his handsome face. But the mark was what drove him, a reminder of what he was fighting for. Six months of physical torture and psychological torment in a MININT prison had given him another diploma in his education—a master's degree in revenge. The last straw had been the photos of his father brutalized almost beyond recognition. At that point, he almost broke. But it also lent a furious energy to fight back. With his fellow prisoner-cadets, he managed to exploit a gap in prison security and engineer a breakout. When he personally slashed the throat of the warden, he felt good. In the handful of isolated attacks against regime personnel since, he and his men spared no lives of communist party cadre. They were summarily shot. Hence, he had earned his moniker, Captain Zero, for zero tolerance for the enemy.

His small band called themselves the Arnaldo Ochoa Brigade in honor of the acclaimed general shot by Fidel in 1989 simply for rivaling himself in popularity. Like Captain Zero, Ochoa also came from modest *guajiro* roots, which gave an added affinity.

At José Maceo, the captain had studied the many rebellions started in the Sierra Maestra Mountains of eastern Cuba, from the Ten Year War and the War of Independence in the nineteenth century to the Castros' own insurgency of the 1950s. He knew what to do and what not to do. These looming karsts, crevices, and precipices were their friends, providing the brigade with sanctuary, cover, and protection. At the academy, he had been taught about force multipliers, those factors that a commander utilizes to enhance his military power. The Sierra Maestra was a force multiplier of a thousandfold.

The five *escopeteros* straggled back to the encampment in the shadow of Cuba's highest peak, Pico Turquino, just before sunset. Along with fresh intelligence and some food provisions, the young men, fellow cadets who had been arrested on trumped up treason charges, brought back two prisoners.

Carlos, the nineteen-year-old chief scout, pushed the two men forward to face Captain Zero. "This one is a CDR block warden and this, a policeman."

"Is it true? That you are a CDR cadre and you are a cop?" Zero asked in an even, detached voice.

The men, shaking with fear, nodded.

Zero pulled out his pistol and shot the CDR man in the head. The man's limp body dropped to the ground. He pointed the pistol at the cop.

"No, Yuri!" Carlos said. "You can't—"

Ignoring his fellow cadet, Zero kept the gun inches from the other man's forehead. "Do you renounce your government and swear allegiance to the Arnaldo Ochoa Brigade?"

The man replied, "You can't do—"

Zero plugged him with a single shot between the eyes. "Photograph their bodies. Then bury them," he ordered as he reholstered his weapon.

With resigned expressions, the men followed the orders.

Zero read their thoughts. "Listen. We are at the very start of a struggle to take our nation back. We've all experienced what mercy the Castros show to their enemies as well as innocents like us. We must spare no measure, or we risk being crushed. We must adopt their tactics and strategy from the early days and turn those against them. And the people must know that there is no middle ground.

"From now on, Party cadre will be liquidated in place. Kill enough of them, and the people become emboldened. Do not bring them here unless they are of intelligence value. Understood?"

The men murmured in the affirmative and continued with the burials.

Nick watched another spider weaving a web, but on his jail cell wall. The creature secreted a substance from its body and deftly spun away, building a nest into which it would trap prey. Just as he was lured and entrapped. He shook his head. And the FBI had actually hired a dope like him?

He had been kept in solitary. Nights blended into days. Time became a blur. But he knew that was their game: throw a guy into solitary and act as if you forgot about him, no more daily interrogations, and deny all human contact. Since the waterboarding and subsequent questioning, he'd been unharmed. He was given three spare meals a day, but was starved for news. Starve a man's emotions and intellect, and mess with his mind— yes, that was their game. Nick Castillo would show them he was tougher than they were. But how? They were playing rope-a-dope. How could he show his strength to the enemy if the latter would no longer play?

He sang and recited literature every day to exercise his voice.

Bulldog, bulldog, bow-wow-wow, Eli Yale!
Bulldog, bulldog, bow-wow-wow, our team will never fail!
When the sons of Eli break through the line,
That is the sign we hail.
Bulldog, bulldog, bow-wow-wow, Eli Yale!

He scrunched his brow to concentrate. He had to occupy his mind. Who won the 2001 Super Bowl? What were the major plays in that game? Then, he would work forward. *Uh, St. Louis beat Tennessee at the Georgia Dome. I was there. Kevin Dyson was tackled on the one-yard-line by Mike Jones as time expired, sealing the Ram win. Good. Super Bowl XXXV. Ravens vs Giants. Ray Lewis. No, wait, Jamal Lewis. Which Lewis? Who won? New York. No, wait. Not sure. On to Super Bowl XXXIV. Patriots vs Buccaneers. Uh, wait. Or was that XXXIII? Who won? Who played?* His under-exercised mind was utterly fatigued.

Was it day or night?

Must be in control.

He pounded the wall.

He cried.

A guard awoke him with a shake. "Get up. You're wanted." He threw a pair of pants and a white shirt at Nick. "Put these on."

Nick obliged and followed the guard down a long corridor of cells and into a small office, where a MININT flunky waited. The MININT guy gestured for Nick to step outside where a second MININT officer was waiting.

Nick looked up. For the first time since he could remember, he saw stars in the sky. The pitch-dark Havana sky was sprayed with twinkling galaxies. Fresh air filled his lungs. Already, he felt rejuvenated.

The second MININT officer ushered Nick into the back of a Toyota sedan with a driver. The two Cuban officers flanked Nick in the rear seat. They sported a plastic badge with *DCI* diagonally in red letters – Directorate for Counterintelligence. Nick knew from debriefing defectors that the IDs, colloquially known as *boniatos*, or sweet potatoes, instilled dread in the average citizen.

"Where are we going?" Nick asked.

"Just get in," the first man said. They flanked Nick in the rear seat as the driver sped out into a somnolent capital. No one uttered a word.

The car turned onto Fifth Avenue and headed west. Fifteen minutes later, they were in an area populated by foreign embassies and sleek office buildings, the upscale neighborhood of Miramar. The driver slowed near the domed San Jesús de Miramar Church, entered a small side street, and stopped before a colonial-style house with a large wrought-iron gate. A guard quickly opened the gate to let the vehicle into a large courtyard with a fountain and lush bougainvillea. The two-story ochre villa featured a roof of curved terra cotta tiles and a set of outdoor stairs leading up to a porch with rounded arches.

A woman opened the front door. Nick's handlers led him into the foyer. General Montilla, in civilian clothes, descended a large, winding staircase. The MININT men saluted. She thanked and dismissed them.

She gestured at Nick. "Come with me."

Nick followed her into an expansive dining room, in the

center of which was a ten-foot antique dining table. Two place settings lay opposite each other at one end.

From the kitchen, aromas of seafood, butter, and spices made Nick almost delirious. Three months on a diet of stale bread, rice and beans, and beans and rice had taken their toll.

"You are dining with me tonight," Montilla said. She sniffed and broke out into a grimace. "You need a bath. And a shave." She called for the the female servant and told her to show him upstairs so he could use the shower.

Nick was led into a bedroom warmly decorated with paintings of rural Cuba, green curtains, and thick rugs. On the bed lay a freshly pressed pair of dress slacks and a white cotton shirt. He took his first hot shower since his arrest, and it felt invigorating. After shaving, he studied himself in the mirror. He looked fine, though thinner. But how much of his soul had he lost? He put on the new clothes and headed back downstairs.

Montilla was waiting for him at the bottom of the staircase. She had changed into a diaphanous white dress, a thin gold necklace, and tasteful gold earrings. Her hair was pinned up. In contrast with his earlier official encounters with her, she was also modestly made up with lipstick and eye shadow, and as in his first encounter with her, a whiff of jasmine. She invited him to have a seat. He remained standing.

"You have nothing to fear. Please sit." She gestured at the chair opposite.

He slowly walked around the table and sat down. He looked around the room—more paintings, mostly contemporary and abstract. The furniture was traditional, heavy, dark, Spanish colonial. From the bemused expression on her face, Nick thought he must have appeared like a little boy in a castle. He quickly adopted a serious demeanor.

"I am told you are a beer man. Have you tried our Hatuey brand? I think you'll like it."

The maid brought out a tall frosty glass of beer and a glass of white wine.

Montilla raised her glass to him and took a sip. "California wine. Sauvignon blanc. Yes, we can get pretty much of anything in spite of your country's blockade."

"Embargo," Nick corrected.

"Semantics," she countered. "Drink," she said with a nod at his glass.

Nick didn't know what to think. From waterboarding to a cold cell in solitary to this sanctuary of comfort. And truth be told, he would have spilled his guts for a cold beer. They even knew his drinking habits. He pondered the foamy lager. The large glass sweated, condensation running down the sides. A bribe, he thought. Or worse.

"Don't worry. It's not spiked," she said with a wry smile. "And no more daiquiris."

He eyed the serrated knife at his place setting.

"Yes. You could injure or kill me," she said evenly. "But then what? You wouldn't make it past the guards. You don't strike me as suicidal."

He stared at her. What was her game? She stared back; the enigmatic and disconcerting Mona Lisa smile sent conflicting messages. Slowly, without averting his gaze, he took the glass and lifted it to his lips. The sensation of the frigid brew flowing down his gullet was ecstasy. It filled his empty stomach. He couldn't stop. He emptied the entire contents of the glass. The effect was immediate. His head whirled, and his body relaxed.

Montilla signaled the server to bring another beer. Nick didn't object. The server returned with another beer and a carpaccio salad, thin slices of rare beef on lettuce, before leaving them alone again.

"Please eat," she said and commenced to dig in.

"What's going on?" he asked.

"Dinner," she replied.

"No. I mean, why am I here?"

"Yes. You deserve an explanation, of course. First, I know that we will not break you. Nor is that my way of doing things. So uncivilized. You owe me a debt of thanks. Only I stand between you and the barbarians at the gate."

"But you were there. At the waterboarding. You questioned me."

"I had to. But my primary purpose was to save you."

"You expect me to believe that?"

"Yes."

"Simple as that. 'Yes.' A sworn enemy of my government, of my agency. Save me? I expected a show trial and a long prison sentence by now."

"That may come, Nick. Don't rule anything out. The U.S. Interests Section has already made inquiries about you, though they concealed your identity, as if we were stupid Latin yokels." She took another sip of her wine.

"Expect to be here a long time, Nick. Years. Perhaps decades. But I will tell you my intentions. It is no secret that a leadership change will come soon to Cuba. Mortality will take care of that. I am in a good position to succeed the old generation, along with others like me. We are neither blind nor rigid. The writing on the wall of history is clear. We are one world, a world that becomes smaller by the day. The old political fault lines fell away when the Soviet Union evaporated in '91. Cuba is late to the game of globalization. We need to catch up."

"Why are you telling me this?" Nick asked. "Tell it to the Secretary of State."

She studied his face. The wheels in her head were turning. "I'd like to start with you. You fell into our lap. But you are unique, a son of the soil of Cuba and an FBI man whose task it is to undermine us. You bridge multiple dimensions. If I can persuade you, well, who knows? And you have courage. Coming here on your own initiative, into the jaws of the lion."

"And the lion swallowed me."

Montilla cocked her head and pursed her lips. The female servant brought in clay pots of piping hot langoustines in garlic-butter sauce. The aroma triggered Nick's salivary glands. Saffron rice and sautéed vegetables completed the entrée. The general was violating Cuban law. Large crustaceans were reserved for export only to garner desperately needed hard currency, in theory anyway.

The second beer put Nick at ease, and he dug in, making a conscious effort not to appear like a starved Visigoth. As the evening went on and his stomach filled with the delicacies, Nick mellowed even further. While he couldn't bring himself to buy into Montilla's story, and suspected a trap, he nonetheless was curious. "You aren't married?" he asked.

"No," she replied curtly.

"Attractive woman like yourself. Why not?"

"I serve the revolution. No time for romance. This course was predestined for me."

"By whom?"

She breathed deeply and trained her lovely eyes on the distance. "By those… those who made me who I am."

Nick shrugged and shook his head slightly. "What? Your parents? Teachers? Mentors?"

"All of those," she said cryptically.

"Did your father fight with Fidel?"

She stroked the stem of her half-empty wine glass and smiled. "Oh, yes. He did indeed."

"Is he still alive?"

"No. He was killed. I never knew my father, but I so know him. I am so much him."

"And your mother?"

"She was a foreigner. Beautiful woman. She died last year."

"What country?" Nick asked. "Your mother, that is."

Montilla looked up. "You ask too many questions. Who is the prisoner here? I do the questioning, *señor* FBI man."

Nick wasn't sure if she was serious or not, but then she smiled.

After a light flan for dessert, Montilla dismissed her household staff. She stood next to Nick and offered to pour him a coffee liqueur. He declined. She remained in place. Nick looked up. She focused her eyes on his.

"What do you see in me? What is it you want?" he asked.

"I've never met any American official before, much less an FBI or CIA officer. Can I say I am fascinated? As a girl, I loved playing with fire. I still do." She bent and pulled open the top of her dress to expose unhaltered breasts. She pressed them against Nick's face. "Do you yearn for the touch of a woman?" she breathed into his ear.

Nick closed his eyes. The soft warm flesh enveloped him, its comfort chasing away what seemed eons of cold jail time, but also too many lonely nights before that. A voice deep inside warned him, told him to flee the witch's spell, but the voice became faint and died.

She took his hand and led him upstairs into the expansive master bedroom. She faced him and proceeded to unbutton his shirt, unzip his pants, and lower his shorts. With one deft move, her dress fell to the floor, revealing a taut, muscle-toned body. She wiggled out of her panties. She put her arms around him and pressed her cheek against his chest.

After a few moments, she raised her head and pressed her lips to his. He kissed her hungrily. She led him to the four-poster bed, where he lay back on the pillows. She hovered over him and gently kissed his neck, abdomen, then his member. Nick trembled and let out a moan. The energy between them intensified. She was in charge, and that was okay. Montilla leaned up and straddled his groin. Her gyrations sent Nick into orbit. He surrendered to her magic.

They collapsed in sweet exhaustion, their sweat-drenched bodies side-by-side.

She turned her face to his ear and circled it playfully with her finger. "So is this what they mean by 'fraternizing with the enemy'?"

"And then some," Nick replied.

After a time, she asked, "Do you like to play games?"

Nick looked at her quizzically.

She went to a dresser, pulled something out, and jumped back into bed. "I am going to torture you to force you to tell me everything." She held up a small riding crop. She playfully swatted him with it. Then again, harder.

"Hey! Cut it out!" He grabbed it from her hand.

"Now you have me." She turned over on her belly.

Nick took in the curve of her waist and the smooth roundness of her bottom. He ran his hand along the contours of her body, then again with his nails. He cracked the riding crop lightly across her buttocks. She moaned. He tapped again, sharper. She squirmed and moaned louder. Nick swatted harder and again until her flesh became rosy. He was whipping his tormentor, a flag officer, no less. It gave him delight, and he hit again and again.

"Yes! Punish me! Punish me!" she squealed.

He stopped and dropped the instrument. "I... I don't think... uh, this isn't right..." He rose, picked up his clothes, and got dressed.

CHAPTER SEVENTEEN

CNN (Havana) Social unrest continues to plague parts of Cuba following mass demonstrations recently in Havana and Santiago, the island's second largest city. The strikes protesting mass layoffs of government employees and tighter rations have eased, but reports of armed attacks in the eastern regions continue to surface.

New policies set forth by Cuba's recent Sixth Party Congress appear to be adding to public discontent. Specifically, cutting back or ending of a range of subsidies for food, agriculture and social welfare are being met with protest. Reports from Cuba's growing blogosphere point to citizens' growing expectations and the Communist Party's inability to meet them as a key factor in fueling the public agitation. They add that there is also growing discontent over the lack of political and travel freedoms.

Unnamed senior officials in the U.S. State Department and intelligence community tell CNN that they are watching developments in Cuba closely. While they cannot confirm the existence of an organized armed resistance on the island, they also do not rule it out. The State Department spokesman reiterated U.S. support for peaceful democratic change in Cuba.

"Only socialism is capable of overcoming the current difficulties and preserving the victories of the revolution."

—*Statement by President Raúl Castro upon releasing the new Guideline Project for Economic Policy.*

Captain Zero's expanding informant networks throughout the island were paying off. He and his small command circle knew well in advance of FAR and police operations in their redoubt in the Sierra Maestra Mountains. That allowed fighters of the Arnaldo Ochoa Brigade to neutralize the attackers through pre-emptive ambushes or simply to recede into the forest. Their intelligence on government forces grew by the day, much of it coming from disaffected rank-and-file officers and soldiers.

The Brigade had just captured a mobile radio truck from the FAR. Soon, Radio Libertad would go on the air, a measure sure to draw a robust armed reaction from the central government. Captain Zero knew guerrilla warfare, having taken to heart the lessons on Maoist strategy taught at José Maceo academy: "The enemy advances, we retreat; the enemy camps, we harass; the enemy tires, we attack; the enemy retreats, we pursue."

A FAR intel informant brought him information that made the hardened young fighter's heart skip a beat and caused him to smile for the first time since he could remember. His father was to be transferred the next day from Boniato Maximum Security Prison in Santiago to the MININT La Campana prison in Havana. Rumor had it that Marcial Senior was to be sentenced and shot. The Arnaldo Ochoa Brigade would be ready.

Boniato Prison stood in the shadow of a four-hundred-meter-high ridge of the Sierra Maestra. At 0700 hours, Zero trained his binoculars onto the prison from his high perch

The informant had reported that the small convoy transporting Marcial would depart at 0730 along the Autopista Nacional A-1 enroute to Bayamo, then westward to Havana. Zero had men positioned at high points astride a gap at Dos Bocas, through which the highway snaked. He had only one shot to rescue his father. Should his plan fail, his father was surely a dead man, and Zero's chances weren't good either. He made his way to the Brigade unit on the north face of the gap.

While they assumed the prisoner would be transported in a prison van, they couldn't be sure. Nor did they know how many vehicles there would be. In any case, they couldn't run the risk of taking out the lead vehicle, which was standard operating procedure in any ambush, lest Marcial might be inside. Weighed against that was the need to strike with lightning speed to prevent the troops from radioing for help. A so-called surgical strike was needed. But all soldiers knew that warfare was rarely surgical, but rather butchery.

Positioned with his main force on the north face, Zero checked his watch—0730. No movement out of Boniato prison. The tropical sun was already high and hot. Sweat soaked Zero's tunic and poured down his brow. Five minutes passed. Ten. Fifteen. Bad intel, he thought, or a ruse by the other side to get the Brigade to expose itself and thereby be vulnerable to attack.

0757. Two vehicles, a GAZ jeep in the lead followed by a van, pulled up to the main administration building in the front of the complex. Men left the building and got into the vehicles. At just after eight, the convoy drove out the front prison gate, turned right onto the road leading away from the prison, then took a left onto highway A-1, heading north and west.

As the convoy entered the pass at Dos Bocas, the Brigade struck. Two snipers shot out the tires on the lead vehicle. As the jeep swerved out of control, the van struck its rear. Zero's men ran up to and surrounded the vehicles, aiming their Kalashnikovs at the still-stunned prison personnel.

A few of Zero's men yanked open the front doors of each vehicle while others remained at a distance, assault rifles trained on their targets. The two men in the lead vehicle stumbled out with their hands raised. The driver of the van slumped over the wheel, unconscious. The man in the van's passenger's seat also got out with his hands held high.

Three of Zero's men approached the rear of the van. One fired a single bullet into the lock and reached out to pull open the door. Before his fingers could reach the handle, the door burst open, and a MININT officer sprayed the rebels with a small submachine gun. Two of Zero's men went down. The third hit the ground, rolled under the van, and fired upward with his pistol. The MININT man's head exploded from the rear cranium, sending blood and brains in all directions.

His killer leapt up and, with both hands gripping his gun, swiveled left and right, ready to take out the next threat. He leveled his weapon on a dark face hovering in the far end of the hold. The prisoner had his hands raised, palms-out on either side of his head.

"Colonel Marcial?" the man with the gun asked.

"Yes."

"Come. Hurry!"

Marcial clumsily frog-marched out with shackled feet and hands.

"Keys!" Zero demanded of his captives. "Keys! Now!"

The men didn't respond.

Zero fired at the left kneecap of a man with lieutenant's insignia. Then, he aimed his gun at the jeep's driver. "Keys!"

The van's front passenger, a sergeant, yanked a set of keys from his trousers and held them up.

"Take them off!" Zero ordered, his pistol three feet from the man's head.

With shaking hands, the man unshackled Marcial's hands and feet.

Marcial grabbed a revolver that had been seized from one of the captives and joined his son.

Zero offered a firm handshake, which Marcial took. Marcial then pulled Zero to him and embraced him in a hearty bear hug.

Zero addressed his prisoners, "You serve a dying regime. Join us and the people or risk going down with a sinking ship."

The prisoners shifted uneasily. One murmured, "We have families, homes."

Zero responded, "Victory is built on sacrifice. I will release all of you. Had any of you been Party men, you would be shot here and now. Tell that to your superiors. Now lie on your bellies!"

"Don't shoot us," the sergeant implored.

"On your bellies! Now!"

The men obliged. At a signal from Zero, his men tied the prisoners' feet and hands, except for the one with the knee wound, who was left to writhe on the ground.

"You will be discovered in due course. Long live the Arnaldo Ochoa Brigade! Long live the cause of freedom! Long live Cuba!"

The two Brigade men who had been shot at by the MININT man had only light wounds. Zero and his troupe receded back into the wilderness.

Nick's circumstances improved markedly after his bizarre tryst with Larisa Montilla. He was moved to a small bungalow on a Havana MININT complex, given better food and plenty to read, albeit carefully screened material: the Cuban Party organ *Granma*, *Juventud Rebelde*, the communist youth paper, and *Trabajadores*, the official organ of Cuban labor. He worked at reading between the lines of the stilted and biased reporting to piece together some of what was going on in the world. He was also supplied with Hemingway's complete works. Nick could listen to music on a small cd player his jailers provided, along with ten cds ranging from classical to rhumba. Finally, he was provided a jump rope and barbells. He also was allowed one hour a day to exercise in a courtyard.

He had plenty of time to reflect on the fact that he should have been convicted in a quickie kangaroo court and sentenced to a long prison term, with accompanying propaganda screeds against Washington.

"That may come, Nick. Don't rule anything out," Montilla had told him.

But his head spun. He'd allowed himself to become compromised by succumbing to the seductive charms of a clever and ruthless senior female Cuban official, a shadowy and effective operative known to the Americans only by her CIA cryptonym, DRIVETRAIN.

If he ever got out, he would have to reveal everything to the FBI. One of two scenarios would then play out. Either he would be quietly dismissed, or to avoid attention and further embarrassment, the Bureau would pull his clearances and assign him to the mailroom or supplies office to dole out toilet paper until he got the message and voluntarily resigned. In any case, his going to Cuba without permission was grounds enough for dismissal. He was screwed any way he looked at it. He wouldn't be able to look his parents in the eye.

But there was more. He looked deep into his soul and didn't like what he saw. Was he losing his mind? Larisa Montilla had a full and detailed dossier on him, clearly methodically collected over a period of years. She knew more about Nick Castillo than anyone else. "Closed book" his ex-girlfriend had called him. But not to Montilla and her operation. Had she cynically preyed upon his emotions to compromise him and ultimately to blackmail him into divulging secrets, or worse, to "turn" him and send him back as a double agent? It made sense. She could add to her tools of coercion a physical or moral threat to his parents, morally by character assassination—exposing their gullibility in supporting the deep cover Cuban agent, María Mirabel de la Cruz, mysteriously killed at a dead drop organized by her handlers. The spider spun her web.

Or was he merely Larisa Montilla's plaything, a kept man, her boy toy? She was an attractive, upwardly mobile, and unattached workaholic soon to be past her sexual prime, as horny as any other human being. A bit gonzo like most top officials in dictatorships. She told him she liked to play with fire. Maybe she saw him as forbidden fruit or as a challenge for conquest, sexual or otherwise.

But the thing that ate at him most, the thing that made him challenge his own strength and integrity was that… he enjoyed it. During his initial interrogation by Montilla, from the moment he looked deep into her inviting eyes, saw her mischievous smile, set eyes on her bosom, and smelled her scent, he had been beguiled. As so often in male-female relations, it was wrong, yet delectable, forbidden, yet enticing. The cerebral and emotional levels clashed. Was he losing his manhood as well as his moral compass? He shook his head. No answers.

Shaken out of his sleep, he was ordered to dress in a replay of an earlier scenario. He was escorted out under the Havana sky, plopped in the back of a sedan between two burly men, and whisked into a slumbering city.

The route was familiar, the same church, same office buildings, until they stopped at an intersection.

The window on the driver's side exploded. Blood flowed from the driver's neck. The shooter stood there, ready to fire again. Two other men wearing black balaclavas rushed to each side at the rear. Before the MININT guards could react, the attackers plugged them with multiple shots in their chests. Blood sprayed over Nick's face and front, not his own, but that of the dead guards. The attacker on the right yanked open the door, pulled out the guard on that side, and kicked the body into the street. He grabbed Nick by his shirt and jerked him out of the car. Two motorcycles pulled up, and Nick was thrown on the back of one. One of the attackers got on the back of the other. The other two disappeared into the night. The bikes roared off, each in opposite directions.

CHAPTER EIGHTEEN

After Arnaldo Ochoa Brigade's first armed strike in the capital, the reaction was swift and harsh. A massive sweep rounded up anybody who had been ratted on by a *chivato* snitch for suspicions of harboring anti-regime sentiments. People were randomly hauled in for questioning. The University of Havana was shut down until further notice. Groups of more than three persons were prohibited from forming in public places. The propaganda organs denounced what they claimed was a cold-blooded murder carried out by reactionaries from Miami with likely support from Washington. All land routes out of the capital were cordoned off; vehicles leaving and entering the city were searched. Police took in for questioning anyone operating a motorcycle. Security cadre appeared edgy and aggressive.

The one area of movement they overlooked was the sea. Small fishing vessels and leisure craft plied the coastal waters unhindered. The Coast Guard was not instructed to stop and board vessels in search of armed fugitives and an escaped American FBI man.

Nick was prone to seasickness, and being passed from one small boat to another over the next four days left him nauseous much of the time. They weaved through the over 2,500 cays and islands of the northeastern coast until finally landing at a point north of Las Tunas. From there, he was transported by truck south to Bayamo, where Zero's agents took him over and smuggled him to the Ochoa Brigade encampment deep inside the Sierra Maestra.

The encampment was as basic as any Nick had seen when in the Marines. The huts were covered in palm fronds, with a few tents interspersed among them. Scrawny young men cleaned their weapons and performed drills. A couple of beat-up jeeps were parked inside the perimeter. Nick was placed in one of the sparely-equipped tents, which contained a cot, a towel, soap, and shaving kit. Four-star conditions in a fleabag guerrilla camp.

He shed Larisa Montilla's dress shirt and pants for the olive drab supplied by Captain Zero.

The guerrilla leader entered the tent and shook Nick's hand. He gestured for Nick to sit on the bunk as he lowered himself on a footlocker opposite. "Are you okay?"

"After a long sleep, I feel fine. Thanks."

One of Zero's men entered the tent with a tray of coffee and *tostones,* fried plantains. Zero took a cup and proffered it to Nick, then took the other for himself. He offered the dish of *tostones.* Nick accepted both with a nod of thanks.

"You are a very hot commodity," Zero said. "You have the distinction of surpassing me as the most wanted man in Cuba. The government is sparing no resources to try to get you back. Their agents here in the east are alternatingly offering bribes and making threats to the country folk to gain leads on your whereabouts. But I don't worry too much. The people here identify with us. They keep us informed of every move of the government."

"I see," Nick said. "But let's walk things back a bit. Who are you? Do you know who I am? How did you know I was incarcerated in Havana?"

"My *nom de guerre* is Captain Zero. My true name is Yuri Marcial. I am the son of Colonel Henrique Marcial. My informants inside the MININT told me of your arrest soon after it happened. I made it my mission to rescue you."

"I know your father. Er, rather I know who your father is. I came here to warn him."

Colonel Marcial entered the tent. Another round of

handshakes. He found a seat on a crate. His even-featured face was a map of healing welts and scars.

"Father, Nick says he came here to warn you," Zero said.

Marcial's face registered surprise. "But I don't know you."

"No. We've never met. But I know of you. Guantanamo. The Line. Your note."

"Ahh!" Marcial exclaimed. "Yes. I must—"

"Just tell me this. Were you genuine in seeking to defect? Or were you set up?"

Marcial clasped his hands together and shook his head. "I was used. They said they chose me because I fit a 'certain profile.' I didn't want to do it, but they made me. I am a simple soldier, not a spy. MININT used me in a carefully crafted operation to lure American agents, then to pounce on them. After I passed the bogus note, they sent me to Havana simply to walk the city. They followed my every move. Then, Badoglio. They got him. I don't know if he is still alive. They tortured him. Then they tortured me." He lightly patted both sides of his injured face. "After Badoglio, now you. Their ploy worked."

"Why would they turn on you? You have a clean record, right?"

"Yes. I do. Well, I did. First, I stumbled into a protest demonstration in Havana, which got me arrested. Then, as conditions deteriorated throughout the country, their paranoia grew. They've begun seeing CIA behind every tree and lamp post. Finally, I refused an order to fire on the people. They arrested me on the spot. In their twisted imaginations, they convinced themselves that I am an enemy agent. I am not the only one wrongly accused." He nodded toward his son.

Zero stiffened. "They shot two of my best friends and arrested and imprisoned others on trumped-up charges. It is sheer madness."

"As you can see, Nick, the revolution is now devouring its children, a sure sign of decline. The end is near. It is only a matter of time."

"And me?" Nick asked.

Zero shrugged. "I suppose you wish to go back home?"

"I need to get back. Yes."

"We can arrange this. But it will take time," Marcial said.

Zero leaned forward, elbows on his knees, eyes focused intently on Nick's. "In the meantime, we could benefit from your knowledge and experience. As you can see, there is much that we need. Better security. Focused intelligence. A set of rules for justice. Improved communications."

Marcial interjected, "And a link to Washington. We need someone who can explain our cause to your government. And… obtain assistance."

Nick let out a long whistle, placed one hand on his forehead, and leaned back. "That, my friends, is one very tall order."

"You are not only FBI. You are also Cuban. It is in your blood to help the land of your forefathers to be free," Marcial said.

Nick took a moment to ponder. "God knows I have nothing to lose at this point. I've broken every rule in the book."

Marcial leaned forward and clasped Nick's hands in his. "We are all in this together."

"For better or worse," Nick replied. "I have one more question."

"Yes?" Marcial said.

"Who's in charge in Havana? I mean, who's really calling the shots?"

"General Montilla," Marcial answered. "She is a dangerous woman. A woman whose ambition has no limits. Nor her paranoia. A woman bent on being at the top. No matter what."

Sleepy San Luís, a town just north of Santiago, was noted for two things. In 1958, Raúl Castro opened the Second Front there, paving the way to victory the following year. And at the present, the simultaneous explosions of seven bombs made history, with the detonations occurring at the local communist party headquarters, the Union of Communist Youth office, the Workers Center of Cuba, the Committee for the Defense of the Revolution, the Federation of Cuban Women, the Association of Combatants of the Cuban Revolution, and the PNR station. The mayhem created the intended effect. Every available law enforcement and military unit rushed to San Luís to deal with the enemy. But the enemy was elsewhere. The timed explosions made a political point, but were merely diversionary.

Three kilometers north of San Luís, forty fighters of the Arnaldo Ochoa Brigade waited patiently astride a rail bridge for the signal of their spotter in the small town of Chile to the northwest, which would alert them to the imminent arrival of the flagship *Tren Francés*, fifteen French-made cars pulled by a Chinese-made diesel locomotive. The train was hauling tons of new arms and ammunition to replenish the stocks of Santiago's FAR garrison. As a bonus, the Chief of the Eastern Region Army, General Marcos López y López, was the train's most distinguished passenger that day, a point not lost on the Marcials.

The explosives were in place to be manually detonated when the train was within six hundred meters, giving the conductor just enough time to brake. The hope was to be able to seize the train before it reached the destroyed bridge. If the train kept going and crashed into the gully, the conflagration resulting from tons of ammunition going up would wipe out attackers and targets alike.

The coms man listened carefully to the voice amid the static. He extended five fingers of his left hand twice, indicating ten minutes. There was a Marcial on each side of the bridge. They signaled for their troops to be at the ready, weapons raised, prepared to attack.

Another spotter a thousand meters up the line radioed in. The coms man raised two fingers. The chug-chug of the diesel locomotive's engine traveled through the air. Marcial, Sr., raised his right arm as he kept one eye on his watch.

The chugging became louder. The tracks vibrated. Every muscle was taut, the men poised to spring like hunters upon a giant wounded beast.

Marcial threw down his right arm, giving the signal to the ordnance man to detonate. The man plunged down the handle. All men then hit the dirt and covered their ears.

Silence.

The ordnance man pushed the handle down again.

Silence.

The train sped toward them.

Nick stood up. "You! And you!" He tapped two young men hard on their shoulders. "Hurry!" Nick ran.

The young men grabbed their RPG-7 rocket-propelled grenade launchers and scurried after him. They reached the side of the rail bed just as the locomotive was upon them. Nick told them where to aim.

"Fire!" Nick commanded.

Two high-explosive anti-tank rockets slammed into the locomotive directly on the right side first and second wheels. The flash explosions at close range hurled the three men twenty feet back like dolls being thrown by a child.

The locomotive let out an ear-splitting screech, the primal scream of a mortally injured monster. The sound of grinding and snapping metal blasted the air. The train veered to the right and completely off the rail bed. It kept going until the cars buckled. The massive wreck spewed towers of smoke, steam, and dust high into the atmosphere.

The attackers cringed, waiting for instant death in the form of a mushroom cloud from ignited munitions.

"Men! Move it!" Nick ordered.

Shaken, but largely unharmed, the raiding party reconstituted themselves. No mushroom cloud. No explosions. Yet.

One of the RPG men had a leg wound. The other had lost his hearing. Nick lifted himself from the pile of sand in which he had landed. Except for scrapes and bruises, he was all right.

Marcial was on his feet, sending some men to check the locomotive and others to open the cargo cars. His son rushed to the passenger cars with additional men.

"Colonel! Ammo and guns here!" a lieutenant shouted.

Marcial sent two of the Brigade's trucks there with orders to load as much weapons and ammunition as possible.

Gunshots broke out. Nick, AK-47 slung over his shoulder, rushed to the other side of the twisted train from where the shots were coming. There he saw men being lined up against the side of the car. An impromptu firing squad was formed. Its head: Captain Zero.

"Fire!" A volley of shots cut down the five men. Five more were hauled out to take their places.

Nick ran out and placed himself between the men and their executioners. "Halt! Do *not* fire!"

"Nick! Get out of the way!" Zero shouted.

"No! What the hell are you doing?"

"They are MININT officers. Now get out of the way!"

"You can't do this, Yuri. It's cold-blooded murder."

"Who are the murderers?" Zero shot back. "If we don't kill them, they'll come after us. Ready! Aim!" The firing squad raised their weapons and took aim.

Nick held his position. A frozen silence hung stiffly in the air.

Zero strutted up to Nick. "If you don't move, I'll have you forcibly removed."

Nick put his face within inches of Zero's. "It's called rule of law. The law of war says you don't gun down enemy prisoners in cold blood."

Colonel Marcial appeared. He glowered at his son. "Yuri!" Marcial nodded at the squad to lower their weapons. They obliged.

Zero stomped off. Two men approached Marcial with another prisoner, a ruffled gray-haired man.

Marcial raised his hand in salute. "General."

General López's face reflected shock and anger. "Marcial. Not you!"

"I refused to gun down our own citizens. So here I am," Marcial replied.

"This is treason, Colonel. You'll be shot for this, and your men too. You're obviously mad!"

"Perhaps I am, General. In any case, you are now a prisoner of the Arnaldo Ochoa Brigade. You will be treated humanely and with respect, more than I got as a prisoner."

The men took General López away. Two colonels would join him in captivity. The MININT officers and a handful of FAR NCOs and enlisted men were bound with plastic ties.

With the two trucks loaded, the men piled into the third with their prisoners and sped away to the Sierra Maestra.

CHAPTER NINETEEN

Due to recent acts of violence on the part of bandit gangs and hooligans, the Council of Ministers hereby declares a state of emergency in the provinces of Holguín, Guantánamo, and Santiago de Cuba. As first steps to suppress the banditry, the Ministry of the Revolutionary Armed Forces orders the immediate deployment of the 95th Infantry Division and 3rd Armored Division to the Sierra Maestra as well as the call-up of units of the Territorial Militia and select special operations units. A curfew will be enforced in all cities and towns of the three affected provinces. Anyone outside his or her home between 2100 and 0600 without special permission will be arrested. Anyone evading arrest will be shot. No groups exceeding three persons are permitted. All institutions of higher learning are ordered closed until further notice. All travelers are subject to thorough inspection at checkpoints. Those who support banditry and other counterrevolutionary activity are guilty of treason and will be subject to punishment under revolutionary justice. Military tribunals in the three eastern provinces now have the authority to try and sentence enemies of the state expeditiously under streamlined procedures.

Cadre of the Association of Combatants of the Cuban Revolution and the Youth Labor Army are instructed to implement security measures at neighborhood and block levels in coordination with the Committees for the Defense of the Revolution.

The CDRs will also step up informational efforts to promote the people's understanding of our revolutionary development and goals. Those expressing negative attitudes or refusing to participate in these efforts will be subject to extended re-education at facilities now being established.

—Council of Ministers

University students were the first targets. Those known to have participated in the recent protests were rounded up and intensively interrogated. Sympathetic professors were fired. FAR veterans who had protested lost their modest pensions. All towns were in lockdown, placed under martial law. Santiago appeared to be under military occupation, with armed troops and security personnel deployed in every neighborhood. Travelers endured intrusive searches at roadblocks. Police carried out knock-on-the-door raids on houses and apartments in the middle of the night. The more the authorities hassled citizens, the less cooperation they received. A dark, dour pall descended on society. Faces reflected resentment and anger.

The FAR's military incursions into the eastern mountain redoubts of the rebels all ended in failure or catastrophe. The armed forces, slimmed down, depleted of resources, and out of action since the demise of the Soviet Union and its allies, were beaten back and humiliated. The rebels' lightning-quick ambushes took their toll in mounting casualties and retreats. Many rebel collaborators caught by the authorities were tried by impromptu military tribunals and summarily executed by firing squad. Others were given long prison sentences. The government publicized the executions with the aim of deterring others. The effect, however, was the opposite. The crackdown only galvanized more people to join or support the Arnaldo Ochoa Brigade. A steady stream of FAR personnel deserted to join the Brigade.

And the young Captain Zero captured the imaginations of millions, particularly the young people. He was likened to Hatuey, the legendary Taino Indian chief who bravely fought Spanish rule and was known as Cuba's first national hero.

"What will you do with the prisoners?" Nick asked.

"Tell Havana that if they don't call off their attacks on our liberated zone within twenty-four hours, they will be executed," Zero said.

"That's terrorism!" Nick protested. "You'll be called the Butcher of the Sierra Maestra, not the Liberator of Cuba."

Zero leapt up and jabbed a finger at Nick. "Do not tell me how to fight a revolution. What do you know about Cuba from your comfortable life in America. You may have Cuban blood, but you are an American. Don't lecture us! We had a hundred years of you Yankees doing that. The Cuban people are rising up. And they are in no mood to give mercy to those who have oppressed us for half a century."

Marcial stepped into the tent. His son, flush with agitation, fell silent, but held his ground physically opposite the FBI man.

"What's this about executions?" Marcial asked.

"I will issue an ultimatum to MINFAR. They have twenty-four hours to pull their troops out, or we will shoot López and his two lapdogs," Zero replied.

"No executions," Marcial declared.

Zero spun on his heel and faced his father. "I am head of this movement. I make the decisions."

"Then you are no better than the Castros. You'll end up replacing one tyranny with another, if you aren't killed by either the enemy or one of your own, that is," Marcial said.

"They only understand strength. And fear. I'll make them tremble at the mere mention of my name. They must be made to realize that their only choices are to bow before the will of the Cuban people or to pay with their blood."

"Your father is right, Yuri," Nick said. "This country now has two generations that have grown up under dictatorship. To be an effective fighter is necessary. But to begin to demonstrate to all Cubans that there is an alternative to tyranny is also required.

You have no concept of democracy, of how to harness the people's strong desire for change, to join the rest of the world in the twenty-first century."

Zero folded his arms. "Okay, American. Lecture us. Tell us how an American would lead Cuba's struggle for freedom."

"I'm not lecturing you. And I'm not speaking as the American. A good leader recognizes his weaknesses as well as his strengths. Yours are twofold. You've experienced only one-party, one-man rule, and you are ignorant of the successful revolutions and the failed revolutions history has to offer us."

"Sorry, but your so-called revolution against Britain was a bourgeois rebellion led by the educated elite. It has no relevance to Cuba today," Zero said.

"I had in mind Poland, Czechoslovakia, East Germany, and Russia," Nick said. "On the one hand, the Bolshevik revolution proved a failure over time due to too many internal contradictions. On the other, the revolutions that overthrew communism in those countries are sustainable. Why? Because wise leaders harnessed the will of the people. They didn't pursue their goals through firing squads."

"All right, then, *yuma*. So tell me. What should we be doing?" Zero asked.

Nick got in Zero's face to command his full attention. "Look at what's been happening. Ordinary citizens give you food and tip you off on the government's movements. FAR soldiers have deserted to your side. Others feed you intel from the inside, at grave risk to their lives."

"Yes," Zero acknowledged.

"And then look at what's been happening in Havana and Santiago. Student protests, joined in by veterans, unemployed workers, many others. Public defiance of the authorities elsewhere. Even the librarians are challenging the government."

"Yes. Good. But what does it have to do with our military struggle?" Zero asked.

"Everything. Don't you see? Two sides of the same struggle.

Popular unrest. Armed rebellion. So far, they've been playing out separately from each other. They need to be harnessed, two oxen pulling together in the same direction. The political movement needs to join up with the armed struggle. The Word and the Gun."

Zero leaned back and pondered.

"José Martí understood this. He said, 'Politics and strategy are one.'"

The young guard strained to read the blue and white *carnet de identidad*, the personal ID all Cubans were required to carry. The eleven digits seemed to stump him. Having a yokel with yams for brains inspecting could be good or bad. His sheer stupidity could cause him to miss key details and wave one through, or the same trait could delay processing to the point at which a clever supervisor would be called in to do some intensive questioning and examination of papers.

"Where you coming from?" the young man asked for a third time.

Nick strained to contain his exasperation and smiled. "From Santiago. I'm on my way back to Holguín."

"What was your business in Santiago?"

"Family. To visit my mother."

"Why did you see your mother?" the oaf asked.

Nick let out a deep breath, but kept the smile frozen in place. "It's her birthday. The family celebrated it."

The clod furrowed his brow.

Still smiling, Nick surveyed the scene carefully. Three trucks and two cars were behind him on the rural road leading out of Santiago. Two of the regime's least finest manned a makeshift roadblock. Young Pedro, assigned by Zero to accompany Nick, fingered the 7.62mm stuffed behind his belt. Pedro was Zero's best assassin. He had participated in Nick's rescue in Havana.

Nick gave a slight shake of his head to Pedro, signaling the man to leave the gun alone. Reluctantly, the younger man pulled his hand away.

The guard looked again at the *carnets*. "Juan An-ton-i-o Or-te-ga," he read with some difficulty.

"Right," Nick answered.

"What kind of work do you do?"

"I'm an accountant at Central Preston Sugar Mill."

"Your accent sounds like Havana."

"Yes. I'm from Havana. But I now work at Holguín."

"And you." He jutted his chin at Pedro. "Where do you live?"

Pedro, less patient than Nick, flashed irritation. "What's it say on the *carnet*?"

Nick was grateful his hotheaded fellow traveler omitted "asshole" at the end of his rude response.

Fortunately, the thickheaded security man missed the sarcasm. He sounded out the words on Pedro's counterfeit *carnet*. "An-dres Vega Ce-ba-llo. Purial, Holguín."

"You can read!" Pedro shot back with a malicious grin, ignoring Nick's reproachful look.

"Yes. Of course I can read." The roadblock guard was obviously not amused. "What is your work?"

"Me? I work at the Purial train station," Pedro said.

"Doing what?"

"Oh. I blow up trains." Pedro's evil grin doubled in size.

Nick elbowed him in the ribs.

"He's got a hangover, officer. From the birthday party. He's a maintenance man at the train station."

"At Purial?"

"Yes."

"That station is closed down."

Nick and Pedro looked at each other, the wheels in their brains in overdrive.

"Still open for freight," Nick responded swiftly.

"Get out," the guard ordered. He slowly circled the vehicle, bending to scrutinize its contents.

Pedro flicked his eyes downward in the direction of his gun. Nick made a slight shake of his head. They exited the car. Pedro's right hand hung close to the weapon on his hip, barely concealed by an old *guayabera* shirt.

"This area has been attacked by bandits. There are many bandits in this area. It is dangerous here," the guard said.

"Is that so?" Nick said.

"You seen any bandits?" the man asked.

"If we did, we'd report it immediately to the police," Nick said.

"You bet. First thing," Pedro chimed in.

"Hey! Can we hurry it up?" the driver of the truck next in line shouted. "I've got seafood in the back. This sun is beating down. I've gotta make time."

The guard took in the growing line of vehicles. He returned the counterfeit IDs to Nick and Pedro. "Okay. Go."

Nick and Pedro jumped into the jeep and drove off, relieved to be rid of the dope who almost lost his life to a well-aimed bullet. Once back on the open road, Nick stopped the car and got out. Pedro followed suit. A green tapestry of open cane fields spread for miles in all directions.

"Are you out of your damned mind?" Nick demanded. "Are you out to get us killed? Here we are sneaking out of the rebel area under aliases, and you crack wise with a cop. Not only that, but your itchy trigger finger just can't keep away from your gun. You're psycho! That's it. Yuri saddled me with a homicidal psychopath!"

"Ah. Cool it, will ya? I'm here to keep *you* alive. That's my job. That dumb pisshead. He wasn't even PNR. Youth Labor Army loser. That's what he was. He couldn't man a kindergarten crossing. I could've taken him out easily. And the other one too."

"Take them out? What the hell are you talking about? You whack a couple of guards, especially in this high state of alert, and they'll put out a dragnet that'll sweep us up in no time. Our mission is to make contact with underground political leaders, and that means calling zero—read my lips: *zero*—attention to ourselves. Yuri and your ilk are too young for this. All you know is killing. That's stupid. You'll get the people against you in no time!"

Pedro lit a cigarette and looked away. "Okay, FBI man, you're in charge. Where to?"

"Jesus, Joseph, and Mary," Nick said in English. "Get back in the car. Put your weapon under the seat, sit still, and shut up. Got me?"

Pedro shook his head and laughed.

Over the following two weeks, Nick made contact with key anti-regime players. With his sixth sense for operational security, Pedro actually proved constructive by ensuring contact was done only after countersurveillance showed the intended contacts were not being monitored by MININT personnel and by ensuring completely clandestine meetings. Nick, under the identity of Juan Antonio Ortega, instructed the contacts on how to form secret cells buffered from one another and how to network with other anti-government units. He also laid the groundwork for coordination between the political agitators and the Arnaldo Ochoa Brigade. That included channeling intelligence to the latter, so central to successful insurgency operations. The cells and networks took on a life form of their own and a broadbased, coherent movement began taking shape. People sensed a wave forming over the land, one that was sweeping more change-starved citizens into its force.

"MININT and its Directorate of Intelligence have ratcheted up their search for you," Marcial said. "They're pulling out all the stops. My sources inform me that General Montilla is livid and beside herself that we got away, but especially you. I am told she has problems sleeping, making her even more temperamental, and that she's seeing a doctor.

Marcial shook his head. "She is intent on tracking down the informant or informants who tipped us off about your being moved from the prison. They've been compelling everybody who was involved with your captivity to undergo lie detector tests and repeated questioning. At least a dozen security and prison personnel are being incarcerated without charges. Now Montilla has dispatched special operations teams throughout the country to sniff out information on your whereabouts. Trouble is, with so many Cuban-Americans having visited the island over the past year, they're spread too thin chasing down false leads. And we're adding to it by spreading false rumors through our psyops. Montilla's cadre are not nice about extracting information. A favorite tactic is beating the soles of suspects' feet. It's painful and leaves them incapacitated for a time, but causes no scars if done correctly."

"Do you think they've made the connection between Nick Castillo and Juan Antonio Ortega?" Nick asked.

"I don't know, but it's just a matter of time. They've always been very adept at infiltrating anti-government groups with informants and spies," Marcial said. "In fact, we can assume they have placed, or soon will place, spies within our ranks here. Your assistance in helping us establish vetting procedures and security checks is invaluable."

"Marcial, it's getting too hot for me on this island. And the last thing the Arnaldo Ochoa Brigade needs now is a radioactive hot potato like me to draw even more fire. I have to leave."

"I understand."

"Now you must remove your uniform," Marcial whispered.

Nick quickly shed his FAR major's uniform and threw on a dark T-shirt and jeans. He kept the army boots. One hundred meters ahead, the Line separating GTMO from Cuban government territory ran like a straight gash across the semi-arid terrain.

"The Frontier Brigade remains loyal to me," Marcial said. "A couple of their men cut a hole in the fence below that pylon directly ahead." He pointed to a tall post illuminated by floodlights. "This area is mine-free. You only need to worry about the pythons, scorpions, and iguanas."

Nick did a double take. "Uh… yeah."

"The Americans have sophisticated motion detectors and cameras all along the perimeter. You will likely be detected, and the Marines will find you very quickly. Just raise your hands and speak English. No sudden moves!"

"How about peeing my pants?" Nick said.

"No time for jokes. On the other side of the fence is a pathway. If the sensors don't catch you for some reason, continue along the path five hundred meters, and you will come to Sherman Avenue. Turn left and continue on. It will lead you to the main base area, including the McDonald's Restaurant with bright yellow arches."

"Yeah, the golden arches, as familiar as the Statue of Liberty."

"Time to go, Nick." Marcial shook Nick's hand and then embraced him heartily. "Thank you for all you have done for us."

"I owe you everything, Marcial."

"I have one last request, Nick. Tell your government about us. Tell them we need America's help. Cuba will be free again." He slapped Nick on the shoulder and pointed to The Line. "Goodbye, my friend." Marcial and his three men then turned and disappeared into the night.

Nick stood facing the formidable razor wire barrier awash in floodlights. America had never looked more uninviting. He made the sign of the cross and sprinted.

CHAPTER TWENTY

United States Marine Corps Base, Quantico, Virginia

"Let's go over this again," said Steele, a blue-eyed, crewcut lifer from the FBI's Security Division. "You just up and fly to Havana because you want to warn this Marcial character, who's an Army officer, that he's in imminent danger… of being arrested by his own government." Steele cocked his head and raised an eyebrow, like a mother who's just caught her child telling a lie.

"Killed," Nick corrected.

"Of being killed. By whom?" Steele asked.

"I don't know," Nick answered.

"If you don't know who, then how did you know?" asked Steele's fellow interrogator, DiMarco, tall, fit, dark, right out of central casting. DiMarco was CI, Counterintelligence Division, tasked with sniffing out spies.

"As I've told you already," Nick replied. "Three Cuban sleepers were methodically assassinated here, one of them a double agent I ran. I believe the other two were also double agents."

"Based on what?" DiMarco asked.

"Just putting two and two together. The puzzle fits."

"So," Steele said, "Marcial was in danger of being killed, but you don't know by who. And you know based on a hunch."

"No, not a hunch—" Nick began.

"You stayed in Cuba for almost half a year," DiMarco interrupted.

"'Stay' isn't quite the word for it," Nick said irritably.

"Well, you stayed at a nice boutique hotel in central Havana," Steele said.

"Yeah, but only until they arrested me."

"In bed with a prostitute," Steele said.

"Yes. But no. I was set up—"

"But at a different place, a motel," DiMarco said. "Then to a prison."

"Where I was waterboarded," Nick added.

"What did you tell them?" Steele asked.

"Nothing," Nick replied.

"But you said earlier you were forced to tell them about Marcial," Steele said.

"Well, I told them I came to warn Marcial—"

"Why?" DiMarco asked.

"Why what?" Nick said.

"Why did you tell them that?"

"Because I was drowning to death, damn it!"

"Then what else?" Steele said.

"What do you mean, 'What else?'"

"What else did you tell them?"

"Nothing."

"Nothing," Steele repeated dubiously. "You're 'drowning to death,' yet you gave up only one secret."

Nick jumped to his feet. His head throbbed. He had lost count how many hours the two clowns had been hammering at him. "You boxed me. Twice. I passed both times!"

"Settle down, Castillo," Steele said. "You know the drill. Guy spends a half year in the Axis of Evil's belly button, a criteria country, AWOL, and well, Mother Bureau has a right to know what you were up to and what you divulged to your hosts."

"This General Montilla," DiMarco said, "tell us more about her."

Nick paused to think. *Careful, Nick.* "Rising star. She might even succeed the Castros."

"Yeah, yeah. You told us that already," DiMarco said. "But what's she like as a person?"

"Smart. Cunning. Ruthless," Nick replied.

"Tall? Fat? How would you describe her physically?"

"Tall for a Cuban. Five-eight, five-nine. Trim and fit. Erect."

"Eye, hair color?"

"Hazel. Light brown, tied back. Usually."

"Except when?" DiMarco pressed.

Nick shot him a sharp look. "I don't know."

"But you said, 'Usually.'"

Nick realized he was walking through a minefield and needed to tread extra carefully. "I think I, uh, saw her with a different hairstyle once or twice."

"How much time did you spend with her?"

"You mean while she watched me being waterboarded?"

"No. Otherwise," DiMarco said.

"I don't like the direction this questioning is taking," Nick said stiffly. "How long will I be held here?"

He could hear troops drilling outside the Marine Corps Brig where he was being held. The FBI shared training facilities at the Quantico base. Funny. He'd graduated from Cuban prisons to an American one. In militarese, his life was FUBAR—Fucked Up Beyond All Recognition. He knew the Bureau suspected he had been broken by the Cubans and had spilled forth a torrent of secrets, or worse, that he was a double agent, all along a Cuban spy, a brainwashed Castro mole inside the belly of the beast. The Caribbean Candidate.

Steele and DiMarco were merely doing their jobs of nitpicking every detail, questioning every claim, and parsing out contradictions and exploiting them. At that moment, waterboarding seemed so much more straightforward and honest than death by a thousand verbal cuts. Nick was wearying, his mind fatigued. Larisa Montilla could learn a few lessons from the Bureau's best.

"Montilla," DiMarco continued, "would you describe her as good-looking? Pretty face? Nice bod?"

Nick remained silent.

"Now, what makes me feel you had a relationship with her that was more than torturer and tortured? Or maybe some combination. How does that song go?" DiMarco sang, "'Hurt so good. Come on, baby. Make it hurt so good.'"

Nick hurled the small table into the two men. They went careening on their butts, taken as much by shock as if a mortar round had landed.

"Go to hell!" Nick banged on the door. Two burly Marine guards burst in, subdued him with an arm lock, and wrestled him to the floor.

Rourke and Morgenstern appeared melancholy and skeptical, though they stood in stark contrast to the previous two Gestapo goons.

"Does it hurt?" Morgenstern asked with a light tap to his own eye.

"Only when I'm awake." Nick's left eye was swollen shut from a blow he took during the scuffle with the guards, who currently stood behind him with arms crossed and billy clubs hanging from their belts. One also had a Taser at the ready.

Rourke leaned forward. "I'm not gonna mince words, Nick. You're in a heap of trouble. Going to Cuba without clearance alone is a fireable offense. Getting yourself caught and jailed compounds the mess. We're lucky we managed to keep it under wraps. The press hasn't picked up on it… yet. CI and Security are deeply concerned you were compromised. Then there are those who…"

"Who what?" Nick asked.

"Well, those who wonder about your loyalties."

"You mean whether I'm a double agent."

"'Fraid so."

"Well, I'm not."

Rourke and Morgenstern exchanged glances and fidgeted.

Nick shook his head. "You guys know me. I'm as true blue as they come. Okay, I blundered in going there. But I felt it was imperative to warn Marcial. My aim was to hightail it out of there as soon as I'd made contact with him."

"Uh-huh," Rourke said.

"So what are my options? They can't just keep me locked up behind twenty-foot-high razor wire fences. Am I going to be charged? If so, with what? If not, I have the right to my freedom now. And is the Bureau going to let me go? Or strip my clearances and assign me to the loading dock until I get the message and quit?"

"I don't know yet, Nick," Rourke said. "Your knocking Steele and DiMarco on their cans hasn't helped your case either. But you're right. It's fish or cut bait time. We're awaiting word from the director's office and from DOJ as soon as the investigation is completed."

"In the meantime," Morgenstern added, "we'd like to pick your brain about what you learned about what's going on there, especially from your time with the rebels. Our sources, as you know, are limited."

Nick gave a full readout of conditions inside Cuba as well as on the Arnaldo Ochoa Brigade. "They want our help. Not military intervention, but some covert aid. Communications equipment, medical supplies, money. More importantly, they want contact. So that when the day comes when they're in power, both sides won't have to start from scratch. And they want us to know that they are fighting for a democratic Cuba."

"Yeah. We've been following events closely. There's lots of doubt as to whether this movement has legs. As for aid... well, once burned, twice shy," Rourke said.

"Another Bay of Pigs, you mean. Like I said, they aren't asking for military support."

"Slippery slope, that," Rourke said. "The Castros are already charging us with fomenting the unrest. Gotta blame it on someone… other than themselves. And the United States is the Rorschach test for blame."

"I'd like to make the case to the White House and State Department," Nick said.

"First things first," Rourke said. "You'll need to make the case to get yourself out of here."

Nick was suspended pending outcome of investigation. His passport had been revoked, as if he would rush back to enjoy further sessions of what Montilla had called the "water carnival." And if he indeed were a Cuban asset, he could escape back to la Patria using forged documents provided by the Cuban DI, unless, of course, he was being surveilled and monitored by his own agency. A small rented efficiency in the Virginia suburbs sure beat the Marine brig in comfort. And solitude beat spending quality time with Steele and DiMarco, hands down.

But the uncertainty was unbearable. Limbo. Neither heaven nor hell. A solid Catholic upbringing very clearly defined all three metaphysical venues. Limbo was for sinners who were fortunate enough to have died in God's good grace but had been denied admittance to heaven until Jesus's redemption allowed for it. *Okay, Son of God. How about it?*

Six months of torture, solitary, kinky lovemaking with a female Cuban alpha-general, blowing up trains, restraining Captain Zero from gratuitous slaughter, breaking into GTMO and being imprisoned yet again by the supposed good guys while undergoing daily marathon interrogations by charmless cops in bad suits had a way of knocking a guy off kilter.

Nick called his parents about every other day. His father thought Nick was out of his mind to have gone to Cuba and lectured him incessantly. His mother fretted about his mental health as well, but in a caring maternal way.

Normalcy. Yes, normalcy was what he needed, the antidote to the famous Chinese curse: "May you live in interesting times."

He hit a few of the bars in the ersatz shopping villages of outer suburbia, places designed to look like an idealized Rockwellian all-American town center where all evil and most minorities were largely absent. They were pleasant, secure soulless places where one could pick up a digital backscratcher at Brookstone or shop for a pod espresso maker at Sur La Table before grabbing a tray of supermarket sushi at Trader Joe's on the way home to a conurbation of identical townhouses looking like they were slapped together by a Hollywood set maker. The denizens were wan, bland, nondescript. Their conversations centered on sales, software, and the perils of navigating Bailey's Crossroads traffic.

The contrast in experiences of assisting rebellion in a third-world communist country to an American suburb was almost too much to digest. Nick was finishing up a Labatt Blue at Houlihan's happy hour, contemplating how he could avoid picking up a tray of supermarket sushi to take home to eat alone.

"Their chile lime shrimp is on special tonight."

Nick swung his head around.

A woman sitting two stools down added, "And their seared rare tuna wontons appetizer is to die for."

"Seared what?" Nick asked.

"Tuna wontons." She was about his age with not overly-coiffed blond hair and wearing corporately safe navy blue business attire.

"Can't say I've ever had those," Nick said.

"Try them. They're delish."

"Delish," he repeated.

"Right."

"Okay. I'm sold. Will you join me?"

"Sure," she said, a tad too eagerly.

He ordered a tuna appetizer and moved over next to her. He offered a hand. "Nick."

She shook his hand. "Meghan."

"What's your claim to fame, Meghan?"

"Ha. You have a funny way of phrasing things. I'm an accounts manager at a reinsurance company."

"Reinsurance?"

"It's like insurance that insurance companies take out to reduce risk on the policies they hold."

"I see."

"I know. It's very dry stuff. But it pays well and my job is secure. And how about you? What's *your* claim to fame?"

"Me? I blow up trains."

Meghan looked at him questioningly.

Nick chuckled. "Actually, I work at the Department of Justice."

"As?"

"As… uh, an accountant."

"Sounds interesting."

"About as interesting as reinsurance, actually."

They both laughed.

She was divorced and had no kids. She enjoyed cooking, "hanging" with friends, and romantic comedies. She had a generically pretty face and came from a happy middle class family in the Midwest. She broadcast normalcy from every pore.

They left Houlihan's together, and he walked her to her apartment in a mid-rise with no architecturally redeeming features. They kissed in the hallway, then she invited him in. Somewhere between the kitchenette and the bedroom, their clothes came off. The lovemaking came like a fast-moving train.

Meghan offset her lack of uniqueness with her bedroom performance. She was full of fire as if tossing away a life of tedium. She taunted him, teased him. Rising to the occasion, Nick flipped her on her belly and tickled her. She squealed and laughed.

"A fighter, are we?" Nick said. He swatted her buttocks with his fingertips.

She giggled.

Nick slapped her bottom. She let out a moan. He slapped again, harder.

"Oohh! You're punishing me! Oohh! Stop it!"

Larisa Montilla's face burst before his eyes like a firebomb, her lustful grin challenging him. All proceedings came to an abrupt halt. Nick perched on the bed's edge and put a hand to his forehead. His eyes were focused a thousand miles away. Sweat poured down his face.

"Nick. Are you okay? Nick?" Meghan shook him gently. "Nick, what is it?"

"Cuba."

CHAPTER TWENTY-ONE

"You traveled a hundred kilometers by open road in a military vehicle dressed in the uniform of a Cuban major?" Rourke asked incredulously.

"It was Marcial's idea," Nick said. "He took his cue from magicians. The art of magic is concealing an object in open sight. In this case, the authorities were rousting rural villagers and urban university students, and tramping through jungle in search of us. It obviously never occurred to them that rebels would drive around openly in FAR uniforms and a captured Army jeep. But it worked."

"And GTMO?"

"Most of the Frontier Brigade remains loyal to Marcial. They arranged for us to get into the security zone and cut a hole in the fence. Once inside, the Marines nabbed me and put me in the brig until the brass came to the realization that they had a genuine American on their hands. They flew me to Norfolk. And that, of course, is where the Bureau took over."

"Impressive, Castillo. But cuckoo. You have a reprimand now in your file, which won't get you any promotions soon. Also, you forfeited your pay from the time of your ill-conceived travel to Cuba 'til now. The good news is that you came out with a clean bill of health from CI and Security. You passed the polygraph, and there's nothing else calling into doubt your loyalty. And of course, your record until now as a fast-tracker in the Bureau speaks for itself.

Rourke shook his head. "There is one puzzling thing, however. The Cubans never trotted you out for propaganda purposes or a show trial."

"I believe they had plans to," Nick said. "Montilla told me that their intention was to use me as a bargaining chip to obtain release of the Cuban Five."

"Then why did they wait?" Rourke asked.

Nick shrugged.

"That General Montilla obviously had plans for you. Don't you think?"

Nick shrugged again. He was concealing a dark secret, one that could be used to blackmail him. If Montilla attempted to do so, however, she would also be burned for revealing that she'd had an affair with an American FBI agent, one who was in her custody no less. As it was, she was probably catching serious heat for having lost him. With luck, she'd be arrested or fired, and he wouldn't have to worry about her any longer. In the meantime, they each possessed what was called in the nuclear arms field "mutual assured destruction"–MAD for short.

"Nick, there's another reason you're getting off relatively light."

Nick leaned forward. "Yeah, what's that?"

"We've got a problem. A very serious problem. And agents with your in-depth expertise and background on Cuba are, well, seriously lacking. In fact, you're virtually it."

"What is it?" Nick asked.

"The USG has been incurring one foreign policy and intelligence failure after another, mostly involving Cuba, but also in other areas—Iran, Venezuela, North Korea."

"And?"

"And we believe there are moles inside our government who are feeding Havana classified information. We think they've been doing so for years. The damage to our national security is immeasurable. We've grabbed a number of them over the years, as you know, but there are others. It's got to stop. The President has ordered us to use whatever resources it takes to sniff them out and catch them."

"It fits in with what happened to me. The Cuban DI was on to me even before I landed. Montilla knew more about me than my own folks."

"You're needed, Nick. If you succeed, it'll put your career back on track. You'll be vindicated. The country will be grateful."

"And if I don't accept, or if I accept, but don't succeed?"

"You can probably look at early retirement as a mid-level agent after assignments in Omaha, Knoxville, and Anchorage."

"Count me in."

"Good. We'll cut orders for your immediate reassignment to headquarters. But I gotta tell you, Nick, you'll be on a short leash. We can't take any more risks with you."

"You won't have to worry about me. I promise."

"Fine. Since the intelligence community is suffering the most damage from the leaks of information, we're assigning an Agency officer to work with you."

"Do I know him?"

"Her."

"Her?"

"That's right. Yes, and somebody you already know. Kate Kovalchuk."

Nick's jaw went slack. "The Ice Princess?"

"Watch it. You're veering into EEO grievance territory," Rourke said.

"She's too young, too inexperienced."

"CIA headquarters doesn't think so. She was the DCI's special assistant. He praises her to the sky. She's a water walker over there. On her way to the top."

"But I—"

"I don't make the terms, Nick. This is a package deal. The CIA doesn't trust you as it is. Whack-job FBI agent flies off to Cuba, gets himself jailed and tortured. Then fights with the rebels in violation of the Neutrality Act. Frankly, they think we're nuts to keep you on. But given your expertise and that you passed security, they're reluctantly willing to give you a chance, provided you work in tandem with one of their own choosing. And that's Kate. The Director has chopped off on it. We're keeping it small at this point. We'll build the team over time with carefully vetted people. Can't risk throwing a ringer in like we did with Aldrich Ames. We've learned our lesson."

Nick leaned back in his chair and placed both hands on his head. "Oh, crap. All right. But I retain the right to be assigned to Anchorage."

"Deal."

The migraines were getting worse, but Amelia Hernández persisted in living her secret life, a lonely life with neither friends nor lovers, with constant risk of arrest and decades-long imprisonment. She was thirty-seven. The biological clock ticked louder each year she got closer to forty, but she blocked it out. She had set herself on her life's mission as a young woman. She had made her choices. She had to live with them. She wasn't so naïve as to think that being a spy for a sworn enemy of her country was something she could just quit. When her youngest sister had taken vows to become a nun in El Salvador, she stated she had become a "bride of Christ," a marriage for eternity. It was the same for traitors.

As she set her canvas lunch bag on her desk, she looked around discreetly. Her office mates were all lunching in the cafeteria downstairs. The office was deserted. She unwrapped her sandwich, separated the bread from the meat, and removed the thumb drive. DIA had a strict policy: no thumb drives and no cell phones allowed inside the building. She wiped off the device with her napkin and quickly inserted it into the USB port of her PC. She then proceeded to download scores of folders containing thousands of classified documents. She had never done such a thing before, and the risk was great. But the newer technology enabled it. And her conviction was strong that Havana needed it. Like a wounded animal, a weakened Cuba became increasingly vulnerable to its decades-long predator, the United States.

It took a few short minutes to steal a wealth of the nation's secrets. Amelia carefully wrapped the thumb drive in a small cellophane bag and inserted it inside the orange she would later eat. This was a temporary measure. Before leaving for the day, it would take the place of her feminine napkin.

Philip Livingston couldn't get enough of Beethoven's Ninth. And in his book, Georg Solti and the Chicago Symphony Orchestra's rendition was, hands down, the best. He often brought the CD with him to work to listen to on his small CD player either on low volume or with earphones. It kept him sane in an institution, the State Department, that was notorious for bad managers and rampant administrative incompetence.

He checked that day's cable traffic take on his classified computer's screen. After he entered the requisite passwords, a long list of cables from Latin American diplomatic posts popped up, covering everything from flawed elections to oil output to human rights. A separate list contained more sensitive documents with strict distribution limitations. Separate passwords were required to access those. Livingston entered his. The first document was classified SECRET NOFORN. It was the National Intelligence Estimate on Cuba, the intelligence community's best assessment on events in that country and where it was headed. After reading the executive summary, he quickly skimmed through the rest.

In the Department's strictly maintained caste system, Livingston was senior enough to enjoy a modicum of quasi-privacy in the form of a corner office with actual walls and a window. He closed his door and placed his phone to his ear.

While pretending to be in a serious conversation with an imaginary interlocutor at the other end, he discreetly placed his Beethoven CD into his computer's CD drive and proceeded to download the NIE as well as the hundreds of cables in that morning's take.

He took the CD out of the drive and returned it to the Beethoven case. He then bade goodbye to the nonexistent person. Livingston went home that evening with Georg Solti and his orchestra in his coat pocket, along with enough official secrets to damage American national security for years to come.

Private Prendergast wanted to tell the sergeant in the worst way that he loved him, loved him with all his heart, but he knew he couldn't. The man was married, happily married, as he phoned his wife from regimental HQ every chance he could.

Of course, what would he lose apart from maybe some broken teeth and a bloody nose should the sergeant take it wrong? After they'd busted him from specialist back to PFC for assaulting another enlisted man, Prendergast had nothing to lose. They were preparing to discharge him, most likely dishonorably.

The sergeant, all six-feet-two of him, glided by, paying Private Prendergast no notice. Prendergast's heart sank. God, he hated the Army. They might have done away with Don't Ask, Don't Tell, but the real world of the rank and file military was as much one of nineteenth century machismo and homophobia as it ever was. He'd assaulted that soldier after the guy called him "faggot maggot."

If he had to be stuck at Task Force Spartan another month, he'd surely kill himself. Ever since the 3rd Brigade Combat Team had taken up positions in eastern Afghanistan, his life had been hell. Boredom day in and day out, mostly. Plenty of drills and mess duty to fill the time. And commo.

He'd already downloaded three CDs worth of military communications. He knew one country that would pay him enough to set him up for life. He had to hang on long enough to maximize his proceeds from selling classified information, as good as gold. He'd show them, all right. Get back at them. While getting rich. Then... freedom.

CHAPTER TWENTY-TWO

Everything about her reminded Nick of ice: glacier-blue eyes, arctic-white skin, solstice tow-blond hair. She lacked the inner warmth and healthy complexion of tropical people. No rhumba in her soul. No conga beat in her heart. No. She was a woman who radiated efficiency, goal-achievement. A northern huntress.

They sat opposite each other in a bare-walled, fluorescent-infused, sparely furnished conference room, one of countless such meeting cells inside the CIA complex at Langley.

"I propose we start with FBI, next State, then DoD," Kate said.

"Start with the Bureau? Why? There've been no red flags coming out of my agency. And what about this place? You didn't even mention CIA," Nick said.

"Well, let's not forget the Hanssen case. The mole hunters spent years looking everywhere but the Bureau. The guy was in the pay of the KGB for twenty-two years."

"And Aldrich Ames? Spied for Moscow for nine years while the Agency was chasing ghosts elsewhere."

"We've cleaned up our act since then. We now conduct polygraphs in a more rigorous manner. Ames managed to fool the box, but that can't happen now. And let's not forget the FBI refuses to box its people. So that's why we need to start with those agencies that don't employ the poly."

"There's a good reason why we don't use it. It's voodoo science."

"Except for you. My understanding is that you were boxed twice."

"You seem to know quite a bit about me," Nick retorted.

"It's called 'due diligence' in the business world. 'Asset validation' in intelligence."

"Oh, I'm an Agency 'asset' now, am I?"

Their voices were now several decibels higher. Her face was flushed.

She held up a hand. "Cease fire. Okay?"

Nick nodded. "Okay. Cease fire."

Kate opened a folder, pulled out a ream of paper, and handed it to him. "This is my proposed CONOPS Plan for going at this. As you can see on page—"

"I beg your pardon?"

"Concept of Operations Plan. It provides the proposed framework for the investi—"

"I know what CONOPS stands for. Who gave you the green light to put one together unilaterally? Isn't this supposed to be a joint effort?"

"I just thought we'd save valuable time. God knows what's being leaked as we speak."

Nick pulled out his own sheaf of papers and placed a folder stamped TOP SECRET in orange-red letters in front of Kate. "I also don't want to waste time. Here's a list of all intel analysts and case officers on the Cuba account at CIA, DIA, State, and DoD, military G-2 level on down, as well as the Bureau. I suggest we start combing through them, access their finances, scrutinize any drinking, substance abuse problems, any sudden change in lifestyle, their—"

"I beg your pardon," Kate said frostily.

"Yes?"

"It's clear we're going off in opposite directions. In any case, we'd need a FISA court warrant—"

"Only for probable cause," Nick corrected. "I'm talking about beginning by reviewing their security files. Active surveillance would be done only on those with probable cause for suspicion."

"But…"

And on went the pissing match over how to go about exposing burrowed moles who were passing some of the nation's deepest secrets to its enemies.

CIA Forward Operating Base Tecumseh Herat, Afghanistan

CIA Base Chief Gregory van Hollen looked out onto the dusty plains beyond the razor-wire perimeter of the Agency's westernmost outpost in Afghanistan and had a bad feeling in the pit of his stomach. Nine months in the desolate place away from Cynthia and their two boys, while working at a burnout pace, was taking a toll on him. He'd lost fifteen pounds, slept badly and was losing his concentration. Three more months and he'd be back at his old job in the Counterterrorism Center. Meanwhile, he waited. The Landcruiser with the informant was already two hours late. He had eaten his millionth MRE of chili and saltines, and his stomach protested. He scanned the horizon with binoculars—no dust trail kicked up by a vehicle. It'd be a long wait. *Afghan time.*

The flow of weapons from Iran had been burgeoning over the past year. The ratlines from Iran's border city of Mashhad into western Afghanistan were multiplying. The resultant increase in Taliban military operations against Afghan government installations and NATO ISAF forces threatened to open another front that the already thinly-stretched foreigners could ill afford.

The informant had been providing a steady stream of actionable intelligence. With that information, Special Ops Forces and drones had been taking out a growing number of Taliban commanders and weapons caches. That whetted

Washington's appetite for more. Added to that was the politically driven desire to bloody the Iranian Revolutionary Guard Qods Force behind the covert aid and its shadowy operative, Colonel Hasan Mortezavi.

Van Hollen had debriefed the informant half a dozen times. A well-placed ethnic Tajik fighter in western Afghanistan, the man had provided useful information both on Iranian involvement and on Herat's growing number of Arab al-Qaeda fighters. But that which attracted Washington's attention most was information he was supplying regarding the whereabouts of Ayman al-Zawahiri, bin Laden's right-hand man and the guy dead center in Uncle Sam's crosshairs since 9/11.

But something about the informant kept nagging at van Hollen. The man was well placed to provide intelligence on the Herat Taliban's commander, Ghulam Akbari, but he steadfastly stated he had nothing on the leader. It took a lead from a much lower-ranking Taliban fighter to lethally target Akbari and twenty-two of his fighters in a lightning helicopter gunship raid.

Nevertheless, the informant had the trust of the CIA, and the top brass wanted to meet him. The Kabul chief of station had arrived to meet the informant. Joining him were the deputy chief of the Counterrorism Center and two senior analysts from Washington. The operational security surrounding the visit was high. Should word leak out that senior CIA officials were in Herat, the Taliban and their al-Qaeda allies would go to extraordinary lengths to launch attacks against them.

The station chief looked impatiently at his watch. Already afflicted with the trots, the other three shifted uneasily on the stiff folding chairs inside the tent where the questioning would take place. Afghan scouts a couple of klicks outside the FOB perimeter radioed in the arrival of the vehicle carrying the informant. Van Hollen informed his guests, who left the tent to get ready to greet the visitor.

As the white Toyota SUV approached the perimeter gate, four XE Services security guards halted it to carry out the routine inspection, including passing a pole-mounted mirror underneath the chassis to check for hidden explosives. They were under instructions, however, not to pat down the informant, lest he feel like he was being treated like a criminal and stop coming for debriefs. Besides, he had been a repeat visitor, one with a proven record of circumspect behavior.

The Toyota was waved through the gate. It stopped ten meters from van Hollen and the CIA VIPs, who were arranged in a sort of receiving line with smiles plastered on their faces, ready to shake hands with the visitor.

The informant got out of the rear of the vehicle. He had a bushy black beard and sported a baggy khaki bush jacket and the Afghans' trademark round pakol hat. He took long strides toward the CIA contingent, then halted and reached inside his jacket.

The white flash blinded van Hollen a half-second before the red-hot ballbearings shot through his body, tearing him to shreds.

Unit 8200 HQ, Glilot Junction, Israel

Millions had gone into development of the Stuxnet worm. It had taken three years to develop by a team comprising dozens of Israel's best information technology experts, nuclear scientists, and industrial engineers. Stuxnet, introduced via infected flash drives, wreaked havoc on Iran's nuclear program, causing thousands of uranium-enriching centrifuges to malfunction. The Natanz enrichment facility and the Bushehr reactor were virtually shut down. Tehran's nuclear program had been set back by at least two years.

The joint top-secret Israeli-U.S. Operation KLINGON had finished creating a 20,000-line code worm jocularly called by the team members, Stuxnet - The Sequel. The malware would finish the job that Stuxnet started: frying the electronic support systems within Iran's nuclear facilities. The aim was to induce a meltdown of the entire nuclear infrastructure of that country, setting back Tehran's nuclear ambitions for many more years.

Like a U-boat captain, Israeli General Yoel Shalev paced back and forth in the cramped Israeli Defense Forces cyber war command center as the countdown proceeded for Cartouche-A's launch, like a torpedo aimed at the government of Iran's heart via the internet. As the digital clock struck zero, he gave the signal to launch. SDF technicians tapped keyboards.

A burst of applause erupted, accompanied by hurrah's, "Eat shit, Iran!" and a host of other epithets. Self-congratulations circulated among the Israeli and American cyber warriors. A job well done, indeed.

The next day, Tehran announced it had successfully blocked a cyber attack against its nuclear facilities. It laid blame on the Zionists and their American masters. Allah had again protected the Islamic Revolution. *Praise be to Allah!*

A small army of handsomely paid Russian and Byelorussian information technology engineers constructed the defenses that deflected the Cartouche-A worm, which was mutated and redirected to cripple electric power plants in Israel and the United States.

U.S. Mission to the United Nations, New York

FM AMEMBASSY BEIJING
TO RUEHC/SECSTATE WASHDC IMMEDIATE
INFO RUEHOO/CHINA POSTS COLLECTIVE
IMMEDIATE
RUEHGG/UN SECURITY COUNCIL
COLLECTIVE IMMEDIATE
RUEKJCS/SECDEF WASHDC IMMEDIATE
RHEHNSC/NSC WASHDC IMMEDIATE
RUEAIIA/CIA WASHDC

RHMFISS/CDR USPACOM HONOLULU HI
CONFIDENTIAL SECTION 01 OF 02 BEIJING
003448

SIPDIS

E.O. 12958: DECL: 07/05/33
TAGS: PREL UNSC CH CU
SUBJECT: FONMIN ZHU REJECTS UNSC AC-
TION ON CUBA

REF: STATE 139560

Classified By: Deputy Chief of Mission Karen S. Bill-
ingsley. Reasons 1.4 (b/d).

1. (C) Foreign Minister Zhu Yuanzhang called in
   Ambassador McKieran today to inform the
   USG that the PRC cannot support UN Security
   Council action on Cuba. Zhu cited China's traditional commitment to noninterference in other
   nations' domestic affairs and its longstanding
   friendship with Cuba. Many countries occasion-
   ally experience domestic unrest, the U.S. and
   China included, Zhu added. It is very seldom
   that such events are taken up by the UNSC, he
   said.

2. (C) Ambassador expressed his disappointment
   in the PRC position. Citing talking points in
   reftel, Ambassador said that Beijing's position
   constitutes a veto of the EU-formulated resolu-
   tion calling for democratic elections in Cuba and
   formation of an inclusive interim government.
   He emphasized the need for concerned nations
   to assist the Cuban people during a critical tran-

sition process, one that hopefully would return stability to the island and provide the framework for holding free and fair elections…

"What the hell is this?" Richard Horowitz demanded, punching the cable with his fingers. "It's like they got Washington's talking points before we did." With thirty years invested in statecraft, the U.S. ambassador to the United Nations could smell a rat a mile away.

"Not only that," Political Counselor Evan Lloyd said, "but PRC ambassadors in the capitals of current UNSC members made their demarches to host governments two hours before State's instruction cable went out. It's weird. The Chinese are almost always plodders. They wait and study an issue to death before making a decision. It's like they're reading our minds, anticipating our every move."

"We're left looking like fools," Horowitz said. "We've been pre-empted before we even finished our breakfast. Either the Chinese are getting much better or they're getting the straight scoop from the inside. Unbelievable."

Since Badoglio's arrest, Eduardo Bermúdez got little sleep. Every creak and bump in his crumbling apartment house jolted him. Any second, he expected the door to his tiny one-room flat to be kicked in. He had nightmares of police goons slamming him onto the tile floor and kicking him. He saw visions of himself in the same cellblock as the Italian, in a countdown to a dawn firing squad.

Since Badoglio had been nabbed, he went into deepfreeze, just doing his archivist work at the Justice Ministry and going home. He no longer provided the Americans with Cuban government secrets, not for a long while anyway. He dreaded the thought of a Badoglio replacement making contact with him.

He made no effort to check the dead drops he had been using to pass and receive messages with his CIA handlers. *What term did the submariners use? Ah, yes. Silent running.* He was running silent, periscope down.

A meticulous man, the middle-aged bachelor put his papers away neatly in labeled boxes and placed his pencils and pens in the top drawer of his ancient desk. It was three p.m., the unofficial quitting time for thousands of civil servants who needed two hours to scrounge for food and other necessities on the black market before going home to prepare dinner out of whatever they managed to scrape together.

He walked out of the garish red and beige Ministry headquarters, turned right onto "La Rampa," the common name for broad 23rd Avenue, and headed toward the Malecón for a breath of fresh sea air before going to the many impromptu trading locales around the city in search of provisions.

The son of fishermen, Bermúdez loved the sea. Its borderless vastness was the embodiment of freedom, and freedom was the breath of life. The Cuban people had been asphyxiating for half a century. Yes, he would resume passing information to the Americans, once things had settled down and he was convinced he was in the clear.

As he approached the Malecón, his hands clasped behind his back, he took a deep breath and closed his eyes. The breath was aborted by a thick arm suddenly locked around his throat. As he blacked out, the full-time archivist/part-time spy was tossed into the back of a sedan and driven off.

CHAPTER TWENTY-THREE

The unremitting chain of intelligence and foreign policy failures and setbacks made it clear that those were no mere coincidences. The White House put out some carefully targeted leaks indicating that there would be a major shakeup in the intelligence community and that the president had lost patience with CIA and FBI bickering. The rumor was circulating that the commander-in-chief was planning to replace the senior leadership at the CIA with military officers who would kick ass and whip the organization into shape. A similar fate faced the FBI, with career agents in the top jobs to be replaced with outsiders, cops and judges who would break the cozy culture of everyone scratching each other's back and managers covering their asses when they screwed up.

To pre-empt White House intervention, the CIA and FBI called a truce. Their leadership read the riot act to all managers, instructing them to cooperate with their other agency counterparts. That trickled down to Nick Castillo and Kate Kovalchuk. They decided to marry her CONOPS Plan with his growing BIGOT List.

"Why do you call it a 'Bigot List'?" she asked. "What's this got to do with bias?"

"Nothing. We took on Bigot List from the Brits during WWII. Some kind of code word: 'going to Gibraltar,' 'to Gib' scrambled: b-i-g-o-t. Something only the Brits could dream up. Anyway, it's just a list of suspects. I've drawn it up in concentric circles. Those names in the bull's eye are individuals who are or were working in the betrayed programs. The second circle encompasses those who had access to the classified information. And the third circle has those who were in a position to overhear talk of the programs. So regarding the Forward Operating Base Tecumseh OP I've come up with almost two hundred sixty names. The Cartouche-A cyber war program, whose access was strictly limited, I have forty-nine names. Through a process of elimination via rigorous investigations over time, we should be able to narrow the list down and eventually ID the mope."

"Mope?"

"The guilty party," he explained.

"And the roll-up of Cuban assets? How many potential mopes?"

"I'm working on it. Also a small list."

"But if we're looking at a bunch of mopes—people on the inside who are working the Iran, Afghanistan, China, Cuba, North Korea, and what-have-you accounts and selling information—it'll take our children and grandchildren to sort them all out. The USG has a grave problem on its hands. Multiple traitors. And why now? Is it something in the water, or what?"

Nick shook his head. "I'm convinced we're looking at a single disseminator. Not necessarily a single traitor, but one adversary who's collecting the secrets from its agent network inside the United States and passing it on to... for want of another name, Axis of Evil countries."

"A wholesaler of secrets?"

"For hard cash and vengeance against the United States."

"Cuba."

"You got it. The Castros have been brokering secrets they've managed to steal from us for years to Tehran, Pyongyang, Moscow, Beijing, others. In return, they receive desperately needed hard currency. It's an important export of theirs. And they get to damage the U.S. to boot."

"Sweet deal for them. Bad deal for us," Kate said.

"Precisely. But there's something more going on here."

"Like what?" she asked.

"We talked about it before. I lost an asset, a double agent I'd been running for several years. My asset was professionally assassinated out in Key West within hours of two Cuban sleeper agents being offed in an identical manner in New Jersey and northern Virginia. But the really interesting thing is not long after that, two Cuban DI operations met with bloody ends. A Cuban agent posing as an Ecuadorian and a known North Korean intelligence officer posing as a Japanese were each shot in the face twice in a Bangkok hotel room, the same manner as the Cuban sleepers here."

"What makes you think they were spies? What was the evidence to back that up? Were cash and classified documents found at the crime scene?" Kate asked.

"No. But everything else fits in place. Then shortly afterward, a group of FARC rebels and their Cuban and Venezuelan advisors was ambushed and annihilated right after they infiltrated into Colombia. Didn't stand a chance. It was clearly a set-up."

"The Colombians did their homework, obviously. Good intel work on the ground," Kate said.

"Well, the Colombian media reported that Bogotá received detailed intel from the U.S. pinpointing the exact location and timing of the Cuban op." Nick bored in on her with a penetrating stare.

Kate averted her eyes. "Hmm. Good work… whoever's responsible."

"Yeah. Sure." Nick leaned forward, elbows on his knees. "It's tit-for-tat."

"I beg your pardon?"

"Something's going on in the background. I see only the tip of the iceberg. How 'bout you, Kate? What can you tell me about all this? Is it 'Need to Know' again?"

Kate crossed her arms and showed a poker face. "Got me."

Operation MOPED, a play on the term "mope," was launched in utter secrecy. The MOPED team was headed by Nick and Kate and included ten others who were briefed into the program after careful vetting and being sworn to utter secrecy. All team members required a full polygraph exam prior to being inducted into the program. Truffle-hog Morgenstern was put in charge of sniffing through the dossiers on BIGOT list personnel and interviewing them. He did that with a couple of career security officers, one CIA, the other FBI. It had to be done without arousing suspicions among the rank and file. Morgenstern and team described the interviews as "routine." Those brought in for the security reviews were selected based on anomalies or contradictions in their files, things like a missing compartmented security clearance, incomplete list of assignments, an overlooked polygraph exam, travel to countries unrelated to their work at a given time, failure to register a divorce, or other missing documentation. Anything that posed a blip on the security screen.

Next, bank and credit card accounts of those who stayed on the BIGOT list were examined for any signs of expenditures well in excess of government salaries. The same type of financial scrutiny had turned investigators onto the FBI-turncoat Robert Hanssen and CIA-traitor Aldrich Ames. No Diamond Jim or Jane Brady's appeared.

"Where there's a mole, there's a handler," Morgenstern told his team. "I want to compile the vacation times of BIGOT list personnel and compare those with the surveillance records of Cuban Interests Section officers. I want a spreadsheet going back ten years. Bore in anywhere there's a match-up of any of our guys and any of their guys being away from Washington at the same time."

Cuban officials were monitored closely inside the U.S. Therefore, a common practice of hostile services was to arrange to meet with their assets in more benign overseas locales, far away from Uncle Sam's prying eyes and ears. Of course, it was simply not possible to keep track of every movement by every diplomat all the time. Surveillance merely gave the government snapshots of time, providing a pattern of activity based on samples of information, rarely twenty-four/seven coverage. And reconstructing the past whereabouts of U.S. public servants was even more of a challenge. The farther back one went, all one had to go on was the official leave records.

"We're looking for a needle in a haystack." Morgenstern sighed. "But we've got to start somewhere."

CHAPTER TWENTY-FOUR

Lt. Col. Sergei Orgonov waited patiently in the visa queue that snaked outside the ornate Palazzo Margherita, home of the U.S. embassy to Italy. He shared company with Africans, Iranians, East Europeans, and Central Asians, a kaleidoscope of the globe's rejected, war ravaged, opportunists and destitute simply seeking the good life. He stood out with his neat suit, good grooming, and erect posture. An Italian security guard checked his passport and visa appointment confirmation letter, then signaled for him to go through the security screening apparatus.

The Russian intelligence officer, a twenty-five-year veteran of the *Sluzhba Vneshney Razvedki* and its predecessor, the KGB, had been involved in many risky operations, some life threatening. But the current one was by far the hardest. His palpitating heart felt as if it would burst any second. Sweat poured down his beefy neck and soaked his shirt collar. Another security guard observed him closely. After Orgonov passed through the detector, the guard gestured for him to step aside, where the man methodically wand-scanned every inch of Orgonov's body, twice.

"What is the purpose of your visit today?" the guard asked.

"To apply for a visa," the SVR officer replied hoarsely.

The guard scrutinized Orgonov's Russian passport. "What kind of visa?"

"Tourism."

"Okay," the guard said tersely and nodded for the Russian to proceed to the bank of teller windows.

Orgonov went to where he was directed and took a deep breath.

"Orgonov," the ceiling-mounted loudspeaker broadcast. He was directed to a security window, behind which stood a blond-haired man in his twenties. The young man studied Orgonov's visa application, which he had submitted online weeks ago.

"You say the purpose of your visit is tourism?" the junior consular officer asked.

"No."

For the first time, the young man looked up.

"I want to defect," the Russian said.

CENTRAL INTELLIGENCE AGENCY
TOP S E C R E T 301515Z AUG STAFF
CITE ROME 51911
TO: IMMEDIATE DIRECTOR
WNINTEL RYBAT
SUBJECT: INITIAL DEBRIEF OF SVR LT. COL.
ORGONOV
REF: A. ROME 51820
         B. DIRECTOR 419577

1. STATION OPS OFFICERS CONDUCTED INITIAL DEBRIEF OF WALK-IN SVR LT. COL. SERGEI VASSILEYEVICH ORGONOV. QUESTIONING BEGAN 1030Z AND FINISHED AT 1830Z. STATION REQUESTS POLYGRAPH ASAP.

2. ORGONOV IS FLUENT IN ENGLISH AND PREFERRED SPEAKING IT DESPITE ONE OPS OFFICER BEING FLUENT IN RUSSIAN. REF A PROVIDED BASIC BIO. FOLLOWING INITIAL NERVOUSNESS,

ORGONOV EASED AS THE DEBRIEF PROCEEDED.

3. SUBJECT STATED GROWING DISILLUSIONMENT WITH HIS GOVERNMENT'S SENIOR LEADERSHIP AND SVR'S CALLOUS MANAGEMENT OF ITS PEOPLE AS HIS REASONS FOR DEFECTING. HE ALSO ALLUDED TO AN ONGOING AFFAIR WITH THE WIFE OF THE COMMERCIAL OFFICER AT RUSSIA CONGEN MONTREAL, RELUCTANTLY STATING HE HOPED TO CONVINCE HER TO JOIN HIM.

4. ORGONOV TOLD OPSOFFS HIS LAST ASSIGNMENT WAS IN THE PR DIRECTORATE LATIN AMERICA DIVISION. HE HAD BEEN IN THIS POSITION SINCE 11 APRIL 2011. PRIOR TO THAT, HE SERVED IN THE HAVANA SVR REZIDENTURA FOR FIVE YEARS, HIS THIRD TOD IN CUBA. HE GRADUATED WITH A BACHELOR'S DEGREE FROM HAVANA UNIVERSITY IN 1985.

5. ORGONOV LIAISED WITH CUBAN DGI ON JOINT AGENT OPS THROUGHOUT HIS HAVANA TOURS. SUBJECT PROVIDED OPSOFFS DETAILS CONCERNING TWO CUBAN AGENTS INSIDE THE USG:

   B. PHILIP RENSSELAER LIVINGS-
      TON, SENIOR LATIN AMERICA

ANALYST IN THE BUREAU OF INTELLIGENCE AND RESEARCH, U.S. STATE DEPT.

C. ARMY PFC JAY LEE PRENDER-GAST, TASK FORCE SPARTAN, AFGHANISTAN.

6. STATION AWAITS INSTRUCTIONS FOR TRANSPORTING ORGONOV TO CONUS AND LIAISING WITH GOI.

7. NO FILE. ALL TOP SECRET

Morgenstern looked at Nick, who returned his incredulous gaze.

"This is too goddamn good to be true," Morgenstern said, tapping the Top Secret cable from Rome Station. "I mean the guy just walks into our embassy, then coughs up the names of two Cuban agents inside our government. This kinda shit just doesn't happen."

Nick's mind went into overdrive as he twirled a pencil nervously in his right hand. "So what are you suggesting?"

"I don't know. But the guy could be a ringer, a double agent sent here to feed us crappola. They've done it before," Morgenstern said.

"Yeah, but not since the Soviet Union collapsed. There've been more SVR and GRU officers turning coat and running."

"Yeah. There was Litvinenko and Poteyev. But Moscow did a Mercader on Litvinov and even had the balls to announce they had one out on Poteyev as well. Last dangle from Moscow was Yurchenko. I still don't believe he was a dangle, but just fucked up personally."

Kate Kovalchuk had entered the room with her morning

coffee just as Nick and his partner had begun their discussion. She scrunched her brow. "Excuse me, but what language are you guys speaking?"

"You'll have to excuse Bart," Nick said. "He talks about spies the way twelve-year-old boys talk about the minutiae of baseball players. If bubble gum manufacturers issued cards on spies, Bart would be blowing pink bubbles his every waking hour. Bart, give her a translation please."

"Alexander Litvinenko was an FSB—Russia's equivalent of the FBI. Anyway, he was an FSB officer who defected to Britain and was fatally poisoned with a radioactive substance. He died in 2006. Alexander Poteyev was an SVR colonel who defected to the U.S. in 2010 just before the 'sleeper' spy network was rolled up by the FBI. Poteyev, a.k.a. Scherbakov, has given away the store to us, dozens of files on sleeper agents and other ultra-secret operations. Vitaly Yurchenko was another colonel—KGB—who 'defected' in 1985, only to turn tail and head back to Russia after claiming the CIA had drugged and kidnapped him. Lotsa folks in our circles believe he was a dangle, a person posing as a defector sent to give false information or find out stuff about how his target service operates. Like I said, the guy had weird shit going on in his personal life. Anyway, the leopard can't change its spots. The Russians still play hardball when it comes to espionage, just like in the old days of the Cold War.

"'Putting out a Mercader on someone refers to Ramón Mercader, the NKVD agent who sank an ice ax into Leon Trotsky's skull in 1940 on orders from the Kremlin. It's the Russian equivalent of the mob expression, 'to put a contract out' on a guy, a directed assassination. They clearly carried out a 'Mercader' on Litvinenko, and like I said, they made no bones about saying they'd put one out on Poteyev as well."

"So what does all this have to do with our Cuban case?" she asked.

"Here we've got this Russian SVR colonel Orgonov just showing up at our embassy in Rome. He says he wants to defect and coughs up two U.S. traitors, but they're working for Havana," Nick said.

"Which isn't so out of line," Morgenstern added. "The Cuban DI is a spawn of the Soviet KGB. Glued at the hip. They've always shared assets and intel. The end of the Soviet Union in '91 really didn't disrupt this cozy relationship. The SVR leaders, as well as the rank and file, merely switched insignia, not their mindset. KGB by another name. Just like Putin." "So, Kate, what do you have on Orgonov?" Nick asked.

"You've seen the cables," she said. "Ideally, our top priority with a walk-in is to send him back as a double agent in place, to turn him and have him feed us information from within the belly of the beast. But Orgonov burned himself. He approached us in a highly visible manner. In doing so, he burned all his bridges. His usefulness as a double agent-in-place is gone. So the next step is to debrief him and milk him for all we can get."

"Has he been polyed yet?" Nick asked.

"Don't know. But he definitely will be within a day's time," Kate said.

"The thing is, plenty of people have fooled the polygraph," Morgenstern said. "There are techniques. And the SVR is highly skilled in these techniques and passing them on to their assets."

"It's just one of the tools. We'll look at the whole composite: hours of debriefs, cross-referencing, more debriefs, another polygraph. It's rigorous. Some defectors break down during the process," Kate said.

"Are we going to have a crack at him?" Nick asked.

She shrugged. "I don't see why not."

Nick nodded. "In the meantime, we've got to blanket these two suspects, Livingston and Prendergast, with twenty-four/seven surveillance to gather evidence. The cases have to be one hundred percent airtight, no wiggle room for some grandstanding sleazebag attorney to get his client off the hook by painting the FBI as a bunch of knuckle-dragging oafs with a rush to judgment. We've fallen down enough times in the past,

Richard Jewell and Mark Hatfield being the most prominent in recent years. The Director held a meeting on this yesterday. We're already on both cases."

"And here's the thing," Morgenstern added. "It's all gotta be done in perfect sync. We can't bust one without also busting the other. Otherwise, let's say we arrest Prendergast, but not Livingston. Upon hearing the news, Livingston will panic, and next thing you know, he's on the next flight to Havana and will be sipping Cuba Libres on Varadero beach before we've had breakfast."

"Army INSCOM and DIA are already onto the little private. It's vitally important that we keep them from jumping the gun and arrest the twerp before we've made our move on Livingston," Nick said.

"Meantime, we need to have at Orgonov. We need to know if this guy is kosher or just blowing smoke out his ass," Morgenstern said.

CHAPTER TWENTY-FIVE

Philip Livingston rose an hour earlier than usual—five a.m. He quickly threw on a pair of jeans and a sweatshirt. He retrieved Bruckner from the CD shelf, opened the case to double check the disk, carefully sealed it in three dark plastic bags, then placed it inside his Ferragamo briefcase, and headed out the door. Dupont Circle was largely devoid of human traffic, but commuters would flood the area within the hour. He sprinted down the Metro escalator, briefcase held tightly, and hopped the red line in the direction of Shady Grove. In fifteen minutes, he got off at the Friendship Heights station, exiting through the upscale shopping complex of Mazza Gallerie. He turned left on Western Avenue and walked briskly until he reached Fort Bayard Park. He climbed a grassy knoll to a tree-shaded spot. Slowly, he scanned the park for any early risers walking their dogs, vagabonds, or FBI tails. He sat on a bench and listened—nothing but pre-commute light traffic. He stood up and walked fifteen steps to a big old stump. He again surveyed the environs. All clear. He squatted and jimmied out a portion of the stump. Livingston then opened his briefcase, took out the package, and carefully placed it inside the stump. He replaced the chunk with a firm tap.

Livingston didn't retrace his steps. Rather, he sauntered two minutes south on River Road until he reached the intersection with Fessenden Street. There, he again carefully surveyed the area, walked in a circle, then paused by a mailbox. From his right pocket, he took out a piece of white chalk and deftly marked a white cross on the container's side.

Livingston then returned to the Friendship Heights station and went home.

The Policy Forum was one in the cluttered constellation of Washington-based think tanks. On whichever side of the podium one might be, the think tanks offered convenient venues for the pretentious, the ambitious, and the wonk power groupies to be seen and to network. Divided along ideological fault lines like confessional duchies of the Holy Roman Empire, each strived to reinforce the agenda du jour of the left or the right. The Policy Forum fell into the former category. The night's topic: "America in Decline: Lessons from Romulus Augustus." Presenter: Philip Livingston.

After a two-minute glowing introduction by a chinless academic fond of the overused cliché "seminal," Livingston tugged at his old tweed jacket, nodded, stepped up to the podium, and proceeded to deliver a tendentious treatise on the similarities of early twenty-first-century America and a late Roman Empire on its way out.

An hour and a half later, he left the Beaux Arts building for the bracing air of Massachusetts Avenue to look for a cab.

"I enjoyed your presentation," a voice said from behind him.

Livingston turned to see a thirtyish man with a pleasant smile.

The man extended his right hand. "Hi. My name is Martín."

Livingston shook his hand. "Thanks very much. Glad to hear it."

"Your thesis that America has overreached with war-making and overspending and linking that to the Roman Empire is very thought-provoking." The man spoke with a slight Spanish accent.

"Are you a scholar of the Roman period?"

"Oh, no. But I know just enough not to get myself into trouble." The man walked alongside Livingston.

"Are you an academic?"

"No. But I graduated from the University of Havana."

Livingston halted in his tracks, speechless. He stared at the man. "No kidding. When did you emigrate?"

"No. I'm not an immigrant." He reached into the breast pocket of his sport coat and pulled out a small packet. "I am asked to give you this small birthday present." He handed it to Livingston.

Livingston accepted and opened the little box. Inside were two Cohiba cigars. He removed one and ran it under his nose. "Ahh. Fidel's favorite."

"Yes, it was. Before *el jefe* was obliged to quit."

"It's a wonderful birthday present. From my… friends?"

"Specifically, from General Montilla."

Livingston smiled. "Larisa. She's a general now? She took care of us that time Deirdre and I saw Fidel in '98. Made all the arrangements. Our secret trip. Marvelous woman. Marvelous."

"Mr. Livingston, your views are sought during this time when changes are occurring in both our countries. Can we meet?"

Livingston stiffened and placed the cigar back in its box. "You know what I told Oscar."

"Oscar," Martín said.

"You guys do coordinate, don't you?"

"Rest assured. We are most careful."

Livingston looked around nervously. "This is too risky, standing in the open."

"Yes, of course."

"I suggest you contact me for a meeting in the usual fashion."

"Certainly. The usual fashion."

"I'll be monitoring my email. Good evening." Livingston walked off into the night.

They played the recording for the tenth time.

"Who the hell is 'Oscar'?" Nick asked.

"His handler, obviously. But the question is, is he a CUBINT officer or some deep cover cutout?" Morgenstern asked.

"I can't tell you how close I came to shitting a brick at that point," Nick said.

"You handled it beautifully. You didn't arouse suspicion."

"We can't be certain of that."

"Don't worry, Nick. I'm telling you the guy thinks you're the real deal. His point of contact. The wire worked just fine. His voice comes out crystal clear."

"Okay," Nick said. "But there are two other things we don't know about that can trip us up. First one is when he says, 'I suggest you contact me for a meeting in the usual fashion.' We've got to get surveillance on all CUBINT officers to find out if one of them is his handler. And we've got to be super-careful 'Martín' and his true handler don't cross paths, or all bets are off. That alone makes this highly time sensitive. Second, he refers to 'monitoring my email.'"

Morgenstern nodded. "That's why we've gotta get the court warrant approved ASAP. We've got to envelope him and his wife in an airtight bubble. Their phone calls, their private conversations, where they go and when. And their emails. They let loose a fart, we gotta not miss it."

"And the Super Gs. We need them, like, yesterday. I've put in a request to Division Five, laying out all our needs. Gone to the seventh floor. Approval should be in the bag."

Morgenstern shifted his prodigious behind in the small office chair.

"What is it?" Nick asked.

The fat man ran his fingers across his balding head. "Just how much of this do we share with Kate?"

"What do you mean?"

Morgenstern looked down at the desk. "I don't fully trust her."

"You've yet to meet a CIA officer you can fully trust."

"That goes for the entire Bureau."

Nick chuckled. "True."

"Anyway, I find her cagey. She's holding something back."

Nick nodded. "I agree."

Livingston left the State Department at five fifteen and hopped the Metro at Foggy Bottom station. He didn't disembark at Dupont as he customarily did, but continued to Friendship Heights. He strolled to the corner of Fessenden and River Road. The chalked cross on the side of the mailbox was gone. Livingston smiled. They'd picked up his package. Another successful dead drop operation.

CHAPTER TWENTY-SIX

The Russian sat erect, his hands folded in front of him on the bare table in the small conference room of a non-descript office building somewhere in northern Virginia. Seated to his left was Nick. To his right sat Morgenstern. Opposite was Kate, who led the questioning. Four other CIA officers observed on a closed-circuit TV monitor in a nearby office.

"You say you came to us because you're 'disillusioned.' What exactly are you disillusioned about?" she asked.

Orgonov rubbed one hand over his walrus moustache. "As I told your people in Rome, Putin is taking my country back to the Soviet Union period. We have a new flag, new anthem, a new constitution, a duma. Even KGB is gone. But it isn't. Just a new name. All these changes have become window dressing. They only care about keeping power for themselves. Just like in days of Soviet Union."

"Why now? You've been an intel officer for twenty-five years. You've served your country faithfully all that time. Suddenly, you have a change of heart?"

"No. This feeling has grown inside me for many years. Living in the West a long time opened my eyes to how a modern country should be like. Open government. Free press. Democracy. Russian people want these things too. But the leadership deceives them.'

"But you've spent many years in Cuba. You mean to tell me *Cuba* opened your eyes?" Kate asked.

"I also served in Mexico and England."

Kate shuffled the papers in her folder and took out a sheet. "True. One year in Mexico and less than that in London. Why so short?"

Orgonov shuffled his feet. "They… they take me out because… I made mistakes." He frowned.

Kate wouldn't let it go. "What mistakes?"

"Personal ones."

Kate sat back and folded her arms. "Look, Sergei Vassileyevich. If you want our help, if you wish to be allowed to resettle in the United States, you're going to have to answer our questions, truthfully and in full," she said in unaccented Russian.

Orgonov raised his eyebrows and looked at her with surprise.

"My parents immigrated from Ukraine," she said. "I retooled my Ukrainian to Russian in college. Now, you made mistakes. Let's hear about them."

"Well, you see, I got involved with some women, and this got me into trouble."

"Yes? And?"

"In Mexico, I had affair with a dancer."

"A dancer."

"Yes."

"A Mexican dancer?"

Orgonov nodded.

"So, why—"

"She was mistress of my ambassador." He shrugged. *Whaddya gonna do?*

"Oohh. I see."

"Of course, he doesn't tell SVR, 'I want Orgonov out of here because he is sleeping with my Mexican mistress.' Nooo. He says to Moscow, 'Orgonov is a security risk. He does not follow the rules. Something like that. And, *fweeet*, I am out of there."

"All right. And London?"

"In London, me and my wife have a falling out—"

"In London only?"

"Well, no, everywhere. Me and my wife are getting divorce."

"You mean, you're still married."

"Yes, technically, this is true."

Nick and Morgenstern exchanged a knowing glance.

"So to continue," Kate said, "in London…"

"My wife first informs me she wants divorce."

"Because?"

"Because I was involved with another woman."

"What other woman?"

"Wife of Russian military attaché. Moscow withdraws him and me and our wives. They do not like such things. All Russian diplomats must be above reproach."

"Then what did they do with you?

"They send me back to Moscow to work in Department Two of First Chief Directorate. This means Latin America affairs. I work on Cuba at a desk in headquarters."

"We'll get to that," Kate said. "Who is Svetlana Volkova?"

The man's eyebrows popped up again.

"Well?" Kate prodded.

"Yes. Svetlana… she is wife of Russian commercial attaché in Montreal."

Kate kept an icy gaze on the Russian.

He squirmed. "I am in love with this Svetlana."

The FBI men rolled their eyes.

"We had affair in Moscow. Now her husband is posted to Montreal. She also loves me. We have plans to run away together."

"To the United States," Kate finished in a flat voice, her chin propped on an open palm.

"Yes. This is our plan."

"And this is where we come in. Am I right?"

"Well, yes."

"And let me kick this can further. We help you pull this Romeo and Juliet scenario off, and you provide us with the crown jewels."

Orgonov look puzzled.

"In other words, we help you get Svetlana in return for your telling us all that you know about the SVR, Cuba, etc."

Orgonov gave one nod. "Yes. This is good."

Kate looked at Nick and Morgenstern for a reaction. Each shifted back in his chair, their faces filled with a mix of resignation and barely concealed disgust.

"The guy's a total douchebag!" Morgenstern flailed his arms. "A girlfriend in every port type of guy. Are you kidding me? Hellooo!"

The three, joined by the four who had been observing remotely, were meeting to discuss next steps to recommend to their superiors.

"You're right. He's certainly that," Nick chimed in.

"Since when have our services been deterred from working with douchebags?" asked Doug, a middle-aged veteran of the Russia Division of the CIA's National Clandestine Service.

They all laughed.

"He's thrown a couple of gems our way already," Mimi, a young analyst, said.

"Those two alleged Cuban assets. We need to get right on that," urged the fourth member of the observation team, Edgar Hanscomb, a crewcut investigator from State's Diplomatic Security.

"*Alleged.* That's the operative word here," Morgenstern interjected. "Think about it. What are the odds this douchebag is a dangle? An agent provocateur sent here to throw monkey wrenches at us, to see how we handle defectors, and to ID people like us. I smell a rat. It stinks to high heaven."

"He's passed a poly," crewcut said.

"That's fine. But it ain't foolproof, my friend," the fat G-man shot back. "The Sovs—I mean Russians—are skilled at beating the box. That's why they don't use it on their own people. Or rarely anyway."

"Anybody know, or know of, Philip Livingston?" Kate asked.

"We're combing through his State Department files—personnel records, travel, financial, background investigations and so on. Should have it all here by COB," crewcut said.

"The Bureau's throwing an invisible net around the guy and his wife. Twenty-four/seven surveillance. We'll know his every move, every phone conversation, every discussion, every email," Nick said. "We got the warrant. Operation MOPED is already in gear."

In a shabby warehouse on upper New York Avenue, far from the raw concrete "brutalist" architecture of FBI headquarters and the other monumental federal buildings created to impress, the MOPED team was taking shape.

Nick selected two young agents, Peter Sacco and Marilee Jones, for the laborious task of monitoring the listening devices in the Livingstons' apartment. To investigate the couple's finances, he chose Doug McManus, a financial forensic expert who excelled in exposing the secret foreign bank accounts and money laundering practices of mafia bosses and the most notorious of America's white-collar criminals. Dale Sondstrom, formerly a professional magician, was in charge of surveillance. His job was to collect evidence on Livingston and his wife, their every move, without their being the least bit aware of it.

Spearheading the surveillance effort was the FBI's Special Surveillance Group. The Super Gs were Investigative Specialists whose job was to envelope a suspect in an invisible bubble using advanced covert surveillance methods. They were young white men, old black ladies, portly Asians, blue-collar Latinos, businessmen, bureaucrats, and street bums—faces in the crowd.

The Super Gs were trained in clandestine photography and shadowing their targets on foot and by car. They weren't called "ghosts" for nothing. They could follow a June bug through a hailstorm.

The first order of business was to track the Livingstons' daily routines and chart a pattern of their movements and absences from home. Weekdays, Philip was out the door at seven thirty a.m. to go to his State Department job. Deirdre worked at an independent bookshop between nine and three. She also did volunteer work at a D.C. social services agency for the mentally handicapped twice a week.

On the fifth day of surveillance, the Super Gs went in. They easily picked the lock to the Livingstons' apartment door. The team swept in and split up. Three team members photographed the interior, then meticulously searched for any incriminating evidence. After their search was done, they referred to the photos when putting things back in place, ensuring all items were restored to their original positions. A group of two placed listening devices and miniature webcams in strategic spots throughout the house. Another two-man squad went into the parking basement, where the Livingstons, who commuted to work by subway, kept their car. One Super G specialist installed a listening device under the dash and a powerful homing apparatus under the plastic molding in the trunk while the other served as lookout.

Other members stood watch outside and in the hallway. Team leaders were equipped with wireless communications. Any sign of danger would be instantly relayed to the others, who would then have precious moments to beat a hasty but silent retreat.

In coordination with State's Diplomatic Security, the FBI team was alerted when Livingston departed for the day. On the second day MOPED was launched, they conducted a thorough search of Livingston's office, including his hard drive as well as a file-by-file inventory of his safe, where classified documents were stored.

Whenever either or both Livingstons took the car, it was followed by eight Super G vehicles that surreptitiously tracked the suspects from behind, ahead, and on one side. Should the Super Gs lose their target, they would re-locate it by means of the homing device inside the Livingstons' car.

If the Livingstons went to a movie, the Super Gs were there. Shopping for groceries? The Super Gs were there. Visiting friends; the Super Gs were nearby. Like phantoms, the Super Gs haunted their targets without revealing themselves. Bag ladies, commuters, garbage men, street repairmen, hawkers. The Super Gs had an infinite array of covers and disguises.

The bubble was complete.

After two weeks, MOPED had precious little to show for the significant resources brought to bear against Philip and Deirdre Livingston. The couple led lives of predictable routines: going to their jobs, returning home, a scotch before dinner, banal mealtime conversation, reading to classical music, a little PBS news, early to bed. There were no brush passes in the supermarkets, covert liaisons with a CUBINT intel officer, or clandestine messages.

Nick sat with his shirtsleeves rolled up and tie loose. He had dark circles under his eyes. "What've we picked up from the apartment?"

Peter Sacco and Marilee Jones turned palms up in the gesture of *nada*. They exhibited the dazed look of having spent fourteen hours a day listening to other people's banal conversations.

"Finances? Anything?" Nick asked.

McManus pushed his thick eyeglasses up on his nose. "I've combed through his bank accounts and investment portfolios going back fifteen years. No unusually large infusions of cash. No funny business."

Nick looked at Dale Sondstrom.

Dale shook his head. "The Super Gs have monitored their

every conversation, every move outside their apartment, every bowel movement. Nothing. Just dull people going about their boring lives. That's all."

"I think this tells us something important," Morgenstern said. "Sometimes it's what you don't see that tips you off."

"What aren't we seeing?" Kate asked.

"We've grown accustomed to Americans spying for the money. In this case, we've got true believers," Morgenstern said. "They've turned down money, I'll bet, and do their treason out of political conviction that the United States is evil and Fidel is a commie Robin Hood. They're of that generation, sixties lefties who still believe in all the crap about Castro being an agrarian reformer, a victim of American imperialism, and so on. Hence, no traces of funny money."

Nick perked up. "You gotta point there, Bart. Motivation. We need to nail down the psychology of the Livingstons spying against their country. Now, what don't we have? What stones remain unturned?"

"Have they been to their boat?" Marilee Jones asked.

Nick looked to Dale Sondstrom for an answer.

Sondstrom looked like a deer caught in headlights. "Holy shit. No, they've not been out to the Chesapeake, where they berth it."

"Why do you say, 'Holy shit?'" Nick asked.

Blushing, Sondstrom said, "We haven't searched it, nor have we bugged it."

"Aw geez, Dale! C'mon! How could you overlook the goddamn boat? Tonight. I want that thing gone through with a fine-tooth comb, and I want it wired so we can hear a dragonfly burp."

Sondstrom got on the STU-IV secure phone immediately to issue the orders.

"And emails?" Nick asked.

Crewcut pulled out a ream of paper. "We've gone through all their emails for the past two weeks. Nothing out of the ordinary."

"Any exchanges with foreign counterparts?" Nick asked.

Peter Sacco answered, "A few with our embassies overseas. Friendly greetings, chatter with friends mostly. Nothing that arouses suspicion. And one exchange with a Mexican art dealer that we're still studying."

"Can I see the last one?" asked Nick.

Sacco handed him a transcript.

From: Pedro Orlando
Subject: New Art Pieces Available

Philip,

I have a fresh consignment of works by Juan Horta and Marco Antonio Martinez. Please let me know when you would like to come and see them.

Pedro

From: Philip R. Livingston
Subject: New Art Pieces Available

Pedro,

We are delighted to hear about the new artwork. We have not made plans for the coming year, but as soon as we do, I'll let you know.

Philip

Nick put down the transcript and massaged his temples. "What sticks with me is this 'Please come' and 'Oh, we will' back and forth. Is this simply a genuine exchange between art seller and collector, or is it disguised verbiage, code between handler and agents?" He looked to Morgenstern for his reaction.

Morgenstern leaned over the paper. "If the Livingstons have been meeting their Cuban handlers outside the country, then there should be a record of their travels. He needs permission from State every time he takes leave. Moreover, it's expected that USG officials notify the U.S. embassy of the country they're visiting. If they're going on USG business, they require country clearance from the embassy. If going on personal travel, then it's simply a matter of professional courtesy to let the embassy know anyway. The thing we especially need to focus on is any time he's told an embassy he's coming to their country, but ends up somewhere else. It's one kind of ruse that's used. Tell your employer you're going to country A on vacation, but in reality go to country B. It's another ploy to cover your tracks."

"How do we figure that out?" Kate asked.

"Compare his leave request records and country clearance messages with his air reservations," Morgenstern said. "It'll take some digging, but it can be done. We've done it before with past traitors."

"I'm worried about 'Oscar.' We still don't know who their handler here is. Livingston told 'Martín'—me—that he'll be monitoring his emails closely," Nick said. "If 'Oscar' picks anything up on 'Martín,' most likely from Livingston himself, then our goose is cooked."

Morgenstern nodded. "That requires us to be on top of his emailing every minute of the day. As soon as we pick up something that's out of the ordinary, disguised code, something fishy, not quite right, then we cover all CUBINT officers for a short period of time with pervasive surveillance. When we identify the guy who's on his way to rendezvous with the Livingstons, then we trip him up."

"And if it's not a CUBINT officer? But some deep cover operative we can't identify?" Kate asked.

"My bet is it's a CUBINT schmuck," Morgenstern said. "But if I'm wrong… well, let's hope I'm not."

CHAPTER TWENTY-SEVEN

Sondstrom produced a thumb drive. "This is an exact duplicate of a thumb drive we found on Livingston's boat in Havre de Grace, Maryland. It was hidden inside a cutout portion of a book titled, *Greek Tragedies: An Anthology*. We downloaded everything on the thumb drive and replaced the original exactly as we found it. It contains encryption and decryption apps for email communications as well as for deciphering code received, we suspect, via shortwave radio broadcasts, which is classic Cuban DI tradecraft. In fact, we also found a Sony shortwave radio in their apartment."

Next, he circulated a set of maps among the MOPED crew. "Navigation maps for Cuban waters. These, of course, are copies. We left the originals on the boat."

Photocopies of handwritten material followed. "Livingston's diary. Look at page forty-five."

July 8, 1998 Havana

> *This may turn out to be the most fascinating day of our lives. To our utter astonishment, we were visited by Fidel! He told us he wanted to meet the "heroes" who have done so much to "help the Cuban people in difficult times." He also presented the Medal for Combatants in the Clandestine Struggle, which will be held in safekeeping for us until the day comes for us to "return home" to this wonderful island.*

We spent four hours with el comandante discussing U.S.-Cuban relations and world events. Fidel may be the most brilliant man I've ever had the good fortune to meet.

"We went back and combed through his travel records going back at least a dozen years. While it's incomplete, we found some interesting anomalies," Hanscomb said. "The most damning is the following." He passed around three documents. The first was Livingston's leave and earnings statements for the pay period June 29 through July 24, 1998. It showed that Livingston took vacation leave July 3-17. The second was a State Department cable to the U.S. embassy in Nassau, Bahamas, sent by Livingston, informing that he would be vacationing in the islands with his wife July 7-16, 1998. The third was an Air Canada manifest for the Toronto-Havana flight of July 3 and the manifest of July 16 of that year showing Philip and Deirdre Livingston as passengers.

"The latter we got from the RCMP, who are very cooperative," Hanscomb said.

"Some of the contents of the Livingstons' home computer are password protected, not accessible using the thumb drive. Our IT specialists are working hard to crack it. As soon as they do, I'll let you all know," Nick said. "What we have here is a developing case, far from airtight. While the evidence thus far is damning, it's not enough to nail Livingston so completely that the slickest grandstanding lawyer will want to avoid a trial and seek a plea agreement: life imprisonment with no parole plus full cooperation as opposed to our seeking the death penalty."

"And we need to safeguard classified information from being dredged up in a public trial," Kate added.

"You got it," Nick said. "It's time for Martín to return and get the Livingstons to spill their guts to a trusted comrade and thereby incriminate themselves beyond all shadow of a doubt."

"Amen to that," Morgenstern said.

From: Oscar
Subject: Meeting

Friends: I would like to schedule another meeting to follow up on the very valuable and helpful information you so kindly provided us last time. I also have something special to convey to you from Havana. I propose that we meet next Saturday at 4:00 pm at the Hilton on upper Connecticut Ave.

Looking forward to seeing you again.

Oscar.

"We intercepted this message six hours ago," Sondstrom told the MOPED team. "We blocked it from getting to the Livingstons. The email address is a private account belonging to one Pedro Estévez Herrera, who happens to be Third Secretary/Press & Cultural Attaché at the Cuban Interests Section."

"Six hours," Morgenstern said. "Meaning we've got to act immediately."

All eyes turned to Nick.

"Now we know the usual form of contact with their handler," Nick said. "I said last time it was time for Martín to return. What we need to do pronto is to repackage this email. Send it on with a couple of edits to Livingston, signed off by Martín."

"Then we have the complication of how to deal with Señor Estévez a.k.a. Oscar," Morgenstern said. "I suggest we send him a phony reply from the Livingstons, saying they're too busy, blah, blah, blah. And if necessary, if Estévez gets in the way, we set up an accident, maybe a car collision, to keep him out of action, even set him up to be PNG'd."

The others stared at Morgenstern incredulously.

"I like the first part, Bart, about the messages. But, as

Hanscomb here can attest, arranging for foreign diplomats to be incapacitated in an accident contrived by us is against international law—"

"The Vienna Convention on Diplomatic Relations, to be exact," Hanscomb interjected.

"Fuck the convention!" Morgenstern spat. "Those schmucks are constantly slashing our people's tires, stealing stuff from them just to drive them to distraction, putting dog shit on their door knobs, you name it—"

"Bart. It's a non-starter," Nick shot back. "We're a nation of laws. Also, if we were to declare one of theirs *persona non grata* and kick him out of the country, then they'd retaliate, and we'd get into a sterile pissing contest of evicting each other's diplomats. I don't think the Secretary of State would be agreeable to that."

"Okay then. I know a bunch of retired special agents who're itching to get the nod. All I gotta do is take care of that thing we've talked about before." He swiped one palm against the other in a gesture of: It's a piece of cake.

Nick chuckled. "Okay, Godfather. Are you willing to be the first to go to jail, lose your pension, and leave in disgrace?"

The other team members burst out laughing.

Nick straightened. "Okay. Let's alter the email as discussed. Get it out immediately to the Livingstons. Get a response signed by Livingston back to Estévez stalling him. Blanket the guy in twenty-four/seven surveillance. But it's got to be absolutely invisible. Got that, Dale?"

Dale nodded.

"Any indications the guy's about to make a direct approach to the Livingstons, we go to red alert status."

"And do what?" Morgenstern asked.

"We'll figure it out if and when it happens. Meanwhile, enter Martín stage left."

From: Martin
Subject: Meeting

Philip: I would like to schedule a meeting to follow up on our pleasant encounter at The Policy Forum. I also have something special to convey to you from Havana. I propose that we meet next Saturday at 4:00 p.m. at the Capitol Hill Hyatt Regency, Room 604. Deirdre should also attend."

Looking forward to seeing you again.

Martin

From: Philip
Subject: Meeting

We will see you on Saturday at the proposed venue and time.

Cheers,
Philip

From: Philip
Subject: Meeting

Dear Oscar,

We cannot make it next Saturday, regrettably. Deirdre's mother is very ill, and Deirdre needs to be at her side. And I need to provide support to my wife in this difficult time. I'll contact you with an alternate date in the near future. Meantime, should you need to convey especially time sensitive information to me, please do so via the usual fashion.

Cheers,
Philip

Nick arrived at the Hyatt Regency two hours in advance of the scheduled meeting with the Livingstons. The MOPED team had discreetly reserved a suite in the name of a fictitious businessman, then wired the place so that every inch was covered by both audio and visual surveillance. Surveillance specialists, including Peter Sacco and Marilee Jones, occupied a neighboring room replete with a full array of electronic monitoring equipment.

"Will you walk into my parlor, said the spider to the fly?" Kate murmured as she stood perusing the suite with her arms crossed.

"What's that?" Nick asked.

"A poem I learned as a girl.

'Will you walk into my parlor?' said the spider to the fly,
'Tis the prettiest little parlor that ever you did spy;
The way into my parlor is up a winding stair,
And I've a many curious thing to show when you are there.'
'Oh no, no,' said the little fly, 'to ask me is in vain,
For who goes up your winding stair can ne'er come down again.'"

Nick smiled. "I like that. With luck, our winding stair will lead the Livingstons directly to a federal prison of our choosing."

"You say, 'With luck.' Are you worried something will go wrong?"

"No. But there's always that little gremlin whispering in my ear: 'The best laid schemes of mice and men go oft awry,'" Nick said.

"Robert Burns. Do you like Burns?" Kate asked.

"'Fraid I don't know him. English lit wasn't my forte."

"What was your forte?"

"The law. After Yale, I went to Fordham Law for a degree in criminal justice."

"So you knew from an early age that you wanted to do this?"

"Pretty much. All those old Elliot Ness shows got me hooked. You were an English major?" Nick asked.

"Yes. I love the truths about human nature that are borne

out in the best of literature. I went to Clarke College on an ROTC scholarship. Ever hear of Clarke?"

"Uh... no."

"Few people have. Small college in Dubuque. I worked two jobs to supplement the scholarship."

"Then what? Did you always know you'd one day be a spy?"

"Oh, no. I did a tour in the Army as payback for the scholarship. The Agency sent a recruiter to my unit. It sounded interesting—see the world, travel, adventure, intrigue, serve your country. I got hooked. I applied, got accepted. And here I am." She looked at Nick and smiled.

She had a twinkle in her pale eyes that Nick hadn't seen before. Accentuated by the dimples in her smile, warmth radiated where before he'd seen only cold.

Nick looked at his watch—one hour to go. "One, two, three. This is a test. Can you hear me? Can you hear me?"

Marilee Jones opened the door to the suite. "For the hundredth time, we can hear just fine. We've got more redundancies built into this operation than Air Force One."

Nick tugged at the sleeves of his shirt and straightened his collar.

"Nervous?" Kate asked.

"Truthfully? Yes. This is big league stuff. We can't blow it. Too much is riding on it. The Bureau's reputation. The U.S. government's image. America's security. Operation MOPED must succeed."

"And if it doesn't?"

"Not in the cards." He looked again at his watch, forty-five minutes.

"Is Martín in full form, ready to go?" Kate asked.

A fleeting smile passed across his face. "Martín is ready and rearing to go," he said in a Spanish accent.

The Livingstons arrived promptly at four o'clock. They were wet from a downpour. Nick took their coats and umbrellas and bade them to sit, then offered coffee.

The patrician, balding Philip looked decidedly ill at ease. Deirdre, her red-gray hair tied into a single braid, was all smiles, a kindly aunt in appearance and demeanor.

Wasting no time on pleasantries, Philip said, "Where's Oscar? How do you two relate to each other?"

"I am gradually taking over Oscar's caseload as he will soon return to Cuba," Nick said. "He sends his regards."

"Why weren't we given advance notice of this?" Philip demanded.

"Well, we apologize for any—" Nick began.

"Darling, don't be so gruff. Martín is simply trying to explain that Oscar will be transferring out. His assignment in Washington is coming to an end. Is that right, Martín?"

"Yes. Exactly," Nick replied. He could see Philip Livingston was going to be a tough customer. *Keep your cool. Don't feed his suspicion.*

"Well, I told Oscar two things last time we did this." Philip leaned forward. "I said meeting in Washington is way too risky. Save your face-to-face business for our overseas travels, and use the Mexican art dealer cover to communicate with us by email. I also told Oscar we're easing out. It's been a long and rewarding run, but I plan to retire soon. We want to spend more time with each other and sailing our boat."

"And with our children and grandchildren," Deirdre added.

"I wouldn't have asked you here today if it weren't important. First, I want to convey to you a message directly from our most senior levels." Nick reached for his briefcase and pulled out some papers. He handed an enlarged photo to the couple. "I have the great pleasure to inform you that you have been awarded the Friends of the Republic of Cuba Medal for your extraordinary contributions to our nation. This is a photo of the medal, which will be safeguarded along with the Medal for Combatants in the Clandestine Struggle that *El Jefe* gave you in '98, until you return to Cuba." Nick watched their reaction.

Philip's face went from sourpuss to glowing. Deirdre beheld the photo as if it were of the grandchildren she just mentioned.

Philip looked up. "I am speechless. I can't begin to express our profound thanks for this glorious award."

"And that is not all," Nick continued. "When you do come back to your second country, if I may, this will be waiting for you." He handed off another photo of a sprawling seashore bungalow swathed in tropical foliage.

"My lord!" Deirdre said. "For us? Really?"

Nick nodded. "Look at it as your retirement home."

Philip hugged his wife. "It's wonderful. Just wonderful."

"It's on Cayo Coco. Perfect retirement place, huh?" Nick said.

Philip reached out to shake Nick's hand. "Splendid. Just splendid."

Deirdre went over and embraced Nick. She then reached into her purse and pulled out her wallet. She opened it to reveal family photos. "This is Jesse, eleven, and Toby, nine, our daughter's children. Jesse plays the violin beautifully already. And Toby's in Little League." She flipped to the next photos. "And these are our son's kids. Four of the most wonderful warm creatures under the sun. We're so proud of them! Aren't we honey?"

"You bet," Philip said. "This is what it's all about for us, quality time with the kids and grandkids. We're a very close-knit family."

"Yes. You are fortunate," Nick said. "Since we are new to each other, I wanted to spend some time getting to know you. We will be working together, mostly long distance, until you actually do retire."

"Don't get us wrong, Martín. We're a little burned out. That's all. Thirty-two years in service to the revolution is a long time."

Nick made a mental note of the year after a quick calculation. "Yes, it is."

"We've lived with the fear and worry for all these years. And still do. We're not quitting. Just think of us as a reserve army to be called up when needed."

Nick nodded. "Of course."

"It was our life," Deirdre added. "And it always will be… in our hearts."

"Absolutely," Philip rejoined. "It's forever. You know, it's like Fidel. It's forever."

"I fully understand," Nick said. "Oscar and I have discussed you at length. But I'd like to hear from you about your motivations and your accomplishments on our behalf."

"Well, you know, with Reagan's coming into office in the eighties, we felt the country and the world were in great danger. And the threats against Cuba by America were simply intolerable," Philip said. "We were convinced that dumb B-movie actor was taking the world to the nuclear brink. Rattling swords all over the globe. When the United States invaded Grenada in '83, it was clear Cuba was next. But Fidel stood up to Reagan and convinced him America would suffer another Bay of Pigs fiasco if he tried. So it was really Reagan who got us to offer our services when we met Gaetano Turró of your office here. He set it all up. Very impressive man, don't you think?"

"Yes, he is," Nick said.

Philip looked at him quizzically. "But he died fifteen years ago."

Nick felt a rush of blood to his head and struggled to maintain a cool composure. "His training texts are still used today in our service."

"Ah, yes. Of course."

Holy shit. Careful. Careful! Nick took a deep breath. "And what did your services consist of then?"

"I was so angry. I gave Gaetano thousands of pages of classified materials, all the way up to Top Secret compartmented information. Not to mention blowing American spies' covers to your service and spotting potential USG recruits for them. And this has continued through his successors. I've lost count, but it's been tens of thousands of pages of U.S. government secrets."

"And I'm mainly the courier," Deirdre interjected. "When we visited Havana in '98, the DGI gave us a crash course on intelligence tradecraft. So I've become very skilled at brush passes with your intelligence people at the supermarket." She giggled.

"Yeah, a real Mata Hari!" Philip said.

Laughter all around.

For four hours, the Livingstons spilled the beans, incriminating themselves beyond all doubt on FBI audio and video. They revealed enough to send them away for the rest of their natural lives.

CHAPTER TWENTY-EIGHT

"Atención! Atención! Cinco-siete-dos-nueve-uno. Ocho-tres-seis-cuatro-siete…"

Deirdre carefully jotted down the code being transmitted from Havana via the shortwave. So did the MOPED team tuned to the same frequency at their base half a city away. With the thumb-drive decryption Sondstrom's crew had obtained, they deciphered Havana's message to the Livingstons in real time.

Your next delivery should be at Crown at 1800 Wednesday. Specific instructions will be left there for you as well. The usual procedures apply. Our sympathies for mother. Please let us know when you will be available for a meeting.

Nick read the deciphered text for the tenth time. "'Crown' is obviously a dead drop. 'The usual procedures' worries me. We don't know what they are. The final two points are very worrisome. The thing about 'mother' must be in response to our phony message about Deirdre's mother being ill. The Livingstons won't get it. That, plus the request for a meeting so soon after their rendezvous with Martín, may arouse suspicions. And Estévez, a.k.a. Oscar, will be mobilized by this message. If anybody's going to catch on that something fishy is up, it'll be him. We need to act fast."

"It gets worse," Morgenstern said. "An emergency signal

to the Livingstons that they're in danger. It's SOP, not just with the Cubes, as all intel services have them to protect their assets. If Estévez senses something funny is up, he'll pull the cord, and the Livingstons will flee like bats out of hell. And if the Cubes have their act together, they have an escape hatch in place, a pre-planned mechanism for hiding and exfiltrating their agents out of the United States."

"What kind of signal? A phone call?" Nick asked.

"Could be. Or a pager. They like pagers because the signals can't be traced. Or some other electronic device. Or even by a personal approach by a sleeper agent."

Nick pointed at Sondstrom. "I want the Super Gs to tighten up on the Livingstons. I want maximum surveillance on them, even if it risks their noticing. And we need to keep Estévez in a box. Whatever it takes!"

The wino vagrant squatting on the metal grate opposite the State Department's E Street entrance murmured into his sleeve. "SEAGULL just exited E Street."

At five fifteen, Philip Livingston trudged along in the light drizzle, Ferragamo attaché case in hand, a gray figure in a gray trench coat against a gray office buildingscape set under a gray sky, blending in with the multitude of other gray commuters, mostly government bureaucrats.

The hot dog vendor on 21st Street talked into his coat collar. "SEAGULL headed toward Foggy Bottom Metro."

A pigtailed coed with a book-laden backpack moved rhythmically as if to music coming through her iPOD earphones as she followed Livingston down the steep escalator to the trains. The music was nonexistent. The iPOD apparatus was a communications device connecting her to MOPED base.

An elderly Asian woman sitting opposite Livingston, her shopping bags at her feet, trained the bag with a hidden webcam directly at the target. A businessman wearing a spiffy Italian-made suit sat behind SEAGULL, keeping a close eye on the subject as he pretended to scan the Wall Street Journal. The three Super Gs disembarked with Livingston at Metro Station, where Livingston made his daily transfer to the red line toward Shady Grove.

The Asian woman and the coed peeled away, to be replaced by a middle-aged African-American man dressed as a mechanic and a nondescript fortyish white woman wearing a department store ensemble and fitting the picture of a classic secretary. The mechanic directed his webcam-equipped lunchbox at Livingston. The secretary mumbled something into her compact as she checked her makeup.

The Super G team awaiting Livingston at Dupont Circle got the word to stand down. Livingston did not get off at his usual place.

"Stick with him. Do *not* let him out of your sight," Sondstrom commanded through the commo system.

"Next stop Friendship Heights," the automated recording announced through the Metro loudspeakers.

Livingston got to his feet. The three watchers glanced at each other furtively. They each exited through separate doors, but kept SEAGULL in their sights every second. Sondstrom scrambled other Super G watchers to get to Friendship Heights as soon as possible.

The mechanic, the businessman, and the secretary went up the escalator with Livingston, the businessman in front and the other two behind, all with the dull look of bored, tired commuters. Strolling leisurely, Livingston turned right on Wisconsin Avenue, then took another right onto Fessenden. The watchers from the subway kept a careful distance from opposite angles, each transmitting SEAGULL's exact location and direction.

A Ford Taurus screeched to a halt at the intersection of Military Road and River Road. Two men and a woman rushed out of the vehicle. The woman, young and made up to appear pregnant, quickly moved to the corner of River Road opposite Fessenden and proceeded to engage in an animated mock chat on her cell phone. A watcher dressed as a UPS deliveryman carefully studied his electronic tasking board a half block further down on River Road. The other man, who one would peg as a young lawyer, directed his briefcase at Livingston, video recording the subject's every move from behind. The mechanic, the businessman, and the secretary then receded, to be held in reserve.

As Livingston approached the mailbox at the intersection of Fessenden and River Roads, he paused briefly and carefully looked over the box. He then turned around and retraced his route back to the Friendship Heights station. He got back on the train heading south, with additional watchers embarking with him.

"Next stop Dupont Circle," the automated voice announced.

When the train stopped, Livingston got off and headed home. MOPED base heard him greet his wife and turn on the CNN news.

A team of Super Gs hovered around Deirdre during the day as well. She reported for work at the bookstore at nine, left at three, did voluntary work at the facility for the mentally handicapped from three-thirty to five-thirty. Then home.

"Nothing. Your guys found nothing?" Nick snapped.

"We went over that site with a fine-tooth comb," Sundstrom replied. "We got the post office to open the box. Just a handful of ordinary envelopes. We searched nearby bushes, trees, gutters, you name it."

"I don't get it," Nick said. "The guy shows up at a street corner right after he gets a coded signal for his next delivery, then he turns around and goes home. Did he catch on we were watching him?"

"Could be. Or maybe he went there looking for some signal and didn't see it," Morgenstern said.

"Surveillance picks up nothing in his conversations with Deirdre after he's home," Sondstrom added.

"What about Estévez?" Nick asked. "Anything unusual in his movements? Communications?"

Sondstrom shook his head. "We're on him like bees on honey."

"I just don't get it." Nick slam-dunked his Styrofoam coffee cup into a wastebasket.

CHAPTER TWENTY-NINE

Task Force Spartan, Nangarhar, Afghanistan

Private Prendergast was having a bad day. The infernal Afghan dust penetrated his sinuses, giving him a terrible headache. His credit card company had canceled his account for non-payment. He was being dishonorably discharged from the Army. And the man he loved, Sergeant Hilliker, was ragging on him for messing up his work.

That was all right. After he downloaded another ten thousand classified messages onto the CD, he would have collected enough of the nation's secrets to set him up for life. The Cuban embassy officer he'd met in New Delhi was really nice to him. The guy promised big bucks in return and asked him to seek employment with a U.S. government contractor with access to classified information. That way, he could continue to sell stuff to the Cubans. He would buy a big sailboat, but first thing, a red Corvette. He definitely wouldn't return to Arkansas. No. Maybe New Orleans. Or Houston. Life would be good. Very good. He sat staring at the ceiling of his office trailer, his mind as far away from Afghanistan as one could get.

His reverie was abruptly terminated by MPs and a counterintel officer from the 902nd Military Intelligence Group bursting into the trailer. Two MPs lifted him from his chair and handcuffed him as another secured his workstation. The counterintel man took photos.

"Private Roger Prendergast. You are under arrest for the crime of espionage," the senior MP declared.

They hauled him away.

The wastebasket went flying across the room, just barely missing Sondstrom's head.

Nick's skills as a placekicker from his football days were as sharp as ever. "Shit! Who told the Army to arrest Prendergast?"

His question was met with shrugs and shaking of heads.

"Jesus Christ almighty! Don't they know what they're risking? What resources we've got committed here? What's at stake?"

Silence.

"All right. This is it, folks. Go after 'em. Take them in. Get the charges formalized. Let's go!" Nick bellowed with a sweep of both arms.

"Nick! Estévez. He's on the move!" Sondstrom declared, one hand supporting a hearing apparatus to his ear.

"Where are the Livingstons?" Nick demanded.

After a moment of listening to reports from the field, Sondstrom said, "Deirdre is at the mental facility. Philip is on the Metro."

"The Super Gs have got to stay on them like glue! Got me? Like glue! And we make the arrests. Send four agents to each one and arrest them! Dale, Bart, you two come with me. We've got a date with Philip Livingston."

"I'll go with you guys," Kate said.

Nick shook his head. "CIA officers at the scene of an arrest? Don't think so, sweetheart. You wait here. Coordinate with your own agency."

Pedro Estévez Herrera pulled out of the rear parking lot of the Cuban Interests Section office and screeched out onto 16th Street, heading toward Euclid. He just made it through a yellow light. He gained speed, expertly maneuvering around rush hour traffic and through two more traffic lights.

As he gained speed, he incurred the wrath of other drivers. "Hey! Fuck you, shithead!" "Screw you, asshole!" "Douchebag!" A rash of vehicular beeping and honking accompanied the epithets.

His luck ran out at the intersection of 16th and U Street. The light was red, and pedestrians crowded the crosswalk. Terror gripped him as he slammed on the brakes, but the car wouldn't stop. People fled in all directions. He hit the brake pedal again with all his might. No response.

The late-model chevy picked up more speed. Like a rocket after launch, it defied gravity and kept shooting forward. The vehicle hit a curb and spun out of control. Estévez's last conscious thought before crashing head-on into an old oak tree was of his family.

"He's headed back to Friendship Heights," Sondstrom reported as the FBI undercover car swerved in and out of traffic, Nick and Bart in the back seat.

"Maybe he's got a rendezvous with Estévez," Morgenstern said. "Or better yet, one or the other is making a delivery at the dead drop, following the instruction from Havana."

Sondstrom held up his hand as he listened intently over the car's secure radiophone. "Estévez is out of the picture."

"What?" Nick asked.

"He flew out of the CUBINT parking lot, floored it down 16th Street, and crashed into a tree at New Hampshire. No word on his condition. Our guys say it looks like his brakes failed."

Nick glared at Morgenstern.

The fat man squirmed, then shrugged. "Musta had car troubles. Go figure. Whaddaya gonna do?" He avoided eye contact with Nick.

"We'll deal with that later," Nick said. "Is the stealth team in place at River Road?"

"Almost there," Sondstrom replied.

Nick looked at his watch. "Shit. Step on it!"

Nick's driver veered left onto River Road, running a red traffic signal and barely avoiding sideswiping another car. Nick signaled for him to pull over two blocks short of Fessenden. The team scrambled out and walked briskly down the street.

Nick spotted a tall figure approaching the mailbox. The balding man wearing a gray trench coat carried a briefcase. The suspect stopped at the box and stared at it, his back to the G-men.

Nick raced ahead of the others and brought one hand down on the man's shoulder. "Philip Livingston. FBI. You are under arrest. You have the right—"

The man turned around, wearing a big smile. "Hi!"

Sondstrom and Morgenstern caught up with Nick and stopped dead in their tracks, their gape-mouthed faces the picture of disbelief.

The man extended his hand. "I'm Ralphie. Missus Deirdre sent me here to give you this." Ralphie spoke slowly and slurred his words. The man was clearly mentally handicapped. He began to open the Ferragamo briefcase.

Nick pulled his gun. "Stop! Put your hands above your head!"

The man's eyes grew wide, and a frown of fear crossed his face. He dropped the briefcase on the sidewalk. A bouquet of flowers fell out of it. Sondstrom picked up the bouquet and opened the attached card. He handed it to Nick.

Dearest Martín,

We've opted for early retirement.

Best,

Phil & Deirdre

Nick threw the card to the ground with all his might and then kicked the mailbox. "Damn you! Goddamn you to hell!" He pressed the heels of his hands against his eyes. *Say it didn't happen. Say it didn't happen.*

They sat at a small table on the sidewalk, nibbling salads at Au Pied de Cochon in Georgetown. The FBI agent was bored with playing nanny to the high-strung Russian.

"So, Sergei, what's next? A house in the 'burbs? Two cars in the garage? The American Dream?"

Orgonov played with his Bibb lettuce. "You know, Frank. In Russia we have a saying: 'One may make up a soft bed, but still it will be hard to sleep in.'" The Russian got up, placed his cloth napkin on the table, and patted the young man on the shoulder. "You are a good boy, Frank. Have a good life."

Before Frank could comprehend what was going on, Lt. Col. Sergei Orgonov had gotten up, sprinted out of the restaurant, and vanished in the maze of small side streets lined with handsome brick Federalist and Georgian homes.

The MSC Orinoco was now in international waters, having left Baltimore loaded with automobile parts and construction equipment. It would arrive at Puerto Cabello, Venezuela's main port, within the week. The endless ocean against a cloudless blue sky painted the perfect picture for the beginning of a long retirement.

Philip popped open a champagne bottle, poured two glasses, and handed one to Deirdre. They toasted the sea from the passenger deck of the Venezuelan cargo ship. Sea spray misted over them, cooling their faces as relief sank in. They breathed deeply of the salt air.

"Here's to a beautiful future," Philip said.

"Here's to Cayo Coco," Deirdre rejoined.

They kissed, clinked glasses, then took in long, slow draughts of the bubbly wine.

CHAPTER THIRTY

The Washington Post

SENIOR RUSSIAN SPY REDEFECTS, QUESTIONS RAISED

Alleged State Department Mole, Wife Flee to Cuba

In a bizarre series of events, the most senior Russian intelligence officer to defect to the United States in decades has returned to Moscow, while a State Department official has fled to Cuba with his wife to escape arrest for espionage. CIA and State Department officials will not comment pending investigation.

Lt. Col. Sergei Orgonov, a senior Russian intelligence operative who defected to the United States amid much publicity last month, has departed Washington for Moscow, insisting he was kidnapped and drugged by CIA officers. "They are political terrorists, violators of international law," Orgonov declared before boarding a Moscow-bound Aeroflot flight at Dulles Airport this morning. Orgonov, 49, claimed that CIA personnel attempted to block him from entering the Russian embassy at Mount Alto, but that he managed to escape them in time to rush through the front gate. He was flanked by Russian embassy officials as he boarded the plane.

Senior U.S. intelligence officials are weighing whether Orgonov was coerced to return by the SVR, the Russian intelligence agency, whether he changed his mind about defecting, or whether he was an agent provocateur, sent here to find out about American covert operations and to sow disinformation.

Ranking intelligence committee members in both houses of Congress are accusing the CIA of botching the vetting and treatment of Orgonov. "Either we should have detected him as a ringer, or the CIA should have had set procedures in place for handling defectors like Orgonov so as not to cause them to have second thoughts about defecting, which may be the case here," said Sen. Rory Harmon (R-TX), chairman of the Senate Select Committee on Intelligence.

Major FBI Failure Seen in State Department Mole Case - Congress to Hold Hearings

In a separate, but possibly related case, an alleged State Department mole spying for Cuba has fled to that country. Philip R. Livingston and his wife, Deirdre, had been under FBI surveillance for weeks, according to administration sources familiar with the case. They would not reveal whether the case was in any way related to that of the Russian Orgonov. The FBI would not comment on how the Livingstons managed to slip that agency's surveillance and depart the country. "A full internal investigation is underway. Pending its outcome, we will withhold comment on this matter," an FBI spokeswoman said. Sen. Harmon is scheduling hearings on what he calls, "The worst counterintelligence failures since the Hanssen and Ames cases..."

Nick put down the paper and rubbed his face. He hadn't slept in two days. He had been suspended with pay while the investigation was underway. He reached for the coffee pot. Empty. He felt too lethargic to get up and make another.

The phone rang, and he reluctantly answered it.

"You gotta hang in there, pal," Morgenstern said. "We've

been had by the best. There are more moles. I'm dead certain of it. It was a perfect setup by the Cubes. Like a game of chess by a master."

"We should've caught on," Nick said. "Orgonov fed us Livingston and Prendergast. If the Agency had done their vetting, they would've nailed him for what he was: a dangle. But why'd he divulge two Cuban assets? I still don't get it."

"SOP tradecraft. They took it straight out of the old KGB playbook. Throw a couple of bones in order to keep us off the trail of the more important assets, bigger fish they'll do anything to protect. And if you look at it closely, you'll see their planning at play. Livingston was going to retire anyway. And they saved his and his wife's asses by getting them out of the country safely. So they did the honorable thing. What traitorous imbecile would want to work for the Cubans if they're seen to throw their assets blithely under the train? Makes perfect sense, and they pulled it all off brilliantly. As for Prendergast, they recognized him for the loser that he is. He was booted out of the Army and had no long-term usefulness to them. Small potatoes. Easy sacrifice."

"And Orgonov? Why a Russian? Why not a Cuban?"

"Simple. The DI has burned all its bridges by sending so many dangles at us over the years that we wouldn't be able to identify a genuine Cuban defector if he came gift wrapped by Santa Claus and certified by the Pope. They knew that any of their own people they sent to us would be polygraphed until they bled, and even then wouldn't be found credible. This was a joint op. They got the SVR to cough up a schmuck like Orgonov, knowing we'd be more inclined to swallow his 'legend.' Pure commie tradecraft. And it worked. It's also revenge for our having rolled up Moscow's sleeper network with that little redheaded tart, Anna Chapman."

"And the mailbox? What did we miss?"

"Oh, yeah. It's so simple. I can't believe we didn't get it. I'm kicking myself."

"Get what?"

"We were looking for *something*. Livingston was looking for the opposite—*nothing*. His handler, Estévez, had *erased* a chalk mark on that box. That was a signal to Livingston that something was wrong. Had the chalk mark not been erased, it would've signaled Livingston that all was okay. Probably also that the delivery was ready for pickup."

"So he immediately went into escape mode."

"That's how I read it," Morgenstern said.

Nick took a deep breath and let it out slowly. "What now?"

"Wait. Wait for the gods to judge our fate. That's all we can do. Meanwhile, there are more Livingstons out there. No doubt about it. Somehow, we've got to convince the higher-ups. But will they be open to listening to us now?"

"They'd be more open to Tommy Flanagan, the Pathological Liar on Saturday Night Live."

Morgenstern chuckled. "Don't let the bastards get you down. Tomorrow's another day."

"Keep the clichés coming, Bart. They're about all I've got to hold onto right now." After hanging up, Nick walked to the bathroom to crack open a bottle of sleep-aid pills. He hadn't actually taken a moment to look at his face in at least two days. He was struck by his reflection in the medicine cabinet mirror. Dark circles appeared under puffy bloodshot eyes. His beard had grown thick, and his hair was unkempt. It was the visage of a man spiraling downward. Where he would land was anybody's guess. He slammed the cabinet door, turned on the faucet, and threw cold water on his face. As he pressed the towel to his face, he saw Philip and Deirdre Livingston staring back, mocking him. "Fool! Fool!" they cackled. He threw the towel against the wall.

The phone rang again. He went back into his bedroom to answer. The crackling sound of long distance static greeted him. "Hello. Hello!"

"Hello," a woman said. "Nick?"

"Yeah, this is Nick. Who's this?"

"Had a bad few days, Nick?"

Nick concentrated. The woman had a Spanish accent, and her voice contained a sultry timbre. "No. It can't be."

"I still think of that beautiful night we had together, Nick. Remember?"

Nick held a hand to his temple. *This can't be happening.* It was *her.* Larisa Montilla. *Holy Christ!* "'A few bad days' is an understatement."

"Aw. Poor Nicky baby. I'm so sorry," she purred. "It wasn't personal, you know."

"You had it all played out from the get-go, didn't you?"

"We had no choice. You guys have been playing rough. We needed to take counteraction."

"What're you talking about?"

"Tsk, tsk. Don't tell me you don't know."

"Know what, goddamn it?"

"Now that's no way to talk to a lady, Nick. By the way, did the lash marks on your bum heal?"

Nick scrunched his eyes and shook his head in a futile effort to throw off a bad memory.

"Mmmm. I've never kissed a man quite like you, Nick—"

"Cut it out! What the hell do you want?"

"Okay, if you're going to be like that, I'll hang up."

Nick struggled to regain his composure. "Uh. No. Don't do that. I'm, uh, sorry. I've been under a lot of stress lately."

"I'll bet you have. And believe me when I tell you that what I... what *we* did in no way was meant as a personal attack on you. In fact, at first, we didn't know you were working on this case. I wish I were there to kiss away the pain."

"Let's stick to business. What did you mean by 'playing rough' and you 'had no choice'?"

Giggles through the static. "Please don't tell me you don't know?"

He waited her out, unwilling to admit he had no idea what she was referring to.

"I guess it's true, then. You really don't know, do you?

My, my, my. So it appears your government is as internally uncommunicative as our own. And you're a democracy. What is this world coming to? Well, it's like this. You may want to sit down and take notes, by the way, Nick."

"Just tell me." He grabbed a pen and pad and cradled the receiver with his shoulder.

"Mirabel de la Cruz in New Jersey, Luís Gabaldón in Virginia, Ulices Peña in Florida. We had to terminate them for two reasons. They were our assets for a long time, but then became traitors; your CIA turned them. And we must safeguard our national security, especially during this time of hooliganism your government is provoking."

"Huh? Uh... and therefore, the hits in Bangkok...?"

"Were revenge by the CIA against us. How do you say? Yes. *Ojo por ojo*. Eye for an eye. Also the ambush killing of our medical team in Colombia. Pure revenge."

"Those guys were guerrilla saboteurs," Nick said.

"It is unimportant what we call them. This is war, Nick. Your CIA will not give up its schemes to destroy our revolution. So now they stir up trouble in eastern Cuba. It's all CIA's doing."

"Why... why are you telling me this?"

"You should know, Nick. It's clear they've kept you in the dark. They're playing you and your Bureau as dupes, pawns in their nefarious plans. And there's another reason I'm being so open."

"Yeah? What's that?"

"We don't need to be enemies, you and I. We proved that, didn't we? Our secret. You love Cuba. It's in your blood. And you love me. I need you to restore peace between our two nations. You can do this, Nick. Work with us. And come and love me again."

Nick hung up.

CHAPTER THIRTY-ONE

Nick hopped in his car and drove to the outer Virginia suburbs, where the sprawl became indistinguishable one block to the next. Like a scene of utopic blandness from a science fiction depiction of the near-future, endless rows of slapped-together cookie cutter townhouse tracts dominated what were a few years ago bucolic farmlands. The masses of buttoned-down denizens of government, insurance companies, law firms, real estate outfits, Beltway Bandits, and contractors of every stripe and persuasion resided in those shoebox complexes. Life there was one of uniformity and conformity.

His GPS guided him to "Heathcrest Estates," one of the innumerable evocations to gauzy green venues of ancient British lore and legend. He turned into the driveway of 5461 Fox Glen Court, a leafy cul-de-sac. He got out and knocked on the townhouse door. A light went on. An eye peered through the peephole.

"Kate, it's me. Nick."

She opened the door a crack, latch chain in place. "It's eleven o'clock. Can it wait 'til tomorrow?"

"It's very important. Can I come in?"

Kate released the latch and opened the door. She was wrapped in a bathrobe, and her hair was wet. "Uh… can I, uh, get you anything?"

"No. I'll cut to the chase. You've been killing Cuban agents. Why?"

Her facial expression went from startled to guarded. "I don't know what you're talking about. How did you know where I live?"

"I'm FBI. We know where everybody lives."

"You look like hell."

"That's what being suspended does to a man who blew a major op and is awaiting transfer orders to Anchorage."

"I'm sorry, Nick."

"Sorry doesn't cut it. I want answers."

Kate backed away a step. "It's late. You're exhausted. I'm tired. Can we continue this conversation another time?"

"No."

"I'm afraid I must ask you to leave."

"Not until I get some answers. There's a dirty little war going on behind the scenes between your agency and the Cuban DI. It's been swirling around me, while I—fat-dumb-and-happy—have been trying to gather evidence and build a case against one of this country's worst traitors. One of my agents, Peña, gets fatally caught in the line of fire. When you said, 'hardliners and progressives are liquidating each other's agents,' you were lying. It was a coverup to mask the CIA and DI killing each other's agents."

Kate crossed her arms. "Need to Know. Need to Know. How many times do I have to tell you? You're not cleared for those compartments. Now go!"

Nick stepped forward until they were almost in physical contact. "I want answers, and I'm not leaving till I get them. Why did they off those three agents? Why did you wipe out their guy and the North Korean in Bangkok?"

Kate looked down and to the side. Nick followed her gaze to a cell phone lying on a side table. She made a lunge for it. Nick blocked her. She attempted to sidestep him, but he blocked her again with his right arm. She fell to the floor. She tried to jump up, but Nick knocked her back down.

"I said I want answers!"

"I'm calling the police!"

Nick grabbed the cell phone and hurled it against the wall. It ricocheted off in pieces.

In a lightning motion, she sprang up and ran for the door. He caught her by the collar. Her robe dropped to her waist, revealing her breasts. Kate instinctively covered them with her arms. She stood motionless for a moment, then swung a knee upward and caught him in the groin. Nick dropped to the floor in paroxysms of pain, holding his crotch.

Kate pulled the robe back up and tied the belt firmly. She again went for the front door, but Nick grabbed her ankle. She landed on top of him. He spun her around so that he hovered above her. He had regained enough strength to pin her hands. She broke one hand free and swung at him, but he blocked it before it could make impact. Kate squirmed under his weight, seeking to free up a leg in order to deliver another testicle-crushing blow. Nick pressed his weight down harder, freezing her in place.

"Tell me, goddammit!" He pressed a forearm onto her throat.

Fear crossed her face. He pressed further, cutting off her oxygen, making major arteries throb.

"Okay!" she croaked.

Nick let up a little. She struggled for breath. Her blond hair was half in her face, the rest in all directions.

"So shoot," Nick commanded.

"They started it."

"What?"

"The Castros are obsessed with us. Their bloated external intelligence apparatus is focused almost entirely on us."

"Tell me something I don't already know."

"Yeah, but they've been sending many more sleepers here, to burrow into American society and build overlapping intel networks. And they've been surprisingly effective."

"Okay. Go on."

"I can't speak comfortably with two hundred pounds of male flesh and bone on me."

"All right. But no funny moves. And I'm one eighty-five."

"Well, then, what am I complaining about?"

He let her get up, but kept close, ready to subdue her again in a flash.

Kate pulled her robe tight and put her hair back in place with her fingers. She sat down on the sofa. "The Cuban Five was only the tip of the iceberg. After they were rolled up in '98, we found out the DI had a training school in Santa Clara dedicated to churning out whole classes of Manchurian candidates to come here and extend their agent networks exponentially.

"In July 2001 alone, we intercepted *fifteen* of their agents in three separate operations. Their missions were to penetrate SOUTHCOM, the exile groups, military bases, and government agencies."

"They didn't make it to U.S. soil?"

"That's right."

"So no trial."

"Yes. No trial."

"Where are they, then?"

"GTMO. In a special facility. Outside the reach of American law, theoretically anyway."

"The murdered sleepers. Mirabel de la Cruz, Luís Gabaldón, and my guy Ulices Peña. What gives?"

"I can't—"

He looked at her menacingly.

"Attack me again, and I swear I'll separate you from your balls," she said coolly.

He took her in—five-feet-nine inches of steeled womanhood, clearly well conditioned. He didn't doubt she'd emasculate him in a second round. And given his lack of rest, poor diet over the past week, and fragile mental state, he had no desire to take her on again.

But he also saw past the ice princess façade. The physical

exertion had filled her fair skin with color. That and her taut frame lent her a fiery beauty—a pagan Norse goddess, alluring yet all-powerful, flawless skin, firm breasts, sleek and powerful legs. Her eyes, while determined, also betrayed passion and curiosity.

He raised his hands in mock surrender. "No trouble. Promise. We're fighting on the same side. You keep talking about Need to Know. I have a *need* to know. I'm FBI, after all, not just another swinging dick. And we're supposed to be working together on the same case, part of the same team."

She studied him for a few seconds. "Okay. We turned Cruz and Gabaldón several years ago. We got them to buy off on a deal. They spill their guts about Cuban intelligence and pass our disinformation onto Havana in return for our not sending them away for life and shaming them before their families as the lying frauds they were. All we had to do was remind them of the Cuban Five—fifteen years to life. They made the right decision and became our double agents-in-place. And they were good. Very good. After so many years living illegally in this country and raising a family, Mirabel de la Cruz realized she'd lost any faith in the system she used to serve. She wanted to help in the end. As for Gabaldón, he was just grateful to turn on his Cuban masters. After all, he was a Dominican who was suborned by their operatives exploiting his financial difficulties."

"And Peña?" Nick asked.

"Poor little Peña. They killed him after they found out he worked for you. Not so different from the others."

"Who killed them?"

Kate shrugged. "They've got wet affairs pros strategically positioned. We may never know who or where they are."

"But wait. *How* did the Cuban DI find out we turned three of their deep cover agents?"

Kate simply looked at his eyes, but said nothing.

"More moles inside our government. The Livingstons aren't the only ones," he said. "And the details we gleaned about their wet affairs hits against the turned agents here–from our own mole inside Cuba."

"All I can tell you is this. You know that Cuba is one of our hardest targets. Only North Korea is harder to penetrate. Recruiting and developing agents inside that country is exceedingly difficult. But we do have assets there, and we protect their identities zealously. If you put a gun to my head and demanded that information, I'd simply tell you to go ahead and shoot. We just lost two valuable assets to the DI, one a Cuban, the other a foreigner. We're convinced at least one was betrayed by a mole inside our government."

"Livingston?"

"No. He didn't have access to that kind of operational intelligence."

"And getting back to the Bangkok hit…"

"All I can tell you is that there was a clear and present danger to our national security. The Cubans were selling secrets that in the hands of Pyongyang risked the lives of American soldiers. It had to be done."

"And they got that intelligence from?"

"Not Livingston. We know that."

"So. Livingston. One down. How many more moles to track down?"

Kate shrugged. Her eyes had softened. Telling him everything seemed to have lifted a burden from her. She shut her eyes in relief, exhaustion, or both. Sitting there, her robe partially open, revealing more of her flawless skin, she seemed so vulnerable, so warm, so inviting.

He leaned over and kissed her softly. She responded in kind.

CHAPTER THIRTY-TWO

Havana

Gen. Larisa Montilla's sedan pulled up to the Palace of the Revolution. She was making more visits to the leadership headquarters since the outbreak of the uprisings in the east, which were spreading to other cities throughout the island. The deaths by heart attack of two of the Politburo's aged leaders within a month of each other and the sclerotic decisionmaking of the remaining thirteen old-guard revolutionaries put more de facto power in her hands. They trusted her implicitly, and sexism hadn't come into play. After decades of seeing up-and-coming young colleagues suddenly purged and marginalized, Cuban civil servants and military officers operated in a state of semiparalysis, afraid to make bold moves or decisions. Montilla, on the other hand, seemed to wear a mantle of invincibility. Rather than being marginalized, she was promoted and given awards. The fact that she wisely kept a below-the-radar public profile was key to her success.

Brig. Gen. Alfredo García Menéndez's car pulled up just behind hers. Getting out of the car, the tall, balding vice minister greeted her with a faint smile. "Difficult times require difficult decisions, eh, Larisa?" he said as they climbed the outside stairs to the main entrance.

"Extraordinary decisions requiring extraordinary measures," she rejoined.

They returned the salutes of two guards at the entrance.

"I fear the harsher we crack down, the greater will be the resistance," García said. "Look at the Middle East."

"I disagree. When the very stability of the country is concerned, when the paramountcy of the revolution is at stake, nothing should be ruled out."

They walked the long corridor and stopped at the elevator. Garcia pressed the Up button.

"We risk massacring our own people," García said in a barely audible voice.

"Correction. Counterrevolutionaries," she replied.

"So is that what you propose we tell them? 'Guns are the answer, comrades'? After the fiasco in Santiago? I worry that units of the Army will revolt. Then what?"

Montilla maintained a stiff bearing. She pressed the button impatiently. The elevator wouldn't come.

"Shit. Does nothing in this country work?" García spat.

They took the stairs to the fourth floor. They were greeted at the President's office by a male aide, who ushered them directly into the power lair of Cuba and asked them to wait in an anteroom. They had been instructed to bring no aides. A minute later, the door to the President's office was opened by the aide, who showed them in. Their salute was returned perfunctorily by the President.

The President rose and gestured for them to be seated at a small table. He opened a folder placed in front of him and flipped through the reports. He looked up with a grave expression. "Demonstrations continue in Santiago. Police beatings are way up here in Havana. There are stirrings in Camagüey, Holguín, and even Pinar del Río. Ten dead in Havana, fifteen in Santiago."

"These uprisings have been quelled, Mr. President," Montilla assured him.

The President nodded to his aide, who pointed a remote control at a video console. A recording came on showing jerky images of mobs overrunning a police station. Several policemen were being pummeled brutally by demonstrators. Others were fleeing for their lives. Smoke emitted from inside the station. The CNN logo graced the bottom of the screen. With another nod from the President, the aide stopped the recording.

"That was in Yaguajay yesterday," the President said. "They tell me ordinary people took those pictures with cellular phones. Do I need to remind you of the importance of the Battle of Yaguajay for the success of our revolution? Cienfuegos and Che became recognized as heroes there."

Montilla cast her eyes downward in shame.

"Mr. President, the crackdowns are only producing more martyrs," García said. "We need to pursue a wholly different approach."

The President lifted an eyebrow. "How?"

"Engage them in dialogue. Engage the people in genuinely implementing the Sixth Party Congress reforms," García urged.

"More mass mobilization?" the leader asked.

"They've had enough of that. Perhaps... allowing more participatory elections. And more rapid implementation of the reforms."

"The new Politburo is working on the latter. As for the former, the party offers a big tent for all," the President said crisply.

"But, Mr. President, two Politburo members recently died. The average age is sixty-eight—"

The President cut Garcia off. "They will soon be replaced."

"Mr. President," Montilla interjected, "the Americans are behind the troubles. Allow me to increase our countermeasures both domestically as well as abroad."

The old man nodded.

"Two American heroes of the revolution recently had to flee here," she said.

"Ah, yes. The Livingstons. I wish to meet them to thank them personally for their service to the revolution."

"Yes, sir. They are now here safely. But just barely. The FBI has stepped up measures to sniff out our agents there. A son of *gusanos* is behind it, but I know how to deal with him. And here in Cuba, we must crush the so-called Arnaldo Ochoa traitors once and for all. Give me a free hand, and I will do both, erase all domestic opposition and keep the *yanquis* at bay."

García stirred but was cut short by a gesture from the President.

"Proceed, General Montilla."

The two were dismissed.

The surge of FAR units into eastern Cuba was expedited just as the rebels were completing their encirclement of Santiago. The route north to Holguín was completely cut off. FAR units from Santiago were stymied in clashes to keep open the Carretera Central west to Bayamo. The MININT commander in Santiago had been sending increasingly urgent messages to Havana, warning of more uprisings, only bigger than previously. Those were accompanied by frantic requests for reinforcements.

The GAZ jeep rocked and bumped along the dirt road circumventing the government stronghold at Guaninao, midway between Bayamo and Santiago. Marcial and Yuri were rushing to meet with Arnaldo Ochoa Brigade subcommanders to finalize the isolation of Santiago and crush demoralized and ammunition-starved FAR troops, so they had broken their own rule of always traveling separately. A two-man jeep led the convoy, while another vehicle with six armed men took up the rear. A culvert lay ahead.

Marcial turned to his son. "Yuri, it is important for Rota's men to link up with those of Irizarry to complete the cutting off of Holguín. This is a strategic encircle—"

Marcial felt intense heat and a sense of floating as a storm of fire lifted his jeep, as well as the lead vehicle, into the air, engulfing them in flames. The boom of the roadside bomb blast echoed off the surrounding hills. Arnaldo Ochoa's commanders flew through the air in opposite directions and landed like marionettes on the hard surface.

The rear jeep screeched to a halt. The soldiers clambered out and ran to their fallen leaders. Just as they arrived, a second explosion erupted, cutting them down.

Hundreds of students gathered near the University of Oriente in Santiago, armed with placards and bullhorns. They were organizing themselves for a procession down Patrice Lumumba Avenue, the same thoroughfare on which the coed Yoandi Álvarez had been raped.

The Black Wasps showed up in ample numbers as well. They were in no mood to put up with rebellious students. They lined up in two flanks in a V-formation, shields and weapons at the ready.

"Freedom now! Freedon now!" the students chanted.

Shots rang out. Protesters fell. Pools of blood formed in the street. The survivors scattered in all directions. Snipers strategically positioned on the top of buildings fired indiscriminately, felling more of the demonstrators. Panic set the young people climbing over each other to get out of the area. Machine gun fire caught those who broke free.

The Black Wasps charged. Scores of students were run down and handcuffed. Rearguard Wasps went in to collect them and throw them into paddy wagons and trucks.

The protest was over almost before it began.

The hastily convened Tribunals for Revolutionary Justice meted out judgments and sentences with more efficiency than any factory had produced anything in Cuba in decades. Thousands of people went through an assembly line process whereby judges passed multiyear jail sentences for offenses ranging from "dangerousness," to "disturbing the socialist order," to "inciting against the socialist state through oral and written enemy propaganda."

Yamilé Acosta, arrested in the wee hours as her eight-year-old daughter cried and her husband stood by helplessly, was given twelve years based on the latter charge.

For captured rebel combatants, the sentences were much harsher. Members of the Arnaldo Ochoa Brigade were quickly convicted of rebellion and sedition, then were summarily shot.

CHAPTER THIRTY-THREE

The information you have been providing has been greatly appreciated by our leadership. Be assured you will be justly recognized for your service in the future. In the meantime, it is imperative that we continue to receive key insights into what your government is planning in a range of areas. Specifically, any information on war games, military maneuvers, and covert operations of any kind is needed urgently.

We also require as much detail as possible on the movements of the CIA director and the Secretary of Defense over the next several weeks and months.

We wish to make a delivery soon. We will be in further contact re details within the next several days.

Finally, we understand and sympathize with your difficult situation and your desire to take a rest from this work. This will be possible once we get through the extraordinary period we are now in. In the meantime, might we suggest you see a specialist regarding your headaches?

Amelia Hernández sat before her laptop screen at a Caribou coffee house near Dupont Circle. She read the decrypted email from Havana one more time, then deleted it. The import of what she had to offer Havana led her to take the extra precaution of doing her espionage communications at an anonymous commercial location.

She took the S1 thumb drive from her handbag and inserted it into her computer. On it was a motherlode of official secrets that she had scanned and downloaded at work. If an alert security officer had been paying the least bit of attention, she'd be sipping tepid jailhouse coffee swill instead of a mocha cappuccino. But she'd had to do it. Cuba was in trouble. Serious trouble.

The first attachment she pulled up from the thumb drive, "OPERATION CHOE-U FREEDOM GUARDIAN," classified SECRET, contained the planning for U.S.-South Korean joint military exercises, one of the largest such operations. The second, "PORTHOLE-12 IMINT SATELLITE OPERATIONS," classified TOP SECRET, was essentially the operating manual for a highly classified spy satellite system. "STU-IV SECURE TELEPHONE KEY CODE DIRECTORY," also TOP SECRET, provided data for unscrambling secure telephonic transmissions. "REPORTING AND COLLECTION NEEDS: POLITICAL LEADERS," was a telegraphic instruction marked SECRET sent to all U.S. embassies outlining Washington's tasking requests for information on foreign leaders. "USSTRATCOM /USCYBERCOM: PLANS & POLICY 2012," a SECRET document of the U.S. Strategic Command laying out priorities for countering cyber-warfare against the United States.

With the click of her mouse, Amelia Hernández sent enough critical information on America's national security to a dedicated enemy to open it to attacks ranging from conventional warfare to terrorism.

The twelve-hour flight from D.C. to Anchorage gave Nick plenty of time to think, about his future, his fallibilities, the predictability of a dead-end career and sullied reputation, and the notion of getting out and working in the private sector. For the time being, he would help enforce the nation's laws in the state ranked forty-seventh by population. The key issues for the Bureau's Anchorage office were methamphetamine trafficking, a bank robber on the loose, a case of child pornography, and one nutcase who threatened to kill a judge.

Exile. He was being sent into exile just as his Miami boss Clement Rourke had predicted could happen. The snowy peaks of the Chugach Mountains lay majestically below. The endless unspoiled wilderness gave Nick a welcome liberating sensation. Perhaps his time in Alaska would be an escape more than an exile. And just maybe opportunity would knock in that last frontier.

As Nick took his time walking to the baggage claim area, his cellphone rang.

"Nick. Clement here."

"Right," was all Nick could muster.

"We've got a problem. A major problem."

Nick's head ached after the long flight. An urgent call about "a major problem" could only mean the system wasn't through with him. Dismissal? Legal charges? What next?

"There's a hemorrhage of classified information. I can't give details over an open line, but all indicators point to your female friend in Havana. Since you're the only individual in the USG who's actually dealt with her and knows her m.o., we're calling you back to work on a new task force, effective immediately."

Nick was stunned. From exile back to the action, just like that. In fact, he hadn't even gotten to experience real exile.

"Nick? You there?"

"Uh, yeah."

"This gives you a second chance, Nick. We who've worked with you and know your capabilities feel you got shafted. Road kill on the way to scapegoating."

"I'll be there." Nick went to ticketing and booked a return flight.

Nick had come to resent PowerPoint. The mind-numbing bullet points outlining one factoid after another had a hypnotic effect on his fatigued mind. And the lousy office coffee he had been chug-a-lugging since his direct return from Alaska was doing more to corrode his digestive tract than to jumpstart his brain.

- *Livingstons defection a great blow*
- *Demonstrates an extensive & effective DI clandestine network here*
- *Ongoing hemorrhage of classified info*
- *Proves DI has additional moles inside our foreign affairs apparatus*
- *Need for increased CI ops tempo*
- *CONOPS for organizing resources to address Cuban espionage*

The presenter, Eric James, was an ambitious, self-assured operator adept at getting others to do his bidding, while never having an original thought or taking a risk that might damage his carefully constructed upward career trajectory. Another careerist lacking a soul. His PowerPoint presentation had all the originality of the ingredients section on a box of corn flakes. Yet James had a knack for making his deliveries sound weighty by dint of his deep voice, direct gaze, and six-foot-four-inch frame.

James was highly skilled at one thing—sucking up to his superiors and bullshitting them into believing he was the best thing since Sunday night football. He was put in charge of the Cuba Counterintelligence Joint Task Force, quickly formed in the wake of the disastrous Operation MOPED.

Nick was beginning to regret leaving Anchorage. Task Force members Nick had known and worked with for years steered clear of him, avoiding any stain of failure from a Special Agent who'd botched one of the most sensitive and sexiest operations in years. It was equally clear to Nick that he was there to be called upon to give brief and concrete answers to direct questions relating to Montilla, the Cuban DI, and the rebels fighting the communist government. Otherwise, he was expected to sit down and shut up. No operational role. Period. He shared a windowless office with two interns.

After the briefing, James asked Nick to see him in his office. As a Special Agent in Charge and task force chief, James had a spacious office overlooking Constitution Avenue. His ego wall, a hallmark of all self-absorbed Washington functionaries, contained meticulously hung bureaucratic awards and photos of James shaking hands with past FBI directors and assorted Washington potentates. His desk had the requisite photos of the wife and trophy children. The papers in his full inbox were neatly piled, nary a sheet sticking out of place. The rest of the workspace was devoid of any mementoes or the routine messes that most office denizens managed to build up in the course of a busy workday.

"Nick, glad we pulled you back in from the Arctic Circle," James said in his baritone. He flashed a perfunctory smile.

"All those years in Miami were ill preparation for The Last Frontier State," Nick said lamely.

"Sorry about MOPED's falling apart like that. CI is a tricky business."

Intended or not, the comment was an insult, addressing Nick as if he were a wide-eyed boy scout out of his depth. But that was typical of James, the alpha-male who habitually pissed out his turf and slam-dunked others in their place to let them know in no uncertain terms who was in charge.

"We had them," Nick said. "The Livingstons. We had them in our sights. But we were betrayed by other Cuban moles inside our govern—"

James held up a hand. "We're pursuing a *fresh* approach. There's enough evidence out there of continued leaking of government secrets."

Tell me something I don't already know, Nick thought.

"Nick, I want you to advise me on what you know about DI operations."

Yeah. Whatever. "Sure. Any way I can help."

"Please have a report on the DI on my desk by COB tomorrow, plus what you know about this woman, Montilla." He pronounced her name Mahn-til-la.

"I can provide a lot of insight on her—"

James got up, gave Nick's shoulder a paternal slap, and shook Nick's hand. "Thanks, Nick."

End of meeting.

CNN (RIYADH) - In a severe blow to Washington's efforts to support Yemen's shaky leadership against al-Qaeda and other militant Islamist groups, CNN has learned that a covert U.S. Special Forces training team in that country was ambushed outside of its base camp near the city of Taiz. Details are sketchy, but initial reports are that at least a dozen Navy SEALs and Delta Force troops were killed in what one administration source described as a "well-planned and well-executed attack." The official, who would not be named, stated that the militants' successful attack "could only have been pulled off with advance detailed information on the Americans' movements. This is the worst attack on our Special Forces personnel since Blackhawk Down in Somalia." A Pentagon spokesman would not comment on the report, citing the classified nature of Special Forces deployments.

Amelia Hernández sat with her feet up, sipping a cup of Jasmine tea as she watched the CNN report.

"Así siempre a los tiranos," she murmured. *Thus always to tyrants.*

CHAPTER THIRTY-FOUR

Havana

Eduardo Bermúdez, a.k.a. CALLICO, never considered himself a brave man. But on his final day of life, he was calm and determined to go out with dignity. As they marched him out of his cell at Combinado del Este prison, the dawn sun settled on his face for the last time. He closed his eyes and took a deep breath. Sea air. How he loved that fresh aroma of life.

In the middle of the large field was a single wooden post. Before they tied him to it, they asked if he had a last request. He whispered it through his parched mouth.

The captain of the squad looked at him in surprise,then gave a brief nod.

Bermúdez approached the six men comprising the firing squad and shook each of their hands. His executioners' reactions ranged from shock to shame. A tear ran down the cheek of a nineteen-year-old.

Bermudez addressed them all. "I forgive you for what you are about to do. You are only doing your duty."

They returned and bound him to the wooden post. He refused a blindfold.

The captain stood back and erect. "*Preparen!*"

The firing squad snapped to attention with rifles shouldered. "*Apunten!*"

They aimed their weapons at the condemned man.

Bermudez shouted, "Down with the Castros! Long live Cu—"

"*Fuego!*"

The simultaneous blasts of six guns echoed off the massive prison walls. Seagulls flocked to the sky from nearby Monumental Highway.

Bermúdez slumped lifeless.

The captain walked over to the body. One more shot rang out as he gave the obligatory coup de grace shot to the head with his pistol.

Marcial and his son were allowed to meet for two minutes prior to their rendezvous with a firing squad at the Special Troops "Black Wasps" base at Baracoa, west of Havana.

Marcial stared longingly at Yuri, his mind going through a mental slideshow of memories of babyhood, boyhood, family outings, days of pride and joy.

"Father."

"Yes, Yuri?"

"Did you love Mama?"

"Oh, yes. As much as any man can love a woman."

"I've missed her so. Do you think she knows what's happening to us?"

Marcial smiled. Yuri the boy had returned. Captain Zero was gone. Marcial shook his head. "I don't know, son." He embraced Yuri, and they wept.

"Father, did we do the right thing? Rebelling?"

"We fought evil, which is always a good thing. Others will carry forth the cause."

"I... I never got to start a family, to truly love a woman." Tears ran down Yuri's cheeks.

"Time's up!" the block warden declared.

Six Black Wasp troops marched to the cell in the dawn light.

Two of them bound Marcial's and Yuri's hands behind their backs. The squad then led them down the brig corridor. Marcial limped from the injury he'd incurred from the IED explosion. Long shadows formed as the new sun appeared.

A single wooden post awaited them at the parade ground. They would be shot in sequence. A six-man firing squad stood at parade rest, rifle butts on the ground, barrels supported in their right hands.

The lantern-jawed captain approached. "Who will go first?"

"Me," Marcial said.

"No, Father—"

"It is wrong for children to die before their parents," Marcial snapped. He nodded at the captain. "Proceed."

Marcial was led to the stake and tied to it.

"Have you any last requests?" the captain asked.

"Yes. That you live productively in a free Cuba," Marcial replied.

A soldier offered a blindfold. Marcial shook his head. "I wish to stare death in the face."

The captain strode back fifteen paces.

"*Preparen!*" he commanded.

The firing squad came to attention, shouldering their rifles.

"*Apunten!*"

They aimed their weapons.

"*Fuego!*"

The deafening explosion of six simultaneous rifle shots shook the atmosphere.

The captain lay dead.

The squad then trained their weapons on the two soldiers assisting the execution. The soldiers raised their hands, shock and fear on their faces.

A member of the squad ran over to the captain to verify that he was dead. Two others untied Marcial and Yuri.

The squad leader saluted Marcial. "We are at your service, Colonel. But we must hurry."

A truck pulled into the parade ground. Marcial and Yuri jumped into the rear, followed by the rebel firing squad. Gunshots rang out as soldiers loyal to the regime rushed onto the scene. The driver floored it, crashed through the barrier at the base entrance gate, and sped off ahead of a hail of bullets.

Gen. Alfredo García Menéndez made sure his face registered shock and anger upon being informed by an aide of the botched execution and bold escape at the Baracoa Barracks. He immediately issued orders to his intelligence staff to get on the case pronto and to keep him informed.

García then closed the door to his office and took his morning cafecito to his desk. He sat back and stretched. The coffee's rich aroma filled his nostrils as he closed his eyes.

Angola. The Loma River. Abandoned by his MPLA troops. Taken prisoner by the South Africans. Two years detention. At first, his captors had been harsh, but they had softened up over time, as did he. And over the months, poring over the generous reading materials they provided, he came to see the world as it really was, not as depicted in the turgid and closed screeds of communist propaganda. Eventually, they introduced him to the nice American who called himself Andy. A young man like himself at the time, Andy, who spoke fluent, accentless Spanish, re-introduced him to García's sister, Luisa, long resettled in Miami. Andy also set up a Swiss bank account for him, into which would be deposited thousands of dollars a month. CIA gave the code name STONEWALL. The money would be waiting for him the day he decided to join Luisa in Miami. But what had really pushed him over the line were the hundreds of Cuban youths whose lives were wasted in quixotic foreign adventures by a delusional dictator. He wanted a role in a new Cuba. Finally, that new page would soon be turned in his country.

If his role in the dramatic escape of the Marcials were uncovered, it would be his turn before a firing squad.

CENTRAL INTELLIGENCE AGENCY
T O P S E C R E T 301515Z DEC STAFF
CITE MEXICO CITY 327914
TO: IMMEDIATE DIRECTOR
WNINTEL RYBAT
SUBJECT: AMSTONEWALL INFO ON DI ASSETS
WITHIN USG

1. LI-WANDERER RETURNED FROM TEN DAYS IN HAVANA 30 DEC WITH FULL REPORT FROM AM STONEWALL WITH FOCUS ON COUNTERINTELLIGENCE. AM-STONEWALL REPORTS A CUBAN DI ASSET HAS BEEN IN PLACE AT DIA IN WASHINGTON FOR THE PAST FIFTEEN YEARS. SOURCE STATES HE DOES NOT KNOW THE NAME OR OTHER SPECIFIC INFORMATION ON THIS ASSET. THE DI'S MOST SENSITIVE ASSETS ARE RUN OUT OF AN OFFICE CALLED THE "SPECIAL ACTIVITIES UNIT," WHICH FUNCTIONS OPERATIONALLY AND PHYSICALLY SEPARATELY FROM DI HEADQUARTERS. THIS UNIT IS COMMANDED BY MAJ. GEN. LARISA MONTILLA (NFI).

2. THE DI REGARDS THE DIA ASSET AS ONE OF ITS MOST PRIZED AND SENSITIVE. AS A RESULT, MG MONTILLA STRICTLY CONFINES DISTRIBUTION OF INTEL PRODUCED BY THIS ASSET TO

THE CUBAN PRESIDENT, COMMUNIST PARTY HEAD AND DEFENSE MINISTER IN EYES ONLY REPORTS AND ORAL BRIEFINGS UNDERTAKEN BY THE GENERAL PERSONALLY. AMSTONEWALL HAS HEARD ABOUT THE DIA ASSET FROM COLLEAGUES OVER THE YEARS. SOURCE, HOWEVER, IS NOT CLEARED INTO THAT PROGRAM. SOURCE BELIEVES DIA ASSET HAS PROVIDED AND CONTINUES TO PROVIDE A WEALTH OF INFORMATION ON SOME OF THE MOST SENSITIVE USG INTEL OPERATIONS AND ANALYSES. FULL REPORT TO FOLLOW SEPTEL.

3. NO FILE. ALL TOP SECRET.

Kate put the cable from the CIA's Mexico City station down and let out a long breath. In the arcane world of CIA cryptonyms, "LI" signified Mexico and "AM" represented Cuba. "Wanderer" was a Mexican national who operated as a cutout agent for the Agency and was able to travel to Cuba frequently under cover as a businessman. "Stonewall" was the Cuban asset he controlled.

"We'll need to get this over to the Bureau and SECDEF immediately." She sat opposite Kent Croswell, the Deputy Director for the National Clandestine Service, the CIA's arm that runs spies. Three underlings flanked Kate at the small conference table.

"Hmm," Croswell murmured. "No. Let's not. It would only 'legalize' the problem. Last thing we want is a bunch of flat-footed fibbies kicking in the doors and bringing everything crashing down. And STONEWALL is an extremely close-held asset, too valuable to risk exposure. This is strictly an intel matter for the time being. We need to sniff out this DIA mole, watch him or her, learn everything we can about the m.o., then turn the bastard around. 'Make them an offer they can't refuse,' to quote the Godfather." Croswell snorted a laugh at his own unoriginal humor. The underlings followed suit, as if on cue.

"Then, once they're turned," Crosswell continued, "we'll bleed 'em dry for everything they know and use 'em as a funnel through which to feed Havana an avalanche of crap intel. We'll bust those Cuban SOBs wide open and finally bring them down, including this mysterious General Montilla. And hopefully, the armed opposition will also benefit. Once the mole is of no further use to us, we'll call in law enforcement and put the traitor away forever—a plea bargain, life without parole in lieu of the execution gurney for having cooperated with us. I'll clear the program, which we'll call Operation COUNTDOWN, with the DNCS, DCI and DNI and DoD, but I foresee no problems."

"And the Cuba Counterintelligence Joint Task Force? Eric James? What do I tell them?" Kate asked.

"Nothing," Croswell replied.

CHAPTER THIRTY-FIVE

Nick reached across the table and took Kate's hand. She seemed distracted, and she only gave him a weak smile before withdrawing her hand. She picked up the menu.

"What's wrong?" he asked.

"Oh. Uh. Nothing. What's good here?"

"The *boliche* is succulent. Best in town." Nick studied her face—unreadable. Her pale eyes had a sweetness to them, but her lovely face withheld emotion. Trained intel operatives were good at concealing their emotions.

"Ah. Yes." She nodded and closed her menu. "I'll take that."

"Kate, I want to apologize for the other night..."

Whatever distraction was preoccupying her left, and she focused on Nick. "Oh. It's... it's... okay. All is forgiven." She flashed a perfunctory grin and fidgeted with her hands.

"No. I really lost it. Something I almost never do."

"You've been under a lot of pressure. As have I," she said.

Nick sat back and took her in. Kate responded in kind. They were silent, yet they were connecting.

The waitress brought their drinks. Nick raised his draft beer, proposing a toast. Kate responded with her iced tea.

"Here's to... here's to truth," he said.

She winced.

"Did I say something wrong?"

"Uh, no. Of course not."

He leaned over the table to kiss her, but she turned away.

He plopped back in his seat, disappointed. "The other thing from the other night. I thought we had something. At least the beginning of something."

Kate stared back at him intently, her expression a mix of emotions: confusion, anger, steeliness. Finally, she said, "I'm a first generation daughter of a Ukrainian factory worker father and a Polish housecleaner mother. I grew up in Chicago and Dubuque, living in small apartments on the wrong side of the tracks. I wore hand-me-downs and went to shitty public schools. But I got myself into Clarke College on a ROTC scholarship. I worked multiple crap jobs to get that degree. I'm twenty-nine, on the cusp of thirty, and here I am, a CIA case officer. I owe nothing to anybody. I'm my own woman, and I'm proud of it. And you?"

Nick was taken aback. "Well, uh… I'm also first generation. Folks from Cuba, as you know. Settled in Miami. I got my B.A., then law degree. I'm a Bureau lifer. Nothing remarkable, really."

"You were comfortably middle class. Upper middle class. Am I right?"

"Yeah. Sure."

"B.A. from Yale. Fordham Law. Paid for by daddy?"

He didn't like the edge in her voice. "What of it?"

"I know people like you. Silver spoon. Sense of entitlement. Look down on people like me."

"What the—"

"Oh, I'm seeing all right. A roll in the hay with some trailer trash. One way to get your kicks!"

Nick got up and threw down his napkin. He signaled for the check. She grabbed her purse and stormed out of the restaurant.

After tossing some cash on the table, Nick ran after her. He caught up with her and blocked her path. She ducked around him and continued on her brisk jaunt.

Nick sprinted up to her and grabbed her shoulder. "I think I'm owed an explanation!"

"I *told* you I'd separate you from your balls if you laid another hand on me!" Kate spat through clenched teeth.

"What the hell's going on? One moment, we're collaborators, maybe even lovers. Or so I thought. Next moment, it's class warfare. What gives?"

Kate glowered at him. Fire shot from her eyes. Blood suffused her face. Veins throbbed in her neck and temples. She was wild. And irresistibly beautiful.

Nick grabbed her and kissed her hungrily. Instead of a knee to the groin, he won her passion. She gave as well as she got. Passersby clapped at the sidewalk lovers, some flashing thumbs up. A passing car honked approval.

When they came up for air, they embraced tightly. He ran his fingers through her hair.

Then she pushed herself from him and looked away.

"What is it?" Nick asked.

"We toasted to the truth."

"Yeah. And?"

"That's something I can't promise."

Amelia Hernández pulled up Intelink-TS on her screen. "JOINT WORLDWIDE INTELLIGENCE COMMUNICATIONS SYSTEM" appeared in bold letters. She entered her username and password, then answered several routine verification questions. The top-secret intranet enabled CIA, DIA, the State Department, and other agencies to share highly sensitive information. Anything entered into it was disseminated through the vast U.S. government secure-intranet system.

She plugged in the thumb drive she had smuggled in that morning, the "delivery" her Cuban handlers had promised in their last message. With a tap-tap-tap of her fingers, Amelia set loose the sophisticated and destructive virus provided to her by her Cuban overseers.

Next, she downloaded the abbreviated schedules of the Secretary of Defense and the CIA Director made available to the intelligence community. Those she would transmit to Havana from her home that evening, fulfilling her overseers' other request.

When the Emergency Action Message, or EAM, flashed across the screen of the operations officer at the 625th Strategic Operations Squadron command center at Offutt Air Force Base in Nebraska, Major Joe Chavez scrambled. It was 0300. Following standard operating procedures, he rousted the Squadron's commander, Lt. Gen. Chet Rankin, out of bed.

"What's it direct us to do?" the bleary-eyed general asked.

"To execute a Major Attack Option immediately," Chavez replied.

"Target?"

"People's Republic of China. Through launches of Minuteman III ICBMs."

"Where's the duty E-6B?"

"Coordinates 45.67 north by 111.03 west."

"Where's that?"

"Uh, Bozeman, Montana, sir."

"What TACAMO links have been activated?"

The major quickly checked with the commo duty officer. "None... none, sir."

"Get me Strike Command. Now!"

The 625th's emergency action staff activated a crisis link with the commanding officer of the Air Force Global Strike Command at Barksdale Air Force Base, Louisiana.

"Hank," Rankin said. "We just received an EAM. But no other links have been activated, and we just heard from the duty E-6B that they didn't receive it. I need to verify now whether this is legit."

Lt. Gen. Hank Schenkmann jumped out of bed and called his duty officer. After a heart-stopping twenty-five seconds, he replied, "There is no such order from the National Command Authority. I repeat. There is no such order. Stand down. I repeat. Stand down. No two-man rule execute. Do you understand, General?"

"Got it. What the fuck just happened?"

"I don't know, but we've already received a JCS counter-order from the NMCC. Some glitch almost got us into a nuclear war with China. Holy Jesus."

Carter Grayson made a last-minute review of his speech before the graduating class of the U.S. Naval War College at Newport, Rhode Island. "Military officers in the twenty-first century must have a broad strategic overview in order to fully comprehend and carry out their mission..." blah, blah. Yet another cookie-cutter address churned out by the SECDEF speech-writing staff. But it fit the bill and hopefully would inspire the fast-track mid-level officers.

He looked out the window of his heavily armored Chevy Suburban followed by two staff cars packed with security guards and aides. Narragansett Bay shone like a sparkling blue-green sapphire. The Secretary made a mental note to again take up his passion for sailing when he retired in six weeks. He'd take the grandkids out on Puget Sound back home.

"And as the President lays out in the National Security Strategy of the United States, the defense of the nation begins with its military personnel..." yadda, yadda. Grayson fought fatigue as the small convoy crossed onto Training Station Road causeway, toward the entrance of the war college. He hadn't had a break in years. He'd revealed it to no one, but his doctor had said his heart wouldn't survive another term as Secretary of Defense. Grayson had simply told the President that he wanted to spend more time with his family as his reason for stepping down.

He was developing another of those blasted headaches brought on by pressure and exhaustion. He reached into his jacket pocket for his medication.

Four IEDs fifteen feet apart on either side of the causeway ended the SECDEF's life as the pentolite explosive seared through the Suburban's armored plating and instantly shredded steel and human flesh alike.

Gen. Montilla's hitman for the mission was already out of the state, settling back into his small Fall River, Massachusetts, apartment. The hitman was a modest, hardworking immigrant mechanic from the Canary Islands and a deep cover agent for the Cuban Directorate of Intelligence.

CHAPTER THIRTY-SIX

Havana

Workmen were putting the finishing touches on the shiny new brass plaque outside the office suite of the new Minister of Interior on the top floor of MININT headquarters. *Gen. Larisa Montilla, Ministro del Interior.*

García entered the suite with trepidation. He had become beholden to her, his nemesis and new boss. She had played her hand masterfully in the high-stakes poker game of Cuban politics. In contrast to so many others who dared to show original thinking or questioned the policies of *los líderes,* Montilla had learned the delicate art of acting boldly while showing absolute allegiance to her superiors and unwavering belief in a system everyone knew to be morally bankrupt and self-destructive in its internal contradictions.

He saluted her as he entered the office. She remained seated, acknowledging his salute with a slight nod.

She motioned him to a chair in front of her large desk. "Well, General, aren't you going to congratulate me?"

"Congratulations."

"I don't need to tell you, General García, that our nation faces difficult times. We face enemies both within and from abroad. As we brace ourselves for new battles, every cadre must demonstrate stiffened resolve and loyalty to the revolution."

García remained silent.

"And I expect you to act on your loyalty in two ways: ferret out and report on those whose loyalty is suspect, and vigorously foil the schemes of our external enemies, who now feel more emboldened than ever to subvert us."

"Bullshit," García responded.

Montilla's eyes widened. "What?"

"Let's speak frankly, if not comradely, shall we? You are the most powerful person in Cuba today because Raúl is in intensive care with his second heart attack, Fidel is sliding deeper into dementia by the day, everyone else is too cowardly to take a breath, and you've managed to pull the wool over their eyes through your feigned ideological purity, cleverly exploiting your femininity and by—"

"By what? I'll have you arrested!"

"—by being the daughter of Che Guevara."

Montilla stiffened. The color drained from her face.

Garcia shook his head. "Oh, come now. You don't deny it."

"I'm proud of it," she said through clenched teeth. "But it is not why I am where I am."

"Nonsense. Of course it is. That's why they, the brothers, fawn all over you. Especially Fidel. But being whispered about as Che's 'bastard' child… well, that's a little too much for our morally hypocritical leadership to take, even on our tropical island of passion-filled people. But what's worse is being half-American, the daughter of an American journalist, Gertrude Rash. Wasn't that her name? Father was U.S. Marine general. Her mother was descended from one of the signers of the Declaration of Independence. About as blue-blooded as one can be in that country. Che had a fling with her. And then came you."

Montilla fidgeted and wrung her hands, the steeliness in her eyes replaced by vulnerability and fear. "How do you know this?"

García flicked his hand dismissively. "It's not important. As one intelligence officer to another, I don't need to educate you on such matters. But I am not so naïve as to think your family tree, if revealed, would do you in. It is the other information that alone, or in tandem with your heritage, would prove fatal, General."

García opened his leather portfolio, reached in and took out a stack of photographs. He tossed them on her desk.

Montilla's face registered horror as she looked through the pictures of Nick Castillo eating dinner, kissing, and making love with her.

"Now, here's what I want," García said. "Full and regular access to all intelligence as well as plans coming out of the Special Activities Unit, policy documents from the Politburo and Armed Forces, and your obedience as I feed you instructions on new and more constructive policy directions our government will take."

"Let me guess. To begin with a rapprochement with the United States?"

García pursed his lips. "Perhaps."

"How long have you been working for them?"

García remained silent.

"Why?" she persisted.

"To save what's left of our country from you and your ilk. Now we face destruction from your reckless and stupid act of assassinating the American Secretary of Defense. Your disguising it as an act of Islamist terrorism won't hold for long. It's only a matter of time that the Americans get to the bottom of it and connect the dots."

"Oh, no. They will not find out," Montilla said.

García was taken aback. "Why not?"

"Because of this." Montilla reached into her top desk drawer, pulled out a Makarov pistol, and fired two shots into García's head.

Defense Intelligence Agency
DIAC, Bolling Air Force Base, Virginia

When Amelia Hernández arrived at work, she detected nothing unusual, but she was still a nervous wreck. Nightmares had been accompanying her increasingly frequent migraines. When she had looked in the mirror that morning, dark circles had lined her puffy eyes.

She had a hard time concentrating on her work. Her boss inquired after her health, which made her even more anxious. Was his suspicion aroused? Would he report her to Security?

The Cubans were getting bolder with more frequent requests for official secrets. She'd been getting sloppy, smuggling way too many materials out, including actual documents, which she had never done before, and emailing that much more out to her handlers. She'd been getting the flash drives confused, further driving up her anxiety level and intensifying her migraines. And every time she informed the Cubans she wanted to take time off, they kept delaying the request.

When she arrived at her cubicle, she sat down, carefully looked around in all directions, then opened her lunch container. She lifted the bread on her turkey and mayo sandwich. The R-1 flash drive was there. She closed her eyes and breathed in deeply. She exhaled slowly, as she had been taught in Pilates. She inhaled again and focused her mind on a faraway island, a tropical island with warm aquamarine waves lapping at the shore. The sky was bright blue, crowned with a golden sun. Ah, yes. That was good.

"Amelia Hernández Colorado. Come with us. Now."

She opened her eyes to a phalanx of beefy men surrounding her. One flashed a badge. Another drew her arms behind her and handcuffed her. Two others lifted her and dragged her away, while others pored over her desk, marking it off with yellow tape as a crime scene. A migraine was coming on.

CHAPTER THIRTY-SEVEN

Rural Virginia

Amelia Hernandez spent the two-hour trip inside a windowless van. The large men who flanked her remained silent during the entire trip. They ignored her demands to see their IDs and to tell her where she was being taken. Finally, the driver parked in front of a rustic cabin.

Inside, three men and a woman sat around a pinewood table. She was promptly shown to a hard wooden chair. Her years inside the U.S. intelligence community told her it was a safe house—generic, devoid of personal trappings, and occupied by several knuckledraggers.

Once seated, she said, "I demand to know who you are and why am I here. Am I under arrest?"

"I am Mr. Smith," one of the men said. He pointed to one of the other men. "And that is Mr. Jones. That's all you need to know for now."

The woman and the third man sat expressionless against the opposite wall.

"If I am not under arrest, then I demand to be set free. I know my constitutional rights. You have no—"

"Shut up," Mr. Smith said. "You've been an agent for Cuban intelligence for fifteen years. We know your M.O. We know your contacts. We know what you've been giving them. Your treason has resulted in the deaths of American personnel and human assets. You're facing the death penalty, Ms. Hernandez."

Amelia feigned shock. She opened her mouth to protest.

Mr. Smith dropped a stack of papers in front of her. "Go ahead. Look at the evidence. Take your time."

Amelia's gaze went from the nondescript, balding Mr. Smith to the pile of papers. She leafed through them: transcripts of her encounters with CUBINT officers, copies of her secure email correspondence with the Cuban Directorate of Intelligence, photographs taken clandestinely of her conducting surveillance detection runs and picking up and leaving materials at drop sites.

Mr. Smith laid a thumb drive on the table. "We found this in your lunch today." He plopped a stack of transcripts next to the drive. "Here are the contents we took off the drive. And if you're wondering how we got all this incriminating evidence off your computer, simply pressing Delete won't erase information from your hard drive. That stuff remains unless you use a special erase function to cleanse it."

Mr. Jones placed yet another stack of documents in front of her. "Here are the charges that will be contained in your indictment. Fifteen counts of espionage. Violations of Title 18, Part I, chapter 37, paragraph 794, the Espionage Act: 'Gathering or delivering defense information to aid a foreign government.'"

Mr. Smith placed both hands on the table and hunched forward, his face inches from hers. "Here's the deal, Amelia. We can call in the FBI to arrest you formally, in which case all of this incriminating stuff will be distilled into a legal indictment. You'll be tried at the Eastern District Court in Alexandria where the District Attorney—at our behest— will seek the death penalty. Think about it, Amelia. You'll be strapped to a gurncy in an antiseptic room and injected with a lethal potion to die like a stray dog at the pound. Your family will be inflicted with shame. They'll read about the details of your execution in the papers."

Amelia no longer could keep her composure. She blinked rapidly. Her pressed lips trembled. Her breathing and heartbeat accelerated. "Or?"

Mr. Smith stood up and crossed his arms. "Or you can cooperate fully with us—unbeknownst to your pals in Havana—

and feed them the information we'll give you. If you play ball, and I mean batting a thousand to the final inning, you'll live."

"What do you mean, 'live'?"

"Life without parole."

"Where?"

"Supermax. The Alcatraz of the Rockies. We might even be willing to back off the Hanssen module."

"Which is?"

"Oh, Bob is in solitary in his cell twenty-three hours every day, with one hour to exercise in the prison yard. Alone. For life."

Amelia began to weep. She covered her face with her hands.

"You decide, Amelia. Life or death. You've got one minute." Mr. Smith made a show of looking at his watch.

Havana

Larisa Montilla stood in front of the window of her ministerial office on the eighth floor of MININT headquarters. She looked past the vacant Plaza de la Revolución, past the concrete erection that was the José Martí Memorial, and stared at the Communist Party headquarters building looming just beyond the memorial. She concentrated. What was it that Che said about power? "Power is the sine qua non strategic objective of the revolutionary forces, and everything must be subordinated to this basic endeavor. There are no borders in this struggle to the death."

"Oh, Papa, I want so to believe what you said about power and defending the revolution to the death. As Che's daughter, I have a sacred commitment to honor. But, Papa, sometimes… sometimes, I am not sure. The world has changed so much since you died, and I never knew you. I just don't know…" She clenched her fists.

There was a knock on the door.

Montilla collected herself. "Enter."

Three MININT officers walked into the room. The senior man, a colonel, saluted. A second set up an easel with posters.

"Proceed," Montilla commanded.

"Yes, comrade Minister," the colonel replied. He turned to the easel. "Operation HATUEY." He turned over a poster to reveal an artistic depiction of the Indian rebel who had fought the Spanish colonizers in the early eighteenth century. "We are prepared to launch this operation at your command, Minister."

"The *yanquis* are again mobilizing against us," Montilla said. "First, they foment counterrevolution throughout our island. Now they are deploying their forces clearly in preparation for an attack on our homeland. There are no borders in this struggle to the death. We must strike at them if we are to safeguard our revolution. And strike hard!"

"Yes, comrade Minister." The colonel flipped over the next graphic.

It was a photo of the President of the United States.

Fall River, Massachusetts

The moonlike glow from the laptop screen reflected on Miguel Guimerá's angular face as he sat in the dark in his one-bedroom apartment in the working class Flint neighborhood of Fall River.

> *Operation Hatuey is hereby launched. Your orders are to activate Cell B and proceed according to the operational plans previously formulated.*

The bogus Canary Islands immigrant nodded. "*Siempre contigo, Fidel,*" he murmured. *Ever with you, Fidel.*

CHAPTER THIRTY-EIGHT

"I'm going back," Nick said. He threw several shirts into the duffel bag.

"Are you crazy?" Kate shot back as she dressed. "You're in so much hot water now. This'll finish you. Not to mention you'll risk getting yourself killed."

"Yeah, well. What was it Bob Dylan said? 'When you got nothin', you got nothin' to lose.'"

"So you're going to save Cuba all by yourself? One man. A foreigner, to boot. Why not pack your Batman cape while you're at it?"

"Kate, I don't need this right now. Lay off! I'm the only officer in the vast USG who knows Montilla and her environs, who has the contacts and knows his way around. And she's got to be stopped before she assassinates the next cabinet officer, or God knows who else."

"That's why we spend eighty billion dollars on the best intel establishment on the planet and another seven hundred billion on the best military. You... *we* are paid to work within the structure, to lend our expertise."

"I tried that. What do I get in return? A windowless cubicle with two interns and no work. And they, the 'best and the brightest,' sit on their hands and dawdle while the so-called decision-makers play Cover Your Ass. Meanwhile, Cuba spirals out of control, leaderless except for one megalomaniacal Bloody Mary whose paranoia and ruthless actions know no bounds."

Kate finished buttoning her blouse, then stepped between Nick and his duffel lying on the unmade bed. "Don't go! This is being taken care of!"

Nick locked his eyes on hers. "What do you mean, 'being taken care of'?"

Kate turned away. She straightened her skirt and checked her face and hair in the bedroom mirror.

He put his hand on her shoulder and swung her back around. "I said, what do you mean, 'being taken care of'?"

Fire shot from her icy blues. She crossed her arms. "Do you really think this government is going to sit idly by after being attacked? It's being taken care of. Let's leave it at that!"

"Oh! Here we go again. Need to Know! Well, sweetheart, I'm fed up with all the secrets, and I'm fed up with being cut out. Screw it!" He scrawled something on a piece of paper and handed it to her. "Here. This is radio frequency, clandestine email, and code words for contacting Colonel Marcial. If anything happens to me, it might come in handy."

"And what about us?" she asked.

"You said not long ago that the truth was something you couldn't promise me. Kate, relationships are based on truth. When you can promise me that, let me know." He zipped the duffel and heaved it over his shoulder, then kissed her one last time before walking out the door.

TOP SECRET
OFFICE OF THE DIRECTOR OF NATIONAL INTELLIGENCE

FROM: DNI – *Oliver J. Haskins, Jr.*
TO: *THE PRESIDENT*

SUBJECT: *Cuban Involvement in the Assassination of SECDEF Carter Grayson*

Multisourced intelligence reveals a clear and undeniable link between the assassination of SECDEF Grayson and Cuban intelligence. VISTRA Program analysis of Cuban Directorate of Intelligence (DI) classified communications, including telegraphic, telephonic, and wireless, shows a burst of communications from Havana to agents inside the United States five days before the incident and a day after. Message decryption reveals two references to "Operation Guama" and an explicit instruction to agent "Miguel" to activate "Cell A" (Attachment A). Geographic coordinates for the attack are described in cryptonyms and are therefore not clear. Decryption of secure emails from Havana DI entities to blind addresses also reveals instructions to "use Package 15" for the attack due to its "exceptional impact against targets" (Attachment B). Earlier analysis of DI traffic has led us to believe that "Package 15" is code for military grade pentolite. Military pentolite comprises a mixture of 50 percent PETN and 50 percent TNT. A 50:50 mixture has a density of 1.65 g/cm3 and a detonation velocity of 7400 m/s. This constitutes a highly potent explosive, one that is off-limits to civilian consumers of pentolite and is a core component of IEDs supplied by Iranian intelligence to Taliban and Iraqi insurgents for their attacks against U.S. military targets.

HUMINT sources report enhanced operational activity on the part of several DI entities in the days leading up to the assassination, including agent-case officer meetings and repeated references to an imminent "wet job." "Wet job" and "wet affairs" are classic Russian and Cuban intelligence terms indicating assassination.

Havana has stepped up intelligence operations against the United States in recent months in response to perceptions that the USG is behind the growing insurrection in Cuba, the turning of DI sleeper agents inside the U.S., the FBI's uncovering of the Livingstons (and thus a major loss to Havana even though they escaped U.S. justice), and the Cubans' recent discovery and liquidation of our asset, STONEWALL in Havana. As in the cases of other au-

thoritarian regimes facing loss of control due to popular uprisings, the Cuban leadership has become increasingly paranoid, blaming its domestic troubles on outside actors, particularly the United States. As more citizens take to the streets, or take up arms, in rebellion to the regime, the harsher the countermeasures by the regime become (see "Insurgency in Cuba: Update and Analysis," Attachment C).

Our reading is that with Raúl Castro in the hospital after reportedly suffering a second heart attack and with Fidel Castro reportedly in a state of dementia, the leadership situation in Havana is fluid, though one figure has emerged as a key actor, perhaps the key actor. Gen. Larisa Montilla (see bio, attachment D) has kept herself carefully in the background until recently. The available intelligence indicates Montilla is a career Ministry of Interior (MININT) intelligence officer associated with hardcore regime elements. Little is known of Montilla's background, including her family connections. Since Raúl fell ill three weeks ago, all leadership declarations out of Havana emanate from the Politburo or the Communist Party headquarters rather than one senior official. Whether this means there is an interim collective leadership or Montilla is cleverly not sticking her neck out in the traditionally treacherous and dangerous context of Fidel Castro's political system is not clear at this time.

SIGINT has picked up additional communications referencing "Operation HATUEY." It is the consensus of the intelligence community that this refers to another imminent violent attack inside the U.S., most likely against another senior official or officials. (Guama and Hatuey were Taino Indian chiefs who fought against Spanish rule.)

Kate re-read the presidential memo and shook her head. "Crazy. Just crazy." She threw the memo on her desk, leaned back, and closed her eyes. Memories of a much simpler past flashed in her brain. Days of sunshine. Parental love. Cuddled in her mother's protective arms. Her golden voice singing,

Uciekaj, myszko, do dziury,
niech cię nie złapie kot bury!
Bo jak cię złapie kot bury,
to cię obedrze ze skóry!

Run little mouse to a hole
so the gray cat will not catch you!
Because if the gray cat catches you
he will pull your skin off!

"Oh, Mama." A tear ran down her cheek.

But she had no time for nostalgia or for pondering the prophetic implications of the old Polish nursery rhyme her mother used to sing to her. As officer-in-charge of intel support for Operation POLECAT, she couldn't afford to miss a beat. People's lives depended on her.

She fought off fatigue and looked up at the clock. COMSEC, communications security, for the operation was tight. Extremely tight. If word leaked that the President had ordered a clandestine Special Forces strike against Cuba, the political and international repercussions would be tremendous. That was why the White House had chosen to cut Congress out of the loop by authorizing POLECAT as a "clandestine" vs a "covert" op. The distinction was important. The latter sought to conceal the sponsor, i.e., the U.S., as well as the action, and fell under a body of law, Title 50, that required Congressional notification and oversight. CIA covert ops were governed by that law.

A clandestine operation, in contrast, sought to conceal the act, but not necessarily the sponsor. Carried out by the military and falling under a different law, it had none of the stringent reporting and oversight requirements of intel operations. Therefore, Congress did not need to be notified.

The President was playing a dangerous game. If revealed, he could not plausibly deny the operation since uniformed American soldiers were carrying it out, but he could invoke the right of a nation to defend itself by taking out the threat: General Larisa Montilla.

A week had passed since Nick had stormed out of Kate's life and into God knew what fate. A sentinel of secrets, she'd told no one in the agency of his plans, his crazy, quixotic quest to rescue Cuba from itself.

CHAPTER THIRTY-NINE

The cigarette boat raced across the waves like the proverbial bat out of hell, its dual 750 horsepower engines pushing the craft at a steady twenty-five knots. They would hit landfall two hours after sundown.

Nick eyed the smugglers who were ferrying him across the Windward Passage from the tip of Haiti's northwest peninsula to eastern Cuba. They were hardened men with scars on their black skin. Could he trust them? They could simply cut his throat right there and throw him overboard as shark bait. He had emptied his government retirement account to pay them the small fortune required for the high-risk undertaking.

But so far, they seemed solid and dependable, even professional. There was no alcohol on board, and they swore they smuggled only humans and cigarettes, not drugs. While the money wasn't as big, it kept the U.S. Drug Enforcement Administration at bay as well as the corrupt Haitian cops and Coast Guard, who received funding from the DEA with one hand and took bribes from smugglers with the other. The bribes were the cost of doing business for the men, who otherwise faced a hand-to-mouth existence.

The ride was bone rattling as the fiberglass boat slammed down from the crests of seven-foot waves. The boat's captain, Josue, invited Nick to eat in the cabin, but Nick gestured to indicate that he preferred to stay out on the deck with the rest of them. He savored the sea spray, rushing fresh air, and the explosion of tropical pastels that painted the sky as the sun set off the bow. It might be his last sunset, he thought. If so, he wanted to take in all its glory. He closed his eyes and took a deep breath.

His mind traveled back to his last encounter with Kate. Their sour parting had left him sad. Kate had grown on him. She was a lot to handle: tempestuous, disciplined, secretive. But there was also a passionate woman beneath that cool Slav exterior. She confessed that the truth was one thing she could not promise him. But a relationship should be based on each partner being totally truthful with the other. That was why the business of espionage crippled so many relationships. How could one be truthful if one's vocation encompassed deceit and lies?

But he had much more urgent matters weighing on his mind, such as returning to Cuba in violation of God-knows-how-many laws, regulations, and policies. He was an FBI agent smuggling himself into a hostile nation, one that had no formal diplomatic relations with the United States. He'd acted more on impulse, not thinking through how things would turn out, even under the rosiest of scenarios. Montilla had to be stopped. Period.

As the sky blackened, glittering stars sprayed across the dark celestial canvas like a trove of scattered diamonds. The boat ran with no lights. A scent of land carried on the warm breeze. Cuba loomed ahead. Josue and his crew were on heightened alert, scanning the horizon with binoculars and monitoring a small radar screen for the presence of other craft.

Nick squinted. He could make out a dark mass in the distance.

Josue cut the engine power to a low rumble and made a wide turn from northwest to southwest. He navigated toward a pre-designated cove in a sparsely populated area east of Barracoa, on Cuba's northeast coast.

In the weeks before his departure, Nick had communicated with the Marcials via intermediaries. They had worked out the rendezvous time and place with no wiggle room for error. Once Nick linked up with Marcial's people, they had to move fast. Cuban forces were not only on heightened alert but itchy-fingered. They would shoot first and ask questions later.

Under a moonless sky, the boat stalked the shoreline, running at a low growl on one engine. Josue strained to see land. His men all squinted in the blackness, hyper-alert to a Cuban vessel or shore activity that would spot them. They'd been in such circumstances countless times over the years, but, like hunters on the prowl in a savage forest, they knew one misstep could cost them their freedom if not their lives. Their faces and torsos dripped in sweat in a stagnant tropical heat made more oppressive by the lack of a sea breeze. And raw nerves only exacerbated the situation.

"*Eh! Mwen wè li sou gen,*" Josue said hoarsely, pointing off the starboard bow.

"What?" Nick asked.

Josue handed Nick his binoculars. "See? Over there. I see it. The place we must go."

Nick trained the binoculars at the indicated location. He could barely make out the contours. The shoreline receded. A cove. "Are you sure?"

"We wait for signal." With a hand moving across his throat, Josue ordered his navigator to cut the engines.

The boat drifted. The shore loomed closer. All was still. Nick could feel every beat of his pounding heart.

"*Li trè fon isit la,*" whispered Josue's man monitoring the depth gauge.

"He say it is very shallow here," Josue translated. "*Evite wòch yo! Sèvi ak pedal yo.*" Josue grabbed two paddles and handed them to the other two men, ordering them to keep the craft away from rocks.

"*Gade. Sou gen!*" one of the men said, pointing in the distance.

The others focused in the direction indicated by the

crewman. Two flashes of light emanated from the west side of the cove, then another three flashes.

Josue grabbed a flashlight and signaled back. His action was reciprocated by two, then three flashes.

"It is them!" Josue said. "Yes. It is them." He switched one engine back on, grasped the wheel, and gassed it.

Slowly, the boat pushed through the still water. The cove greeted them like two huge jaws ready to clamp down. Deep into the cove, the water appeared stagnant and brackish. The lights flashed again, now much closer. Josue flashed back.

The outlines of two men appeared on the embankment. Each shouldered an assault rifle.

"*Bienvenidos a Cuba*," one of them said.

"*Gracias. Yo soy Nick*," Nick said.

One of the men got into a small boat and rowed over to the starboard side where Nick waited. Nick quickly climbed in, his duffel in hand. After a quick farewell, Josue gunned an engine and eased out of the cove, back out to sea, back to Haiti, another delivery safely completed.

"Colonel Marcial and Captain Zero extend their warm greetings and look forward to having you back," the thirtyish man said. "My name is Manuel. We must hurry. It is not safe here."

When they reached land, an erect young man with a military bearing shook hands with Nick. "Colonel Marcial welcomes you back," the man said.

The three men plodded off into the interior along a narrow path.

The Arnaldo Ochoa Brigade's sprawling jungle redoubt was a far cry from the rudimentary base in a clearing where Nick had first met Marcial and Yuri. Scores of men moved about purposefully amid neatly arranged barracks and office huts. Jeeps loaded with armed men and supplies sped through the encampment, kicking up dust. A commo building bristled with antennas connected to an array of wireless equipment and computers manned by trained operators; generators hummed just outside the perimeter. Trucks were parked in neat rows under camouflage netting. The area was a picture of military commotion and activity.

"Welcome to Camp Martí." The fit, erect figure of Colonel Marcial stood in the doorway of Nick's hooch, a broad smile on his face.

The two men embraced and exchanged hearty backslaps.

"Henrique! Ah, so good to see you!" Nick exclaimed.

"And you, my friend!"

Yuri stepped in, and more bear hugs ensued.

"I told you you'd be back!" Yuri said.

"These days, I'm feeling more Cuban than American," Nick replied with a smile.

Marcial gestured for Nick to have a seat on his made-up bunk while he and Yuri pulled up two simple chairs. Yuri signaled an aide-de-camp to bring refreshments.

"I'm impressed," Nick said with a broad sweep of his arm at the bustling complex called Camp Martí.

"We have come a long way since you were here," Marcial answered.

"And we are expanding. We have new bases going up all over eastern and central Cuba," Yuri said. "It is only a matter of time. Soon Cuba will be free."

The three caught up with each other over malt soda and pork sandwiches.

"As strong as we've become, we can use your help and expertise," Marcial said.

"I am flattered. But my goal is to take down Larisa Montilla. By whatever means necessary," Nick said.

Father and son looked at each other. Then Marcial said, "This is our goal too, Nick. But to get to the head, we must first attack and vanquish the beast's body."

"And we are succeeding," Yuri added. "Every day we make gains. And every day the communists find themselves on the run. Look." He pointed at a large pole barn where about a dozen men milled about. "See those men over there? They are deserters from the FAR. They join our ranks to fight for freedom."

"This is good. But it takes time. And we've got no time," Nick said. "Montilla ordered the assassination of our Defense Secretary. We know she has similar operations in the works. Washington will soon strike back. How, I don't know. Probably something covert. But don't rule out an outright intervention."

"And so, Washington sent you here to assist us," Marcial said.

"No. I'm afraid not. I'm also a rebel. From my own government." Nick went on to explain the circumstances that had driven him to leave his job and country and smuggle himself back into Cuba.

"You play a doubly dangerous game," Marcial said. "But that's what we like about you. You are bold and bad!"

The men broke into laughter.

"'The guerrilla must move amongst the people as a fish swims in the sea.' Mao Tse-tung understood the true nature of guerrilla war," Yuri said. "We studied him at José Maceo."

"We are two of the three most wanted men in Cuba. And here we are deep in enemy territory in the back of a truck with a bunch of average citizens," Nick said. He shook his head and smiled.

The breeze coming into the rear of the open claptrap truck blew Nick's hair in all directions. The air was intermingled with black diesel vapor belching from the vehicle's topside exhaust pipe. Yuri held onto his tattered straw farmhand's hat. Then, as the truck hit a crater in the middle of the dirt road, the men were jolted upward and jostled together, causing all twelve of the truck's passengers to grab for the wooden railing, a common happening on Cuba's rural roads.

Nick and Yuri resumed their positions in the front corner where the wind hit them flush and muffled their voices. They, like their co-passengers, were dressed in the basic tattered white shirt and coarse cut-offs of sugarcane workers. Stubble covered their faces. Fish in the sea.

They were wending their way westward, toward the capital. Their forged travel documents listed them as Yasmani Dominguez and Sergio Espinosa, migrant cane harvesters. Road checkpoints did cursory inspections at best of such everyday vehicles. The police routinely waved them through.

They were approaching Matanzas, a city an hour and a half from Havana. Once there, Yasmani Dominguez and Sergio Espinosa would cease to exist. Shed of their peasant garb, Nick and Yuri would rendezvous with a cell of the Arnaldo Ochoa Brigade and go underground.

CHAPTER FORTY

Captain Hank Cartwright surveyed the computer screens in the command center of the USS Virginia. The latest class of USN attack submarine had replaced the periscope with sensor-filled photonic masts that sent thermal and laser as well as optical images to the control room Q-70 touch control consoles.

The latest stealth technology virtually guaranteed that the Virginia would remain undetected as it patrolled off the coast of eastern Cuba. The first OPORD, or operational order, had arrived twenty minutes ago. Six Navy SEALS were already in the lock chamber, ready for launch on their covert mission.

Cartwright dreaded the second OPORD, which could come any minute, or the next day, or hopefully never. Sixteen Tomahawk missiles sat in a dozen vertical launch tubes and four torpedo tubes, a hair trigger away from raining untold devastation upon pre-targeted Cuban military and intelligence sites in retaliation for the communist regime's assassination of Defense Secretary Carter Grayson. Through signals intelligence, SIGINT, the intel community had been able to uncover the tracks Gen. Montilla had so elaborately labored to conceal; her disinformation efforts to pin the assassination on Islamist terrorists couldn't fool an American national security apparatus that had the globe wired as never before in the decade since 9/11.

The SEAL team headed to the Cuban coast in the U.S. Navy's only Dry Combat Submersible, so called because it kept its passengers in a protective watertight enclosure that zipped along at five knots and fifty feet in depth. Cartwright prayed that the unproven rushed-to-service prototype submersible would not malfunction, or worse, be detected by Cuba's Coast Guard. Operation POLECAT was launched.

Yuri's hit squad consisted of seven of his best covert operators plus Nick. Three were highly trained ex-FAR Special Forces soldiers. Split into four two-man teams in order not to draw attention, the eight linked up under cover of darkness at a safe house apartment in west Havana, a mere four blocks from their target in upscale Miramar.

They were armed with the implements of expert assassins: Russian-made 5.45mm PRI automatic pistols with suppressors, NR-2 combat knives that included 7.62mm gun barrels for extra lethality, stun grenades and several short-barreled AK-74u assault rifles.

In three cars, they drove separate routes toward the Casa Central de las Fuerzas Armadas Cubanas, the Miramar Yacht Club in pre-revolution days that had become an R&R facility for Army personnel and their families. The facility hugged the shoreline.

The Marcials' inside sources told them that Gen. Montilla worked out at the Casa Central every Tuesday and Friday after work. They had compiled a detailed layout of the place. One of the assassin team members had even spent recreation time there while in the Army. He guided the team.

The eight men would infiltrate the grounds from an alley bordering the baseball diamond, storm the workout area, and kill everybody they encountered on their way to the main target. Two PRI pistol-bearing attackers were tasked with taking out Montilla by plugging two bullets in her brain and two in the chest. Then, all eight would make a quick getaway in separate directions.

Nick made the sign of the cross.

The SEAL team debarked from their submersible fifty meters from shore. They cut through the choppy waters in a straight line as if pulled by gravity. Clouds blocked the moon, deepening the cover of darkness. They breached concrete breakers and entered a calm, shallow basin for boats and swimmers. Their senses hyper-alert, they slowly crossed into the sandy-bottomed shore area and waded onto a remote corner of the beach under a cluster of coconut trees. They quickly removed and stashed their amphibious gear, then switched off the safeties on their weapons: MK23 .45 caliber handguns with supressors, M4A1 assault rifles, an HK MP5 submachine gun, and one M4 Super 90 shotgun. At close range, one of the designated hitters would fire one shot in Larisa Montilla's chest and one in her head—a clean kill to end a vexing national security threat in the form a rogue female Cuban general. The POLECAT team would then quickly slither back into the sea and to their home sub.

Larisa Montilla breathed deeply with each accelerating pump of the stationary exercise cycle. A headband kept her hair from her eyes. Beads of sweat glistened on her taut, muscle-toned skin. She always looked forward to her workouts. They cleared her mind and released endorphins that relieved the stress of running a bankrupt nation nominally ruled by two delusional and incapacitated octogenarians.

Montilla excluded all others from the ground-floor workout space on her gym evenings, needing the space and privacy to recharge her batteries and keep her focus. Two bodyguards kept vigil just outside the room.

As she quickened her pace on the cycle, she closed her eyes and hummed *La Bayamesa*. The patriotic lyrics and stirring beat helped her maintain a steady rhythm to her exercise.

Al combate, corred, Bayameses!,
Que la patria os contempla orgullosa;
No temáis una muerte gloriosa,
Que morir por la patria es vivir.

Hasten to battle, men of Bayamo!
The motherland looks proudly to you;
Do not fear a glorious death,
Because to die for the fatherland is to live.

Yuri and his partner skirted the unlit baseball diamond, keeping low to the ground. Nick and another man flitted down the dark diamond's middle. Two of the AK-74-bearing squad members followed a sand path between the two team leaders and broad Third Avenue, securing the left flank. The remaining AK-bearing squad member reached the gravel drive between the baseball field and the main FAR clubhouse where Montilla worked out.

Yuri and Nick linked up on the western edge of the diamond. They and the other two men lay on their stomachs while the other squad members took up support positions farther away. One of the bodyguards leaned against a pillar on the western side, smoking a cigarette. The other, adjacent to the courtyard on the northern side of the rec building, paced slowly back and forth. Exterior floodlights illuminated both of the men.

Yuri gave the signal, and the two hitmen, keeping approximately ten meters apart, crept carefully across a grassy area until they reached the edge of the gravel driveway. Each man took careful aim with his KRS-suppressored Kalashnikov. Yuri threw his arm downward. Two bullets simultaneously found their marks. The bodyguard on the west side slammed against the building. His cigarette fell from his lips as he slumped to the pavement, leaving a big red blotch of blood on the wall. The other bodyguard clutched his chest, and he fell hard onto the ground.

Nick and Yuri rushed forward. Nick flung open the door to the workout room, pistol ready, barrel directed upward. The familiar green eyes of Larisa Montilla locked with his. Nick froze. Montilla sat unmoving on her exercise cycle.

Yuri stepped in front of Nick, both hands clutching his PRI pistol, and aimed squarely at Montilla's face. He squeezed the trigger twice. The bullets ripped into the gym mat on the floor as Nick's hand fell hard onto Yuri's arms.

With a swift counterstrike, Yuri backhanded Nick in the face, sending him reeling backward.

Montilla threw herself to the floor. She plunged her hand into a gym bag and brought out a Makarov. She spun onto her back and squeezed off two shots at Yuri, but missed.

Nick threw himself on her, pinning her to the floor. The Makarov flew from her hand.

"Get off her! God help me, Nick! I'll kill you as well as her!" Yuri yelled while clutching his gun with both hands. His face was a tense grimace. Veins throbbed. Sweat beaded on his forehead.

Recalling his wrestling training, Nick swiftly flipped Montilla on her belly and locked her right arm high on her back.

"We're taking her with us!" Nick said.

Yuri's face was a mask of incomprehension. "Are you crazy? No. We kill her. Here and now! Get out of my way!" He strained to aim a clear shot at Montilla.

"Listen! We need to take her hostage. We kill her, and all hell will break loose. Keep her alive, and we can use her to command communist loyalists to lay down their arms in the name of reconciliation."

"Is it your soft American nature? Or did she get to you when she had you in her custody? What is it, Nick? Something happened between you and her. People talk. Plenty of rumors have been going around."

Laughter erupted from Montilla. It ended abruptly as another round from Yuri's pistol tore the mat an inch from her head, kicking up strands of her hair.

Gunshots broke out outside. Yuri ducked and pulled aside the nearest window curtain.

"I can tell you what is happening." Montilla grunted as she labored to breathe under Nick's weight.

Yuri shot a look at her, then quickly focused on what was going on outside the building, gun at the ready.

Nick crunched her arm further. "What? What is it? Tell us!"

Montilla groaned. "You're breaking my arm."

Nick eased up slightly, but maintained a knee-press on her back.

"You are surrounded," she said.

"Bullshit!" Yuri lunged and brought his pistol down on her face.

Blood streamed from her temple into her left eye.

Nick let up a little more and allowed her to free one hand.

Montilla touched her face. "You can kill me. But you two are dead men. Along with those from your submarine."

Nick furrowed his brow. He exchanged a quizzical look with Yuri.

Montilla caught on to their confusion. "Oh. You don't know?"

"Know what?" Nick asked guardedly.

Montilla managed a pained laugh.

Yuri shoved the barrel of his pistol into the bruise on her face. "Talk, bitch! Or they'll be mopping your brains up from the mat."

"You really don't know, do you?" she said. "I cannot believe it! Let me sit up. In minutes, we'll all be dead if you don't listen to me."

Yuri gave a slight nod to Nick. Nick let her sit upright against the wall.

Montilla placed her palm against the bruise. "A battalion of Black Wasps is converging on this area. Your men are likely all dead or captured by now. You gentlemen have brilliantly stumbled into a major military assault. Your American SEALs infiltrated from the sea. They've fallen into a trap. We are not stupid, in case you have not noticed over the past fifty-plus years."

"What's their mission?" Nick demanded.

"To kill me. As I assume is also your mission?"

A blast blew the room's windows into a million flying shards. Yuri flew several meters and slammed against a wall. Nick covered Montilla with his body in a reflexive act of protection.

When they regained their senses, Montilla turned her face up to Nick's. Her nose touched his. She stared into his eyes. "Nick, we can have it back. We don't need this. We don't need to die. Dying in one another's arms is for Cervantes's and Shakespeare's lovers. Not for us."

Nick gazed down at her. He had come to kill her. But...

"And do not forget. I am also American. Will you kill a kinsman? Cuban. American. We are both, Nick. You and I."

Yuri tried to get up, but fell back down.

Nick crawled to the nearest window, gun in hand. He squinted to see what was happening outside. The electricity to the compound had been shut off. All he could make out were dark figures flitting across the courtyard and baseball diamond. More explosions and gunfire pierced the air.

Nick ran over to Yuri. "Yuri! Get up! Yuri!"

Yuri shook his head and slowly rose to a sitting position. Blood poured down his forehead where glass shards had made their mark. Nick steadied him with a firm grip on his elbow.

A grenade flew into the room and hissed. Tear gas began to fill the area. Nick rolled over, grabbed the grenade, and flung it back out the window.

"Grab her!" Yuri commanded. He ran to the hallway door.

Nick followed, holding Montilla firmly by the arm. The hallway was pitch-black. Machine gun fire ripped through the night air outside the building.

Pistol aimed ahead of him, Yuri leapt into the blackened corridor. Nick pulled Montilla along as he stayed near Yuri.

Slowly, they crept ahead, feeling their way along the right wall.

The shuffle of feet sounded just ahead. Yuri fired blindly.

Nick heard a moan followed by the thump of a body hitting the hard floor.

Tension filled the control room in the USS Virginia as the last message burst from the POLECAT team was followed by the sound of static.

Capt. Hank Cartwright wiped the perspiration from his brow. "All channels are open? You sure?" he asked the radioman.

"Yes, sir," the man replied, double checking the controls. "No contact, sir."

Cartwright exchanged a knowing glance with his XO, Lieutenant Commander Brett Holstrom.

"Try again," Holstrom ordered the radioman.

"Base to White Rook. Do you read? Over. Base to White Rook. Do you read? Over." The radioman looked forlornly at Cartwright and Holstrom.

The captain rubbed his hand across his chin. "Shit."

CHAPTER FORTY-ONE

TOP SECRET
SITREP

SUBJECT: COMMANDERS SITREP 3
UNIT: USS VIRGINIA
PARENT ORGANIZATION: USSOUTHCOM
BOX ID: BX000269

FROM: CDR USS VIRGINIA//
TO: COMUSSOUTHCOM //
           CNO//NOO/N09/N3/N5//
           JOINT STAFF/J-1/J-5//
           DIRCIA WASHDC//

CLASSIFICATION: TOP SECRET
SUBJECT: COMMANDER SITREP 3
PRECEDENCE: FLASH
REPORTING PERIOD: 0830Z TO 0905Z APR
L(TS).W OPERATIONS SUMMARY.

    1.   (TS) POLECAT TEAM ARRIVED SHORE
          AT COORDINATES 23.105174478315717N
          / -82.44732856750488 AT 0331. IMMEDI-
          ATE CONTACT WITH HOSTILE FORCES.
          LAST COMMUNICATION AT 0902Z. NO
          CONTACT RPT NO CONTACT SINCE

0902Z. POLECAT TEAM PRESUMED CAP-
TURED/KILLED.

2. (S) REQUEST FURTHER INSTRUCTIONS.

(2)(TS) (E) 1AD.
TOP SECRET

On the surface, she was a cool, steady professional. But underneath, Kate was a nervous wreck. Operation POLECAT had fallen into a trap. Six SEALs had been captured or killed. The expected gloating announcement over Cuban official media hadn't appeared yet. Above all, POLECAT was an intel failure. Her intel failure. As officer in charge of intel support for the operation, it was her duty to ferret out any traps in advance. And she'd missed them. Nothing in the all-source intelligence revealed any foreknowledge on the part of Havana of the operation. How could it have happened? She covered her face with her hands, as much to conceal her tears as to hide her shame.

The consequences were dire. A National Security Council Principals meeting was deliberating counteractions. Having run out of options, the President would have no other recourse but to launch an all-out attack on Cuba. The wrath of the world would come down on Washington for what would be called "rash interventionism," nothing new in the years since 9/11.

The Joint Chiefs' planning branch, J-5, had already drawn up contingency invasion plans, and the Defense Intelligence Agency updated its list of tactical targets. Working Groups had been operating twenty-four/seven to coordinate military, intelligence, and diplomatic aspects. The news media hadn't yet picked up on the preparations, but it was only a matter of time before *the Washington Post* had a banner headline along the lines of, "U.S. Prepares Cuba Strike."

Kate focused on her own future. Years of personal investment and sacrifice in her Agency career were going down the tubes. It was time to contemplate an alternate career. The business sector had never held an attraction for her. Academia also wasn't her cup of tea. What, then? She'd always envisioned herself as a government lifer. U.S. Army. CIA. The USG was all she knew and all she ever cared to work for. General MacArthur's farewell speech resonated in her fatigued mind: "My last conscious thoughts will be of the Corps, and the Corps, and the Corps." She nodded off.

"Ms. Kovalchuk, you have a call," said the office assistant, a matronly African-American woman whose face reflected concern. "Line one." She nodded at the blinking phone on Kate's paper-strewn desk.

Kate jerked back to wakefulness. "Oh, thanks, Alice." She picked up the receiver.

Static. "Kate. You there, Kate?" came a familiar voice, one that echoed over the poor link.

"Nick! Is that you, Nick?"

"Listen, Kate. You know where I am. This has to be short."

"Are you safe?"

"I'm okay. Now listen up. Write this down."

Kate fumbled for a pen and piece of paper. "Go ahead."

"I'm aware what they're up to back there. Kate, it's dangerous. They've got to rein in. The worst thing Washington can do is to intervene. Let the Cubans take care of their own problems."

She stiffened. "This is an open line, Nick." She was too aware that any number of the world's intelligence agencies could be eavesdropping.

"I can't help that, Kate. Just listen up. I'll make it quick."

Kate readied the pen. "Okay, go ahead."

"One, the assault on the FAR facility. They were ambushed. Montilla knew it was coming. I don't know the fate of our guys. I barely escaped with my own life. Two, the rebels' reach is growing.

They'll take Havana on their own. Let them do it. U.S. intervention will only bollix things up. We can get the perps behind SECDEF's murder after liberation.

"Three: I know what they think of me back there, but you've got to convince them I'm all they've got. I'm the USG's inside man here. I'm no crackpot, no renegade. I'll forward regular reports securely. I'm it. I am all they've got. Last: Regarding Montilla—"

Static filled the line.

"Nick? Nick! You there, Nick?"

Nick folded his cell phone and pocketed it as Yuri yanked him by the arm.

"It's not safe here," Yuri said.

They wore baseball caps and large sunglasses. Chairman Mao's dictum on swimming with the fish in the sea came into play again, along with the magician's trick of hiding in plain sight. Two of the most wanted men in Cuba were promenading along the Malecón, blending in with the diminishing numbers of European and South American tourists while planning their next move.

Yuri headed for a café.

"Slow down!" Nick barked. "We're tourists, remember? Tourists don't move like they're running for their lives."

Yuri eased his pace a notch. Once in the café, they chose a table, sat, and ordered drinks. Slowly, but deliberately, they scanned their surroundings for anything or anybody suspicious. The drinks arrived.

Nick downed his in one gulp. His hand trembled slightly.

"You are so nervous?" Yuri asked.

Nick set down the glass. "Not nervous so much as rattled from last night."

"Yes. So am I. We are lucky to be alive," Yuri said in a low voice.

"I just can't believe it," Nick said, hunched forward and also speaking in a hushed tone. "We had her. She was our prisoner. Then pfft! Gone."

Yuri had his eyes set on Havana Bay. "If you hadn't interfered, she would be dead now. You should have let me kill her as we originally planned."

Nick was silent.

"It was in that dark corridor that she got away," Yuri said. "After I shot that security guard. Too much confusion. And she's as slippery as the snake she is. And we pick the same moment of the same day to execute our operation as when your government launches theirs?" He shook his head. "I don't know if I believe in God, but if he exists, he's fucking with us."

Nick let out a chuckle.

Yuri looked at him, obviously unamused, then fixed his gaze back onto the sea.

"So now what?" Nick asked.

"We rendezvous with one of our cells and exfiltrate back to our lines. It's too hot for us here. Our day of reckoning with Montilla will come." He looked back at Nick. "She's not a lover, Nick. Next time, I kill her. And you too if you pull another stunt like last night." He was not smiling.

Nick sat quietly, contemplating the blue expanse of water in the distance.

A foreign couple took a table at the opposite end of the café. The tall man with thinning gray hair pulled out a chair for his wife. They ordered.

Nick barely paid attention until he heard them speak American English in familiar voices. He peered over his sunglasses to catch a better glimpse. "Holy shit."

"What?" Yuri asked.

"Talk about God fucking with us."

"What? Those people? You know them?"

"Not only do I know them, but I almost arrested them. They're the ones I told you about."

"You mean that's them over there? There?" Yuri's voice rose a little on the last word.

"Shh. Don't draw attention. We're already half a step away from a firing squad."

Yuri leaned forward. "You're sure? Those two *yanquis* are the traitors who spied for Fidel and got away?"

Nick studied them closely. "Yes. One hundred percent sure." As he fumbled to put his sunglasses back on, they fell and clanged onto the metal table.

The Livingstons both looked Nick's way. Philip went slackjawed. Deirdre gasped. They sprang to their feet.

Yuri shot up, strode over to the Livingstons' table with three long paces, pulled his Makarov out of his belt, and plugged each in the forehead. Both crashed to the tiled floor, eyes open in death stares. Yuri then methodically shoved the gun barrel into each mouth and fired another round, sending brains, blood, and patrons in all directions.

Nick and Yuri bolted out of the café and ran toward the city center, hugging the walls of one dilapidated apartment house after another. The sound of police sirens filled the air. Residents poured out onto the streets to see what was happening. Yuri dove through a large frame once containing a window into an abandoned building, its roof having collapsed years ago. Nick followed. They took refuge in a dark corner. Rats roamed the premises freely.

Between gasps, Yuri said, "The police now will have descriptions of us from the clients in the café. They'll cordon the entire area tight as a drum."

"Why did you shoot them?" Nick demanded, his lungs heaving.

"Because they needed to die, that's why. And they ID'd you."

"You risked getting us both caught!"

"No. We will escape. As always."

"Yuri, you killed them because of Montilla, right? You've

had so much rage pent up inside you over her getaway that you just had to take it out on the next available target."

"Don't psychoanalyze me, my friend. I killed them because traitorous spies like that do not deserve to live. Killing them sends a message to all such turncoats and sellouts to the Castro regime. I did America a favor."

Nick shook his head. "Sometimes I think you're incapable of seeing past your nose. You're just too impulsive. How can you hope to lead a revolution, much less govern a country, without thinking things through?"

"No time for this." Carefully, Yuri crawled back to the window frame and peered outside. A gun barrel greeted him between his eyes. The click of a round being chambered followed. Yuri shut his eyes.

CHAPTER FORTY-TWO

TOP SECRET
SUBJECT: WARNO
PARENT ORGANIZATION: USSOUTHCOM
UNIT: CDR
BOX ID: BX000269

FROM: COMUSSOUTHCOM //
TO: CDR USS VIRGINIA//

INFO: CNO//NOO/N09/N3/N5//
        JOINT STAFF/J-1/J-5//
        SECDEF/HDASA/ISA/SO/LIC//
        DIRCIA WASHDC//

CLASSIFICATION: TOP SECRET
SUBJECT: WARNING ORDER 1: OPERATION
IRON FORGE
PRECEDENCE: FLASH
l(TS).W WARNING ORDER

1. (TS) SITUATION: GOC HAS CARRIED OUT
MULTIPLE TERRORIST ATTACKS ON
U.S. SOIL, INCLUDING ASSASSINATION
OF SECDEF. NCA HAS DETERMINED
COUNTERACTION IS TO BE TAKEN.

USN ASSETS UNDER DIRECTION OF SOUTHCOM TO SPEARHEAD COUNTER-ACTIONS IN OPERATION IRON FORGE.

2. (TS) MISSION: CDR USS VIRGINIA WILL PREPARE FOR IMMEDIATE LAUNCH FIVE TLAM-D MISSILES PER PRE-PROGRAMMED TARGET DATA. ADDITIONAL LAUNCH ORDERS TO BE EXECUTED PER DESIGNATED OPORDS. PRIMARY TARGETS INCLUDE CUBAN COMMAND, CONTROL & COMMUNICA-TIONS NODES, FAR BASES, MININT HQ AND RELATED MININT SITES. SECOND-ARY TARGETS PER PRE-SELECTED AIF LISTS.

3. (S) EXECUTION: SOP IMMEDIATE PER OPORD UPON RECEIPT.

4. (S) SERVICE SUPPORT: PER SOP.

5. (S) COMMAND AND SIGNAL: PER SOP.

(2)(TS) (e) 1AD.
TOP SECRET

GRANMA
Official Organ of the Central Committee of the Communist Party of Cuba

YANQUI INVASION DEFEATED!
U.S. Commandos Killed – Chief Terrorist and FBI Agent to Meet Justice

A six-man U.S. commando team was intercepted and annihilated by Cuban forces today near Havana. The invaders, who attempted to infiltrate at 4:00 am at the Casa Central of the FAR, apparently had as its mission to assassinate senior Cuban military officials. Vigilant security personnel, however, crushed this scheme and, after a brief shootout, killed all six members. The Americans wore uniforms of the U.S. Navy special operations forces called the SEALS.

Also intercepted and killed were a number of domestic terrorists who conspired with the invasion force. The terrorist leader, Yuri Marcial Dominguez, was captured along with an agent of the American Federal Bureau of Investigation. Marcial, who has called himself "Captain Zero," is one of Cuba's most wanted criminals. The American, Nicholas Castillo, is the only American attacker to survive.

The Central Committee of the Communist Party of Cuba denounced the attack in the strongest terms and praised security personnel for courageously defending the Fatherland. Foreign Minister Espinoza has called for this despicable aggression to be brought immediately before the United Nations Security Council and for the world to condemn it, the first by yanqui imperialists since the failed Bay of Pigs assault in 1961.

The government has announced it will try the traitor Marcial and his American accomplice before a military tribunal. The sentence for seeking the overthrow of the government is death by firing squad.

CENTRAL INTELLIGENCE AGENCY

TOP SECRET
MEMORANDUM

FROM: *NCS/SAD/IS – Kate Kovalchuk*
THROUGH: DDNCS
TO: DNCS
             DCI

SUBJECT: Failure of Operation POLECAT – Need for Restraint

The failure of Operation POLECAT follows a series of intelligence setbacks concerning Cuba. As senior intelligence support officer for the operation, I take full responsibility for not having foreseen indicators of GOC preparations to intercept the SEAL team. It is clear, however, that Havana had advance warning of this mission.

FBI agent Nicholas Castillo, who is inside Cuba and was at the scene of the ambush, told me in a phonecon that it was very clear that the GOC knew of Operation POLECAT in advance and set out to intercept the SEAL team. Mr. Castillo was captured following the aborted mission and is now in Cuban custody. According to Cuban official media, Castillo and a rebel accomplice will be tried before a military tribunal very soon and likely executed. Castillo went to Cuba on a personal basis. His travel was sanctioned by neither his home agency nor the State Department. Castillo's parents emigrated from Cuba to the U.S. Therefore, Havana is asserting that he is a Cuban citizen and will be tried as such.

Mr. Castillo told me before his capture that it was imperative that the U.S. not intervene in Cuba despite the acts of terrorism its leadership has directed against us. Having spent ample time with the rebels, he states it is only a matter of time before they take over, after which those guilty of terrorism will be brought to justice.

Even though he has disobeyed policy and gone to Cuba without permission, Mr. Castillo's advice is sound. Furthermore, our government needs to do all in its power to secure his release, or at least a commitment from the Cubans that he not be executed. Our positive actions now will benefit future U.S.-Cuban relations.

At the bottom of Kate's memo was scrawled, "Denied. You are too close to Mr. Castillo and this case. Furthermore, policy is not your or our purview, but rather that of the White House and State Department. See me. Kent Croswell, DDNCS."

After a terse face-to-face with the Deputy Director of the National Clandestine Service, Kate received assignment orders detailing her to the Department of Health and Human Services to assist that domestic agency with collating intelligence on disease outbreaks in underdeveloped countries. It was a one-way ticket to bureaucratic Siberia.

The walls were closing in on her. The clinically cold overhead fluorescent lighting blinded her. Her co-workers steered clear, averting their eyes, as if to avoid a contagion. The gray hallways of CIA headquarters befitted a morgue. She needed to get out. Escape.

Kate walked briskly to the main cafeteria. With shaky hands, she poured a cup of coffee to go, spilling some as she took it to the cashier.

She headed out to the courtyard. She sat on a bench, closed her eyes, and basked in the glow of the brilliant sun. Slowly, she sipped the coffee. The hot liquid gave inner warmth. The cadaverous otherworld of spy bureaucracy was loosening its cold grip. Her mind wandered. The soothing sensation of sunlight and hot arabica lulled her into a stupor. For the first time in weeks, perhaps even months, she truly relaxed. The heavy burdens that had been her cross to bear for so long lifted. She smiled.

A breeze tousled her hair. As she cracked open her eyes, Kate focused on "Kryptos," a sculpture in the shape of a large coppery scroll dedicated to intelligence gathering. It sat before her like some alien spacecraft. Covered in random letters and question marks, the cipher-art pulled her back to the real world, the world that threatened to destroy her lover, the arcane world that had offered her a false sense of home.

Kryptos, the Greek word for "hidden," contained four cryptograms, befitting the intelligence profession. After years of concerted effort by legions of codebreaking nerds, all but one of the encrypted messages had been deciphered. Kate recalled the first:

Between subtle shading and the absence of light lies the nuance of illusion.

Thus was the universe of spies, where nothing was clear, where right and wrong became blurred, where all was relative and the practitioners of the dark craft of espionage sat comfortably in a closed cocoon of elastic morality.

Upon returning home that evening, Kate went to her desk and booted up her PC. She then took down her Webster's dictionary and removed the book jacket. She peeled off the slip of paper she had taped inside the fold. It was the paper on which Nick had jotted down the clandestine contact information for Col. Marcial.

She logged into the site Nick had written down: *LatinSingles-Connection.com*. She entered the username, *AmorVerdadero1878*, and the password, *GallEgO*6231!*

When the account loaded, the screen displayed one connection: *SweetButterfly*, which included a photo of an attractive young woman. Kate clicked on the mailbox—no stored messages. She clicked the button to create a new message and typed,

From: AmorVerdadero1878
To: SweetButterfly

I miss you very much. So does Messenger. Messenger asked me to send his warm greetings. Yours, AmorV.

After clicking Send, Kate lowered her head and wept.

She awoke in the morning with a sore back, having fallen asleep at her desk, bent over the computer keyboard. Her head ached as well. Still in her office clothing, she felt scuzzy. She blinked and shook her head. Like a junkie badly in need of a fix, she craved coffee. Caffeine. Then a shower.

The computer screen glowed. *SweetButterfly.*

Kate went into the history cache and clicked on *LatinSingles-Connection.com.* She rubbed her temples to try to dissipate the ache in her head.

The mailbox showed one incoming message. She clicked it.

From: SweetButterfly
To: AmorVerdadero1878

Thank you for your greetings, AmorV. I've been concerned about Messenger and his friend. Please click on the following SSL-enabled website. Log in using Messenger's name and birth date. We are standing by.

Kate did so, using Nick's name and birthday.

KK: Hello. Please respond.

HM: We read you. Please identify yourself.

KK: I'm Kate, Nick's friend and colleague.

HM: I am Col. Henrique Marcial Arribe, commander of the Arnaldo Ochoa Brigade. We have little time to try to save the lives of Nick and my son, Yuri. But we will do everything possible. Please explain what your govt plans to do.

KK: Washington has run out of useful options. The only option left is military intervention.

HM: This would be disastrous. You will only become bogged down in a morass. We Cubans must settle our affairs ourselves. Tell your govt to stay out. We have need of some covert materiel. But no intervention. Such an act would only complicate and even reverse our momentum toward victory.

KK: They won't listen to me. And I fear action could commence any time. I urge you to announce your views publicly. You need to call on Washington to stand down and explain why. Your message should be clear and firm, and it should be issued as soon as possible.

HM: This we will do. Thank you.

The Washington Post

CUBAN REBEL LEADER CALLS ON U.S. TO STAY OUT OF CONFLICT

Pentagon Poised to Launch Strikes

Cuba's rebel leader, Colonel Henrique Marcial Arribe has called on Washington not to intervene in that country's civil conflict. In an interview with the AP wire service, Col. Marical stated, "We ask our American friends not to intervene in our country. The struggle to overthrow the communist tyranny must be accomplished by Cubans and Cubans alone. After this is done, we will welcome outside assistance in helping us to rebuild Cuba. Victory and freedom are only a matter of time. We Cubans can do it ourselves."

The White House spokesman declined to comment on Marcial's statement, formal printed copies of which have been received at the State Department and at the office of the United Nations Secretary General.

Pentagon Deploys Forces Near Cuba

The Defense Department has ordered U.S. naval vessels and units of the Second Marine Division to be on high alert status and ready to strike at Cuba at any moment, according to official sources. A senior intelligence official told the Washington Post *that Washington has "irrefutable evidence" that elements in the Cuban regime were behind the assassination of Defense Secretary Carter Grayson.*

The military alert also follows a failed raid in the Cuban capital of Havana, according to Cuban official media.

USS Virginia

Capt. Hank Cartwright read the latest OPORD again. "NCA ORDERS STANDDOWN. REPEAT. STANDDOWN. THIS OPORD SUPERSEDES PREVIOUS."

Cartwright looked at his XO, Brett Holstrum, and breathed a sigh of relief. Their years of intensive training to make war would be put to a test another day.

Cartwright issued the orders to put distance between the SSN-774 and the Republic of Cuba.

CHAPTER FORTY-THREE

Nick awoke in a fog of confusion and pain. He was naked and cold. Vaguely aware that violence had been inflicted on him, he feared moving and knowing how much. So he lay as still as possible as his addled mind struggled to return to consciousness. One of his eyes pulsed with pain and wouldn't open.

Back in a Cuban prison. Just how stupid can he get? Yes, guilty of stupidity. Nick wanted to shake his head in self-disapproval, but the throbbing between his ears and sharp pain down his neck checked such a movement.

A black spider made a beeline toward his face on the concrete floor. If he didn't move, the creature would soon be spinning a web from his eyelids to his nose. He blew hard at it. That small action triggered a convulsive fit that brought blood and bile into his mouth. He gagged, then vomited. The paroxysms made his whole body tighten. The full extent of his injuries came crashing home. He groaned.

Every part of his bare body telegraphed pain, but especially his head and groin. He had to move, lift himself off the cold, hard surface, and get up to wash out his mouth. Nick labored to sit up so he could look around. He was in a six-by-ten-foot cell. A slit of a window was well above head level. A squat-hole in the floor served as toilet. A bucket of water sat next to a blanketless concrete bunk. One bare, dim bulb hung from the high ceiling. From the fading light, he deduced the sun was setting.

Nick rubbed his neck. A storm raged inside his head. His stomach felt as if someone had brought a sledgehammer down on it. He was in need of prodigious amounts of painkillers, but knew none would be forthcoming. He struggled to come to life, but his battered body, craving the healing powers of rest, lulled him back to unconsciousness, sprawled naked on the cold floor.

Pangs of hunger woke him. How many hours later, he did not know, but daylight no longer streamed through the slit window. His head pounded, and his mouth was dry. With great effort, Nick sat up, rubbed his aching neck. He felt wet. Looking down, he saw that he was sitting in a pool of his own piss. "Oh, Christ."

The lock of his cell clanked, and the door opened with a metallic creak. Three people entered—two males, one female. His vision was too blurred to make them out clearly.

"Tsk, tsk, tsk," Larisa Montilla said. "Look at you. Big FBI man sitting in his own urine, naked. What is your bureau's motto? Ah, yes. 'Fidelity, Bravery, Integrity.'" She chuckled. "If your bosses could only see you now." With a flick of her head, she signaled to one of the males.

The guard walked over to the water bucket, lifted it, and dumped the contents over Nick.

Montilla tossed a coarse blanket at Nick. "Cover yourself. We need to talk."

As soon as Nick wrapped the blanket around himself, the guards lifted him by his armpits and frog-marched him out the cell door and down a long corridor. The sudden motion caused Nick to pass out. He came to upon being shoved onto a metal chair. He was in a small, bare-walled room. A high wattage floodlamp two feet from his face blinded him, compelling him to squint. His head felt as if a grenade had gone off inside it. He fought to stay conscious.

As his eyes adjusted to the bright light, he could make out Montilla seated in a chair opposite him. She was flanked by the guards.

"Señor Castillo, what is your mission in Cuba?" she asked.

Nick attempted a riposte, but his parched mouth and throat emitted only a croak.

Montilla signaled again. A guard left the room and returned moments later with a glass of water.

Nick downed the liquid in one desperate gulp. His stomach tightened then eased. He felt life returning. "More," he gasped, holding out the glass.

Montilla gave a slight nod, and the guard took the glass, left again, and returned with the refill. Nick drank the second more slowly. With his body rehydrating, the pounding inside Nick's head let up. Warmth and feeling returned to his limbs.

"Now, again. What is your mission in Cuba?" Montilla repeated.

"Oh, to see the sights. Share a daiquiri with Papa Hemingway's ghost at La Bodeguita."

One of the guards sent Nick flying across the room and into a wall. The burly guard lifted him with little effort and plopped him back onto the chair. Nick shook his head and blinked to try to keep his mind clear.

"Now, let's try again," Montilla said in an even voice. "What is your mission in Cuba?"

Nick shook his head. "No mission. I'm here on my own."

"Ah. I feel now you are taking us seriously."

Nick's mind raced to grasp his situation and to plot his next moves. How much could he divulge without spilling his guts, but still managing avoid further bodily harm? He'd been there before, Montilla grilling him in a small room in a dank prison. But he had good reason to believe he would be cut no slack. Gone were the cat and mouse games. Montilla had barely escaped with her life when she'd made the slip from Yuri and Nick at the FAR compound. And her back was against the wall politically as the communist system further crumbled from internal decay and the rebel movement seized more territory and population.

"You have been collaborating with the traitor, Marcial. At the FAR compound, was your mission to kill me?"

Nick stared blankly ahead. He'd never felt so vulnerable in his life, sitting naked before her, clutching a dirty blanket around himself in a pathetic effort to retain a shred of dignity.

"Our waterboarding team is standing by, Señor Castillo. You have exactly twenty seconds to respond. If you do not, be prepared to more than slake your thirst."

Nick thought hard. Montilla was holding all the cards. His choice was stark: spill the beans or sacrifice himself. The end, however, would be the same. He'd used up his nine lives. He could tell them all he knew or clam up; the outcome would be the same. He knew the shrewd Montilla well enough by then. She was coldly calculating and ruthless.

He looked her straight in the eye and smirked. "Shoot me. You've already written the final chapter, Larisa. Unless I become a turncoat and propaganda tool for your dying regime, my fate is sealed. You'll try me as a 'Cuban citizen' in a kangaroo court, then execute me whether I talk or not. So let's skip the waterboarding, which got you nowhere last time you had me, and get on with the firing squad. The way I see it, I've nothing to lose."

The guards started for him, but halted at Montilla's command.

She stared at Nick coldly, then a twinkle came to her eyes, followed by a wry smile. "Leave us," she ordered the guards.

"But, General—" one said.

"Go!" she commanded.

They left the room.

When the door closed behind them, Montilla cracked a smile. She rose and paced around Nick. "That's what I like about you, Nick. You are the only Cuban male I know who is macho yet without the flamboyant Latin swagger. Maybe it's the American in you.

She stopped in front of him. "You are right, Nick. Unless you publicly renounce your government and slavishly work for the revolution as an open turncoat, I have no use for you. It is too late in the game to try to use you as a bargaining chip with Washington. In their eyes, you are already a turncoat, or at least a rogue agent. Your crimes against us are not only too great to allow you get off easy, but you return to do us more damage. You're an incorrigible. And murdering the Livingstons in cold blood like that? They were old. So what if they had helped us? Their spying only contributed to peace. But it wasn't you, was it? Captain Zero did it. Bloodthirsty fool. Well, we have a few more tricks up our sleeve. Your country will pay. "In any case, we need to make an example of you in order to deter others and to show we are strong and in control."

She leaned a little closer. "Nicky. Nicky. I will make a confession. Sometimes I have fantasized: what if my life had taken an entirely different turn and I had followed in my American mother's tracks? And I think about having a normal American life, an unassuming woman with a solid business career in Miami. And then we met, you and I. What would have followed?"

She fell silent for a moment. "Too bad." She caressed his cheek.

Nick's first reaction was to grab her arm and break it and her neck before the guards could respond. But the warmth of her touch disarmed him. He caught that hint of jasmine. The contrast to the cold and violence he'd been suffering made him crave it more.

She removed her hand and stood erect before him. "In exactly seven days, you will be tried before a special military tribunal. The day following your conviction, you will get your wish. At oh-six-hundred sharp, you and the young Marcial will be shot in the courtyard of this prison. Sorry, Nicky. Goodbye."

Montilla turned sharply and exited the room.

"Here's my letter of resignation." Kate handed the paper across Jake Coburn's desk.

Her supervisor frowned, his eyes quickly skimming the letter. "Now, listen, Kate—"

"No, let me speak, please."

Coburn set the letter aside, folded his hands across his paunch, and nodded.

"I failed the POLECAT team. Six Navy SEALS are dead because I let them down. I simply cannot continue in this career with their blood on my hands."

Coburn leaned forward, supporting himself on his sleeve-rolled forearms. "Let me share something with you I rarely talk about because it's just too painful. I was Station Beirut's security officer in 1983 when Hezbollah took out seventeen Americans, eight of them Station personnel, with two thousand pounds of explosives in a delivery van driven by a suicide bomber. My station chief and good friend, Ken Haas, was one of the victims. I was about your age and took my job deadly seriously. That I managed to walk away from that scene alive was a miracle. But I knew I'd failed. I hadn't seen it coming, had no reporting to alert us of an imminent planned attack. I had the blood of sixty-three people on my hands, I told myself. I just couldn't live with it. I turned in my resignation."

"What happened?" Kate asked.

"My branch chief here at headquarters talked me out of it. He himself had lost people serving under him in Vietnam. He'd been around the horn and knew the drill. He told me two things: 'Nobody ever said this line of work was without risk; we all put our lives on the line in the service of Uncle Sam. And nobody can expect to be Nostradamus.' From Pearl Harbor to 9/11, we've missed some doozies. You aren't at fault for what happened. We aren't at fault. Shit happens. That's all. We pick ourselves up, try to learn from what happened, and do a better job. That's all we can do."

"But the Cubans clearly knew what was about to happen. They ambushed our guys."

"You know that for a fact?"

"Well, Nick told me. Nick Castillo phoned me from Havana the next day—"

Coburn waved her off. "He's a renegade. A nutcase. Or worse, a traitor. The FBI wants his ass. And bad. But it looks like the Cubans already have it. Don't believe anything that comes from his sorry mouth, Kate." He wagged an index finger at her. "Steer clear of that bastard. Leave him to the Bureau."

Kate looked away.

"Kate, you need to unwind, have some extended down time. Take a couple months leave of absence. More if you need it. I'll authorize it."

"Maybe you're right."

"Get away from this place. Go see your folks. Travel. Don't read any newspapers. Watch soap operas instead of CNN. Your job, or *a* job, will be waiting for you when you come back."

"Sure. Thanks." Kate got up to leave, then paused. "One other thing."

"Shoot."

"RAPTOR. If she isn't already, she needs to be activated. The timing is crucial with what's happening on the ground in Cuba."

"Rest assured, Kate. She's already earning her keep." He jabbed his chest. "Mr. Smith is seeing to that."

Upon returning to her townhouse, Kate began to pack. She pulled from her home safe an Irish passport. "Una O'Dalaigh, born 9/4/1983, Balgriffen, Eire." It had been issued to her on her last covert mission to meet an Iranian physicist she had recruited in Europe for the Agency. She had neglected to return the bogus passport to her cover officer. She decided to make use of it again – as a tourist going to Havana.

CHAPTER FORTY-FOUR

Kate was exhausted to the marrow. The eleven-and-a-half-hour flight from Washington/Dulles to Dublin hadn't been so bad. But following that with another twelve-hour leg from Dublin to Havana in the bosom of a tour group comprised of loudmouthed, hard-drinking Irish blue-collar workers was taxing in the extreme.

The travel method was part of her cover story: Irish secretary on a group vacation to Cuba's sunny tourist trap resorts. She'd been practicing an Irish accent for days, but decided the safer course was to pass herself off as Irish-born, but American-raised. Beyond that, her story got dangerously thin, as she had never even stepped foot in Ireland, and her European bloodlines ran to Lvov rather than to Limerick.

She therefore made her cover identity, Una O'Dalaigh, a shy, mousy recluse, along for the ride, but not the party. She'd been already hit on by a couple of the males. They backed off after she responded in a wispy voice, averted her eyes, and acted fidgety—not the type to bring to bed or back to Mom.

When the tour organizer, a woman in her early fifties with supreme organizational skills, asked about Una, Kate replied in a rapid staccato, "I was born outside of Dublin. My folks immigrated to Baltimore when I was very young. I'm visiting relatives and decided to vacation in Cuba on my Irish passport. I work in an accounting firm catering to pet food producers, yadda, yadda, yadda." She gave a nervous laugh, shrugged, and averted her eyes.

The tour lady, eyes glazed, quickly moved on to other members of the group.

On day two of her stay at Varadero Beach, Kate departed her hotel room at noon, sporting sunglasses, a large straw hat, and a generous slathering of sunblock. She began a leisurely promenade along Avenida de la Playa, which ran the length of the narrow white sand peninsula of Cuba's most popular resort.

Varadero was Cuba's pallid answer to Mexico's Cancún. The area had over sixty resort hotels, with restaurants that served food ranging from passable to detestable and service staff who put in effort commensurate with their one dollar per day salary. Unless working there, the average Cuban was barred from entering, access being controlled by a police checkpoint at the western end, and plainclothes agents monitored locals and visitors alike. Pristine beaches, snorkeling, wind surfing, and the other accoutrements of modern tropical tourism was all represented. Yet, vitality was lacking from the Potemkin village designed to suck hard currency out of sunburned northerners.

Kate allotted ninety minutes to conduct a surveillance detection run. She started by hiring a coco-taxi to take her on a relaxing tour of a stretch of the Hicacos peninsula. The coco-taxi was a miniature, fiberglass yellow and red vehicle resembling an open Easter egg shell on three wheels. She asked the driver to show her the hotels, the beach, and commercial areas. Every ten minutes or so, she instructed him to make a sudden right or left turn, or to drive around a block.

Eyes concealed by her large sunglasses, Kate stared intensely, memorizing every face, studying every individual, noting every car to the front as well as to the rear, any sign that she was being surveilled. She took digital photos of selected persons in the guise of snapping shots of the sea, luxury hotels, and street scenes. Discreetly, she would review the photos to see if she could detect a face or vehicle that might be tailing her.

A couple of times, she had the driver drop her off at one of the crafts markets, a paltry affair with lethargic vendors selling

T-shirts and cheap Chinese-made souvenirs. She took a T-shirt sporting Che Guevara's bearded, bereted visage off a rack. As she held it out at arm's length, she looked past it to First Avenue. A stocky middle-aged Cuban stood on the corner, doing nothing special. She memorized his face. Kate held the shirt against her torso to check the fit. In doing so, she made a half-turn and glanced at the narrow 48th Street. A young woman in a billowy white dress walked by, bag in hand. Again, Kate made a mental snapshot.

Kate quit the crafts market and strolled down First Avenue until she came upon Librería Hanoi. She stood in front of the small bookshop to pretend to peruse the leftist literature in the display window. She focused on the window's surface, scanning the reflections for any signs of surveillance.

She walked into the store, randomly picked up a book, *African Socialism*, and flipped through the pages. She looked around as she put the book back on its shelf. Her mind took in the people within her view, inside and outside. Was that stocky man loitering outside the door the same man she had seen earlier on a street corner? Was that woman in a white dress the same one she had seen outside?

Small spaces like a bookstore compelled watchers to converge on a narrower platform, thereby increasing the risk of revealing their presence. Those trained in countersurveillance, like Kate, used such spaces to funnel people by carefully studying faces they may have encountered during their meanderings.

She departed the bookstore. Her time spent performing countersurveillance had turned up no definite watchers. She turned the corner and headed for the Coppelia ice cream shop. There, she ordered two scoops of *mamey*, a Caribbean fruit tasting of pumpkin and maraschino cherries. She took a seat with her back to a wall, setting her canvas shopping bag on the floor.

"Are you Canadian?" asked a woman from behind her.

Kate turned to see a pretty young woman, dark in complexion, with ear-length hair and wearing a white fluffy dress.

"No. I'm from Ireland."

"Ah. I see you like *mamey* too." The woman spoke barely accented English.

"Yes. I've recently discovered it. I love the flavor."

"Well, enjoy your stay on Varadero." The Cuban woman rose and smiled. As she passed Kate, something dropped from her hand and into Kate's open bag with a barely perceptible plunk.

Kate finished her ice cream and departed Coppelia. She returned to her hotel room, where she fished out the item the woman had dropped in her bag. It was a key from the same hotel, marked "612."

Kate left her room and climbed the stairs to the sixth floor. Looking around carefully, she made her way to Room 612. She spotted no staff or guests. She unlocked the door, flitted into the room, and quietly shut the door behind her.

In the darkness, she felt for a lightswitch and flipped it. Sitting on the edge of the bed was the same woman she had encountered at Coppelia.

The woman smiled, stood up, and extended her hand. "My name is Rosa. Isn't *mamey* a heavenly flavor?"

"Sure. I'm glad Marcial's instructions worked so well. We should hurry."

"Yes, we must." Rosa opened a bag and pulled out some clothes and a bottle, the latter of which she tossed to Kate.

Kate read the label. "Hair Dye–Black." She looked back at Rosa, puzzled.

"Use the bathroom." Rosa nodded toward an open door. "We can't have a woman with hair the color of sugar cane joining us. You'll stand out like a lighthouse. When you are done, we will both change into these hotel maid outfits."

"What about my things?"

"Don't worry. They are being collected. And we're checking you out of the hotel. Please. Quick!"

As Kate was applying the dye, she asked, "How long have you been with the Brigade?"

Rosa hesitated before replying, "Not long."

"What drove you to join the rebels?"

"My father. He is high up in the party. My mother too. They are committed *fidelistas*. They named me after Rosa Luxemburg, the martyred Marxist revolutionary. I am therefore a child of the revolution. But their blindness to the injustices and bankruptcy of the system made me question it all. The massacres of students in Santiago led me to support the new revolution. Anyway, we can talk about these things later on. First, we must get you out of here."

Kate dried her hair and studied her new look in the bathroom mirror. "Wow. I always wondered what I'd look like as a brunette. What do you think?"

"Less conspicuous. Your name now is Yelina. How is your Spanish?"

Kate pulled down a corner of her mouth.

Rosa chuckled. "Keep your mouth shut and let me do all the talking."

They changed into the hotel uniforms and left the room. They slowly wended their way down the stairwell to the rear service area. A supply van backed up to the rear entrance, and the rear door opened. A man hunched inside the back gestured for the women to jump in. The van roared off.

Over the next three days, Kate traveled clandestinely eastward, sequestered in safehouses in Matanzas, Ciego de Ávila, and Las Tunas. Her escorts expertly avoided roadblocks and used the ever-growing Arnaldo Ochoa Brigade underground network to pass through government-controlled territory.

From Bayamo, they entered rebel-held domain. Over bumpy dirt tracks, they made their way to Marcial's jungle redoubt in the northern Santiago province.

The constant military vehicle traffic kicked up a continuous blanket of dust. Men drilled in surrounding fields. Trucks groaned under loads of ordnance and ammunition headed for frontline troops. ZPU-4 anti-aircraft guns, manned by alert Army defectors, were aimed mutely skyward. Other men armed with Strela-2 shoulder-fired, surface-to-air missile launchers manned stationary posts throughout the encampment. Marcial had built his guerrilla headquarters into a *Festung*, bristling with armaments and bustling with purposeful activity.

Kate was led to the command HQ, a basic wooden structure packed with communications equipment, battle maps, a Cuban flag and the Brigade's own banner mounted on a pole in front.

The aide escorting Kate tapped on a door bearing a painted wooden sign reading, *Comandante.* Inside, Col. Marcial and several officers stood before a wall-mounted map, animatedly plotting battle moves.

Marcial turned around. "You are *AmorVerdadero1878*?" he asked with a smile.

"The one and only. And you must be *SweetButterfly*."

"Yes. Isn't it obvious?"

They laughed. Marcial dismissed the others and pulled out a wooden chair for her. They sat opposite each other at the conference table.

"Did your CIA send you here?" Marcial asked.

"No. I came on my own accord."

"Therefore, you fall into the same status as Nick, a rebel?"

Kate lowered her head, then lifted her eyes coyly. "Yep, afraid so."

"Well, we are all rebels here. You come here to try to save him?"

Kate leaned forward. "Yes! Any way I can. They will execute him if we don't save him."

"And my son, too."

"Like before? With insiders?"

Marcial shook his head. "No. I am afraid lightning strikes only once."

"What, then?"

"Montilla has assigned her personal protection detail to carry out the executions. She can trust them, and does, with her own life. They will follow any order she gives them. But we must act fast."

CHAPTER FORTY-FIVE

"Lieutenant Marcial is guilty of violating Article 65 of the Cuban Constitution and of betraying the confidence placed in him by the people, the revolution, the party, and his comrades, a most repugnant fact that demands the severest disciplinary and legal measures."

Nick felt as if he were floating in suspension. Everthing was just too surreal. Standing in a drab, nondescript courtroom, flanked by two guards, he faced a tribunal of Cuban military officers. He anticipated a pre-scripted outcome—death by firing squad. Montilla had said his execution would take place at dawn the day after the kangaroo court. She observed the tribunal from her seat at an elevated table to one side. Her demeanor was stony. But all in the room had one eye on the "General of the Western Army," Cuba's third most powerful figure. She channeled the ailing Castro brothers, her presence ensuring that revolutionary justice would be meted in tried and true fashion.

"He will bear the full weight of the law for his crimes through death by firing squad at oh-six-hundred tomorrow."

Nick looked across the front row at Yuri, who sat erect, exhibiting no emotion as his death sentence was read by the presiding colonel. Yuri caught Nick's glimpse with a shift of his eyes and gave Nick a slight comradely nod.

Nick tuned out as the military prosecutor read the long litany of charges against him. He thought of his parents, of how he had betrayed their pride in him and how he would never be able to say goodbye. His heart sank not for his own sorry, self-inflicted fate, but for his parents losing their only child. He had never given them grandchildren. That and his betraying the FBI made his eyes tear.

And he thought of Kate. For the first time in his adult life, he had truly bonded emotionally with a woman. She'd tried vainly to steer him from his self-destructive course. Maybe he deserved a firing squad. He had disappointed everyone close to him. He had disappointed himself. His life was the definition of failure.

"Nicolás Castillo, a Cuban citizen, is guilty of espionage, sabotage, and activities directed at undermining the Revolution. The punishment is death by firing squad. Sentence will be carried out at oh-six-hundred tomorrow."

Strangely, Nick felt no emotion. No fear. No self-pity. No anger. His life would end within hours. He would face it like a man. He had played a dangerous game and was paying the ultimate price. So be it.

He looked at Montilla. If he could read anything in her expression, he would guess she was feeling triumphant.

The presiding colonel dropped the gavel. The guards shackled Nick and Yuri and led them in separate directions.

Twenty miles southeast of Havana, situated on flat, open terrain, the San José de las Lajas Maximum Security Prison, also known as Ganuza, was among the most difficult of hard targets. Reserved for military prisoners, prominent dissidents, and hardened criminals, Ganuza was as impenetrable from an intelligence angle as it was from a physical one. Marcial had no inside agents, no one to help him pull off a spectacular breakout like the one at Baracoa where he'd had an entire firing squad in his hip pocket, enabling him and Yuri to flee.

His men told him it was a suicide mission. But what choice

did he have? Yuri was hours from being summarily shot. His only son.

The plan was big and bold, typical of Marcial. *Do what the enemy cannot imagine you'd do. Think outside the box.* His revolution was built on such a strategy, just as Fidel's had been before it had ossified into a political fossil.

"Appear at places to which the enemy must hasten. Move swiftly where he does not expect you... and release the attack like a lightning bolt from above the nine-layered heavens," the great Chinese strategist Sun Tzu had said almost three millennia ago. Marcial had taken that advice to heart while he was a cadet at the General Máximo Gómez Academy, back when he and García had loyally served Fidel, before Angola, before being used as a pawn in a silly spy game, before his son's arrest, before he had lost faith in a hollow ideology that propped up doddering old men who refused to accept change.

The cement plant just north of San José de las Lajas was typical of all state-owned enterprises in Cuba's moribund economic sector. Only quasi-functional during the day, it was positively dead at night, a pushover target. Marcial assigned his crack José Martí Strike Force to pull off Operation Zero.

Ten men took over the plant within a matter of minutes, overpowering the single napping guard. With keys given up by the frightened guard, the men started the plant's five aging cement trucks and headed out the gate, turning onto the Carretera Central before heading south. No one in San José de las Lajas paid attention to the pre-dawn diesel exhaust-belching cement truck convoy barreling through the sleepy town center.

Within minutes, the convoy swung right onto a dirt road south of the city, kicking up clouds of red dust, then a sharp left onto another small road. Running past a neat baseball diamond on their left, the drivers floored it. With a loud roar, the vehicles bored headlong through the modest gate of a small FAR infantry base. The first truck crashed into the base's command office, sending splintering wood in all directions.

Two other trucks veered right, and two more veered left along the base's perimeter tracks and slammed to a halt. Men of the strike force leapt from the trucks on either side, took up positions, and let loose a hail of rocket-launched high explosive and incendiary grenades on the barracks. Other force members opened fire with assault weapons as FAR soldiers ran screaming from the building, some writhing in flames.

A siren sounded. Those FAR troops not caught in ambush fire mustered under their officers to organize counterfire. But the rain of grenades and mortar rounds from Marcial's men wreaked havoc on them.

The first explosions alerted the staff of Ganuza Maximum Security Prison diagonally across from the FAR base. Seeing the base go up in flames and come under siege, guards scrambled to put on riot gear and grab weapons. Under the direction of a senior guard, they stormed out of the prison front gate to help rescue their Army comrades.

Twenty more men of the José Martí Strike Force who flanked the prison entrance opened fire on the guards.

Nick stared intently at the narrow window high in the wall of his cell. He could see the glow of moonlight. He fixed his eyes, unblinking, on the pale light. Gradually, his peripheral vision blackened. Round and round and round, he swirled into another consciousness. He was no longer of the earthly realm, but in an ethereal one. His mind cleared of life's clutter. No pain, no hunger, no fear. His life story played out on a mental stage in fast forward: fragmented memories of early childhood, his mother's caress, his father's strong embrace, scenes from school, English, Spanish, laughter, weeping, first love, college, the FBI, Kate, Cuba. Yoruba drumbeats synchronized with his heartbeat. Babalú. *God of the earth appears. He smiles down. "Exile, debilitation will become resurrection. Be at peace, my son."*

In his trance-like state, every muscle untensed, and warmth enveloped Nick until he felt like a baby still in the womb. Babalú opened the sky, a welcoming entrance to somewhere better. Bliss. Repose. Carefree. Nick smiled and succumbed.

A flash of yellow-red light flared through the slat. A second later, the sounds of explosions and gunfire reverberated off the concrete walls, jarring Nick out of his deep contemplation.

The metallic squeak of coarse metal followed as the lock on his cell door turned. The door swung open with a loud clang. Two guards entered, grabbed Nick by the armpits, and dragged him out into the corridor.

A flustered FAR sergeant looked at him coldly. "You are condemned to die. Sentence is now to be carried out."

A wall clock displayed 0410, nearly two hours before the time laid down by the court.

After the guards had tied his hands, the sergeant motioned for Nick to be hauled away.

The explosions and gunfire outside the prison intensified. Inmates shouted and banged their cell doors with tin cups and whatever else they had found to make noise. The atmosphere was one of panic and growing chaos. Whatever was happening on the outside would make its way into the prison, but the question was whether it would storm the place fast enough to stop his execution.

Nick was rushed outside to the prison courtyard, where he saw an abbreviated firing squad of four nervous men. Another set of guards shoved Yuri out into the courtyard. Yuri's face was bruised and swollen.

"Nick!" Yuri said. "My father is coming for us. We will be spared!"

"Shut up!" the sergeant commanded.

A guard slammed his forearm down hard on the back of Yuri's neck. Yuri fell to his knees.

The guards pulled Nick and Yuri to stakes three meters apart and quickly tied their hands to the stakes. The harried sergeant winced when a mortar round exploded just within the far prison wall.

The firing squad separated into two two-man units and stood at an uneasy attention as tracer rounds lit the night sky above their heads. No blindfolds were proffered or last words solicited.

"*Preparen!*" the sergeant shouted.

The two-man squad before Yuri shouldered their rifles.

Yuri turned to Nick. "Nicky!" His eyes were filled with fiery intensity. The veins of his head and neck throbbed.

"*Apunten!*"

The squad aimed.

"This is not the end. It is the beginn—"

"*Fuego!*"

Gunshots erupted. Nick instinctively shut his eyes. He opened them to see Yuri's body slumped at the stake, his chest torn open and hemorrhaging blood.

A guard strode to the stake and cut Yuri's body free with a bayonet. The body fell to the ground with a soft thud.

The sergeant then strutted over, pulled out his service revolver, and delivered the ritual coup de grace, a bullet through Yuri's head. The sergeant reholstered his revolver and returned to the flank of the firing squad.

Another mortar round exploded inside the prison perimeter. The battle on the outside raged nearer and louder.

"*Preparen!*" the sergeant commanded the second two-man team.

They shouldered their rifles.

"*Apunten!*"

Nick raised his eyes to the star-filled night sky. "God save me."

"*Fuego!*"

Kate listened to the annoying tick-tock, tick-tock of *Radio Reloj* – Clock Radio, the government radio station. The incessant sound of a ticking clock was forever in the background of the broadcasts. And at the top of every minute, the announcer identified the station, *Radio Reloj,* followed by a beep, a time announcement, and finally, the letters "RR" tapped out in Morse code. At the top of the hour, *Radio Reloj* announced the top headlines.

Today, two traitors were executed for crimes against the Cuban people and attempting the violent overthrow of the government of Cuba. The Ministry of Defense spokesman stated that the traitors, Yuri Marcial Arribe and Nicolás Castillo Fernánadez, were put to death by firing squad at dawn today, carrying out the sentence imposed by the Extraordinary Military Tribunal a week ago. The two were responsible for the deaths of scores of innocent citizens and the destruction of the people's property valued at many millions of pesos. The spokesman said that the executions removed two very dangerous elements from the scene...

Kate and Marcial sat motionless in Marcial's office. Marcial stood, frozen, jaws clenched, eyes staring into space. When the news sank in, Kate ran out of the building.

Kate raced into the woodland surrounding the rebel base, brambles scratching her arms and legs. Arriving in a clearing, she dropped to her knees, raised her arms to the sky, and let out a primal scream

CHAPTER FORTY-SIX

Amelia Hernández Colorado had been feeding disinformation to Cuban intelligence for several months, ever since she had been apprehended and turned by CIA and DIA counterintel officers. Amelia, codenamed RAPTOR, was a haunted woman. She cared about one thing and one thing only: saving her own skin. She lived under house arrest in a nondescript building somewhere in southern Virginia, as far as she could tell. The place had armed guards twenty-four/seven, and everything she did was observed by her counterintelligence controllers. They worked in shifts. She had zero privacy. Shortly after she had been picked up, Mr. Smith handed her text that she had to transcribe into a letter to her family, stating that she was away on a classified assignment and would be incommunicado for several months.

Each day, U.S. intelligence officers monitored the covert email channels the DI had set up for Amelia for any new messages as well as shortwave radio instructions. When a message arrived from Havana, the monitors would print it out and deliver it to a special CI team, which would draw up a reply. The Cubans had requested a face-to-face meeting for Amelia with a cutout agent, but they immediately honored "her" request to defer the meeting due to increased CI vigilance at DIA and the other agencies. The Cubans went out of their way to protect prized assets like Amelia, code-named RAPTOR by her USG handlers.

Jake Coburn, a.k.a. Mr. Smith, was in charge of the RAPTOR operation. His mission was twofold: a) feed disinformation with the objective of disrupting DI operations, and b) fish for insights on the DI's modus operandi and plans.

His standing orders to Amelia's handlers were to "stay on her like spit to gum." Handling a turned double agent was exceedingly tricky. Having been coerced to turn sides, a turned double agent had every incentive to tip off her sponsors. One way of doing that would be to omit a pre-agreed security code in outgoing messages. The omission could be a deliberate typo or a misplaced number. Or a warning that the Americans had turned her could be conveyed by using a certain word or word order, something that would be missed by Amelia's new handlers, yet instantly picked up by Cuban intel. But there was one huge disincentive to exercising those ploys: the polygraph. Amelia had to undergo regular lie detector examinations. Should the box reveal she was lying or trying to fool the machine, all deals would be canceled. The death sentence would be sought.

Havana heaped praise on her after she transmitted a phony National Intelligence Estimate on Cuba that falsely concluded the latter's influence in Venezuela and Nicaragua was waning and that the Castro regime would likely survive and overcome the rebellion. Her report on a concocted Presidential Finding that instructed U.S. intelligence agencies to be in contact with Arnaldo Ochoa Brigade representatives but to lend no assistance was received by a grateful Havana along with pleas for more classified information. The DI was ecstatic with her list of CIA officers recently posted around Latin America whom she judged ripe for recruitment by Cuban intelligence. The CIA officers, of course, were "dangles," pre-positioned to be approached by Havana's agents with the aim of teasing out their modus operandi and any other useful information they could garner, not least of which would be the identities of the Cuban agents pitching them. And on it went for months—a steady stream of carefully confected lies, partial lies and disinformation. To add further weight to their source, Coburn "promoted" Amelia to a special White House task force on intelligence.

The operation worked for a while, but then the DI started losing spies.

Since the yacht Granma launched from Veracruz on November 25, 1956, with eighty-two revolutionaries of Fidel's 26 of July Movement to begin the armed struggle against Batista, Mexico had been a chessboard for Cuban political machinations against Washington. Mexico City had long been the DI's biggest spy station, or Center. Cuba's bloated embassy of fifty-two accredited diplomats and its four consulates scattered around the country were oriented heavily toward intelligence gathering on the United States. Fully half of those diplomats were in fact DI agents under diplomatic cover.

The DEA and ATF are running a covert program involving letting Mexican cartel criminals purchase assault rifles and other weapons from commercial arms vendors in U.S. border states and smuggle them into Mexico for use in combating rival gangs as well as Mexican military and law enforcement authorities. Increasingly, these weapons are turning up in Mexican government seizures. The Mexicans are furious that the United States is doing nothing to curb this arms trafficking. But they are unaware of the U.S. covert program, called Operation WALKER. The purpose of the program is to let the arms "walk" to cartel gang leaders, thereby revealing those calling the shots, which will lead to their arrest, interception of drugs, and closing down drug smuggling routes into the U.S.

U.S. law enforcement agents are divided over the wisdom and legality of the WALKER operation. It is a high-risk program that, if discovered by the Mexican government, would severely damage relations with Washington.

My source in DEA informs me that Los Zetas cartel plans to ship 2,000 AR-15's from Texas into Tamaulipas ten days hence in a trailer truck ostensibly transporting tractor parts. Mexican border agents and police have been bribed to look the other way. Washington is fully knowledgeable of this operation, but is withholding the information in order to observe the "walking" of the arms as part of Operation WALKER.

The CIA man encrypted the message into the S-1 thumb drive, just as Amelia had done for many months before being apprehended, and pressed Send. He then took a coffee break.

Montilla ordered her agents to sabotage the smuggling vehicle soon after it crossed into Mexico. Next, there would be well-placed tip-offs to the Mexican media about "a covert American plot to subvert Mexican security by shipping arms to major criminal gangs."

The Kenworth semi-trailer whose manifest listed farm equipment parts crossed the border from Interstate 35 into Nuevo Laredo on a sun-drenched weekday morning. A Mexican border agent waved the truck through. The vehicle headed west along the less traveled route to Monterey. Several miles before reaching the rendezvous point outside the dusty town of Anáhuac, the rig blew a tire. Then another. And another.

The two Cuban snipers hit their marks from positions five hundred meters from either side of the road. Their ops chief radioed in the news of success to the DI Center chief at the Cuban embassy in Mexico City.

Scores of heavily armed Mexican *federales* swooped in to arrest the Cubans and secure the truck.

Troops killed Los Zetas gang leaders and arrested others in Monterey.

El Universal

(Mexico City) – Federal Police busted a major arms smuggling operation today in Nuevo Leon, killing seven members of Los Zetas cartel and arresting twenty. Also arrested were an undisclosed number of Cuban diplomats who were at the scene where a tractor-trailer carrying some 2,000 arms from the United States was seized by the police. Unconfirmed reports state that the Cubans were armed and carrying radio communications equipment. Their role in the incident is not known at the present time. The Foreign Ministry issued a statement that the matter is being investigated.

A top Mexican official who wishes to remain unnamed credited the United States with helping Mexican authorities in a joint operation to allow the arms to enter Mexico unhindered in order to track their destination to cartel leaders who used narco-money to purchase them in Texas. American ATF agents simultaneously arrested the sellers of the arms. The senior Mexican official lauded the operation as "a success of Mexican-U.S. intelligence-sharing and law enforcement collaboration."

The Washington Post

(Mexico City) – In a major rupture in Cuban-Mexican relations, the Mexican government has declared the Cuban ambassador and twenty-five Cuban diplomats persona non grata and has withdrawn its ambassador from Havana. The move comes on the heels of an investigation of Cuban government involvement in a narcotics-for-arms deal gone wrong with the Los Zetas crime cartel. The Cubans were given twenty-four hours to leave the country. A Mexican Foreign Ministry spokeswoman called the Cuban actions "unconscionable and a gross interference in Mexico's internal affairs." Manuel

Guzman Romero, chief National Security Advisor to Mexican President Alfonso Aguilar, told reporters, "We have been increasingly concerned about the activities of Cuban intelligence agents on Mexican soil. This case brought to the surface just how brazen and lawless their behavior has become."

According to Mexican and U.S. law enforcement officials, the Cubans stumbled into a carefully planned joint covert program to ensnare Los Zetas in a sting operation. The CIA has declined to comment on the operation, reportedly launched as an intelligence operation as well as anti-crime action.

Jake Coburn put the newspaper down and poured himself another cup of coffee. He re-read the *Post* story and then erupted into uncontrolled laughter. He bunched his right hand into the shape of a pistol and pointed it at the newspaper.

"Attaway, Larisa. Gotcha!"

CHAPTER FORTY-SEVEN

Havana

"You are all worthless pygmies! You have dog shit for brains!" Pacing the conference room with her hands behind her back, Larisa Montilla looked every inch a beast of prey ready to strike. Her face flushed red, jugulars throbbing, brow furrowed.

"General, if I may—"

"You may go to hell!" Montilla shot back.

The MININT colonel shrank back in his chair. His fellow officers stared blankly at the conference table.

"Do you see what has happened? Or are you all blind as well as stupid?" Montilla asked. "We've been taken in. The Americans set an elaborate disinformation trap, and we stumbled right into it. I can't believe we fell for it. And now, over fifty years of warm Cuban-Mexican relations are in the garbage can! Not to mention our extensive intelligence network targeted against the United States. How did this happen?"

The senior colonel spoke up meekly. "We acted on inside intelligence given to us by Amelia Hernández." He removed a sheaf of top-secret communications from a folder. "These are her reports on Operation WALKER. They contain detailed information on how Washington was allowing guns to enter Mexico in order to track them into the hands of narcotraffickers. They were not informing the Mexicans."

Montilla grabbed the papers and skimmed fast. "Pull all of

Amelia's reports. I want a close analysis of all the information she has provided us with and an assessment of its value and truthfulness. I want it in exactly forty-eight hours."

The signal coming from the TETRA encrypted radiophone was surprisingly clear.

"Jake," Kate said, "I'm in eastern Cuba with the rebels."

Jake Coburn didn't respond.

"I know what you're probably thinking, Jake. She's run amok just like Nick Castillo. Something in that damn Cuban water." She let out a chuckle that sounded lame even to her own ears.

"K-Kate? Is… is that you?"

"Yes. It's Kate. I'm calling from Cuba over the Brigade's secure phone system. They've got good COMSEC here. They're thoroughly professional and disciplined."

"Kate, are you out of your bleeping mind?"

"Listen. No time to chew me out. I'm a big girl. I know what I'm doing."

"Okay. I'm all ears. But understand, you can now consider yourself a security risk, likely out of a job. Maybe even subject to federal prosecution."

"But my mother still loves me. Now listen up. They… they shot Nick."

"I know. State's been trying to get them to turn over his body. I'm sorry, Kate. I'm very sorry."

"But that's not why I'm calling. I'm calling to offer myself as the Agency's point person with the Cuban freedom—"

"Kate! Stop there. What you're asking is impos—"

"Just hear me out. Please."

Coburn let out a loud sigh. "Okay. Shoot."

"These guys are going to win, Jake. Better to be in on the ground floor, know what they're up to, and offer modest non-lethal support. Sending in the SEAL team was simply the wrong thing to do. But we shouldn't let that mistake make us stick our heads in the ground. Let me stay in place. I can be headquarters' eyes and ears on the ground as well as a means to channel our government's views and positions. They don't want military intervention from us. They just want a channel open. And when they're in charge in Havana, we'll already have the contacts and the inside dope, which will keep us from having to play catch-up. Who are we going to piss off by doing this anyway? The Castros? A government we don't even have diplomatic relations with?"

"I'll tell you what I'll do, Kate. I'll run it up the flagpole. But I can't promise anything."

"Jake, if I were there, I'd give you a big fat kiss!"

"Save your kisses for your sorry ass, sweetheart."

The analysis of Amelia Hernández's reporting arrived on Montilla's desk in exactly two days, just as she had ordered.

From her recruitment up until six months ago, Hernández's reporting was accurate and closely mirrored that from our other sources. In many instances, events bore out what she had told us. Simply put, she was consistently the best sensitive source we had on American intentions and actions. A close traffic analysis of the information coming to us from Hernández shows that, six months ago, a pattern of deception began. Equally disturbing is her consistent failure to use one set of security code signals in each of her reports. She used two of the three in her reports, but kept leaving out the third, a double period in the next to last sentence of each report. Señora Hernández, in our view, has been turned by the Americans, who have used the clandestine channel we set up with her to feed us carefully crafted disinformation. Some of this information has contributed to strategic losses as well as to the deaths and disappearances of a number of our agents. Many covers were blown. We can assume some of our DI agents have been co-opted by U.S. intelligence. We are conducting a damage assessment.

Montilla convened a meeting of her Special Activities Unit. "Operation HATUEY. Where does it stand?"

"Our sleeper agent, Miguel Guimerá, is carefully laying the groundwork," a senior colonel replied.

"Details?" Montilla asked tersely.

"Guimerá is one of our best, General. His father was on the Granma with Fidel and fought at the Bay of Pigs. He has lived in the United States for fifteen years. He is methodical and extremely security conscious. He doesn't provide interim reports. He fears being exposed. It also protects us should he be revealed."

"Or micro-managed," Montilla interjected. "Timing? How much longer?"

"We have no precise timeframe, General. But his strike against the American Secretary of Defense was clean, bold, and trace-free."

"Ah, yes. Let me know when you learn anything further. I also want Amelia Hernández taken care of. A message must be sent: 'Thus always to traitors.'"

As the months passed, Amelia's handlers granted her slightly more freedom of movement, but always still within the confines of the small isolated property in the middle of a forest. She deduced from the climate, the low blue mountains in the west, and the mostly north-south airplane traffic that she indeed was being held in southern Virginia, not very far from coastal naval bases. They let her start a small garden, a gesture for which she was most grateful. Her time spent tilling the soil, planting, and starting new life took her mind off her predicament, if only for an hour or two each day. She offered to make a *salpicón* beef and tomato dish with *curtido* cabbage salad for her controllers once her veggies were ripe for harvesting.

Just after breakfast, she put on her overalls and plunged her hands into the soft cool earth. That gave Amelia great pleasure. Life. Nature. She relished it, for who knew how long it would be until she found herself in solitary confinement at a supermax prison, surrounded by cold cinderblock walls, fluorescent lights, alone in a lifeless existence ?

Only when gardening did a smile return to Amelia's face. The sun was brilliant. She stood up, turned her face up to welcome the warmth, and took a deep breath of the crisp forest air.

No immediate sound accompanied the .50 caliber bullet that ripped Amelia's head from her body. The distant boom arrived a second or two after, too late to offer the stunned security guard who watched over her a clue as from which direction the lethal lead had come.

Thus always to traitors.

CHAPTER FORTY-EIGHT

The surroundings were familiar: a bedroom warmly decorated with paintings of rural Cuba, green curtains covering tall windows, and thick rugs on the floor, heavy Spanish colonial furniture, a four-poster bed. And the lovely green eyes boring into him from above, the cunning eyes of a female Cuban general.

She held a cup to his lips. "Drink. Drink up."

He drank. Some of the sweet elixir dripped from his mouth, landing on the soft bedsheets. His head spun. He strained to get up, but couldn't. Nylon cord secured his arms and legs to the bedposts. And the more he strained against them, the dizzier he got. He blinked repeatedly and shook his head in a vain attempt to clear his muddled mind.

"*No. No, querido.*" Montilla stroked his forehead, then gently kissed him. "I will remove the cord. But first you must obey me. There's a good boy."

Nick felt as if he were on a fast-moving carousel. Images swirled around him, too fast for his stultified brain to process. All he could make out was the beautiful succubus hovering over him. Everything else around her was a blur. He could muster no resistance to her enticements. Her breasts rubbing against his face only caused him to yield more to her. The faint aroma of jasmine lulled him further into her witchery.

His inner self, deep in his consciousness, told him to resist. That faint, yet solid core of his being knew what was happening, knew it was wrong, and screamed for him to fight it, but its signals dissipated before reaching his limbs. And the pleasure side of him, overrun with endorphins, told him to give in, yield to the pleasures being administered to his damaged body.

Her hands rubbed his naked chest, nails scratching his skin tantalizingly. Further down they went. Deft touching of his manhood brought on an involuntary reaction. Nails raked his thighs. Teeth lightly bit his neck. Hot breath blew against his face. Wet lips pressed on his.

Nick was alternatingly aware and not aware of what she was doing to him. He felt as if he were floating in air, every inch of his body titillated and aroused. He gave himself fully. Resistance was futile. Surrender was his only choice.

Through his mental fog, he saw her atop him, straddling his torso, and begin writhing in naked glory. No inhibitions. Each thrust of her strong body brought spasms of increasingly intense pleasure in his own. Faster and faster she went until he heard her scream, which caused his own explosive release. She collapsed, smothering his sweat-drenched body with hers. They both panted, hearts racing against each other.

When he awoke, only the dull glow of the outside security lights shone through the drawn curtains. Nick blinked to full consciousness. His head was clearer. Whatever drug she had slipped him had worn off.

Her naked body was nestled close to his, one arm resting across his chest. She was deep in slumber, breathing deeply and regularly.

Nick tried to lift an arm, but couldn't. His limbs were still constrained by cords tied to the bedposts. He pulled each leg as hard as he could, but it was useless. He was as helpless as Gulliver. He raised his head and surveyed his immediate surroundings, searching for a sharp object he might be able to reach. Nothing. She had roped him as securely as a rodeo calf.

She stirred and raised her head slightly. She peeked at him through bleary eyes, then nuzzled against his neck and sighed, sinking back into slumber.

"Hey," he said.

She was unperturbed. No movement.

"Hey!" he said louder. He bumped her thigh with his knee.

Montilla stirred.

"Larisa, wake up!"

She slowly raised her head and peered at him through half-closed lids. "What is it, *querido?*"

"I've got to go to the bathroom. Untie me."

Montilla came fully awake. She propped her head on one arm, her light brown tresses cascading onto the sheets. She ran the index finger of her other hand playfully across Nick's chest.

"Larisa, take off these ropes."

"Oh. But I like you like this. You are my captive, *querido.*" She raised herself directly over him, her hair swaying playfully across his face, neck, and chest as she nibbled and kissed his body.

Nick strained again against the ropes.

Her mouth and tongue brushed his groin, ending between his legs. "Ahh! That's better."

"Larisa, listen to me! You can't keep me this way."

"Oh, yes, I can!" she answered mischievously, continuing with her ministrations.

"At least let me go to the bathroom. If you don't..."

"All right." She got up and freed one of his hands, then the other.

Nick sat up with a start only to be met with the business end of a 9mm pistol.

"Not so fast, *querido.*" Montilla stood before him, her bare femininity offset by the hard metal weapon in her right hand. She unbound Nick's legs using one hand. "No fast moves. No funny business."

Nick sat frozen. One minute, she was making love to him. The next, she was threatening him with a loaded gun.

She indicated the location of the bathroom with a flick of the gun barrel.

Nick rose cautiously and made his way to the toilet. As soon as he turned on the light and closed the door, he quickly checked out the room. Medicine chest, sink, cabinet. Nothing that remotely could be used as a weapon, clearly a detail Montilla had attended to earlier. He did his business, then threw some water on his face. He studied himself in the mirror. He looked ragged and worn with puffy, dark-circled eyes, a well-past-five-o'clock shadow, and wild hair. He could only think of himself as a caged animal and Larisa Montilla as his keeper. She had staged the execution episode so that the firing squad used real bullets on Yuri, but blanks for him. Why?

He opened the door, expecting to be greeted by the gun barrel again. Instead, he saw Montilla sprawled on the bed, leaning on one elbow, sporting a wicked smile.

She patted the bed. "Come."

Step by halting step, he obeyed and made his way back to the bed.

She took his hand and guided him to her. She lifted his hand to her breasts and leaned forward so her lips were a centimeter from his. "You want this, Nick. You know you do." Her breath was hot and smelled of rum. Her eyes broadcast lust.

One part of him tried to resist; one part succumbed. Their lips met, and he covered her with his body. Their lovemaking quickened.

"Take me! Yes! Yes! Yes!" she panted.

He made no effort to be gentle with her. They moved in unison, their movements becoming more and more frantic. She moaned, finally squealing in climax. Seized by a force of nature beyond his control, Nick let himself go. They reached the erotic summit together, then collapsed in each other's arms.

In the afterglow, they lay on their backs, staring into space, silent.

She turned to him. Her face was serious. "Nick."

"Yes."

"I can imagine what is going through your mind."

"Like?"

She leaned on her elbow and faced him. "Why I spared you, for example."

"And killed Yuri. You had him shot. But you spared me. Why?"

She placed a hand on her forehead and leaned back, a troubled expression on her face. "Oh, Nicky. We live in such complicated times. I had no choice. Can't you see? It is kill or be killed in this environment. A zero-sum game. Yuri Marcial was an enemy of the state, of our revolution. He mercilessly slaughtered many of our people. He paid with his life. But he died honorably in a military execution, if that is important to you."

"And me?"

She looked searchingly into his eyes. "I-I love you." Tears ran down her cheeks. "From the first moment I laid eyes on you, I felt something... special."

"And where do you expect this to lead?"

Montilla grasped his hand and put herself nose-to-nose with him. "Nicky, listen to what I have to say. Stay here. With me. You have no future in America. You are seen by your own FBI as a turncoat. You can't return. Your bridges are burned. If you stay in Cuba, I can give you a secure and good future. Once we bring these insurrectionists under control, we will embark on reforms. Real reforms. We will open up the economy. Hold elections. Cuba must move forward into the world of today and tomorrow. I know this. And I will move to open up relations with your country. Raúl and Fidel... they will soon draw their last breaths. And this will allow change to come. Real change. And you can be part of it. After all, you are also Cuban. The blood of Cuba runs through your veins. Join us. Stay with me." She placed her head on his chest.

He smiled and stroked her hair, but said nothing.

"Nicky, I am not asking you to betray your country. I loathe traitors. But there is going to be a leadership change in Washington. Very soon."

Nick stirred. "What do you mean?"

"Ah, it's the rum talking. Nothing. It's nothing."

"But—"

"Shh." She placed her forefinger against his lips and nuzzled up against his neck. "What can I do to persuade you to join me here?" Her long fingers played with the hair on his stomach, then danced down his groin and between his legs. Her wet lips teased his ear. "I am now going to administer some of our most effective torture to get you to say yes." She placed herself on top of him and rubbed her body against his.

He locked his mouth on hers. In one powerful move, he reversed positions, causing her to squeal. On top of her, Nick pinned her arms against the bed. "Now who's torturing whom?"

"Ah, but you underestimate MININT." With a quick thrust of a thigh, she sent Nick onto his side.

The two gripped each other in a wrestlers' test of wills and strength.

Nick leapt off the bed onto his feet. "You want torture? I'll show you what we Yanks can dish out." He dashed to the large dresser, opened a drawer, and pulled out the riding crop. He plunged to the bed, turned a giggling Montilla over on her stomach, and playfully thrashed her buttocks with the small whip. "All right. Time to cough up some secrets! What do you mean by a leadership change in Washington? Explain!"

"Ouch! No, *señor* FBI agent. I shall not talk. Oww!" Giggle.

Her buttocks were reddening with each light swat. Her unconvincing protestations melted into purring. "Don't stop. Harder!"

Nick obliged. The redness changed to crimson. Montilla squirmed.

Nick stopped.

She opened her eyes. "Why did you stop? Continue. I promise I'll reveal a secret."

With one of the cords that had restrained him, Nick deftly bound her hands behind her back.

"Whoa!" Montilla yelped. "This is getting exciting. What role are you playing? My jailer?"

"No. Your executioner." Nick placed her gun behind her ear and cocked it.

"Nicky. This is getting to be too realistic."

He pulled the trigger. All he heard was the hollow metallic click of an empty gun. He pulled back the slide and again pressed the trigger. Click. He pressed the barrel hard against her cheek. "The only reason you're alive right now is an empty magazine. I should've known. You're methodical to a fault. No loaded guns in the same room as a prisoner, eh, Larisa?"

Nick heard men's voices and the heavy tramping of boots up the stairs. He dropped the gun, climbed out of the tall window and onto the front portico roof, then sprang to the ground and ran out into the night.

CHAPTER FORTY-NINE

Miguel Guimerá showed up at the Elk Run Ranch outside of Dallas at seven o'clock for his new job as a farm laborer. He gave his name as José Gutiérrez, lately of Nicaragua. Having fulfilled his "internationalist duty" in that country in years past, he easily spoke its Spanish dialect when mingling with the other Latino workers. Mostly, however, he intended to keep to himself, in keeping with his cover as the middle-aged, nose-to-the-grindstone immigrant worker earning dollars to remit to his family "back home."

Hank, the burly tobacco-chewing supervisor, led Guimerá to a corral. Inside were three large Holsteins. "Them there's Bertha, Gertie, and Nellie."

Guimerá nodded and smiled.

"Girls! This here's Ho-zay. He's gonna be seein' to yer needs and takin' good care of ya from here on in."

One of the cows mooed.

"Now, Ho-zay, these are our prime dairy cattle. The beauty queens. They've won all kinds of ribbons at the state fair and our own county fair. Ya unnerstan'?"

Guimerá nodded.

"Now, we've hired you to work full time with these beauties. They got special food. They gotta be exercised, but don't run 'em ragged. They gotta be groomed. A vet comes by regular-like to check on their health and give 'em their medicines. I want you to make sure everything gets done when it's s'posed to and keep these lovely ladies happy." Hank opened the gate and led Guimerá into the corral.

Guimerá slowly approached the cows, then reached out and stroked their flanks. The animals nuzzled his hand.

"Looks like you got a natural way with bovines," Hank said. "Good."

"I know cows since I was a boy. My dad, me, and my brothers worked on a ranch in Nicaragua."

"Great. First order of business is to make sure they don't get hardware disease—loose metal they pick up while grazing that gets stuck in their honeycombs." Hank placed a hand over his prodigious paunch. "Their first stomach chamber."

Hank reached over and grabbed a short metallic pole with a three-ringed triggering device at the end. With the other hand, he lifted a box packed with three-inch cylindrical objects rounded at the ends. "These're the cow magnets we insert to pick up all the loose metal. Now, this here's a balling gun. We'll insert magnets in them Holsteins over there." He pointed to a small herd of cows in a nearby corral. "In a few days, we'll do the same to Bertha, Gertie, and Nellie. Got it?"

"Yes, boss. I got it," Guimerá said with a grin.

"These babies gotta be at the top of their form when the President comes to the Texas State Fair in two weeks. Shit. The whole area'll be like a zoo." Hank spat black juice into the dirt.

Billows of dust engulfed the two-truck convoy as it barreled into Camp Martí. Kate vainly waved the air in front of her face and coughed. Dust covered everything. She manned the radio equipment much of the day, sending encrypted concise reports to Langley. The dust filled her skin pores, giving life to pimples and other blemishes. Her hair felt and looked like straw from daily washings with rough soap.

Brakes screeched. Metal doors slammed. She heard a commotion, the familiar sounds of men returning from the front, then a loud "Hurrah!" and the quickening footsteps of other men running to the scene. The noise grew louder. Kate signed off and left the commo hut to see what all the fuss was about.

Outside, she placed a hand above her eyes to shield them from the blinding sun.

A raucous gaggle of soldiers was celebrating, one man hoisted on their shoulders. "*Hurra! Hurra! Viva!*" they shouted in unison as they jostled their returning hero.

Kate squinted to make out who the man was. The raucous procession made its way toward her. The men paused in front of her. The good-looking man being regaled smiled down on her.

"Nicky!" she screamed. "Nick!"

The men lowered him. Beaming, he walked toward her. She threw herself at him. As they embraced, another round of *hurrahs* erupted. They kissed hungrily. Kate then pressed her cheek against Nick's chest and shut her eyes. His heartbeat, life affirming, renewed her life. Tears ran down her face, wetting his smudged tunic.

"Oh, Nicky! You're alive. My God! You're alive."

He kissed her head. "I've only used up eight of my nine lives, baby. Takes more than a firing squad to kill this *guajiro*."

She looked up at him and placed her hands on either side of his head. "After this, after Cuba, the ninth life, we share together. Without firing squads. Promise me?"

"Promise."

Marcial dismissed his aides after Nick was escorted to his command center. The men embraced then sat with Kate at the conference table.

Nick described the Havana café scene, Yuri's impromptu

assassination of the Livingstons, their flight, and subsequent capture. "Colonel, your son died bravely for Cuba."

Marcial stood and faced a window overlooking a small parade ground in the center of which was a flagpole with Cuba's banner waving in a light breeze. Hands clenched behind his back, the rebel leader remained silent.

"He told me, 'This is not the end. It is the beginning,' just before… before they shot him. He expressed his undying faith in you, Henrique. He sacrificed his life so Cuba would be free. His name will go down in the annals of the great Cuban heroes."

Marcial half-turned his head in Nick's direction. "Before… before they… killed him… did he suffer? Did they… did they…"

"He was strong, unbowed. Full of life. He accepted his fate. You can be proud of your son."

Marcial's eyes welled with tears. "Yes. Very proud. But my son was a hothead, impulsive." Marcial breathed deeply and collected himself. He then called for his staff to return. He stepped up to the large map on the far wall and pointed at Santiago. "The city is surrounded. All lines of communication are cut. Government troops are short of ammunition, provisions, everything. And the people are rising up. Tomorrow, there will be a mass strike. The government there is crumbling from within, and they cannot withstand our imminent assault.

He indicated an area toward the center of the country. "Santa Clara, the center of gravity for the regime; once it falls, the whole rotten edifice collapses, and Havana is ours. I will lead the assault on Santiago in two days' time. You, Nick, shall lead a column to attack Santa Clara."

Nick was stunned. An FBI agent wasn't supposed to involve himself in foreign conflicts, much less help lead one. But in for a centavo, in for a peso, he thought. He straddled two existences now: American and Cuban. And his foothold in the former had been becoming more and more tenuous.

"You will be our William Alexander Morgan," Marcial said, referring to the young American adventurer who had become a commander of rebel forces during the anti-Batista insurrection ultimately won by Castro. He didn't mention that Castro later had Morgan shot before a firing squad for being a CIA spy. "I am putting a thousand men under your command. They are battle tested. Many of them served under Yuri. Therefore, they know you from the San Luís operation when we attacked the government train and captured General López y López.

"We have intelligence that another train loaded with tons of ammunition, equipment, troops, and senior officers will be sent to Santa Clara in two days. They mean to strengthen the government garrison there. By capturing this train, we will not only deprive the garrison of needed supplies, but with those supplies, we can cut off the head of the snake: Havana."

"It's not quite the honeymoon suite, I'm afraid," Kate said with a shrug.

Two army bunks stood side-by-side in the corner of a spare thatch hut with a tarp for a door and two small window openings. An empty ammo box served as a table, on top of which sat a well-used oil lamp. Another box was used as an improvised dresser. A mosquito net was tied above the bunks. The roar of truck engines and diesel generators created constant background noise.

"It's just fine," Nick said as he put his arms around Kate's waist.

They kissed, tentative at first, then hungrily. Their passion surged. Seconds later, they were on the bunks. He reached under her tunic, released her belt, and pulled at her pants. He was eager, impatient, rushing things.

Kate placed her fingers on his lips. "Slow," she said gently. "I want us to take our time. I want to savor you. I want to relish every second." She kissed him lingeringly. With one hand, she unbuttoned his shirt and ran it up his chest.

Nick looked deeply into her eyes. "I love you."

After their lovemaking, they lay still in each other's arms.

"Kate, I need to tell you—"

She interrupted. "Larisa Montilla."

Nick raised his head to look at her. "She has this power over people. And I don't mean jackbooted power. It's her personality. Charisma. Guile. It's hard to put a word on it. Almost witch-like."

"Sexual?"

"Kate—"

"And you gave in?" she asked.

"Yes. I mean, no. I mean—"

"Nick, I think you need help. Counseling." Kate jumped up and began to dress.

"Yes. Maybe I do! But first, get yourself captured, imprisoned, beaten, interrogated, waterboarded, then suddenly given comfort, a human touch. Know what it's like to be kept in solitary, naked, fed state propaganda, face a firing squad, see your friend's chest explode, but you're spared. Then... then..." He lowered his head into his hands and broke down weeping.

Kate rushed to him and enveloped him in her arms. "I'm sorry. I didn't know. I didn't know."

"I'm coming," Kate said. She tossed her duffel onto the back of the lead truck.

Nick tried to block her way. "Kate, it's too dangerous. Besides, you've got a job to do here. Man the commo gear and send reports back."

"I've trained a young lady to do that. And her English is impeccable. I'm coming." She climbed into the cab.

Nick stood glowering at her, arms crossed. "Kate, I don't have time for this."

"Neither does this revolution. You'll have to arrest me to keep from being part of history."

Nick continued to glower, but was at a loss for words. The fire in her eyes and that contrast of femininity and dogged determination were what so attracted her to him. "Hell. Neither of us has anything left to lose. Just do as I say. We don't need any dead Americans in this adventure. Agreed?"

"Agreed."

The column pulled out with a loud roar and a cloud of mushrooming dust.

CHAPTER FIFTY

The normally sleepy city of Yaguajay, hugging the Bay of Buena Vista on the north coast, had turned into a bustling garrison town. Its capture by Marcial's fighters months earlier had been an enormous embarrassment to the central government. The Battle of Yaguajay in late 1958 lent hero status to Che Guevara and Camilo Cienfuegos and accelerated the downfall of Fulgencio Batista. The town was the launching point of choice for the Arnaldo Ochoa Brigade. Target: Santa Clara.

The truck column rumbled north toward the coastal port of Caibarién. Intelligence on the force's size had reached the city's defenders. Rather than face such an enemy, the FAR troops charged with defending the place turned on their officers, shooting some before melting away.

A similar scenario played out at Remedios and Camajuaní on the route westward toward Santa Clara. As the Arnaldo Ochoa Brigade rolled through Camajuaní's town center along Independence Avenue, citizens lined the road waving Cuban flags and cheering wildly, greeting the Brigade as liberators.

As the convoy left Camajuaní heading west toward Santa Clara, the roar of fighter jets tore through the clouds. One, two, then three MiG-29s swooped down like birds of prey and fired 30mm rounds, which chewed up jeeps and trucks, setting them ablaze. Bodies burst into bloody pieces. Men scattered away from the column.

Nick shoved Kate from the cab of the lead truck. She

landed roughly on the roadside, injuring an arm. Nick leapt after her and pulled her into the brush.

The MiGs circled to make another swoop. As they bore down, they fired S-24 rockets at the column, destroying more vehicles and killing more men. From the north came a different sound, one no less lethal. The chop-chop-chop of military helicopters. Six Mi-24 Hind choppers shredded the air with their five-bladed main rotors. The flying behemoths spat out death at four thousand rounds per minute with Yak-B Gatling guns and more explosive force from S-8 rockets. As they swept over the Brigade at one hundred sixty miles per hour, the air impact from the rotors flattened most vegetation and sent fighters to the ground. They tag-teamed in their attacks so that firepower was dealt out continuously.

Amid the confusion, Nick and Kate, hunched low to the ground, ran toward two vehicles towing ZU-23-2 23mm anti-aircraft twin-barreled autocannons.

"Get on it. Fire back, godammit!" Nick ordered the equipment's operators, who hovered in a nearby drainage ditch. When they didn't respond, Nick took his pistol from its holster and fired in the air. "I said, get on it!"

Refinding their courage, the men hopped on the guns and began blasting away at jets and choppers.

Nick pointed to another group. "You! You guys with the SAMs. Get your asses in gear!"

Several rebels scrambled to their trucks and took out shoulder-fired SA-7s. They positioned themselves in an arc astride the stalled convoy.

A Hind swooped in, firing its Gatling gun. Nick signaled to one SA-7 operator to fire. The Grail round whooshed upward, catching the attack helicopter in the nose. The aircraft burst into flames, spun wildly, and crashed fifty meters away.

Nick signaled another man to launch just as the second Hind was homing in to fire its S-8 rockets. The second Grail missed its mark. An S-8 slammed into a now-empty troop carrier, setting off another ground explosion. As the hovering chopper's powerful blades blew away hats, tunics, and light equipment, Nick ordered the third and fourth SA-7 operators to fire. The fourth rocket hit the Hind squarely in its belly, setting off a blast of burning fuel groundward.

The rebels ran for their lives as liquid fire descended on them. Two men were enveloped in flames. Their screams pierced the air as they writhed in death throes.

Another Hind was hit, sending black smoke from its exhaust. It beat a retreat to safe territory.

The anti-aircraft guns continued to blaze away. A third joined the fray, firing over a thousand rounds per minute at one incoming MiG fighter. At nine hundred meters out, the jet fired rockets at the column. They barely missed it, exploding a stand of trees on the right flank. When the jet swooped up, its right vertical stabilizer split off in a thousand pieces as anti-aircraft rounds found their mark. The MiG lurched out of control and lunged at the earth. A huge ball of flame mushroomed skyward in the distance at the point of impact.

Brigade men cheered.

"Great job, men! You just destroyed one-third of Cuba's MiG-29 fleet," Nick shouted, alluding to the cash-strapped regime's deteriorating Army.

The remaining two MiGs and four operable helicopters receded beyond the horizon toward Havana.

Nick held up his hands. "This is no time to celebrate. This was only meant to soften us up. The next attack will be by ground forces. Get back to your positions. Onward to Santa Clara!"

Students at the Central University of La Villas, on the northeastern outskirts of Santa Clara, had seized control of their campus, followed quickly by students at the ironically named Comandante Ernesto Che Guevara Vocational Institute of Hard Sciences. After being welcomed as liberators, the Brigade garrisoned themselves at the schools.

The armored train reached the foot of the hill of Capiro, northeast of the city. The FAR force established a command post at the nearby Camilo Cienfuegos Military School, just outside Santa Clara's beltway. As night fell, both sides settled in, reinforcing their positions and keeping a wary watch on each other.

"Who was William Alexander Morgan exactly?" Kate asked. "Marcial said you were his 'William Alexander Morgan.'"

They sat in an impromptu command center in the rector's office, relaying orders to field units and reviewing the latest incoming tactical intelligence.

"He was a young adventurer from Toledo, Ohio, who went to Cuba in 1957 to join the battle to oust Batista. With his U.S. Army experience, his pluck, and charisma, he took command of a group of noncommunist rebels. Along with Che Guevara, he helped liberate Santa Clara at the end of 1958."

"How come I've never heard of him? What happened to him?"

"He died young at only thirty-two. Castro had him shot before a firing squad, having accused him of being a CIA spy. Then, Castro imprisoned his widow for a decade. They had two toddlers."

"Oh, my God! It gives me the shivers."

"It always was a zero-sum game with Fidel. And his paranoia is the hallmark of all dictators."

"And here we are," Kate said, "over fifty years later, an American leading Cuban rebels in the second Battle of Santa Clara."

"But no firing squad at game's end."

"Amen to that."

The holiest shrine to Cuban communism, the Che Guevara Mausoleum, on the western side of Santa Clara, exhibited trouble. Someone had scaled the ten-meter-tall concrete pillar that supported the bronze heroic statue of "El Che." They had defaced the late revolutionary's trademark slogan, *"Hasta la Victoria*

Siempre," crossing out *"la Victoria"* with red spray paint and crudely writing, *"al Infierno."* So the slogan changed to *"Hasta al Infierno Siempre"*—"Ever Onward to Hell."

The city was coming apart.

Comandante Nick Castillo sent two columns of troops out before dawn, one to seize Capiro Hill and the government train, the other to probe the southern sector of the city. As news spread that anti-government forces were poised for attack on the outskirts of the city, residents became restive. A series of skirmishes broke out between armed residents and government troops. Rebel supporters hurled Molotov cocktails at FAR vehicles and offices.

From his armored vehicle, Nick surveilled the city through binoculars. Flames and explosions lit the sky. He radioed the southern column leader to attack in force. Then he pointed at a unit leader. "Méndez, link up with the partisans. Take two tractors from the agriculture school here. Get them to infiltrate those tractors inside the beltway. Then use them to tear up the tracks so the government train can't retreat when we assault Capiro Hill." He turned to address a twenty-three-year-old guerrilla unit commander known affectionately as el Torito, Little Bull, for his aggressive, speedy attacks on enemy positions. "Capiro Hill, that's your mission, Medina."

The subcommanders took off on their missions. The small G-2 military intelligence unit was in contact with partisans inside the city and collected vital information on enemy positions and movements. They were Nick's eyes and ears inside the city.

"Kate. Can you collate the reports on..." He looked around. "Kate? Where's Kate?"

In a clearing, Kate set up the portable SatLink communications unit provided to her by the CIA. Two weathertight metal briefcases contained compact digital equipment that could send and receive secure phone calls, faxes, photos, and data as well as locate positions through GPS via a direct INMARSAT satellite link. After activating the link, she would send in short reports to Langley in real time.

"Kingfisher. Kingfisher. Do you read me?" Nick's voice crackled over the walkie-talkie on Kate's belt. Kingfisher was her code name.

El Torito was organizing his men for a mortar attack on the Camilo Cienfuegos Military School as a diversionary tactic while sending a separate team to take Capiro Hill, the highest point in Santa Clara. Control of the hill would give them fire superiority as well as a clear view on the enemy's movements, which Kate would also report to Nick.

"Kingfisher. Get your ass back here now!"

"No can do, Comandante. Operation in progress. Will keep you posted. Over." Kate switched off the walkie-talkie and resumed setting up the SatLink.

As the first column penetrated the city from the south, Medina hit the military school with a barrage of 82mm mortar rounds and opened fire with infantry weapons from three sides. Those FAR troops defending the hill withdrew with surprising speed to help defend the school. The train command post with officers and troops, pulled back toward the city center until it came to the rails pulled up by the tractors. The train went off the tracks, sliding cockeyed into a field.

Attacks by Hind choppers missed their mark. Two were taken down by SA-7 surface-to-air missiles.

Santa Clara partisans emerged armed with a hodge podge of captured weaponry and Molotov cocktails. They drew near the train and began lobbing the fire bombs at it. Over three hundred officers and men fled through whatever openings they could as the cars became veritable ovens. Demoralized and disoriented, they surrendered.

At the same time, the two FAR garrisons in the city succumbed to the combined forces of the southern Brigade column and local partisans.

Shortly after, *Radio Libertad* announced that all government troops in Santa Clara had surrendered.

Kate stood up to get a clear look at the sight of hundreds of surrendering government troops. It was too soon.

A single shot rang out. Kate felt a dull pain in her back as she fell to the ground.

CHAPTER FIFTY-ONE

Havana

The throbbing in her head was such that she thought it would explode. Her heart pumped to the bursting point. Sweat flowed from every pore. Larisa Montilla couldn't believe what she was reading and hearing. Santa Clara in rebel hands. Santiago on the verge. The whole country was falling from the government's grip.

She got up to issue more orders, but found the offices eerily vacant, her staff having flown the coop. Havana's Party Secretary had reportedly commandeered a government Yak jet to fly to Caracas. The president of the National Assembly, a Fidel stalwart from the early days of the revolution, had vanished. The first vice president had been shot by citizens as he tried to flee his home with his family. There were unconfirmed reports that members of the Army general staff had defected to the other side. Havana residents were pouring into the streets, challenging the police and throwing bricks into the windows of government offices. Flames and explosions erupted on the capital's outskirts. The walled-off world that had been in place for over half a century was collapsing.

Montilla stormed out of her office. "Hermanos Almejeiras Hospital. Step on it!" she barked to her nervous driver.

The driver skirted off Salvador Allende Avenue in the face of growing crowds and impromptu roadblocks. They passed a

CDR office being trashed by a mob. Taking side streets, they raced to Central Havana and the towering showcase hospital that catered to the country's political elite and hard-currency-paying foreigners.

The cavernous, muraled foyer was filled with confused, fearful staff, patients, and visitors. Cool-tempered MININT security personnel met Montilla and escorted her to the top floor in a private elevator.

They entered the floor reserved exclusively for top party, government, and military officials to find a klatsch of distraught and weeping hospital staff, who parted as Montilla strode in.

"I am here to see the President," she snapped.

Doctors and nurses looked at each other. Then, the senior staff physician said, *"Está muerto, general."*

"Dead?" The blood drained from Montilla's head. "Show me."

The physician led her to a VIP room in the intensive care unit. The stonelike body of the President lay with a sheet over his face.

Montilla pulled back the cloth. "When?"

"A few minutes ago. The latest news… it was too much for his weak heart."

Montilla stormed out. "Jaimanitas!" she ordered her driver.

They sped along a clogged and chaotic Fifth Avenue to the western suburb of Jaimanitas, once a favorite haunt of "Papa" Hemingway. Code-named *Punto Cero*—Point Zero— by MININT personnel in charge of VIP protection, the place hosted the residence of Fidel. The four-bedroom house was sandwiched between a farm and an Army garrison.

Montilla's vehicle screeched to a halt in front of a gate manned by a score of jumpy machine-gun-toting security guards. The officer-in-charge scrutinized her ID, saluted, and ordered the gate opened. The tranquility of the small pine-tree-ringed compound stood in stark contrast to the growing chaos in the rest of the capital.

Montilla was met at the house by another phalanx of armed men, who closely checked her papers before escorting her inside the marble-floored, simply-appointed residence.

She was led by an aide to the master bedroom. Inside were Fidel's wife Dalia and their four children, faces drawn. The former Maximum Leader lay on his bed, eyes closed, breathing heavily. His personal physician was checking his vital signs.

Montilla looked questioningly at Fidel's son Antonio, a surgeon.

Antonio shook his head. "He collapsed upon hearing the news about Uncle Raúl. He hadn't slept since Santa Clara fell. It was too much for him."

The physician said, "Stroke. It is too dangerous to move him with the chaos out there."

"Has he been conscious?" she asked.

Fidel stirred and mumbled something.

Montilla knelt at his bedside. She took his hand and caressed it.

"Is… is that you?" he rasped.

"It's Larisa, *jefe.*"

The old man's half-opened eyes tried to focus. "Che?"

"Che's daughter," she answered.

"Che! When you attack Santa Clara, you must do so quickly from the south. Camilo, he should seize Capiro. Understand me, Che? "

Montilla looked up at the others. "He's back in 1958," she said softly. She again caressed his hand. "This is not 1958, *jefe.* Santa Clara fell to the rebels, *our* rebels, yesterday."

He gasped. "Huh?"

"Everything is falling apart. The revolution. Collapsing. What do I do, Comandante? What do I do?"

His hand tightened around hers. *"Patria o muerte. Patria o…"* His eyes widened, then closed.

Montilla let go of his hand. She rose, eyes still transfixed on him. She then looked blankly at the others, all sobbing, turned, and strode toward the door.

"What do we do, General?" one shouted in desperation.

"You heard him. *Patria o muerte.*" Fatherland or death. And she left.

"Where the hell did you get body armor?" Nick asked as he applied ice to the swelling on Kate's back.

"Jake Coburn gave it to me. He suspected what I was up to and made me promise to wear it any time I found myself in a shooting environment." She winced as Nick placed his hand gently on the injured spot.

"How did you get it through Cuban customs?"

"I wore it."

"Oh. Well, the armor panel on the back deflected the bullet. Good material. It saved your life. But you disobeyed my explicit orders to hang back."

"Shoot me."

"Funny. Someone already did. I want you to promise me never to do anything like that again."

She raised her right hand in a scout salute. "I promise never to knowingly get myself shot."

"Ha, ha. Funny. I may want to shoot you myself."

"What's next, Comandante?"

"Think you can sit in a truck? We're moving out in an hour."

"Yeah, with the help of a painkiller. Destination?"

"Havana."

Just after the fall of Santa Clara, the Council for the Restoration of Freedom and Democracy in Cuba (CRLDC) called for a general strike in all areas still under government control. With Marcial at its head, the body was to begin governing Cuba until free elections could bring about a democratically chosen government.

Santiago fell shortly after Santa Clara. Marcial's multi-flank attacks combined with another student-led uprising overwhelmed the weakened regime forces in that city. Brigade forces struggled to bring control over the newly liberated city where reprisals against party figures, secret police agents, and CDR cadre were threatening to turn into a bloodbath. The CRDLC was tasked with restoring order.

Habaneros took to launching a general strike with gusto. As government control evaporated in advance of the arrival of Brigade forces, the city descended into chaos. More reprisals arose against communist officials. Worse, looters went on a rampage of theft and vandalism against not only all icons of the Castro regime, but also tourist hotels, restaurants, and shops. Embassies were evacuating their citizens.

Larisa Montilla shed her MININT uniform for a plain dress and dyed her hair black. She ditched her government ID, replacing it with a forged citizen's *carnet* in the name of Gloria Rodríguez. She commandeered a civilian vehicle and headed to Vedado, past billowing black smoke from torched government buildings, drunken looters, and stolen vehicles driven wildly by men with guns.

She crashed through the gate of her unguarded house. Fortunately, the neighborhood had yet to be targeted by looters or enemies of the communist government. She ran upstairs to collect some personal items, fifty thousand dollars, and forged passports she had stashed in a hidden wall safe for just such an emergency.

She threw some clothes into a small suitcase. Out of a bureau drawer, she retrieved a Makarov pistol and two clips. She jammed one clip into the gun and stuck the weapon into a handbag. Then she ran to a wall at the far end of the room and carefully removed a panel, revealing a safe. With trembling fingers, she began dialing the combination lock. Sweat poured down her forehead.

"Shit!" she murmured under her breath when the first

attempt failed. She closed her eyes, took a deep breath, and started again.

The safe door sprang open. She reached inside and shoveled the crisp note stacks into her suitcase and the passports into her handbag. Her heart pounded as if it would burst from her chest.

"What? Aren't you going to pack your whip?" a man asked.

The adrenalin that shot through her body almost caused her to pass out. She spun around.

Nick stood in the doorway with a gun aimed at her. "I believe it's in the top right drawer of that dresser."

"You!" she hissed.

"The one and only."

"I should have issued the firing squad live bullets."

"Tsk, tsk, Larisa. Now is not a time to cry over spilt milk. Hands up. And back away slowly."

Keeping her eyes on him, she stepped back and sat on the bed.

He peeked at the greenbacks in the suitcase and fingered the passports. "Planning a trip, Larisa? A nice Caribbean cruise perhaps? What's this? An American passport in the name of Sally Montego. *Sally Montego?* Funny. You just don't strike me as a Sally. And besides, with your mother being American, you could get a genuine one in your real name."

"We could go off together, Nicky. After all, what do you have to go back to? You're considered a renegade by your own government. As for me, I no longer have a government. But I do have financial resources. I have millions that I've carefully stashed overseas over many years. We're both outcasts now, with no going back from where we came. We're made for each other."

Nick hesitated a moment. "So where would we go?"

"Oh, I have options. And I have many friends in position to help us. But we must act fast."

"And you embezzled public funds that you hid away in foreign banks?"

"Embezzled? No. I looked at it as insurance. Everybody did it. It's part of survival in such a system. You can't imagine."

He moved closer to her and lowered his gun. He sat down beside her. She turned to him, her lips almost touching his, and closed her eyes. Nick placed a hand on her head and released her hair clasp. With a flick of her head, her hair fell to her shoulders. Gently, he brushed his lips against her neck.

"Hmm," she purred as she responded to his touch.

"We're too volatile, you and I," Nick whispered. "Nitro and glycerin."

"Ah, but that's the spark that sets fire to love. It's the fire that attracts us to each other." She caressed his cheek with one hand.

"I couldn't live with a woman so full of secrets, I'm afraid," he said, nuzzling her neck. "Secrets defeat trust."

"We each came close to killing the other. But we did not. Why? There is something there. Between us." She stared deeply into his eyes. "You are the only man I've ever truly loved. I was always kept on a pedestal. El Che's daughter couldn't take just any man. And any man not a member of the communist aristocracy was chased away, not good enough for Che's daughter. And those they tried to arrange for me were arrogant, privileged members of the old guard. So I devoted myself completely to the revolution and its goals. Now, there is no more revolution. No more Fidel. No future for me here." She took his hand in hers. "So let us go together. Start fresh. And not look back. Now."

"As an act of trust, I want you to answer me one thing."

"And that is?"

"Before, you told me there was going to be a 'leadership change in Washington.' What did you mean?"

She hesitated.

"Well?" he prompted.

She averted her gaze and fidgeted. She looked back at him. "Your president," she said hoarsely.

"What about him?"

"An assassin will kill him."

"How? Where? When?" Nick asked.

"I don't know."

"Larisa, this is important. Tell me!"

"I truly don't know! We issue orders, and he carries them out. We never know how or when. It's his way of protecting himself. Operational security. We don't even know where he lives. He moves around."

"What's his name?"

"Miguel Guimerá. His father fought with Fidel. He lives under assumed names and identities. We don't know those either. It was war! Your CIA killed our agents and threatened to roll up our entire network of agents in your country. We put them there to keep tabs on the reactionary Cuban exile community, who pose a security threat to Cuba. And the CIA was undermining the revolution. Our very existence! We had to strike back. Like in 1963..."

"What?"

Montilla turned away.

He took her chin in his hand and forced her to look at him. "What about 1963? What do you mean?"

Tears rolled down her cheeks as she gazed up at him. "Yes, we knew. Beforehand. Oswald came to us and told us his plans to kill Kennedy. Che told Fidel to let it play out. The CIA was trying to assassinate Fidel. There was the Bay of Pigs invasion. We were constantly under siege. They had no choice in the face of such threats from the United States."

"You weren't even born then. How do you know this?"

"I am Che's daughter. I was being groomed. They let me in on all the revolution's secrets. Fidel and Raúl treated me like their daughter, but more. I was their heir. Therefore, I needed to know all."

"How can we stop this Guimerá?"

"My staff communicated with him and all of our sleepers

abroad. Shortwave, internet, brush passes, cutouts. Various means."

"Okay. Do it! Stop him!"

"I told you my staff carried out all communications. MININT and DI are gone. Pfft!" She swept the air with her hand.

The bedroom door opened, and Kate and several Brigade members entered, all armed.

"What is this?" Montilla demanded.

"It's out of my hands, Larisa," Nick said. You will be judged and dealt with by your countrymen. But if you can neutralize your man, Guimerá, I can go to bat for you. Maybe get you a better deal."

"Betrayal! *Betrayal!*" She lunged to the floor and reached under the bed. She popped up with a KLIN PP-9 submachine gun and sprayed the room.

Two Brigade men fell dead on the floor. The rest scattered in search of cover. In an instant, Montilla jammed another clip into her weapon and resumed firing as she backed out the door, locking it behind her.

She killed two more men rushing up the stairway. She flew out of the house and got into her car. She backed out with a screech of tires and stomped on the gas. She headed west, away from Havana.

CHAPTER FIFTY-TWO

Miguel Guimerá, a.k.a. José Gutiérrez, got a lot of practice inserting cow magnets inside the first stomachs of cattle using the balling gun. That day, it was the turn of prize winners Nellie, Gertie, and Bertha. Only instead of cow magnets, he inserted two Semtex high explosive cylinders into each bovine. Armed with tiny magnetic sensor detonators, the devices would be triggered when the cows ate feed laced with magnetized steel filaments, care of Miguel. It took him mere minutes to complete the task.

Guimerá didn't care what the headlines said about the revolution's death or the deaths of the Castros. The job would be his last, he knew, but it would also be his last act of fealty.

"I don't know, Kate. The guy's got several screws loose, and I hear DOJ is investigating whether to slap him with some indictments, violating the Neutrality Act being the least of them. He's seen as a loose cannon, a renegade FBI agent, maybe even a turncoat," Jake Coburn said through a scratchy satellite signal.

"Did you hear me, Jake? Montilla told him they had a hit out on the President," Kate said with exasperation.

"Whose President?"

"*Our* President, dammit!"

"Right."

"Are you listening to me, Jake? Nick—"

"Kate, shut up. I've already put myself out on a limb with the seventh floor in—"

"Powerholders, Jake! They're the ones in charge now."

"Point made. And without you there, we would've been blindsided. I'm putting you in for an award."

"Never mind that! This is too important. *Please*, Jake."

"All I can promise is to pass it along. Bear in mind the Secret Service has placed Nick on its watch list after he called them directly, sounding like a raving lunatic."

"We'll deliver Montilla to you and get her to confess all."

"Kate, listen to me! You will under no circumstances do any such thing. Let the Cubans deal with her. The White House has issued orders for us not to interfere. The new leadership will have to deal with the former rulers. State is already gearing up a program to help them out on setting up a new judiciary. So *stay out*. Do you read me?"

"Read you? Yes. Comprehend you? No. Signing off."

"Kate! Ka—"

She knew the window of opportunity for escape was small. Someone once said, in chaos lies greatest opportunity. The old regime had fallen, yet a new one wasn't in place. The airport was closed, but departure by boat was still possible. As she raced along Fifth Avenue, she kept one eye on the rearview mirror. So far, she'd seen no signs of Nick Castillo or any other pursuers.

She arrived at Hemingway Marina to find hundreds of other officials like herself jamming the docks, desperately trying to find a way out by sea. Boats overloaded with *fidelistas* listed precariously in the aquamarine sea. After decades of driving tens of thousands of Cuban citizens into the treacherous Caribbean waters, many to their deaths, it was their turn.

A unit of FAR soldiers was in control of the outermost of four fingerlike extensions of the marina. Armed with assault rifles, they kept out all but the most senior officials of the defunct communist government, leaving the rest to fight amongst themselves over whatever floated. Having commandeered the biggest and most seaworthy craft, they methodically loaded the boats with officials and their family members and sent them off, out of Cuba.

"General Larisa Montilla!" she shouted, brandishing her government ID. The soldiers took her in without saluting. No more salutes in the fading slice of a failed revolution. Survival was the only motivator, every man for himself, or woman, as the case might be.

A frazzled major pointed Montilla to a group of VIPs boarding a Coast Guard vessel. Montilla eagerly joined them. Perspiring in the relentless afternoon sun, she looked nervously at her watch, then behind her for the enemy who would soon arrive to take control and make arrests, or worse. Her heart felt as if it would jump out of her chest.

"Where is this boat going?" she asked the major.

"Venezuelan cargo ship five kilometers out," he said.

Montilla closed her eyes, took a deep breath, and held it. *Almost there.* Just as she stepped aboard the vessel, gunfire broke out. Everybody ducked for cover.

Two armored personnel carriers bearing markings of the Arnaldo Ochoa Brigade crashed through the marina barrier, with fighters fanning out to seize the area. The FAR troops lay cover fire as the last VIP boat loaded up and pushed off with engines roaring, Larisa Montilla aboard.

Their GAZ jeep careened to a screeching halt behind the Brigade fighters. Out jumped Nick, Kate, and two soldiers.

The battle with the outnumbered FAR contingent came to an abrupt halt, and the FAR soldiers surrendered. Quickly, the attackers rounded up the rest of the would-be escapees amid screams and weeping. Some leapt into the sea in a vain attempt to evade capture. The least fit sank below the waves.

Nick ran to the dock's edge. The Coast Guard vessel was a hundred meters away. Nick grabbed an AK-47 from one of his own troops, took careful aim, and fired a full magazine at the boat. The effort was futile.

A speedboat crammed with communist officials and their family members, caught up in the melee, bobbed at the dock under the menacing shadows of a dozen Kalashnikov rifles pointed at them.

Nick ran to the boat, fired in the air, and ordered, "Get out! Now!"

Fearing they'd be slaughtered, the would-be refugees held their hands high, crying, "Don't shoot! Please. Don't shoot!"

"Get them all out. Hurry," Nick commanded his troops.

The soldiers scrambled to pull the people off the boat. Children screamed, unassuaged by the frantic comforting gestures of their mothers.

Before the last few had disembarked, Nick jumped onto the deck and started the engine. "RPGs! Bring RPGs!"

Soldiers rushed rocket propelled grenade launchers to the vessel. With a handful of fighters aboard, Nick steered the boat in the direction of the fleeing Coast Guard craft.

After twenty minutes of cutting through choppy waters, they spotted the boat sidled up against a gleaming gray freighter—MSC Orinoco—Maracaibo—and a fluttering red-blue-yellow ensign on its stern identified its Venezuelan registry. The crew members were assisting the Cubans to board the ship via rope ladders.

As the speedboat zipped closer, Nick ordered three men to prepare the RPGs for fire and two others to ready their Kalashnikovs.

Cuban naval crew raked the waves with 30mm fire, several rounds ripping through the fiberglass speedboat's stern. A quick evasive move by the boat's steersman sent the others falling onto the deck. Seaspray drenched all.

Nick took over the wheel and maneuvered the craft toward the bow of the Venezuelan ship. Staring down at him from amidships and the bow were two 50mm guns, manned, cocked, and ready to tear his little speed boat to shreds. Three Venezuelan Bolivarian Marines directed RPG-7s at him as well.

Nick's men aimed their RPGs at the Cuban craft and the ship. But Nick knew it was useless. One shot fired from his side would bring on enough destructive power in return that there wouldn't be enough of them left to be fish bait.

As the two sides stared each other down, a decision needed to be made. And fast.

"Lower your weapons. Let's get out of here. Slowly now," Nick ordered his men.

As he turned the speedboat around, Nick looked back. Climbing onto the deck of the Orinoco was a woman. Steadying herself, she shielded her eyes from the sun as she looked down. She blew a kiss to Nick.

The speedboat roared off.

"She got away! She got away, dammit!" Nick told Marcial in the central office of the José Martí Military Technical Institute, adjacent to Libertad Airport in west Havana, where the Provisional Government had set up temporary headquarters.

"She will face justice. As will they all. It's only a matter of time. But we have other priorities. We have to wash away a half-century of stunted development, stifled dreams, and fear. We need to show the Cuban people the way of freedom, of being part of today's world," Marcial said.

"You've got your hands full, my friend," Nick said.

"I need help."

"The world will be eager to help Cuba."

"Yes. But I need good men and women here to help rebuild the country. I need a Minister of Interior to build a law enforcement system from the ground up." Marcial crossed his arms and looked at Nick expectantly.

"Me?"

"Yes, you. Or if you prefer Minister of Defense…"

"No, no. That's out of the question. You want Cubans for those posts."

"But you are Cuban."

"Well, yes and no… I mean, yes, Cuban in my heart, but American through and through."

"I understand," Marcial said. "Nick Castillo always has a place here."

"Which I value. But I have urgent, unfinished business back home."

They shook hands.

"*Vaya con Dios.*"

"*Y contigo.*"

"Jake Coburn told me you're considered to be a renegade by your own FBI and possibly a turncoat, that you may come under indictment," Kate said.

"Indictment? What for?" Nick asked.

"Not sure. Bottom line, however, is you can't just hop a flight to Miami, or anywhere. You're on watchlists, including that of the Secret Service. They classify you as a potential threat to the president. What did you tell them?"

"Damn it. I called them to warn them about a plot hatched by Montilla, undoubtedly at Fidel's instigation, to assassinate the president. Maybe I came off a little too edgy. I hadn't slept in days."

"That, combined with your unauthorized activities down here. Unfortunately, Nick, you're seen as a loose cannon, not to be trusted."

"What did Coburn say when you told him about the plot?"

"He didn't buy it. He's one of the zillion officials in D.C. who sees you as a whack job at best, a rogue at worst."

Nick sipped his icy drink. "Mm hm. God, that's good. Best daiquiri I've ever had."

Kate did a double take. "What?"

"I said this—"

"I know what you said. One second, we're brainstorming on stopping an assassination threat against the President of the United States, your status as a pariah, my sinking credibility with my own agency and you... you go all gaga over a daiquiri? I'm sorry, but are you finally losing it, Nick?"

Nick raised his glass and held it high in a toast. "Here's to El Floridita. Home for tragic, doomed Yankees. Ezra Pound was nuts, and Ernest Hemingway blew his brains out." He gulped down the drink, then signaled the bartender for another. The place was deserted in the interregnum between conflict's end and the resumption of tourism.

He scanned the long retro red and black bar, at the far end of which was a bronze sculpture of Hemingway leaning against it. He raised his glass again. "Papa, you had it right."

"What're you talking about?" Kate asked.

"'Never confuse movement with action,' Papa said. We can sit here pretending to do something while bureaucrats have their heads up their collective asses, or we can get up off our own asses and do something."

"I love it when you're angry." Kate grasped Nick's face in her hands and planted a firm kiss on his lips.

CHAPTER FIFTY-THREE

They left after midnight from Hemingway Marina in the same speedboat Nick had used in his futile chase after Larisa Montilla. They traveled blind, no lights and fast, but not so fast as to draw attention. Any time the radar picked up other vessels, they cut the engine and waited until it was clear. When they could see lights from Marathon in the Florida Keys, they slowed to a crawl, patiently making their way toward land. The Brigade soldier steering the craft took it cautiously toward undeveloped Vaca Key where the Americans jumped off, arriving back on American soil without having to worry about being caught on any agency's watchlist.

With backpacks, they walked to Marathon's center, killing time at a twenty-four-hour fast food restaurant until they caught the 0810 bus to Florida City. There, they took Metrorail to downtown Miami, then a local bus to Miami Springs. After that, they made the short walk to LaBaron Drive.

Serafina looked as if she had seen a ghost. After the initial shock, she and Rolando embraced their son and peppered him with rapid-fire questions.

"Where have you been?"

"What have you been up to?"

"How is your health?"

"Are you in trouble?"

"Has the FBI fired you?"

"Who is this lovely young lady?"

"This is my coworker I told you about a while back. Kate, my parents. Mom, Pop, this is Kate."

Settling in the small living room over cafecitos and biscuits gave Rolando and Serafina the opportunity they needed to check out the young woman about whom Nick had made but a brief dismissive comment months ago.

"Ukrainian-Polish?" they asked politely. "So you are Catholic, then?"

"And then some," Kate quipped.

"Ahh," they uttered approvingly.

"Mom, Pop, we don't have a lot of time. There's something urgent we need to work on," Nick said.

"But you just got here," Serafina objected.

"It concerns the president. Once we're done with this assignment, we can take the time to really catch up on things," Nick replied.

"Including getting to know Kate better…"

"You bet, Mom. But first, I need to buy a used car and do some shopping. Then we've gotta get going."

"Where to?"

"Texas."

"You're going seventy miles an hour, and we've got twenty-three hours of driving time ahead of us," Kate said as they zoomed along I-75 north.

"Yeah, so?" Nick replied.

"How confident are you that a '97 Mustang with a hundred forty thousand miles is going to stand up to such a marathon?"

"Got no choice." Nick offered her a Cuban pork sandwich made by Serafina for the trip.

She took it and nibbled. "All right. So we googled the President's schedule and found out he's appearing at a rodeo thingy in Dallas. We might as well throw a dart at a map. Why Dallas?"

"Has to be. She told me Fidel knew in advance about Oswald's plan to kill Kennedy. Then she confessed about one of their sleeper agents, a guy named Guimerá, who's been set in motion to assassinate POTUS soon… very soon. Just look at the symmetry. And I'm betting this killer's their best, which means he's careful, calculating, mathematical even. He's been in their service so long, you can bet he's a dedicated, hardcore dead-ender. He'll carry out this job as his last act of faithfulness to the Castros, a posthumous homage. The thing is, he's gotta been living in the U.S. for many years. So he knows how to move around while living under the radar. I'm betting he carried out the jobs in New Jersey, Virginia, and Florida. It's obvious they had their best man on those cases. He wants to drive home a point—the two U.S. presidents who posed the greatest threat to the Cuban revolution, JFK and Brogan, killed in the same U.S. city."

"So we arrive there, two civilians, not FBI agent and CIA ops officer, and what do we do? How do we get access? And last but not least, how do we identify the perp, and how do we deal with him?"

"Details. Details. We'll figure it out." He looked at her with mock seriousness.

She gazed at him with a serious expression. Then, they both burst into laughter.

Miguel Guimerá looked forward to killing the President of the United States. Nine minutes from Dealy Plaza. The act would be just revenge for Washington's many crimes against the Cuban revolution. His last act might even return pride to the Cuban people, who one day would yearn to bring back the revolution and again stand up to a superpower bound to bring social pollution and exploitation back to Cuba under the new so-called democratic government.

"You must use this feed and no other," he instructed the Plano chapter students of the Future Farmers of America as he pointed to three large buckets of feed laced with magnetized steel filaments. "They like this kind of feed. Give it to Bertha, Gertie, and Nellie when the President comes to inspect them and no sooner. It will make for a great photo shoot. Understand?" He smiled benevolently at the nodding youths and patted them affectionately on their cheeks. So sad they would all die that afternoon. What was that term the Pentagon used when it murdered civilians? *Ah, yes. Collateral damage.*

They stood in the expansive, low-slung Livestock Judging Pavilion at Dallas's Fair Park. The Texas State Fair was in full swing, and security for the president's visit in two hours was tight. Texas state troopers and Dallas police manned all entrances and exits as well as patrolled strategic areas of the fair grounds. Uniformed Secret Service personnel screened people who would attend the same events as the President through banks of magnetometers. K-9 Unit agents led sniffer dogs throughout the area to check for explosives. Guimerá's practiced eyes also identified plainclothes Texas Rangers and Secret Service personnel interspersed among the crowds. But Guimerá paid special attention to two heavily armed five-man Secret Service Counter Assault Teams, one inside a Chevy Suburban in the parking lot south of the pavilion, the other in a Ford 550 at the north entrance. He also spied Secret Service sniper teams atop the rim of Cotton Bowl Stadium and the Coliseum building overlooking the pavilion.

The odors nauseated Guimerá: deep fried biscuits and gravy, deep fried brownies, deep fried chicken skins, deep fried mashed potatoes with bacon and cheese, deep fried chocolate sandwiches. The stench of hot overused grease permeated the atmosphere. Its consumption was visible in the multitude of lard asses lumbering around the fair grounds. That was why Americans were so fat and so stupid, he thought. And such foolish overindulgences marked a declining civilization.

But he must stay fully concentrated on the mission. He had prepared the operation in meticulous detail weeks in advance. It was by far his biggest ever. And he must ensure completion of the mission. For Fidel. For Cuba.

He stuck close to the Livestock Judging Pavilion, overseeing the children's grooming and care of Bertha, Nellie, and Gertie in the final moments of the bovines' pampered lives. He kept his cool, but it wasn't easy. Guimerá had killed coolheadedly without so much as a tremble in his hands. He had nearly died in battle in El Salvador and Nicaragua. He'd barely escaped with his life after his failed hits on Pinochet and Savimbi. The close calls had merely hardened him, focused his resolve. But the current mission was different. The stakes couldn't be higher. And his overseers and the system he had so faithfully served for so many years were gone. Should he survive it, there would be no more. Perhaps that was just as well. He was getting too old. He couldn't keep killing forever.

He could hear the U.S. Marine Corps Band warming up in the stadium. Sousa was regularly interrupted by the piercing *wooh-wooh-wooh* of police sirens as more law enforcement vehicles arrived.

Ninety minutes 'til zero hour.

Kate grimaced as she watched Nick devour a pile of fried mashed potatoes with bacon and cheese. "How can you eat that? It's gross."

"Gotta eat something," he said. "If you can find a nice healthy salad here at cholesterol central, let me know. Otherwise, when in Rome…"

"Right. Right. Maybe a corn dog for me. It'll take only one year off my life rather the five that slop will take off of yours. Meanwhile, the clock's ticking down. The Prez is due in exactly seventy minutes. No time to eat."

Nick, sporting a cheap Josey Wales knock-off hat, and Kate, her face nearly concealed by a too-cute straw Stetson, stood in the shadow of the Cotton Bowl. She fumbled with a map of the fairgrounds while he ate, making them look every bit the stereotypical couple from Nacogdoches on their annual pilgrimage to the big fair.

"I don't know how they can wear those leather boots in such a hot climate," Kate complained, looking down forlornly at her stiff new embroidered buckaroos.

"Leave it. We've got bigger things. Let's see. Pig Races. Peewee Stampede. Hog Heaven Stage."

"What're you doing?" Kate demanded. "Don't you see on the schedule? POTUS at Livestock Judging Pavilion at fourteen hundred. Cotton Bowl at fourteen thirty. Depart fair grounds fifteen thirty."

"Right. Right." Nick dumped the remainder of his heartbuster lunch in the trash. "It's this stagnant heat. Muddles my brain."

"It's only ten degrees above normal. Bear with it."

They walked briskly past the horse barn. Then they encountered the manned barricades, magnetometers, and K-9 Unit sniffer dogs. Nick approached the first checkpoint, which was manned by fair employees carefully checking the tickets of attendees before sending them to the metal detectors and further Secret Service scrutiny.

"We'd like two tickets, please," Nick said.

The ticket checker looked at him as if he were crazy. "Sold out. And you needed to be here six hours before the event anyway," a large-framed woman with a beehive hairdo responded.

"Oh." Nick exchanged a worried glance with Kate. "Any way we can get squeezed in?" he asked

The woman took a second, long look at them. Suspicion shadowed her face. "Wait right here."

Nick grabbed Kate's arm. "Let's get out of here." When they were at a safe distance, Nick said, "You can bet your bottom dollar they've got my photo among their rogue's gallery of potential threats to the President."

"All right, then. I say we turn ourselves in. Warn them. Tell them to cancel the whole shebang due to a clear and present danger," Kate said.

Nick shook his head. "We have zero credibility. Don't you get it? They think I'm a threat. They'll just haul us away, content they neutralized the 'rogue FBI agent.' And you're the Bonnie to my Clyde. Understand?"

"So now what?"

"I don't know." Nick suddenly got an idea. "Wait a minute." He reached inside his back pocket, pulled out his wallet, and flipped it open to reveal his FBI badge and ID. "There it is. License to roam."

Kate reached into her fanny bag and pulled out her CIA ID attached to a chain around her neck. "These won't get us inside the Secret Service Presidential Protection Detail, but they should get us into the building."

They ditched their hats, circled the pavilion to a checkpoint for security personnel, and presented their ID's. And they were let in.

Confident that everything was on track, Guimerá discreetly departed the pavilion, crossed the train tracks on the northern edge of the park, and exited the Texas State Fair.

The seventeen-car presidential motorcade entered the park on time and pulled up to the entrance of the Livestock Judging Pavilion. The usual coterie of official greeters was lined up to formally receive the President: the governor and his retinue, the state fair managers, Dallas's mayor, a group of Future Farmers of America kids.

From the Beast—the President's state of-the-art armored black Cadillac—emerged the chief executive sporting an open-collar shirt befitting the venue and a resplendent smile. Flanked by Secret Service agents, the President vigorously shook hands with and exchanged pleasantries with the greeters. Making his way into the pavilion, he waved to the enthusiastic crowd.

He stepped up to the podium. "Well, I'm glad to come see y'all today!" The apt use of "y'all" elicited another raucous applause from the audience.

As the POTUS launched into a speech about cattle ranching's importance in the nation's economy and the need to educate youth in modern farming techniques, Nick and Kate headed to the low bleachers behind the steel barriers around the inside perimeter of the building.

"What're we looking for?" Kate asked.

"Anything, anybody suspicious. And act official. Keep your ID displayed. We also need to keep our sunglasses on like most of the Secret Service agents here, as much to disguise ourselves as to blend in."

Moving at a brisk, deliberate pace, Nick moved through the crowd, scrutinizing each face for the one that would stand out in a sea of enthusiasm. The grave, determined one. The nervous, sweaty one. The crazed one. Any that simply didn't fit. He glommed onto snippets of conversation, listening for Spanish or a Cuban accent.

The pavilion, decked out in American and Texas state flags from the high convex roof, was filled with warring odors. Cow dung. Deep-fried crap. Flowers. Scent of jasmine...

He stopped in his tracks. That aroma. Familiar. Dangerous. He swung his head to the left, then to the right, sniffing the air carefully.

"You. Let's see your ID!" a deep voice ordered.

Nick trained his eyes on a stocky male figure approaching him. A second figure came from the opposite direction.

Seeing what was happening, Kate retreated toward a wall.

Nick struggled to remain calm as the two Secret Service agents cornered him. "What's the problem?" he asked as he handed over his FBI badge.

"No fibbies are attached to this detail," the stocky one said as he studied Nick's ID. "Castillo, huh?"

"Yeah, that's right. Special Agent Nick Castillo. I'm TDY here, ordered to help coordinate the locals."

"Where's your special access pin, Castillo?" Stocky turned to the other agent. "Run his name through, Al."

The emcee announced the winners of the dairy Holstein competition held earlier. The Plano Future Farmers of America youth proudly stood by Bertha, Gertie, and Nellie as the President was handed a blue ribbon to take to the Elk Run bovines and their human handlers some fifteen feet away. The prize-winning cows contentedly chewed their feed.

Jasmine. Nick strained to locate the origin of that too familiar smell.

A woman in the next row of bleachers turned her head in the direction of the commotion among the agents. Hazel eyes. Light brown hair tied back. Nick knew the shock on her face was reflected equally on his own.

"Come with us, Castillo," the stocky Secret Service agent ordered.

"It's her!" Nick lunged toward Larisa Montilla. "It's her!"

The Secret Service agents threw themselves on top of Nick, quickly subduing him in an arm lock.

"Get the President out! Now!" Nick yelled at the top of his lungs, despite the four hundred pounds of muscled Secret Service flesh piled on him.

The Future Farmers beamed as the President walked toward them, ribbon in hand.

Nick's shout and the struggle in the bleachers catalyzed the Secret Service's presidential protection detail into lightning action. Just as two agents hustled the nation's top leader by both elbows toward the main entrance, a muffled explosion erupted, followed by another and another. Blood sprayed all over. Chunks of flesh, hide, and bone flew through the air, making their marks on scores of panic-stricken spectators and fair organizers fleeing in all directions or taking cover.

"Get her! Montilla! Not me, dammit! Get her!" were Nick's last words before being tasered into unconsciousness.

The Counter Assault Teams stormed into the pavilion, covering the entrance with MP5 submachine guns, AR-15 assault rifles, SIG Sauer pistols, and Remington pump-action shotguns to ensure a safe getaway for the Beast. State and local police SWAT teams fanned out in and around the pavilion to suppress potential armed attackers.

Amid the pandemonium, dead and injured Future Farmers and state fair staff sprawled in the arena center. Pieces of the shredded carcasses of Bertha, Nellie, and Gertie were scattered everywhere.

The Beast, sirens in full blare, screeched up the fairground's Pennsylvania Avenue to turn right onto Gaisford and connect with a major artery leading to Military Parkway away from the city, according to pre-set contingency plans. A fireball blew the metal maintenance building on the east corner of Pennsylvania Avenue into a million hot shards, causing the Beast's driver to veer off course. Then the maintenance building on the opposite side exploded.

The Beast and its back-up vehicles slammed into a reverse-J turn, backtracked, and entered McKenzie Street, adjacent to the Livestock Judging Pavilion. They sped away from the fairground to get onto four-lane Haskell Avenue. As they entered an underpass beneath the rail tracks, in lightning-quick succession, semtex charges destroyed the twenty-two brick and concrete columns holding up the tunnel. Tons of it collapsed onto the presidential motorcade, burying the Beast and its occupants.

Kate caught up with Montilla in a parking lot due east of the pavilion and wrestled her to the ground. But a sharp upward knee-ram to the stomach sent Kate into spasms of pain and lost breath. The Cuban tore off Kate's shoes and, with them in hand, absconded across busy Haskell Avenue. Her lungs heaving, unable to run in her bare feet, Kate sat up and watched helplessly as Montilla disappeared into the residential neighborhood opposite the thoroughfare.

CHAPTER FIFTY-FOUR

"Nobody knows what to make of you, Castillo," Clement Rourke said. "'Marches to the beat of his own drum' is an understatement. 'I am become Death, the destroyer of worlds,' is more like it."

"But if I didn't go—"

Rourke held up a hand. "Just shut up for once and listen. Headquarters sent me up here to deal with you because they know I'll jump kick your face in if you get out of hand again."

Nick sat back and let out a deep breath. He was beyond tired. He had lived more than one lifetime in the past year. He felt as though he'd aged decades. And his brain, so preoccupied with immediate survival instincts, seemed incapable of reflection.

"You saved the president's life in that pavilion. The Secret Service had you on their watch list."

"So am I off the hook, then?"

Rourke looked at Jake Coburn.

Coburn cocked an eyebrow. "You and Kate not only gave us our best intel from inside Cuba, you steered U.S. policy in a positive direction, making friends for Washington. And you passed the poly with flying colors."

Kate smiled.

Nick grinned, too. It was good to be back at the FBI Miami office, belonging instead of rejected. The sounds of traffic along busy I-95 were a welcome change from the crack of AK-47 and RPG fire. He glanced at Rourke's desk and the miniature sculpture of three figures representing Fidelity, Bravery, and Integrity, copied from the original in the J. Edgar Hoover Building courtyard. Fidelity, a seated female, looked up at the standing male figure representing Bravery. On the other side, Integrity, a kneeling male figure, also looked up to Bravery against a backdrop of an oversized Old Glory waving in the breeze.

"Fortunately, the Beast saved the President's life," Rourke continued. "It would take more than a few tons of rubble to crush that thing. And the vehicle's internal oxygen supply literally gave the occupants breathing room until we could get heavy equipment in there to dig them out."

"And we now urgently need you and Kate to help us track down Larisa Montilla and her hitman, Miguel Guimerá," Coburn said.

"They're always two steps ahead of the rest of us," Nick said. "But nobody knows her like I do."

Rourke cocked his head with brow raised.

Nick realized what he'd said. "Uh, I meant… I know her M.O. better than anyone. But there are others. The Castros burrowed networks of moles deep into our government and society for decades. They're still there, ready to serve another master."

An agent rushed into Rourke's office. "There's an agent down."

Rourke's face drained. "Who? Where?"

"Bart Morgenstern. Twenty minutes ago." The agent kept his phone to his hear, receiving real-time reports. "Double tap to the head as he was walking out of the Deli Donuts shop with a coffee three blocks from here." The agent listened again, then shook his head. "Bart's dead."

Rourke nodded. "Let's go!"

As they ran out of the building, Nick pulled out his cell phone and dialed his parents' house. No answer. He dialed his mother's cell phone. No answer. "Shit!" He broke from the others and sprinted to his car in the adjacent parking lot.

"Nick! Nick!" Rourke shouted.

Nick jumped into the driver's seat of his Mustang, jammed the key into the ignition, and backed out with a smoking screech. He barreled out of the building onto NW 2nd Avenue. Hitting 60 miles per hour, he stormed through the red traffic light at 167th, causing three cars with the right of way to collide with each other and a semi-trailer to career into a power transformer station on the northeast corner, setting off a cascade of electrical fireworks.

He made a sharp left onto the ramp to I-95 South. Speeding up to eighty, he weaved perilously through traffic, incurring loud honks, obscene gestures, and profanities.

Barely easing up on the gas as he got onto 112 West, he reached inside his jacket, unsnapped his shoulder holster, and took out the Glock 22. He held the weapon in his right hand as he gripped the steering wheel with his left. Only when he blew onto four-lane West 36th did he become aware that his clothing was soaked with his perspiration. He took out his handkerchief and wiped the sweat from his eyes.

The wail of police sirens grew louder to his rear. He glanced at his rearview mirror. A police squad car was closing in. He ran another light and screeched onto South Avenue, tires smoking. He drove four blocks up South Avenue, then took a hard right onto LaBaron. One block from his parents' house, he slammed on the brakes, flung open the door, and leapt out, Glock in hand.

His folks' Honda was parked in the driveway. The police car, siren sounding and dome lights flashing, came to an abrupt halt right behind his Mustang.

He had no time to reconnoiter. And the police, unaware they were on the tail of an FBI agent, could take him down, seeing only an armed man running from them after tearing up Miami's roadways.

"Stop! Drop your weapon!"

Nick rushed to the front door. Locked. He shot the lock and kicked open the door. His Glock grasped in both hands, he skirted into the living room. Nothing. He quickly ran to the kitchen.

His parents were tied to chairs, mouths covered in duct tape.

A shot rang out. Nick hit the floor. Another shot. A male figure rushed at him.

Rolling to one side to evade the next shot, Nick fired off five rounds.

The man fell to the floor and groaned. Nick leapt up and stood over his target, Glock pointed at the man's sternum. The man lay unmoving, bloody froth pouring from the sides of his mouth. His wide eyes mirrored the fear and desperation of a man soon to breathe his last breath. Nick kicked the guy's weapon out of reach.

"Police! Drop it!" a cop commanded from the doorway behind Nick.

"FBI!" Nick shouted, knowing the cop would have a gun aimed at him, but refusing to lower his weapon from Guimerá's chest.

"ID. Left hand. Real slow," the cop ordered.

Carefully, Nick obliged, lowering his badge onto the floor.

"This man's wanted for attempting to assassinate the President," Nick said.

From the corner of his eye, Nick saw a police officer step forward and cut loose Nick's parents. The first cop came around and cautiously approached Nick and the dying Cuban.

The assassin strained to speak. Nick bent over to hear the man's last words.

"Fidel!" the man managed hoarsely. "Fidel." His eyes froze in a dead man's stare as his breathing stopped.

Nick patted Guimerá's pockets and retrieved a cell phone. He flipped it open and scrolled. The contacts list contained a single number. He dialed it.

After two rings, a woman answered, *"Guimerá? Qué esta pasando? Dígame!"*

"Larisa," Nick said.

She didn't respond.

Nick hissed, "We've got your number."

The line went dead.

EPILOGUE

Havana

Like a freshly watered garden after a long drought, south Old Havana was coming to life. The air was filled with the scent of paint and the sounds of banging hammers and construction machinery. The streets were alive with the bustle of people on the go, eager to earn a living unconstrained by the rigor mortised hand of a dead ideology. New restaurants, bars, beauty salons, and shops of all sorts sprang up, brimming with consumer products considered virtually out of reach in the past. New fashion bloomed. Chicly dressed women dodged around newly cemented sidewalks along with suited yuppie entrepreneurs, half-naked skateboarders, mohawked *punqueros,* and tourists.

"Let a hundred flowers bloom and a hundred schools of thought contend," Mao Tse-tung once said. The legendary communist revolutionary would be rolling in his grave if he could see what was happening in the land of his once close ally.

"Vote Raúl Fernández!" blurted loudspeakers from a slowly passing new Toyota pickup truck. "A new man for a new Cuba! Vote Raúl Fernández!" Walls and lampposts were plastered with posters of the smiling visages of politicians competing in upcoming elections for the new National Assembly, mayor, prime minister, and a host of local offices.

Cubans moved with purpose and optimism. Gone was the guardedness that protected one from the eavesdropping *chivato* and intrusiveness of the CDR bully. Gone was the shame of having to steal from the state to survive. And gone was the hypocrisy of giving lip service to revolutionary cant while plotting one's escape.

Yamilé Acosta sat in a rattan chair and ordered an iced coffee. She took her notes from her attaché bag and spread them on the contemporary Italian-made table. She opened and booted up her laptop. The spiffy new cybercafé had replaced a pile of rubble in a vacant lot, the product of seed money from Miami investors. Packed with a mostly young crowd making deals, flirting, exchanging gossip, and carrying on political debates, the place looked as if it could have been lifted straight out of Stockholm, Chicago, or Tokyo. With its retro art-deco architecture, sleek furniture, avant-garde paintings, and the latest coffee-making technology straight from Milano, the place was popular. However, it would have competitors throughout the city.

Yamilé scrunched her brow and pinched her lips in thought. When the inevitable brainstorm hit, her eyes lit up, and she set her long fingers to work on the keyboard.

CUBASIEMPRE.COM

BLOG BY YAMILÉ ACOSTA

As I recounted not long ago, Cubans have a saying: "A lie runs until it is overtaken by the truth." Well, the truth has arrived. It hit us directly between the eyes like a bullet. Now what do we do?

The Provisional Government has scheduled free elections in the coming weeks. That's good, but what is it doing to combat the corruption seeping into our newly formed political life? How will it deal with the urgent needs of our people for jobs, decent health care, and women's equality? Have we replaced one set of mismanagers with another? As I ponder these issues in the new La Reina, Cubans have many questions and demands...

ABOUT THE AUTHOR

James Bruno is the author of Amazon Kindle Bestsellers ***PERMANENT INTERESTS, CHASM,*** and ***TRIBE***. A former diplomat and military intelligence analyst, he resides in Upstate New York.